Counterfeit Rodeos

A Nathan Wolf Novel

Books by James Duermeyer

Nathan Wolf *series*
Trail of the Outlaw
Singing Creek
Counterfeit Rodeos

Novels
Flint Bluff
Market Time Conspiracy

Nonfiction Books
Heroes in Obscurity
The Capture of the USS Pueblo; the Incident, the Aftermath, and the Motives of North Korea

Counterfeit Rodeos

A Nathan Wolf Novel

James Duermeyer

SPEAKING VOLUMES, LLC
NAPLES, FLORIDA
2022

Counterfeit Rodeos

Cover design by Hannah Linder

ISBN 978-1-64540-668-6

Chapter One:
The Reprieve

June 1879

St. Louis, Missouri

Victor Carelli was a mobster, a gangster, a killer, and to those who knew him, he was also, quite literally, a heartless bastard. He had not reached his criminal pinnacle by being scrupled. Carelli had clawed and scratched his way to the top of a criminal empire, dislodging or killing those persons who showed signs of opposing him in his ascent. In the decades that passed in his quest, the story was that at least twenty unsolved murder cases languished in the St. Louis police files, never to be solved while payoff money crossed the palms of key members of the law enforcement constabulary. Bodies, small businesses that had refused to pay "insurance" money, broken families, and other small-time criminals' endeavors lay strewn to the side of the path of Carelli's rise to power. And now, Carelli was head of one of the most powerful criminal syndicates in the Midwest, with tentacles in racketeering, bootlegging, counterfeiting, prostitution, gambling, as well as murder when necessary to protect the Carelli empire.

Only his most trusted cohorts at the top of his criminal hierarchy could call him by his nickname, "Vico," and for the most part, even his most loyal lieutenants called him Mr. Carelli. Two of those subordinate, ever-present body guards stood at each side of Carelli, as the gangster sat facing the windows behind the desk. His office was on the upper floor of a two story, non-descript warehouse. From his window, Carelli could see the warehouse activity below, as horse-drawn wagons filled with illicit liquor, counterfeit currency, and other black market goods came and went during the day. Periodically, individual mounted men rode their horses up an inclined ramp into the warehouse, away from the eyes of passersby. They carried satchels burdened with real currency taken from merchants in Carelli's protection racket. Carelli's tentacles were far reaching.

On this day, a man sat in a chair facing Carelli's desk, staring at the back side of Carelli's high-back leather chair. His eyes, with a look of foreboding, roamed over his surroundings. The office was painted in a deep maroon color. The décor was old and garish and was in dire need of a more modern remodel. Carelli did not care, as he liked it just the way it was. Bright brass lamps sat on the desk, a credenza, and a sideboard cupboard. Expensive, yet dusty and decadent, paintings adorned one wall, and a brass and crystal chandelier hung over the desk. It was the gaudy lair of an underworld boss comfortable in his private domain.

After being forcefully escorted into Carelli's office and taking his seat, the man had been left sitting in his chair for a full ten minutes while staring at the back of Carelli's chair. He had yet to see or speak to the mob boss, and a bead of sweat trickled down the middle of his back. In due time, Carelli turned slowly around in his chair and faced the man across the desk, still not making direct eye contact with him.

Carelli was a self-made gangster. Abandoned as a child to the streets of a seedier neighborhood in St. Louis, he scraped a livelihood from the street, selling stolen cigarettes, picking pockets, running errands for figures in the underworld, and taking on other assorted unpleasant tasks through which he acquired the knowledge of the undesirable quirks and intricacies of the local hoodlums. Over the years, Carelli gained an ever-growing reputation, that of a hood who used terror and bloodshed to bolster the word on the street that he would not be crossed without suffering consequences. With his reputation growing, so did his criminal enterprise, to the point that his organization was one that oversaw a great sphere of underworld influence in St. Louis. He was a man who was known to grant favors, but just as quickly end the lives of those who competed with or crossed him.

Carelli was corpulent, so fat that he filled the width of the leather chair in which he sat. But his fine, smooth Australian worsted wool suit and silk vest with its gold buttons were cleverly cut by his favorite tailor to visually diminish his wide girth. His face was clean shaven, and his slightly-graying hair was lightly oiled to remain in place. His cheeks and his flat nose were ruddy and crisscrossed with spider-web veins that divulged his penchant for rich foods accompanied by multiple glasses of wine and his favorite after-dinner sherry. Among his other vices, Carelli was a glutton. His culinary tastes were well known in his favorite dining establishments where he indulged in his rich diet and left much-appreciated gratuities.

Carelli continued to look down. In one of his short-fingered fat hands was a long, hand-rolled cheroot. In his other hand he held a gold-plated cigar cutter, which he had just used to trim the cigar. He placed the cigar cutter on the desk and stared at the cigar momentarily before he stuck it in his mouth, thereby giving him the appearance of a pig with a root stuck in its mouth. One of the gangster's bodyguards produced a match, which he struck on his shoe sole before holding the flickering flame at the end of his boss's cigar. A thick haze of gray cigar smoke soon swirled around Carelli's head. He exhaled, waved and blew the smoke aside, finally letting his gaze rest on the apprehensive man across the desk from him.

Marcus Zima, up until this point in his career, had been one of the many bookkeepers employed by Carelli's criminal enterprise. Zima was the son of an Eastern European immigrant, a man who would take on small jobs, legal or illegal, to feed his family, and who had accidentally met and later began working for Carelli when Carelli was selling bootleg liquor out of the back of horse-drawn freight wagons and slowly amassing his criminal enterprise. After the younger Zima attended a business and bookkeeping school, his father had respectfully asked Carelli to hire Marcus. All had gone well for the Zimas until the elder Zima had been accidentally killed by the explosion of one of Carelli's liquor stills. Then again, according to discreet sources at the fire department, perhaps it was not necessarily an accident, as Carelli quickly began to "look after" Marcus's mother, the comely widow Zima along with a few of his other girlfriends, all of whom together had produced a raft of illegitimate children. Nearly all of those offspring had found their way into orphanages after anonymous monetary contributions had been made for their support. Marriage and raising children did not fit into Carelli's life plan.

A number of sweat droplets now showed on the sides of Zima's forehead. He knew exactly why he had been brought to Carelli's office. Cooking the books for Carelli's crime syndicate was part of Zima's job. Syphoning money off for his personal use was the fateful step that put Zima in front of Carelli's desk and would be the reason for Zima's pending demise. Zima had worked for the crime boss for over five years and had seen what had happened to other Carelli employees who did not measure up to Carelli's standards. Those men had disappeared or been found on a seldom-used street with a single bullet hole in their heads. They were murders that would never be solved. With that knowledge, Zima had resigned himself to being a walking dead man. Carelli watched as one of the sweat droplets wandered down the side of Zima's face to hang on his jowl before dropping onto his vest. Carelli had always found it fascinating to watch men who knew that they might die momentarily at the hands of his enforcers.

Marcus Zima was in awe and deathly afraid of his boss. Zima, too, was on the portly side, but his clothes came nowhere near to matching the quality and cut of his boss's sartorial garb. His ready-made black frock coat and vest matched with tan wool pants bore the fashion mark of working-class men.

Zima carefully watched Carelli's small brown eyes, the eyes of a badger on the trail of a crippled rabbit. The thought crossed Zima's mind that he should leap from his chair and run for the door, but he quickly realized that he could not make it to the door before he was clubbed to the floor or killed for his stupidity. He watched as more cigar smoke wreathed Carelli's seemingly neckless head. Carelli then turned his full attention to Zima.

"Why are you here, Marcus?" asked Carelli, in a quiet tone.

Zima did not reply, but only looked down into his lap. Another sweat droplet fell from his jowl.

Carelli then shouted, "Look at me, you son of a bitch and tell me why you are here."

Zima looked up but could not form the words to reply to Carelli. Instead, his lips simply quivered.

Carelli suddenly lunged from his chair, stood up, pulled the cigar from his mouth, and threw it at Zima. It struck Zima on the cheek, and fell to the floor, where it continued to smoke. One of the Carelli bodyguards came around the desk, bent over and picked up the cigar, grabbed Zima's hand, and snuffed out the cigar on the top of Zima's hand. Zima loudly groaned, twisted his arm in pain, and tried in vain to pull his hand back from the vice-like grip of the bodyguard. After the cigar had been extinguished, Zima's hand was released. An ugly black and red circle remained on the top of Zima's hand. The bodyguard threw the cigar butt into a trash can and returned to his former place at the side of Carelli.

Carelli remained standing, leaning on the desk as he shouted at Zima. "I'll tell you why you're here. You're a goddam thief, that's why! You're a smart ass, punk, wise guy. What the hell got into you to steal from the hand that feeds you?" Carelli's face was beet red. His fleshy jowls shook as he continued shouting.

"For years, I have taken care of your family. Your papa worked for me and asked me to hire you, which at this moment I deeply regret. Your mama, a fine woman, still works for me to this day, bless her soul, and you go and steal from me to dirty your papa and mama's names."

Carelli paused. He opened a desk drawer and withdrew a small, pedestalled glass, which he placed on the desk. A bodyguard turned and opened a cabinet door behind Carelli and retrieved a bottle of cognac. The man pulled the cork from the bottle and poured a small amount of the brandy into Carelli's glass, before returning the bottle to the cabinet. Carelli took a small sip of the liquid, held it in his mouth, then swallowed before setting the glass back on the desk. He slowly licked his lips, pulled a handkerchief from his pocket and wiped his mouth, then put the cloth back in his pocket.

In a quieter, ominous tone, Carelli continued. "Marcus, it pains me to think that you would steal from my pocket. In my organization, there is only one consequence for your cowardly behavior, and you know damn well what that is."

Carelli waved to his bodyguards who walked to the front of his desk, and with a man on each side of him, Marcus Zima was literally lifted from the chair on which he had been sitting. As the bodyguards pulled him upright, there was a small rap on Carelli's office door. Carelli's male secretary opened the door slowly and put his upper body into the room. "Boss, there's someone here to see you."

"Who the hell is it?" asked Carelli.

The secretary replied, "I don't know her name. She wouldn't tell me, but she says it's very important and threatened to come in here herself. I think you might want to see her," he said.

"What the hell is the matter with you?" Carelli shouted at the secretary. "Can't you see I'm busy? This better be important," said Carelli, and he strode around the side of his desk and followed the secretary.

"Hang on to him," said Carelli as he tromped out of his office and angrily slammed the door behind him.

The two bodyguards roughly shoved Zima back into the chair and stood on each side of him.

"I sure as hell wouldn't want to be in your shoes, Zima," said one of the men. "You're gonna be a dead man real soon." The other bodyguard snorted a short laugh as the two men stood in front of Zima's chair starting at the bookkeeper who would soon have an end brought to his life.

As those words left the mouth of the bodyguard, a commotion could be heard outside the office through the closed door. Raised voices from Carelli and a woman could be heard in muffled tones. The words could not be understood by the bodyguards or Zima because Carelli and his visitor were speaking in a foreign tongue, but it was plainly understood that the speakers were very angry. One of the bodyguards walked to the door and quietly opened it only enough to make sure that his boss was in no danger. He then closed the door, turned and shrugged his shoulders to the questioning look of his cohort, and returned to Zima's chair.

The loud, angry shouting went on for several minutes, at the end of which it became quiet again, almost as if the speakers were murmuring to each other. In a moment, Carelli briskly opened the office door, entered, and slammed the door behind himself. He returned to his desk, sat down, and placed a finger on the top of the wine glass. The bodyguard retrieved the bottle and refilled the glass. This time, Carelli quickly swallowed the contents of the glass and laid his finger atop the glass once more, and the pouring and quick swallowing repeated itself.

Carelli brusquely set the wine glass on the desk with a sharp bang and sat back in his chair glaring at Zima. His face was still bright red, and now he was also sweating. Beads of moisture dotted his forehead. It was clear that the unseen argument had further added to Carelli's angry agitation. He slowly rose from his chair, walked around the desk, and with all his strength, smashed his fist into Zima's face. The force of the blow, knocked Zima's head back and rolled both Zima and the chair backwards, loudly crashing to the floor where Zima lay unmoving, tangled in the chair. The bodyguards lifted Zima and the chair, put Zima in the chair, and slapped him until he slowly came around and opened his eyes. Blood flowed from a gash under Zima's left eye. He slowly opened his eyes, only to see Carelli glaring at him from across the desk.

Unbeknownst to Zima, the woman who had been shouting at Carelli outside the office door was his mother, Veronica Zima, a woman who was still handsome after the many years of working for Carelli. She was the manager of one of Carelli's many food and drink establishments, several of which carried out a second function, that of laundering the dirty money received by Carelli's criminal ventures. The widow Zima was loyal to her boss and maintained a mutually agreeable physical arrangement with him. In turn, she was a favorite of Carelli's and was still discreetly called upon on a regular basis for their intimate pleasure. Her calm demeanor and accommodating nature helped Carelli relax and spend many pleasant evenings in her company. As a result of this special arrangement, Carelli found a niche in his icy heart for Veronica Zima, and at this moment, shouting into that small chasm, she had made her wishes known. Those wishes were that her son's life would be spared. Carelli was still considering their conversation as he returned to his seat behind his desk, still glowering at Zima and stymied by this turn of events. He was trying to conjure up a plan that would allow him to kill the pathetic traitor sitting across the desk from him, yet somehow either appease the widow Zima or make an airtight plan whereby she would never find out what happened to her son. For the moment, he could think of no solution.

"Marcus, you disgust me. You are the lowest scum I know at the moment," said the mobster. "You're such a little mama's boy that Mrs. Zima had to come and beg me for your pitiful life. I think if I had a gun, I would take care of this right now."

Suddenly, one of the bodyguards reached inside his jacket, pulled out a large revolver, and offered it to his boss. Carelli took the pistol and turned it to aim at Zima. He then pulled back the hammer, which made a loud metallic click sound as he cocked the gun. He paused for a few seconds while pointing the gun at Zima. Then Carelli loudly shouted, "Bang!" Zima physically jumped in his chair and began shaking uncontrollably. Carelli gave a quick snorting laugh, eased the pistol's hammer back down to safe position, and handed the gun back to its owner.

"Get this cockroach out of my sight," he said and waved to the bodyguards. "Take him downstairs and make sure he's locked in."

The bodyguards lifted Zima from his chair and left the office by a side door. They dragged Zima downstairs to a dusky and damp basement and chained him to a gray, concrete bench used just for that purpose. They left Zima still wondering when his death sentence would be carried out. He couldn't help but think how stupid he had been to be in this situation. It was not as if he was not paid well by Carelli, but he had finally become too greedy after years of handling money taken in at the expense of others. Initially, he had not needed the money, but after developing a gambling habit and frequenting ever more expensive pleasure dens, he had used the stolen funds for his own enjoyment. Fine women, fine food, rolls of the dice, and good booze all cost money, money that Zima had skimmed from his gangster employer.

Hours passed in the darkness of the basement. Zima had received no food or water, and his whole face hurt whenever he moved a facial muscle. He probed three loose teeth with his tongue to see how much they wiggled when he pushed his tongue against them. He thought it was odd that the teeth had remained connected to his jaw considering the force of the blow that had hit his face. Dried blood made up a macabre mask across the lower half of his face. He breathed with difficulty through his blocked nose that was pushed to the side. A large purple and black contusion wreathed the left side of his face, and the left eye was swollen closed. At this time, his only wish was that his demise would be quick and painless.

After more time had transpired, Zima heard the door to the basement being opened, and footfalls coming down the stairs. This was it, he thought. I'll soon be dead. But mindful of Veronica Zima's plea, Vico Carelli had other plans for the traitor and, for the time being, immediate death was not to be. After untying him, the bodyguards yanked Zima from the bench, saying, "Let's go, rat. You've got a train to catch."

The next day, after hours of monotonous stops at small towns across Missouri, the train rolled into the vast rail yard of Kansas City and lurched to a stop. The train engineer announced the arrival with a short blast from the steam whistle. Directed by the train's conductor, travel-weary passengers made their way to the exits and were met by family members or business associates. The Carelli lieutenant who had ridden with Zima, rose from his seat and pulled Zima to his feet.

"This is where you get off, Zima," and the two men walked to the steps of the rail car.

Carelli's henchman scanned the people standing on the train platform, gave a small "hmmph" sound, and began walking while holding Zima's arm. They approached two men who had been standing to the side of the platform, both of whom were known by Carelli's man. They were each dressed in poor fitting suits and wore soft, flat hats. One of the men had a small knife in his hand as was idly trimming his fingernails. The other man, from whose mouth a cigarette dangled, stared at Carelli's man and Zima as they approached.

Carelli's lieutenant shook hands with the two men on the train platform, as he had known them for a number of years. He then turned to Zima, grabbed his arm, and thrust him toward the two men, one of whom immediately slapped Zima across the face. Zima groaned and put a hand to his previously-injured face.

"This traitor is now your responsibility, my friends," said Carelli's man. "I've got a train to catch back to St. Louis." He shook hands again with his cronies, glared at Zima, and calmly walked away. Zima was led away by the other two men. He had no idea what was in store for him, but at least he was still alive, he thought to himself.

Chapter Two: Robert Owen Wolf

June 1900, Saturday Morning
Summer Prairie Ranch
Two miles southeast of Tioga, Kansas

U.S. Marshal Nathan Wolf felt awed and somewhat helpless as he watched his son, Robert Owen, being fed at Claire May's breast. When the baby turned his head, signifying that he was satisfied, Claire May wiped his face, gave him a kiss, handed the baby to Nathan, and began readjusting her clothing. Nathan placed the baby against his shoulder and gently patted his back until he heard a healthy burp from the infant. Nathan then laid him on the rug beside him. Nathan never tired of watching the baby. Three-month-old Bobby, as he was called by the proud parents, lay on his back, contentedly moving both his arms and legs while uttering baby sounds. Nathan smiled and quietly laughed to himself at the sight of his son lying there wiggling his extremities. When he had viewed this scene for the first time, it had somehow reminded Nathan of an old Mississippi River story about a turtle that had inadvertently been rolled over onto its shell by a rogue wave of water and helplessly moved its legs to right itself. The turtle could not right itself without help, or another passing wave. He had seen several of those hapless turtles after river flooding when he was growing up along the Mississippi in Iowa. He had wisely kept that turtle thought to himself rather than mentioning it to his beautiful wife. Claire May worshipped the baby and would probably not take kindly to Nathan's little turtle joke comparison. Claire May sidled up next to her husband on the floor, leaned into Nathan, and draped an arm across his shoulders, while they both looked in awe at their own baby boy.

"Isn't he just the most precious thing you've ever seen?" she said.

Nathan quietly replied, "Mmm, hmm." Short on words, but long on love, Nathan could only look on the baby with wonder. For the past year, he had watched in amazement as Claire May had slowly grown larger to accommodate the baby's growth within her. So many times Nathan had gently stroked his wife's belly, occasionally feeling the movement of the fetus within Claire May. And while he had known that there was a child developing within his wife, when Bobby's birth had finally taken place, with Claire May's mother, Virginia Summers, acting as midwife, he still felt that it was a bit unbelievable that a new life had been produced from the union of he and his wife. He asked himself, how could such a beautiful miracle happen? He was humble enough to know that there was a force much more powerful than his understanding at work in the process of creation.

"Mom and Rosa have breakfast ready by now, I'm sure. You bring Bobby and let's go eat," said Claire May. "I think they made eggs, bacon, and biscuits, and I'm hungry." She kissed Nathan on the cheek and rose to walk into the kitchen.

Nathan picked up Bobby and stood, momentarily looking down onto the cherubic face of his son. When Bobby started waving his arms, Nathan laughed and began walking toward breakfast. In the kitchen, Rosa came quickly to Nathan and took the baby. She began a litany of cooing sounds directed at Bobby. The melodic words she spoke were a mixture of motherly English mixed with Spanish endearments. Rosa's children were all grown, so she lovingly doted on the new baby at the Summer Prairie Ranch.

Claire May's brother, Will, was already seated at the table. He had just returned from the bunk house to check on the hands, seeing that they were fed and accounted for, and also to make sure the ranch work tasks for the day were understood. The work on a cattle ranch never ended, and Sunday was still a day with accompanying chores. A steaming plate of scrambled eggs and bacon was on the table in front of him, and he had his finger through the handle of his coffee mug as he sat waiting for the others to join him at the table. Since the untimely death of his father years ago, and as Will had grown older, he had taken over most of the duties of running Summer Prairie. But Virginia Summers, Will and Claire May's mother, still kept the books for the ranch and had the final say in any business matters that were out of the ordinary.

Will was a handsome man, who everyone said took after his late father, Robert. His shock of dark brown hair refused to be tamed in places, exacerbated by clamping a large, wide-brimmed hat on his head from morning to night. The lighter shade of ruddy color on his upper face attested to the hat's ability to block part of the intense Kansas sun. He sat with his dusty boots crossed at the ankle and stretched out in front of him, idly watching Rosa fuss over the baby. He slowly turned his coffee mug back and forth with his thumb and index finger. His thoughts turned to his fiancé, Alice Morgan, who lived on the neighboring ranch. Several months ago, Will had finally bolstered his courage and asked Alice to be his bride. Alice had enthusiastically agreed, and their wedding was being planned, but setting a date had not yet been finalized. With a pending marriage, and still watching his nephew, Will's thoughts strayed to the prospect of his own future children, an idea that often times made him nervous. He was not sure how fatherhood would suit him. Yet, he was pleasantly surprised to see his tough-as-nails brother-in-law, Nathan, wilt under the wiles of his own child and wondered how fatherhood would affect him when the time came. And as far as being an uncle, to Will it seemed that he was just a bit young to be called uncle. Claire May, Nathan, and Virginia joined him at the table, while at the end of the table, Rosa beamed while she gently rocked Bobby in her arms.

"Will, did you get enough sleep last night?" asked Virginia, as she carefully looked at her son.

"Yep. I feel OK, Mom. Why, do I look bad to you?" Will asked.

"No, I just worry about you is all. Lately, it seems like you are putting in a lot of hours," she answered.

"Always work to do on a ranch, Mom, as we all know." He continued. "Not much on my plate today, though. We need to keep working on the winter calves, getting them inoculated and castrated. Probably go ahead and do the branding, too. Nathan volunteered last night to help out today."

Claire May sat silently munching her griddle-toasted bread. She wondered how many times she had listened to discussions of the work being planned for the day on the ranch as she sat at this table. Thousands of times, she guessed. She remembered her dad discussing the same subjects when he was alive. Ranch life was demanding when there were nearly three hundred head of cattle wandering over the twelve hundred acres of prairie grassland of the Summer Prairie Ranch. It was taxing work with long hours, and it could very well be dangerous. Cantankerous cattle had been known to charge cowboys, injuring them or even killing them. Being kicked by a steer or heifer was common. Fast moving winter blizzards could kill cattle or cow hands without warning. Yet the ranch hands were the guardians of the cattle that provided their livelihood, even in the dead of winter amidst bone-chilling storms. While looking out for a stranded calf in a winter storm, Claire May's father, Robert, had been killed in a winter-time storm when Claire May was young. And even on a Sunday, the chores continued.

The quiet talk at the table was soon interrupted. Bobby had begun fussing in Rosa's arms. Claire May rose and retrieved the baby. She did a quick sniff test, and said, "Ugh. All right, little man, let's get a clean diaper for you," and she carried Bobby from the kitchen. Rosa immediately began making lunches for Will, Nathan, and the hands and began packing a large basket with the food items and water jugs. She would have it ready for the men when they left.

"Let me check on Claire May, and then I'll meet you at the corral," said Nathan to Will.

Will rose, took another swig of his coffee, set the mug back on the table, and walked out the side door. He paused for a few seconds to look at a row of rose bushes that bloomed in the morning sun next to the house. They were his mother's pride and joy. He then made his way to the barn next to the corral to retrieve his gear. His horse watched him from the corral. Will could see that the buckboard was already hitched for one of the hands to drive. Two others would also join them, and their horses were saddled and tied off to the rear corners of the buckboard.

Back in the house, Nathan had checked to make sure everything was all right with Claire May and gave her a kiss as she finished up with the baby. "I'll see you at dinner," he said, and headed out of the house toward the corral. The day had dawned warm, with a light layer of clouds that would burn off before noon. It would be a sunny, warm day, a good day for working the cattle, thought Nathan. Nathan's horse, Wander, stood eyeing the marshal as he passed the corral to get his gear in the barn. Nathan returned to the corral and put the saddle and blanket on the top rail. Then he noticed that Wander had moved to the far side of the corral.

Wander was the horse Will had given Nathan to use over a year ago, and Nathan rode the gelding nearly every day. Will claimed, and probably rightly so, that Wander just didn't have the attention span to be a good cow horse but was a perfectly fine horse otherwise. But Wander had his quirks. Just as his name implied, the horse would have bouts where he simply walked away from a trail or a task, sometimes even while being ridden, and was just as likely to walk away from a ground tie to find tasty fodder.

"Gonna be one of them days, huh," muttered Nathan.

With the bridle in his hand, Nathan walked toward Wander, but the horse slowly moved around the corral, keeping just ahead of Nathan. It was not as if the horse was avoiding the inevitable by being cantankerous. Instead, Wander simply saw this as a kind of game to be played. Sooner or later he would submit to Nathan, but Nathan preferred it to be sooner.

"Damn horse," Nathan mumbled.

Nathan bent down and passed through the corral rails and returned to the barn, where he put the bridle over his arm, scooped two handfuls of oats from a barrel and walked back to the corral. Will had nearly completed getting ready and was standing outside the corral where he had tied off his horse. "Wander's got you trained pretty good, Nathan," he said, and laughed.

Nathan had slipped back between the corral rails, carefully holding his cupped hands in front of him. "Yeah, I reckon so. Other than being dumb as a rock, he's OK, though." Both men laughed.

Nathan shook his hands holding the oats so the horse could hear, and Wander walked over to him and began lipping up the oats. When the oats were gone, and the horse stood still, noisily munching the last of the oats, Nathan slipped the bridle over the horse's head and buckled it up. He led Wander out of the corral and tied him to the top rail while he saddled the horse.

Rosa soon came from the house, struggling to carry the heavy basket of food. One of the hands hurried to her, took the basket, and loaded it into the buckboard. The men had already loaded a wooden medicine box, branding irons, an ax, and other tools they would need into the wagon. Will confirmed where they were going with the hand who was driving the wagon, because the wagon would take longer than the riders to get there. They would stop periodically along their route to pick up deadfall wood, chopping it into pieces that would fit in the wagon and that would be used for a branding and cooking fire. The men set off, heading to the southeast section of the ranch, where they would set up camp and begin building a fire. With the fire glowing and branding irons in the coals, Will and one of the cowhands rode toward the nearby cattle and began cutting out and roping unbranded calves. Each roper in turn pulled his calf to the fire, leaped from his horse, ran down the rope holding the calf and wrestled the calf to the ground, then kneeled on the calf's neck to keep it still. While the calf laid on its side, Nathan and another cowboy branded the calf and castrated the bulls. This process went on repetitiously until the men finally broke for lunch.

They all sat in the shade of the wagon to eat, their metal plates resting in their laps. A much-used, dented metal coffee pot rested on a metal grill above the red coals of the fire.

"I don't know if I want to sit real close to you, Nathan. You're getting too good with that castrating knife," joked Will as he sat down next to his brother-in-law.

The men ate in silence, and Will's plate was soon empty except for a few chicken bones from Rosa's cold fried chicken. Will sat quietly, drinking his coffee and watching the cattle in the near distance as they foraged for grass.

"I never get tired of this," said Will. "Just listen to how quiet it is," he said to Nathan. "The only sound is the breeze roughing up the grass and the heifers calling their calves. There's nothing like this in the city." He was quiet again for a moment and then asked Nathan, "What are you thinking about, Nathan."

"Nothing much, I guess," said Nathan. "Except I know that there will be work piled on my desk at the office tomorrow. Between the new sheriff in town, and my marshaling territory, there's always something going on."

Will picked at a piece of chicken in his teeth, then replied, "Well, I guess if I had to have a job off the ranch, I guess yours would be a good job. Bringing bad guys to justice is a fine thing. But sometimes it gets to be a bit too dangerous. You and Claire May found that out a year or so ago. I'll never forget how that Crenshaw gang kidnapped Claire May." Will was referring to Claire May's being kidnapped and held in the old Tioga railroad station by Arthur Crenshaw's gang last year, a situation wherein Claire May was thankfully able to escape before the gang was able to carry out its plan to murder her.

Nathan visibly shuddered at the thought of that incident. He did not know what would have happened with his life if his wife had been killed. She was his world, and he knew he could not imagine going through life without his wife, and now his son. Life would hold little meaning without them. He wished that Will had not brought up that chapter in his life. Just the thought of it made Nathan's stomach churn. He rose and said, "Let's get back to work." He flung the last of his coffee from his mug and walked over and put his dirty plate and mug into the back of the buckboard.

Will watched Nathan's back as his brother-in-law walked away. In the two years that he had known Nathan, Will had grown to like Nathan more as a true brother rather than an in-law. It was easy to see how Claire May had fallen for the soft spoken, muscular, tall, and handsome man from Iowa. He knew his sister adored Nathan and was very happy with her life, even more so since Bobby's arrival. For those reasons, he hoped that Nathan came to no harm in his dangerous work. He also wished that Nathan would quit his marshaling, and stay on the ranch, but he knew Nathan loved his job too much to quit.

Late in the afternoon, the men had finished their work, repacked the buckboard, and were very nearly ready to start back to the ranch house. Nathan saw her first, and a slight smile crossed his face. Will saw him looking off in the distance, smiled, and shook his head from side to side. Both the men knew who was riding toward them.

"Can't keep a wife at home, I reckon," said Will.

Nathan chuckled, "Yeah, I guess not," he replied, as Claire May got closer.

She pulled to a stop, leaned down toward Will, and asked, "Are you almost finished?"

Nathan mounted Wander, rode over to his wife's side and leaned over and kissed her. "What are you doing here?" he asked. "Not that I mind, of course."

The hands had turned the wagon and were already rolling toward home. "I just decided to come out and ride back to the house with you," said Claire May.

Nathan knew better and chuckled to himself. Claire May generally did not ride out from the house to visit him and Will when they were working. And while it might be true that she had wanted to join him, there was usually a secondary motive when his wife played coy with him. The couple rode side by side as their horses moved toward the ranch house. After Claire May had cleared her throat three or four times, Nathan finally asked, "Anything bothering you, dear?"

Claire May looked at him. "I just needed to get out of the house for a few minutes to get some fresh air," she said.

"Well, I'm glad you came out," said Nathan, but he thought there might be more. Sure enough Claire May then said, "You got a telegram from Ralph Gilman. He wants you to telegraph him first thing in the morning when you get to town."

Ralph Gilman was Nathan's boss. Gilman's office was in Kansas City, and he was the regional director for the U.S. Marshal Service. It was Gilman who generally gave Nathan assignments, or jobs that fell under the marshal's purview within Nathan's territory. Yet there were other incidents that Nathan attended to without receiving instructions from Kansas City. For those items, Nathan simply wrote up a post incident report and forwarded it to Gilman. Whenever Gilman contacted Nathan, it usually turned out to be something out of the ordinary and perhaps fraught with risk. Claire May was well aware that the working relationship between Nathan and Gilman was very good, and that Nathan took his special assignments in stride, but that didn't take the stress from Claire May when she saw her husband riding away after being contacted by his boss. Nathan knew what Claire May was thinking because he had witnessed this situation several times in the past.

Nathan tried to console his wife as they rode. "Stop fretting, Claire May. You know everything will turn out all right, it always does. He reached over and put his hand on her shoulder as they continued riding.

"Yes," she replied. "I know it will, but you can't blame me for worrying," and she raised her free hand and put it on his hand on her shoulder. They stopped their horses for a moment, and each leaned over and they kissed, but then Wander decided that he had seen a bit of green grass at the side, and he moved away while the couple was still in a kiss. Nathan nearly tumbled from the saddle before he righted himself and brought the horse under control.

"Damn horse," said Nathan, while Claire May laughed.

When she stopped laughing, she said, "All right, Marshal, I'll race you home."

"Nothing doing," said Nathan. "You know the doctor said you were to take it easy for a while longer."

"Oh, what does an old doctor know, anyway," said Claire May, and she spurred her horse into a lope and quickly passed the buckboard. Nathan just shook his head and put Wander into a canter. He was not going to try to catch Claire May. He had learned long ago that she would not allow herself to be caught in a horse race, and Nathan thought it was more prudent to let her go.

Will had joined him as they rode toward home. "Your wife is a pistol," he said.

"Yeah, yeah, so is your sister," said Nathan, and the men laughed and loped toward the house.

Chapter Three:
Snake Eyes Skinner

June 1900
Monday, six a.m.
Kansas State Penitentiary
Lansing, Kansas

Hank Skinner was sweating profusely, and his sinuses were swollen and blocked from the foul odors of the surrounding bed sheets. He did his best not to think of the disgusting sweat and filth of those sheets that had recently lain on the soiled, thin bunk mattresses in each cell of the prison. Skinner was laying at the bottom of a laundry cart that was being rolled out of the prison to be lifted and placed on a wagon destined for a commercial laundry nearby where the bed clothes would be washed. The cart was jostled roughly but was then lifted onto the wagon. One of the prison trustees lifting the cart remarked that this cart seemed heavier than the others, but the men did not stop to investigate. Skinner listened as other carts were added to the load in the enclosed wagon. In a few moments he heard the bang of the wagon's rear doors being closed and latched, followed by muffled talking as the laundry wagon driver received the go-ahead from the prison guards to drive through the prison wall gates.

Skinner was regarded as one of the nastiest men housed in the most secure area of the Lansing, Kansas, prison. By normal standards, he was considered a giant of a man, standing over six feet tall and weighing over 250 pounds. He was a man whom nobody cared to challenge. Coupled with his size, Skinner was just plain mean. His criminal record included armed robbery and the murder of at least six men, including a Pinkerton detective, an act that intensified an all-out manhunt for him and ultimately led to his incarceration. His prison moniker was "Snake Eyes," a name that he had earned after killing a gambling foe whom he believed had rigged the dice in a craps game to roll one pip per die, a losing throw. It was coincidental that Skinner also had green-hued eyes that seemed to be placed too close together, giving him a feral, snake-eyed look. The "snake eye murder," seen by many witnesses, had necessitated Skinner's life of running from the law and his Snake Eyes nickname. But running from the law had its disadvantages for Skinner, primarily reducing his ability to stay in one place long enough to plan his next crime. As a result, his fugitive life meant that he struggled to find food and shelter, and he was forced to find refuge wherever he could. Skinner had been relentlessly tracked and finally found in a Kansas City opium den where he had lain for several days under the influence of the drug on which he had spent his last stolen dime. After a speedy trial, Skinner was sentenced to life without parole and thrown into the Kansas State Prison in Lansing, where he had spent the past four years. But on this late morning, he would be free of the prison walls.

The driver of the laundry wagon was an employee of a drayage company that held a contract with the prison to pick up and deliver the weekly laundry. He was an older gentleman, content with his driving job, a profession he had followed all of his life. His team of nearly identical black horses knew the route, and on this seldom travelled road, while the horses walked ahead, he relaxed his hold on the reins so that he could fish in his pocket for his tobacco quid. He also removed a small sharp folding knife from a pocket and began to cut a piece of the quid to put in his mouth. The driver's full attention was on cutting the tobacco, and he could not see what was transpiring behind him. Hank Skinner had quietly climbed out of the laundry cart and was approaching the driver from behind. Skinner bent down on one knee reached up his pant leg to the pocket sown into the inside of his trouser leg. From that pocket, he retrieved a prison-made knife, fashioned from a piece of scrap iron carelessly left on the floor of a prison workshop. From that scrap iron, Skinner had made a deadly knife, the blade of which was razor sharp.

Skinner, who was left-handed, carefully came up behind the driver and began to raise his knife-wielding hand to strike the driver in the neck. But the old driver, a veteran of several Civil War battles, had been through numerous scrapes in his lifetime, including a period in his much younger days as an Indian fighter. He was not as frail as he appeared. At the last second, he saw Skinner's raised arm. The driver immediately lurched to the side of the wagon seat and twisted his body. Skinner's blade missed its mark and entered the top of the drivers left shoulder. The driver quickly grabbed Skinner's wrist, pulled it from his shoulder, and with his own knife, stabbed Skinner's left wrist with the filthy tobacco-encrusted blade, and twisted the knife, severing two tendons in Skinner's wrist. Skinner screamed in pain, but retrieved the knife with his right hand. He managed to move to his right to reach around the neck of the driver, and immediately slashed the driver's throat. The driver sighed heavily and slumped to the foot well of the wagon where he lay bleeding profusely. Skinner looked at his bloody, oozing wrist and discovered that he could not move the middle three fingers of that hand.

"You old son of a bitch," he mumbled and bent over to superfluously stab the driver again. He then grabbed the reins, stopped the horses, and tied them off on the wagon brake handle. Using strips he cut from the bed sheets, he managed to securely wrap his wrist to staunch the bleeding. His wound was heatedly painful, especially if he tried to move the fingers on his left hand. Straining with his right hand and partial use of his left, he was able to pull the driver into the back of the wagon, where he stripped the clothes from the driver and went through the man's pockets. Skinner was surprised to find that the old man was carrying a few dollars, but even more surprised to find a small, wood-gripped .32 caliber revolver in the man's pocket. Even though they did not fit him well, Skinner changed into the driver's clothes, wrapped more cloth strips around his wrist, and threw dirty sheets over the man's body. He then moved to the front of the wagon and stepped to the ground.

For a moment, he studied the harnesses of the horses and decided which of the two horses he would unhitch. He began unbuckling the breeching straps and was moving up to the collar. But before he could unbuckle it, he noticed a two-wheeled, single-horse drawn cart approaching him from the distance. His hand went into his trouser pocket and felt the small revolver, then withdrew his hand and moved back to the rear of the horse.

The driver of the cart stopped, and the gray horse pulling the cart hung its head to rest, paying no attention to the two blacks that were hitched to the laundry wagon. By the well-worn clothes he was wearing, the cart driver appeared to be a farmer returning home from an early morning trip to town. "Do you need some help there, stranger," he said, while studying Skinner.

Skinner quickly answered. "I had a strap come loose. I'm just tightening it up and I'll be on my way."

"Looks like you've got the prison's laundry there," said the farmer.

Skinner was slowly rebuckling the straps he had loosened only moments before. He tensed in response to the farmer's remark and wished this interloper would get on his way. "Yep, it's the weekly laundry run from the prison. Now, if you don't mind, I'll just get this fixed and head on into town."

The farmer did not move but continued to study Skinner. "Don't believe I've seen you around here before. Did Ray Leonard just hire you?" he asked.

Well, dammit, thought Skinner, why won't this old hayseed leave? "Yeah, just a few days ago. I think I'd best get finished here, so Mr. Leonard won't get mad," lied Skinner, and his unwounded hand moved toward his trouser pocket.

The farmer spat a brown glob of tobacco juice off the side of his cart. "OK then, it looks like you don't need any help, so I'll mosey on," he said. He touched his hat, gave his reins a flick, and began receding down the road.

"Dumb hayseed," mumbled Skinner, and again began unbuckling the harness. After a few moments all the trappings were removed leaving only the head harness and reins attached to the horse. Skinner quickly used his knife and cut the reins shorter, led the horse next to the wagon, stood on the axle hub and jumped on the horse's back. He was soon heading south, riding the black horse at a fast walk, Skinner holding the reins and trying his best not to slide off the back of the horse.

Meanwhile, the farmer followed the westward road, where he soon heard an odd noise. As he approached the prison, the sound became clear. It was the sound of a hand-cranked siren, modulating in pitch as its operator cranked the handle in a circular motion. Uh-oh, thought the farmer. Something has happened at the prison. He stopped his cart at the end of the drive of the prison. It was not long before a uniformed man hurriedly came from the gate and approached the farmer.

"What happened?" asked the farmer.

"Prison break," responded the guard. "Did you happen to see a laundry wagon on your way here?" he asked.

"Sure did," said the farmer. "I passed it up the road a ways."

"Did you see the driver. Did you get a good look at him?" asked the guard.

"Heck, I spoke with the fella for a few minutes," replied the farmer.

"Tell me what he looked like," said the guard.

“He weren’t nothin’ special,” said the man. “’Cept he had kinda funny eyes. Kinda close together like.”

“Dammit,” said the guard. “One more thing,” said the guard. “What color were those laundry wagon horses?”

“Black,” said the farmer. “Yep, they were both nearly all black,”

“Much obliged,” said the guard, and he began running back toward the gate.

The farmer scratched his bewhiskered cheek for a moment. “Hmm,” he mumbled, then clucked to his horse and continued on his way home.

By telegraph, the prison soon sent messages to all the surrounding law enforcement entities including the U.S. Marshal Service, wherein they described the prison break, the physical appearance of Hank “Snake Eyes” Skinner, and the fact that he was probably riding a black horse. The hunt was on for the dangerous felon.

Chapter Four: Pursuit of Snake Eyes

June 1900
Monday 10 a.m.
Chanute, Kansas

The good people of Chanute had seen their city slowly grow to the point that they needed more direct, on-the-scene law enforcement, and had elected Tom Barnes to be their sheriff in a special election nearly six months ago. This was no reflection on Marshal Nathan Wolf and Deputy Bill Ward. Their duties sometimes took them out into the territory for days at a time, leaving the local area without law enforcement. Barnes was a young single man lacking in experience, but the city fathers felt that he would grow into the job and could be reelected to office for as long as he wanted the job. But with both a marshal and a sheriff, more office space was required. Rather than find a convenient office for their new sheriff, the city had knocked out a wall of the jail and U.S. Marshal's office to enlarge it to make room for the sheriff and added a few more pieces of second-hand furniture. Marshal Nathan Wolf, Deputy Marshal Bill Ward, and Sheriff Tom Barnes and his deputies all shared the one well-worn location. And while the group of law enforcement men got along well together, none of them felt that case work between the two agencies should co-mingle, even though it often could not be helped. U.S. Marshal Service Regional Director Ralph Gilman was vehemently opposed to the arrangement, but his agency could not afford to build a new office for Nathan and Bill. He was sure that any message he sent to Nathan was more than likely being read by the sheriff, which was true many times, but neither Nathan nor Tom saw it as a problem.

As Nathan, Bill, and Tom sat in the office drinking their second mugs of morning coffee, they were idly discussing a wire that had come in to the telegraph office the previous day and subsequently had been delivered to their office. It was the contact that Claire May had mentioned to Nathan the day before when she told him that Gilman wanted to alert Nathan to a situation. According to Gilman's telegram, there had been a report in the Kansas City area of counterfeit currency being passed among retail merchants. These innocent, small-businessmen were hopping mad because they had accepted bogus money from customers, and their banks were turning down this currency when they attempted to make deposits. The Secret Service, in turn, was contacting other law enforcement agencies to be on the lookout for bogus currency in their areas of responsibility. As a result, Gilman had been contacted by his counterpart at the Secret Service and had been briefed on a growing concern that the fake currency could spread.

Counterfeiting was not a new problem in the United States. During the Civil War, and even more so after the war, commerce in America was flooded with counterfeit money. As a result, the U.S. Secret Service had been formed with the express, primary purpose of finding and prosecuting counterfeiters. They had been successful in carrying out their mission, but according to Gilman's wire, there was a concern that more fake currency could appear on a widespread basis, and he wanted his marshals to be on the lookout for counterfeit money. In true bureaucratic fashion, Gilman did not want his agency to be accused of allowing the bogus money to spread into their territories, even though the primary responsibility for stopping the spread of the currency belonged to the Secret Service. In addition, the U.S. Marshals were not sufficiently trained to identify fake currency if it were to pass through their respective territories.

"Sounds like our boss is worried over something that isn't even our job," said Bill. Never one to mince words, Bill saw Gilman's wire as trying to rope the Marshal Service into helping the Secret Service. "Just wait and see," said Bill, "if any of this funny money shows up in our territory, we wouldn't know it from a pig's ear, and we'll probably get blamed for letting it happen."

Nathan initially did not respond. He was smart enough to know that whatever he might say could find its way outside the office, and he did not feel that the town should be privy to their objection to helping the Secret Service. But he had to agree with Bill in that it seemed that the Marshal Service acted as the first repository of citizens' discontent with the federal government when things were not going well, but conversely were praised when the Marshals clamped down on criminal activity. Nathan preferred to keep a low profile.

The clacking of the telegraph key broke into their discussion of counterfeiters.

"That's Gilman's office sending again," said Bill. "Hope he wasn't reading my thoughts."

The men laughed. "Yeah, Bill, you better watch out what you're thinking," said Tom.

Bill got up and moved to the key and tapped it to let the sender know he was ready to receive. For the next few minutes, he scribbled down the letters on a sheet of paper. Nathan knew Morse code and what was being sent, and mentally, he pieced the letters together in his head. He sat upright in his chair and listened intently. Tom Barnes didn't know the code and could only wait until Bill had completed the message. In a few minutes, Bill tapped the key again, acknowledging receipt of the message.

Bill looked at the message for a bit, made some corrections to it, and handed it to Nathan. "Looks like we've got some work to do," said Bill. The telegram read:

Gilman sending:

Word received - Hank Skinner, highly dangerous felon escaped Lansing this day. In for murder and robbery. Fought and killed a prison delivery man and stole black horse. Thought to be heading your direction. Mentioned Texas to a cell mate. Directing Wolf immediately pursue and capture escapee. Ht. 6 ft. Wt. 240. Dark hair. No visible scars. Close set green eyes. Observe caution - consider Skinner to be armed, extremely dangerous. Good hunting. Gilman

"What's up?" asked Tom.

Nathan didn't answer right away. He was thinking, trying to reason or put himself in the shoes of the fugitive. In his mind, he was seeing a visual image of the man, riding a black horse and allegedly heading for Texas, which meant that he would pass close to their territory.

"Guess it's time I earned my paycheck," said Nathan, and he showed Tom the written message. He rose from his chair, finished his coffee, and hung his tin mug on its peg by the wood stove. "You boys ready for some lunch? I figure I better put some grub away since I'll be on the road awhile."

When the lawmen returned from lunch, Nathan gathered up his bedroll and saddle bags from the bunk in the back room that he used when he was staying overnight in town. He rolled his rain poncho into the bedroll and tied it. He then carefully put extra newspaper wrap around the sandwiches he had brought from the cafe and put them in the saddle bags. He retrieved a set of brand new binoculars from a hook on the wall and put them in the saddlebags. Finally, he looked over his Winchester 1892, worked the action, and loaded the rifle. He did the same with the Colt 1892 pistol, putting a drop of oil in the cylinder turning mechanism, loaded it with the higher powered .41 caliber cartridges, and shoved it into the gun belt before buckling it around his waist. He patted his back pocket, ensuring that his blackjack was there. He then walked over, sat down in front of the telegraph key, and keyed in the call sign for the Summer Prairie Ranch. He was soon answered with Claire May's key code letters. He relayed to her the details of his assignment to track an escaped convict, leaving out the fact that Skinner was extremely dangerous. He told her that he would be home in a few days, that he loved her, and to kiss Bobby for him. Claire May answered that she loved him, and that he should be careful. Then they both signed off.

At Summer Prairie Ranch, Claire May sat in the ranch office for a moment thinking about Nathan. She was worried about him and said a silent prayer to keep him safe. Stoically, she walked through the house to stand over Bobby's crib. The baby was sleeping peacefully, and she leaned over and kissed his forehead.

Nathan carried his bed roll, saddlebags, and rifle to the livery stable, *Mullins and Son Livery,* and entered the barn door. Hay dust hung in the sun beams entering the east windows of the building. "Headed out, Nathan?" asked Dwight Mullins, the stable owner. He and his son, Ed, had run the livery for years, and they both owed Nathan a great deal of respect for the manner in which he had handled Ed's unwilling involvement with the Ku Klux Klan before Nathan had disbanded and prosecuted the gang for their crimes a year ago. Ed was at his usual place at the forge, heating and shaping horseshoes for customers as well as making special order iron projects. A horse was tied nearby to a tether ring, awaiting the product of Ed's hammering. Ed put his tongs down, wiped his brow and hands on a rag he withdrew from his back pocket, and walked over to shake hands with the marshal. His blackened leather apron was evidence of many years spent smithing.

"Yeah, Dwight. I've got to be gone a couple days," answered Nathan.

Dwight left to get Nathan's horse ready.

Nathan turned to Ed. "Everything going OK, Ed?" asked Nathan.

"Yeah, it sure is. I've gotta say that life is going a lot better than it was a year ago," replied Ed. "Heck, I've even started courting a young lady."

"Glad to hear it," said Nathan, and the men chatted a few more minutes, waiting for Dwight's return.

Dwight walked Wander from his stall, where he had already saddled and bridled the gelding. Wander danced a bit when he saw Nathan. He knew he was going to hit the road with the marshal, and that was more exciting than sleep-standing in his cramped stall. The horse was well rested, grained up, and ready to go.

While Dwight watched, Nathan led the horse outside, tied him to a hitch rack, shoved his Winchester into its scabbard, and tied the bedroll to the saddle cantle. He shook hands with Dwight, untied Wander, and climbed into the saddle.

"I'll see you in a couple days," said Nathan. "And thanks for looking after knucklehead for me."

"Ah, he ain't no trouble," said Dwight. "That horse is too dumb to be trouble."

Both men laughed as Nathan turned Wander and heard Dwight say, "You stay safe, Marshal."

Nathan waved and headed north out of town.

He rode for the rest of the day, all the while looking from right to left as he moved north, using the binoculars when he saw distant objects of interest. Throughout the afternoon, he only met two riders going south, and both were ranchers going to town for supplies. As darkness began to fall, he reached Garnett, a small farming and ranching community.

He could tell that Wander was bushed, and he made his way to the livery stable. He spoke to the proprietor and gave instructions for boarding the horse. He then grabbed his saddle bags and rifle, leaving the bed roll on the saddle. The livery man unsaddled Wander and put the saddle on a saddle rack with the blanket on top to air and came back to Nathan.

"Could you recommend a decent hotel and place to get some supper?" asked Nathan.

"Sure," the livery owner replied. "Up the street is the Garnett Hotel, and they've got a little restaurant that serves good roast beef and gravy and some mighty fine pie."

"Much obliged," answered Nathan, and turned to walk away. But then he stopped and walked back to the owner.

"Say, you didn't happen to see a stranger passing through here today, did you?" asked Nathan. "He would have been riding a black horse."

Immediately the livery owner answered. "Oh, sure. I saw a fella like that. He came in here riding a lathered up black horse that looked like it was going to keel over. He was a mean lookin' sort of fella. I grained and rubbed down the horse while the man went to eat. He came back and peeled a couple dollars out of his pocket and bought an old saddle I had handy. Then he got on that horse and left town heading south. I feel sorry for that horse," he said.

Nathan peeled back his vest and showed the livery man his badge. "What did the man look like?" asked Nathan.

"Big fella," said the livery man. "Mighty tall and broad, but he had these funny little eyes that 'pert near looked through you. Kinda squinty and narrow-like."

Nathan cursed under his breath. He had somehow missed Skinner on the road.

"I'll be back at sunup to get my horse," said Nathan, and he turned to walk to the hotel.

"Marshal," shouted the livery man. "One more thing I just remembered. He had a bunch of dirty bloody rags wrapped around his hand."

Nathan had stopped and listened, "You mean it looked like he had injured it somehow?"

"Looked that way," said the livery man, "and he wasn't using it at all. Left hand as I recall," he said.

"Hmm. Much obliged," said Nathan and turned back to the hotel. So it appeared that Skinner, the escaped felon, may have been injured, thought Nathan. Must have gotten hurt in the struggle with the delivery man. Even so, thought Nathan, I don't want to forget that this character has killed quite a few men. But he struggled to figure out how he had missed the fugitive on the road. He felt certain that they had passed each other somehow. He continued walking toward the hotel for the night.

Tuesday 6 a.m.

Nathan was up with the sun. He hurriedly ate breakfast in the hotel restaurant, paid for his meal, and started off for the livery stable carrying his rifle and saddlebags. In another twenty minutes he was back on the road. But this time he was headed south, away from Garnett.

Wander was a large quarter horse, just a bit over fifteen hands, bred for endurance and stamina. Unfortunately, the horse didn't seem to have "cow sense" and was not useful as a cutting horse on the Summer Prairie Ranch. But what the horse lacked in cattle skills, and sometimes common sense, he made up for in stamina. Wander could trail nearly all day, as long as Nathan altered the horse's gait between a fast walk and a trot with an occasional rest. In this manner, Nathan was able to cover a good distance in the course of a day without overtiring the horse. That traveling rhythm of Wander's changing gaits had started as Nathan trotted to the south.

Nathan had not seen Hank Skinner the previous day because the fugitive had left the road for a couple of hours in the late afternoon. He had made his way to a nearby creek for water, tying his horse in a clump of bushes in order to be hidden from the road. His left wrist was giving him a great deal of pain. After watering and tying the horse, he had walked to the creek, where he unwrapped the bandages from his wound. The wound was ugly, raw and red. Skinner washed the soiled bandages in the cold creek water, laid them out on the grass, and painfully rinsed the ugly wound on his wrist.

That son-of-a-bitch laundry man, thought Skinner, while he stared at the raw wound. He tried to move his fingers on his left hand and winced in intense pain. "Dammit," he shouted. The black horse lifted its head and stared at Skinner, grass protruding from both sides of its mouth. Little did Skinner know that the strips of bandages made from the soiled bed sheets and the germ-laden blade of the delivery man's knife had already introduced an enormous amount of germs and bacteria into the wrist wound, creating pain that had now extended up Skinner's arm. He had no way of knowing that the beginnings of gangrene had already started in the left wrist due to lack of blood flow and a harmful infection. All he really knew for sure was that the wound and his hand and arm hurt like the devil.

As Skinner had rewrapped the damp bandages around the wound, the pain caused him to be lightheaded. When he finished with the bandages, he had lain on his back in the grass to let the light-headedness pass. Shadows lengthened into dusk. It had been a hell of a day, he thought, and he had begun pondering what his life might be like as he increased the distance between him and Lansing. Then he had closed his eyes and fallen asleep. He was sleeping when U.S. Marshal Nathan Wolf had passed on the road near his location. Skinner had slept through the night in the same clump of grass. When he awoke, the sun was already up.

He raised himself to a sitting position and gripped his left arm as it throbbed in pain. He noticed that his left fingers appeared to be darker in color, taking on a dark, deep red hue. He knew that could not be a good sign. He rose, stumbled to the creek, splashed water on his face, and drank the water. Instead of a normal, sweet taste, the water tasted like iron, and he spit it out. He rose and walked to the black horse that appeared to be dozing with its head down and one upturned rear hoof. It started awake as Skinner neared and suspiciously eyeballed the criminal. Checking the cinches for tightness, Skinner climbed to the saddle and got back on the road heading south. Every jostling step the horse took shot pain up Skinner's arm.

Tuesday, Early Evening

Hank Skinner wasn't the only one in pain. U.S. Marshal Nathan Wolf was sure that he had bruised his entire body. Twelve hours in the saddle with few breaks would jostle even the best of riders, and he was sore all over. Wander was at the end of his stamina as Nathan rode to the Mullins' livery stable in Chanute. Dwight Mullins sat on a chair at the large entrance door, a beat-up pipe curling smoke from its bowl. He rose quickly when he saw Nathan.

"You don't look so good, Marshal," said Dwight. Indeed, Nathan was bone tired, but quitting was not part of the plan.

"I don't doubt it, Dwight. I'm just a bit tired. Take Wander, here, and saddle me one of your fastest and best horses. I'm going over to the office and then I'll be right back. I want to keep riding tonight," said Nathan, and he turned and walked up the street to the office, aching with every step.

The office was empty. Bill Ward and the Sheriff had left for the day. Nathan felt the side of the coffee pot on the stove. It was warm, so he poured a mug and sat down at the telegraph key. He keyed the Summer

Prairie Ranch. In a moment he received an answer. Virginia Summers was at the key. Virginia told him that Claire May was out on the ranch with Will. Nathan responded and asked Virginia to tell Claire May that he loved her and that his fugitive was heading south. He would see her in a couple more days. Virginia acknowledged and told Nathan to be very careful. Through a neighbor who had been to town and had spoken to Sheriff Tom Barnes, she had learned about the felon that Nathan was chasing. Finally, she told him that everyone, including the baby, missed him. Nathan was motionless for a moment. Finally he acknowledged and signed off. Virginia did the same. Nathan swallowed the lump in his throat, and then his coffee. He stood and stretched and then left the office for the livery stable.

Dwight had the horse ready, a red roan gelding that looked like it could run. Dwight had already shifted Nathan's bed roll, saddlebags, and rifle to the new horse. Overcoming his weariness, Nathan climbed in the saddle. "Thanks, Dwight. I hope to see you in a couple days," said Nathan, and he leaned down and shook Dwight's hand. He then wheeled the horse and turned south out of town. When he felt the horse was warm, he broke into a canter, keeping up an alternating canter and walk routine through the darkness. He hoped to close the distance between him and Skinner in the next few hours.

At nearly three a.m., Nathan had had enough. In the dim moon light, he found a grassy copse by a stream. He dismounted, watered the horse, and hobbled the animal. He removed the bridle so the horse could graze, retrieved his bed roll, and nearly fell asleep before he hit the ground.

Wednesday 6:30 a.m.

As he lay on the grass waking up, he opened his eyes and saw the roan nearly eyeball to eyeball. It startled Nathan for a second until he realized where he was. He shoved at the horse's head. He said aloud, "I guess I'm lying on the best grass, huh." The horse moved off a couple feet and continued chewing.

Nathan rose, walked to the stream, and splashed water on his face. He drank some water then went to the horse. He reached into his saddlebag and retrieved one of the two-day-old sandwiches. Nathan did not care that it was stale. Hunger overcomes taste sometimes, he thought. He mumbled to the horse, "At least your grass is fresh."

He finished the stale sandwich, returned to the stream with his canteen, filled it, and drank more water. In ten more minutes, he had screwed on his hat and was back in the saddle. The sun was just hurdling the horizon, and the clear sky of the cool morning gave promise of a pretty day as Nathan rode south. He was figuring he would reach the border with Oklahoma before the day was over. He thought that if he did not find Skinner before that, he would have to turn back at the border and transfer the chase to the marshal in Oklahoma.

Throughout the morning, Nathan would stop periodically, scan his surroundings, and use the binoculars when he spied any object of interest. There was only one indication that he was on the right track. In all of the many horse and wagon tracks that comprised the travelled road, only one set appeared fresh, with fresh horse droppings. Those tracks were heading south, and by the look of the horse scat, the horse and rider were not far ahead of him. Nathan nudged the horse back into a lope.

In mid-afternoon, Nathan figured that he was nearing the state border. From the top of a long rise where he had paused, he could see smoke rising from buildings in the far distance, a sure sign of a town. He reasoned that it had to be Coffeyville, the last Kansas town before the border with Oklahoma. As he sat for a moment letting the horse blow, his eyes caught a discoloration in the distance away from the road. He retrieved the binoculars, training them on what appeared to be a dilapidated farmhouse. Such an old, abandoned house was not unusual, but the black horse standing at the side of the house was odd. The horse was still saddled, and stood head down, not moving. Nathan thought to himself, Snake Eyes, I believe I've caught you. Nathan also noticed that neat rows of corn marched across the back of the house, giving the appearance that someone was tending to the crop.

He eased the roan off the road and walked to a small grove of trees where he dismounted, tied off the horse, and retrieved his rifle. He checked his pistol and the rifle to make sure they were operating properly and walked slowly out of the grove. He crouched as he approached the side of the weathered-gray board house until he reached the black horse. One look at the dried crusty salt on the horse and the fact that the horse did not raise its head to acknowledge him, told Nathan that the horse was sadly, near death. Nathan slowly walked around to the front of the house, where the scarred and broken front door was hanging askance by one hinge.

"Skinner, this is Marshal Nathan Wolf. I know you're in there," shouted Nathan. "You need to come out with your hands in the air." While Nathan crouched to the side of the small front porch of the house, he heard no response, although Skinner had heard Nathan.

Skinner's wound had gotten more serious. The fugitive was delirious with fever from blood poisoning, and his breathing had become labored. Just like the horse he had been riding, Skinner was nearing death. The outlaw was near dying from the spreading gangrene, yet, he remained dangerous. While the deliriums were upon him, they caused Skinner to be in a state of frenzy. In such a condition, he could easily lash out at any threat. He had heard Nathan's shout, and in fact, had seen Nathan approach the house. Yet, even wounded, he was determined to eliminate the threat and make his escape. He remembered that the black horse was a goner, but the marshal was riding a good-looking animal. He would make his escape by stealing the lawman's horse. He slipped out the back door of the house and made his way into some tall grassy weeds, where he slipped down on hands and knees and began crawling to where Nathan's horse was tied. The pistol was tucked into his belt in the small of his back.

Nathan shouted again. "Skinner, get yourself out here, I know you're in there."

Skinner paid no attention and continued crawling in the grass. But suddenly, he came to a section of ground where shade from an oak tree had stunted the growth of grass. The criminal would have to cross the bare ground to get to the marshal's horse. He decided to make a break for it and stood to run. But at the same instant, Nathan saw him, raised his rifle, and placed a shot at the feet of the fugitive.

"The next one will have your name on it, Skinner," shouted Nathan.

Skinner turned to face Nathan as the marshal approached. His fever was making Skinner irrational. He raised his hands as Nathan continued nearing. Nathan drew his pistol and laid the rifle on the ground.

"Turn around Skinner and put your hands behind your back. I don't want any trouble out of you and we'll get along just fine," said Nathan. Nathan, seeing the fugitive for the first time, thought to himself that Skinner matched the description he had been given. Skinner really was a big man, and he did not look forward to riding with this fugitive all the way back to Lansing.

"Yeah, yeah," said Skinner, and he slowly began to turn.

But in the instant as he twisted, Skinner flashed his right hand back and retrieved the pistol from his waist band. He quickly turned the pistol on Nathan and fired. The bullet struck Nathan just under the collar bone and passed up into his shoulder. Blood began flowing from the wound. But Nathan, too, fired his Colt and the bullet struck Skinner in the stomach. In pain, Skinner fired his weapon again, striking Nathan in the upper leg, partially breaking the femur, sending Nathan to the ground. That wound, too, began bleeding. As he lay there, Skinner closed the distance between him and the marshal, and then stood on Nathan's wrist. He bent down and pulled Nathan's pistol from his hand, tossing it to the side. But Nathan was not idle. With his good arm, Nathan retrieved the blackjack from his rear pocket and using all his strength, he swung the blackjack, striking Skinner on the top of his pistol hand, breaking bones in the hand. The pain caused Skinner to scream and involuntarily drop the pistol. In an instant, Nathan retrieved the pistol, aimed quickly, and fired, continuing to shoot Skinner until the gun was empty. Skinner stood motionless, his face a mask of bewilderment. Ever so slowly, his knees buckled, he went down on his knees, and sighed. He then fell forward on his face. Half his body lay on Nathan, with one of Skinner's arms crossing Nathan's chest. The two men lay in repose.

After another moment, Nathan was able to painfully extricate himself from Skinner's death embrace. But then he looked at the blood oozing from his leg and upper body wounds. He could not walk, and with only one arm, he could not rise anyway. He now knew he was in a serious, deadly situation. He looked over at the fugitive lying face down in the dirt. After emptying the pistol at Skinner, Nathan had no reason to believe that the criminal was alive.

When he raised his head, Nathan could see the horse, still tied where he had left him. If I can make it to the horse, he thought, maybe I could pull myself up on him. Nathan began to drag himself, using one arm and one leg to move across the dirt. He gave up after a few moments. The loss of blood was sapping his strength.

The shadows were lengthening. Day was nearly at an end. After a bit, darkness fell. Nathan still lay in the dirt, his breath growing more shallow. His last thought before losing consciousness, was that he would never see Claire May and Bobby again.

Four Days Later, Sunday 8 a.m.
Yoder Family Farm
Coffeyville, Kansas

Paul Yoder was returning to the house after milking the eight Guernsey cows by hand, one by one, in his barn. When he finished milking, he opened a combination of door and gates to let the cows return to the pasture. A vendor's wagon would come to the farm in an hour or so to take the milk to the local creamery. After shoveling the cow manure into an iron-wheeled spreader, he set the shovel aside and walked to the pump outside the back door of the house. He washed his hands and face, walked to the back door, and removed his boots. He could smell coffee brewing and bacon cooking as he entered the kitchen. His wife, Martha, was busy at the stove, finishing the bacon and keeping a watchful eye on the biscuits browning in the oven. Three of the six Yoder children were helping their mother by setting the table and keeping the youngest children from being underfoot.

The Yoders were Amish. Paul's great grandfather emigrated from Germany, first settling in the Northeast. But in 1801, when the United States acquired the Louisiana Purchase, Paul's grandfather resettled in Kansas and filed for his own homestead. The farm had now been owned and managed first by Paul's grandfather, then his father, and now Paul. The Yoders had six children, all of whom had assigned tasks for helping make their farm self-sustaining. In addition to the dairy cattle, the Yoders raised row crops of corn and oats. Eight large draft horses and four cart and riding horses toiled to work the crop fields and carry the family on the surrounding rutted dirt roads. The men of the family all wore similar overalls and shirts, while Martha and the girls wore plain, clean dresses, aprons, and crisp white bonnets when they were out in public. The family was hurrying through their daily chores because they would need to leave for a neighbor's house in a couple of hours for regular worship services, followed by a picnic lunch and general visiting, or as they termed it, socializing. The family looked forward to this bi-weekly gathering so they could catch up on the events shaping the lives of their friends, neighbors, and families living close by.

"What news of the Englishman, Martha?" asked Paul to Martha. Paul was speaking German to his wife, although both adults spoke both German and English. In accordance with their culture, the Amish referred to anyone outside of the Amish faith as "English," no matter what the stranger's ancestry might be.

"While you were out choring, he awoke," replied Martha. "I haven't had a chance yet to talk much with him, except to assure him that he is safe. After we eat breakfast, I'll take a small portion up to him to see if he will eat," she said.

The Yoders sat down to eat breakfast, and after saying grace, the table was quiet while they ate. Like all farm families, they discussed the various chores that would need to be accomplished before they set out for their meeting with friends.

"Will Jenna stay here with the English when we go?" asked Paul. Jenna was the oldest of the Yoder children. She was eighteen years old and would soon marry. As the oldest of the girls, Jenna had stayed with the Englishman before when the family had to leave the farm for various reasons. She did not mind, except that by staying home, she did not have the opportunity to visit with her fiancé, John, who lived nearby. Secretly, though, she was hoping to talk to the outsider while her parents were away.

"Yes," answered Martha. "I will get him his breakfast before we leave, and Jenna has sewing to do while she stays here." The parents looked at Jenna, who merely nodded her head. The Yoders finished their tasks in the house, then carried large, covered baskets of food to the horse-drawn wagon that Paul had brought from the barn. In less than an hour, the family would leave to meet their other Amish friends. But Martha would first need to feed the stranger.

Chapter Five: Recovery

Sunday Noon, Yoder Family Farm
Coffeyville, Kansas

For nearly a week, Nathan had lain on a plain bed in the loft of the Yoder home, only semi-conscious and being attended to by Martha and Jenna Yoder. The Yoders had struggled but managed to get him to drink water and thin broth by propping him up in the bed. Nathan would rouse just enough to swallow the liquids before he fell asleep again. But on this morning, he was awake, letting his eyes roam the small loft room, and seeing the sunshine coming into the only window next to a stair railing at the end of the room. He had no idea where he was. The peak of a roof line rose above his bed. He painfully turned his head to see shelves stacked with various boxes behind the bed. He now presumed that he was in an attic room. He wondered to himself; how did he get here?

Nathan was vaguely aware that a woman had come into the room a few minutes ago, but though she had attended to him for the past few days, his head had not cleared enough to be able to recognize her. In a few moments, he heard footsteps coming up the stairs to the loft. He looked over to see two women, one older and one younger. The older woman carried a woven willow tray. She came to his bed and sat down on a stool to the side of the bed, placing the tray on her lap.

Nathan looked at her. In a hoarse whisper, he asked, “Who are you?”

“My name is Martha Yoder,” the woman answered, “and this is my daughter, Jenna. Now don’t try to talk too much. You’re in no condition to exert yourself." She turned to her daughter. "Jenna, grab his good arm to sit him up and put the pillows behind his back."

Jenna came around the bed and pulled Nathan's right arm to help him sit up. To Nathan, the effort was excruciatingly painful. Jenna placed another pillow behind Nathan's back. It was then that Nathan could see that his left arm was tightly bandaged to his side and across his chest. He could also see the homemade slats strapped to his right leg as a splint. His head throbbed from the pain of sitting up.

"Englishman, what is your name?" asked Martha.

"Nathan Wolf," he answered and watched as Martha Yoder fed him small bites of scrambled egg and buttered toast. When he was finished, the women laid Nathan back down, and he immediately fell asleep again.

Later, in the afternoon, he woke again. Turning his head slightly, he could see Jenna Yoder sitting in a chair near the window. She appeared to be sewing a pair of men's trousers. She looked up from her sewing and saw Nathan looking at her.

Jenna said quietly, "Are you awake, Englishman?"

"Yes," Nathan replied.

"Ah, good," replied Jenna. Her pronunciation of good sounded like "goot." "I'll go get you some tea."

In a few moments, she returned up the stairs with the same willow tray which she set on her chair. She then came to the bed and helped Nathan sit up to sip the tea and nibble at more buttered toast. Again, he laid back down and fell asleep after the bit of food. While he slept, the Yoder family returned home from their social gathering.

Later, when he woke, Nathan could see from the dimmed light coming through the window that the sun had faded. He was also vaguely aware that his stomach was telling him it was hungry. He could hear talking, laughter and the chatter of children from downstairs. He smiled slightly. He knew from the sounds that he was in a safe place. In a moment, he saw Jenna's head appear at the top of the stairs. She quickly darted back down the stairs, but Nathan heard her say rather loudly, "Yes, he's awake."

In a few more minutes, Nathan heard several footsteps on the stair. A large, burly man with a dark brown full beard reached the top of the stairs followed by Martha, Jenna, and the rest of the Yoder children. Nathan now knew how he had gotten to the upstairs room. The man appeared capable of lifting a loaded wagon. The man came to the bedside and stared down at Nathan with kindly blue eyes. "Hmm, I think you are going to live, Mr. Wolf," said the man, and in response to Nathan's wide eyes, the man laughed. It was a deep, friendly laugh, and his beard bobbed while he laughed.

"Martha has some vittles for you, and after you eat, we will talk." He turned and walked over to sit in the chair by the window. The women brought a bowl of steaming chicken noodle soup that Nathan was convinced was the best he had ever eaten. The chicken fat broth held small chunks of chicken and buttery homemade noodles. Small pieces of carrot and celery swam among the noodles. All the while he ate, Nathan watched the smaller children as they warily stared at the strange man who was eating in their attic. Nathan smiled at them, and the small children turned their heads and giggled.

When Nathan was finished eating, Jenna took the tray. "Downstairs, children," she said, and the children scampered down the stairs ahead of their older sister. Mr. Yoder stood and carried the chair closer to Nathan's bed. He stuck out his beefy hand, saying, "I'm Paul Yoder, and my daughter told me your name is Wolf. Is that right?" Nathan weakly took his hand.

"Yes, I'm Nathan Wolf. How did I get here?"

Paul Yoder laughed his deep laugh once again and sat down. "Well, Mr. Wolf, I guess the Almighty wasn't ready for the likes of you.

Instead, He gave you to us for a while. Do I presume correctly that you are a man of the law?" As Yoder spoke, he held up Nathan's badge.

"Yes, I'm the U.S. Marshal for eastern Kansas," said Nathan. Then he continued, "For a while, you said. How long have I been here? What day of the week is it?"

"It's the Lord's day of rest, Mr. Wolf. It's Sunday," said Yoder.

"Sunday," mumbled Nathan. "What day was it when you found me?"

"I believe that was Wednesday," replied Yoder.

Nathan was silent for a moment, and then asked, "How did you find me?"

"Oh, that old house where you had your difficulty belonged to my great grandfather. He passed on many years ago, and we just haven't taken the time to raze the house. It sits on the edge of our farm, so we go past the house almost every day. The day we found you, we had driven the wagon over to hoe weeds in the corn on that side of the farm, and we found you and another big fellow laying there waiting on the buzzards."

"Mmm. That other fellow was an outlaw that I had been trailing," said Nathan. "What happened to him?"

"Well, your outlaw appeared to die of gangrene poisoning. 'Course, he had a couple bullet holes in him, but it was probably the gangrene that killed him. He was just a bit of a mess since the turkey buzzards seemed to take a liking to him. We buried him over there by where he died. Do you know if he had any family, Mr. Wolf?" asked Yoder.

"The only family that man had was the devil," said Nathan. "He had already killed a half dozen men and aimed to add me to his list."

"Yes, sir, Mr. Wolf. I'd say you were pretty lucky," said Yoder as he stroked his beard and showed his large smile. "The Lord wasn't ready for you yet."

"Who fixed me up?" asked Nathan. "Do you have a doctor close by?"

Yoder's eyes glistened as he laughed again. "I'm your doctor. When you've been tending to animals on the farm as long as I have, you know a thing or two about fixing up wounds. It's a good thing that both bullets that hit you went clean through you, so I didn't have to go digging in those wounds. But with all the blood you lost, you're going to be gimpy for a while. But I figure you'll heal up just fine. Now you tell me, Mr. Wolf. Do have any family that might wonder where you've got to?"

Nathan was suddenly alarmed. "Oh Lord," he said. "My family is really going to be worried. I told them I would be back long before this, and here it is almost a week since I left home. How far is it into Coffeyville? I've got to get a telegram to them."

Yoder chuckled. "You aren't going anywhere, anytime soon. But don't you worry none. I've got to go into town tomorrow, and I'll stop at the telegraph office. You just let me know where to send the wire."

The men talked for a few more minutes before Nathan fell asleep again. Yoder rose and muttered to himself as he made for the stairs. "Yes, sir, just doggone lucky we found him."

Monday Morning 5:30 a.m.
Summer Prairie Ranch
Near Tioga, Kansas

Claire May looked down into his face and watched as Bobby's cheeks and jaw moved while he was suckling. They were sitting in a chair in the kitchen. A tepid mug of coffee was perched on the table within her reach. A tear welled in her eyes as she marveled at the wonder of her son. But there was another reason for the tears. Nathan had been gone nearly a week and the only word from him had been a hasty telegram while he was in pursuit of an escaped convict. Claire May was worried that something terrible had happened to her husband, and that she might be faced with raising the baby without a father. The very thought of such an occurrence brought more tears to her eyes, one of which fell on the baby's forehead. She gently wiped it away. She quietly whispered to Bobby, "No matter what happens, Bobby, we will get through it, even if it means your daddy isn't with us. But your daddy is tough, and I just know that he will be coming home soon." She thought to herself that she wished she could be more certain.

Virginia Summers had risen from bed when she heard stirring in the kitchen. She stood at the doorway and watched her daughter feed her grandson. She could see the heartache being experienced by her daughter. She tightened the belt on her robe, walked over to Claire May, and kissed her on the cheek. "Good morning, sweetheart," she said.

"Morning, Mom." Claire May answered as she wiped the tears from her eyes. She gently handed a satiated Bobby to her mother while she buttoned her night shirt and tied her robe.

"Maybe we'll hear something today. Surely the sheriff will let us know if he hears anything," said Virginia, as she handed the baby back to Claire May and poured herself a mug of coffee from the stove, then came back to sit by her daughter.

The outer door opened, and Will came in from outdoors. He had made the coffee just before he went to the barn to make sure the chores were being completed by the ranch hands. The women watched him as he poured himself a mug of coffee and sat down with them. "Looks like one of the mares is about ready to foal," he said. "She's stopped eating, so I figure she's . . ." He didn't finish his words, as he looked at the women who were paying no attention to him.

"Hmmm, at least I thought it was interesting," said Will as he shrugged his shoulders. But then, he figured it out and thought to himself that he did not really know what to say in these circumstances.

"I wonder how Nathan is getting along," said Will. The two women just stared stonily at him. "Well, I'm worried about him too," he said, a hangdog look crossing his face.

His mother patted his arm. "We're all worried, honey," she said.

Rubbing her eyes, Rosa came into the kitchen. "You all got up too early. I didn't know I was supposed to be up already," she said.

"It's OK, Rosa. We couldn't sleep, so it just happened that we all got up early," said Virginia.

"I'll have breakfast ready in a little bit," said Rosa, and she stirred the coals in the stove and added wood to the fire.

Five hours later, the group reconvened at the kitchen table for lunch. Rosa had baked bread to accompany their beef cutlets and gravy. Rosa sat at the end of the table cooing to the baby as she held him. The table was quiet but for the sound of forks and knives on the plates. It was quiet enough that they all heard the clicking noise of the telegraph in Virginia's office. Claire May looked at Virginia, who quietly said, "Oh Lord, please . . ."

They hurried into the office, and Virginia keyed a response. In a moment, the telegraph began clacking while Virginia copied down the letters. Bill Ward was passing on a message he had received from the sheriff in Coffeyville.

Ward Sending:

Recd word Marshal Wolf is at Coffeyville. Was shot twice by escaped convict. Being cared for by local family and getting better. May be able to come home in a week or two. Escaped convict dead. Stop.

Virginia read the message while Claire May and Will looked over her shoulder. Claire May began crying again. "He was shot," she sobbed.

Will put his arm around his sister. "Now Claire May, Nathan is a pretty damn tough fella. I don't think you should be too worried. He's liable to be just fine."

Virginia joined in. "Be thankful, Claire May. He's alive and it sounds like he is mending well. I have faith that it will be all right," she said and hugged her daughter.

Claire May snuffed her nose and quietly said, "At least, he is alive."

Six Days Later, The Following Saturday
Yoder Farm, Coffeyville, Kansas

Nathan sat on the back porch of the Yoder home. He was feeling pretty proud of himself. He had walked down the lane to the family's mailbox twice that morning, using just a cane for support. His leg still ached, but it felt better and was healing well. His arm was now in a loose sling because of the lingering pain when he moved it, and to allow the wound to continue healing. In spite of the aches and pains, Nathan knew that in a few days he would be able to board the train for home. He could hardly contain his excitement at the thought of seeing Claire May and Bobby, and to sleep in his own bed once again.

The previous day, Nathan had had a pleasant visit from the U.S. Marshal from eastern Oklahoma. He had ridden the train up from Tulsa to visit Nathan after receiving a wire from Kansas U.S. Marshal Director Ralph Gilman letting him know that Nathan was in Coffeyville, Kansas. It was the first time that the men had met, but they had so much in common that they were kindred spirits. The Tulsa marshal told Nathan that the story of him being shot by Hank Skinner had rattled up and down the telegraph lines between U.S. Marshal offices. He had told

Nathan that he was a bit of a celebrity in the marshal service. The Tulsa ranger also told Nathan that as soon as Hank Skinner had broken out of prison, there was a reward posted by the Federal Prison System for his capture, dead or alive. The reward was $1,000, and Frank Gilman had told the Tulsa ranger to tell Nathan that Gilman was going to make sure that Nathan got the reward. Nathan felt that the gesture by Gilman was an appropriate show of appreciation for the hard work of tracking down and killing the notorious outlaw. Nathan was proud of his work even though it meant nearly getting killed and a long healing process. During their visit, the ranger from Tulsa also let Nathan know that there had been a warning sent to the offices of the marshals, letting them know that there were rumors of more counterfeit bills showing up, especially in the Kansas City area. Both the men had laughed, because neither had seen any sign of bogus money in their territories and remarked that they probably would not know it was fake even if they saw it. The Tulsa Marshal had wished Nathan well in his recovery, thanked the Yoders for taking care of a fellow marshal, and headed back to Oklahoma. Nathan was appreciative of the visit.

A Week and a half Later, Thursday, Noon
Chanute, Kansas Railroad Depot

Will had parked the phaeton nearby while they stood on the platform waiting for the train from Coffeyville. He had retrieved Nathan's horse, Wander, from the livery stable, and paid Dwight Mullins for the horse Nathan had borrowed. Wander was tied to the back of the carriage. Before he left Coffeyville, Nathan had given the borrowed horse to the Yoder family in appreciation for all they had done for him. The Yoders had thanked him profusely. Another riding horse for the growing Amish family was greatly appreciated. While he was waiting for the train to leave Coffeyville, Nathan had wired Will of his intention to leave the horse with Yoders. In Chanute, Claire May, Will, and Virginia waited patiently on the train platform.

With loud whistling and clouds of steam, the train arrived on time and sighed with a great blast of steam as it came to a stop. The Summer Prairie group studied the passengers as they stepped off of the train cars. When all the passengers had cleared, the conductor stood at one of the train car steps and offered his arm to the last passenger. Nathan Wolf came down the steps, slowly, one leg at a time, with his left arm secured in a sling. A walking stick was in his other hand, and he stood for a moment leaning on it. To his concerned family, it appeared that Nathan had lost weight and was pale and gaunt. But when Nathan spied Claire May, Virginia, and Will, he managed a huge smile. They rushed to him, and Claire May embraced him, kissing him repeatedly.

Nathan laughed, his first laugh in many days. "Easy there, Claire May. People might talk," and he laughed again.

"Let them talk, darling. How are you? Are you in any pain?" asked Claire May.

With his free arm, he embraced his wife. "I think I'm finally feeling pretty darn good," he said. "Let's go home."

Ten Days Later 10 a.m.
Sherriff and Marshal's Office
Chanute, Kansas

"I thought I missed your coffee, Bill. Guess I was mistaken," said Nathan, and then he laughed. Bill and Tom Barnes stared at their friend. Nathan was walking better now, but still using a cane, and his shoulder needed a few more days in the sling. He could not yet ride a horse and had driven a buggy into town to visit and to have coffee with Bill and Tom.

"Well, it might taste better after your women folk stop pampering you out at the ranch," said Bill. "You got spoiled on their good coffee, I 'spect."

Nathan laughed. "Yeah, it's surprising what some good vittles will do for you. Rosa makes a mighty good cobbler." He went on, "My arm and leg get better every day, and I've been target practicing to keep up my gun hand. I'll get rid of this cane and sling in a few days and make Wander start earning his keep."

"Well, you haven't missed much," said Bill. "We got another telegram from our boss, Gilman. I reckon the Secret Service is pestering him. They want us to keep an eye out for any counterfeit money," said Bill. "I swear, Gilman is determined to make revenuers out of us yet." The men laughed.

"And other than Tom and me transporting a few prisoners, things have been slow," said Bill.

Tom changed the subject and asked, "How's the baby, Nathan? Is Claire May getting any sleep?"

"Bobby's fine, Tom. I swear, between Claire May, Virginia, and Rosa, that boy is going to be spoiled rotten for the rest of his life. How about you, Tom? Things going OK here in town?" asked Nathan.

"Yep, everything is fine. Just trying to keep the drunks off the streets, and the kids from bothering the old folks. But I'm not looking forward to two weeks from now," said Tom. He continued. "We've got the county fair starting, so one of those damn carnivals is coming to town. And there will also be a rodeo, so every cowboy in these parts will be here. That means a lot of late nights and a whole lot more drunks in the jail. And somebody always gets hurt when that many people get together."

"Well, if we don't have anything serious going on, we can help you keep the peace," said Nathan. "Besides, I haven't been to a rodeo for quite a while. Might be fun."

Chapter Six: The Carnival and Rodeo

Fifteen Days Later, Sunday, Mid-afternoon

Fair Grounds, Chanute, Kansas

He was not sure how Claire May had talked him into it, but Nathan found himself walking the midway of the Sterling Traveling Carnival. He was not a fan of traveling shows, but Claire May could talk him into jumping off of a cliff if she had a mind to. However, he was enjoying the walk since he was now walking without a cane, and his arm was free of its sling. He still moved his arm gingerly, and he was a bit sore with some lingering aches, but he felt much better, especially walking arm in arm with his gorgeous wife amidst the throng of ogle-eyed patrons who had come to see the exotic oddity shows, animals, and rides that made up the traveling carnival. Brightly painted banners depicting scenes of bizarre-looking people, quirks of nature, and sights that could be seen behind the facades, hung in a long row above tent entrance flaps. At each entrance, a man dressed in garish attire attempted to entice passers-by to stop and pay their money to see the mysterious offerings.

In addition to the sounds of the barkers shouting their come-ons, the calliope music, and the fair goers' talk and laughter, a constant machine and loud hissing sound came forth from the small steam generators behind every ride and side show facade. They created the power for the motors and the rows and rows of sparkling lights throughout the mid-way. As Nathan and Claire May walked slowly along, they passed the oddity show facades where hawkers barked the enticing details of strange-looking persons and creatures that could be seen inside for the small sum of a nickel or a dime. A man wrapped with a large snake stood on one of the stages. Another stage held a woman covered from head to foot with tattoos. They stopped for a moment to take in all of the gaudily painted banners depicting the sights that could be seen for paying a small entry fee. A brightly attired barker, who wore a tall stove-pipe hat, stood next to a banner showing an obese woman sitting on a throne-like chair. Nathan and Claire May listened to the monotone spiel of the barker.

Ladies and gentlemen, you have never before in your lives witnessed such a spectacle. Little Miko, the princess daughter of a barbaric chieftain from a faraway tribe of headhunters, reigns supreme on her throne within this tent. Her weight will astound you. She comes from the far away exotic Polynesian island of Guamara where she was the daughter of the chief of a blood-thirsty tribe of headhunters. She was brought to our show by great safari hunters and has been tamed for your entertainment. She will answer your questions and you will behold the fattest woman in the whole United States and maybe the world. For a mere ten cents, a small thin dime, you can enter and see the wonder of the carnival. Little Miko, the fattest woman you will ever see, awaits your visit. Step right up and for a ten-cent admission you can see Little Miko.

In truth, Little Miko was a very obese blonde woman named Priscilla Dillman of the Philadelphia Dillmans. Her family was wealthy, so rich that they belonged to every high society organization in the city. The Dillmans had three children, two daughters and a son. The son and one of the daughters were the picture of high society, slim, handsome, and chic. Priscilla, called "Priz" by acquaintances, was the opposite of her siblings. She had always been chubby, and not altogether pleasing to the eye. Hence, she was ignored by her parents and excluded from society's gatherings as her parents felt she was not a desirable representative for their wealthy family. Her childhood rearing had been left to a family servant, a nanny, and her world consisted for the most part of the four walls of her lavishly appointed room that was also home to a menagerie of toy animals and other children's toys. Priz spent most of her days in her room, save her frequent trips to the kitchen where the staff of servants fed her copious amounts of food in addition to her meals. Her proclivity to gain weight increased as time passed, until her parents completely ignored their disgustingly obese offspring.

One thing that Priz Dillman had enjoyed in her teen-age years were rides in the surrounding countryside in her custom-made buggy, pulled by a spirited chestnut gelding. While driving alone, she could take in the air and the sights of the neighboring countryside with no one to bother or chastise her for her massive weight. It was on one of these outings when she met a passing train of wagons, the Sterling Traveling Carnival. She had paused to watch them pass, mesmerized by the gaudy paintings of carnival attractions on the sides of the wagons. Unfortunately, as the wagons passed, her horse had been spooked by two caged lions that chose to bellow at the moment their wagon came into view. Priz's horse reared in its traces, then bolted and began to run, but the wheel of the buggy got caught on one of the carnival wagons and spilled the buggy, tossing Miss Priscilla to the ground where she struck her head, knocking her unconscious. The manager of the carnival walked to the prostrate body of Priz Dillman and immediately saw dollar signs in the fall of the finely dressed fat woman. Wishing to avoid a civil suit, and recognizing a money-making opportunity, he instructed his staff to bring the fat woman with them as they journeyed onward. In other words, he kidnapped Priz Dillman. He had a use for such an obese person. When Priscilla awakened, she found herself gently rocking in a traveling carnival wagon and was told that she was now in the employ of the Sterling Carnival as the resident Fat Lady. Taking a few moments to digest her situation, she had agreed to stay, at least temporarily. Time passed, and she had now been the fat lady of the carnival for several years. Her family never knew where she had gone, except for an occasional post card from Priz to let them know she was still alive, as if they cared. The post cards originated from various towns around the country, causing her family to give only an occasional wondering thought as to what had happened to their strange daughter. Priz did not mind her life, and rather enjoyed her role, placing a large, full, black wig over her blond hair and donning appropriate make up when she was seen by the public. With this bit of chicanery regarding her background and the notoriety and attention she received, she was at peace. She had found a family in the carnival, including what she considered to be the man of her dreams.

Nathan and Claire May passed from the fat lady's barker and continued on to where they paused to watch the merry-go-round with its gaily painted animals and bobbing horses, all marching to the tune of the calliope. Then they strolled on to watch as young men threw rings onto glass plates, attempting to win a bisque doll for their sweethearts. One of the carnival rides caught Claire May's attention. She looked up to watch the "Swing of Terror," a turning post with several two-person swings hanging from the top of the post by chains. As the center post turned, the swings turned faster and caused the swings to draw away from the post, rising ever higher in their flight. As the seats of the swings moved faster, the riders screamed, either in fright or delight. The "Swing of Terror" was an exhilaratingly popular attraction.

"I don't believe I would like to ride that contraption," said Claire May. "It makes my tummy queasy just watching those people swinging around up there."

"I'm with you, sweetheart. I prefer staying on the ground," said Nathan.

They walked on and found themselves watching a large wheel with seats attached. The ride was called "The Pleasure Wheel." Two-seat chairs were attached to the wheel's framework and swung freely on their mounts as the wheel turned slowly. Many of the couples in the seats held hands as the wheel turned. When patrons reached the top of the turning wheel, they were treated to a broad view of the fair grounds.

"Nathan, let's ride this one," said Claire May.

Nathan was not convinced that he should board any contraption that raised him twenty or thirty feet in the air in a small swinging seat, but he dutifully followed Clair May. They stood in line, bought their tickets, and were soon rising as the wheel turned. At the top of the turning wheel, they marveled at the bright lights that glowed even during the afternoon, and they were able to observe the crowd spread out beneath them. Rows of wagons, used for transporting the carnival attractions, were parked behind the midway along with the gaily painted caravan wagons in which the fair workers lived. Carnival goers parked their wagons and horses in a vacant field near the fairgrounds. As Claire May and Nathan looked over the fairgrounds, they saw that preparations were underway for the evening's rodeo. They could see hostlers who were removing rodeo stock animals from large wagons and herding them into holding pens. They watched pole-mounted blinking lights in the arena that were being tested for the evening rodeo.

Later, as they continued to stroll the fairgrounds, and the sun got lower, the lights of the carnival became more striking. To Claire May and Nathan, the generator-driven lights were fascinating. The Summer Prairie Ranch was without electricity, just as nearly all of the other homesteads in the country. In Chanute, only a small number of locations had electricity. Seeing so many electric lights all at the same time was a novelty.

"Isn't it marvelous," said Claire May. "It's like something out of a story book."

Nathan did not comment. As he continued walking amidst the milling crowd, he thought to himself that he would rather be sitting on the porch at the ranch with just a couple of oil lamps casting a warm light, listening to the crickets and owls, and holding his wife's hand. He kept his opinion to himself.

It was nearing seven o'clock, the time that the rodeo was to begin, so the couple walked to the arena, bought their tickets and found bleacher seats. The judges and a large man with a megaphone were seated on a raised platform next to the stock chutes. Beneath their platform, a small brass band was assembling.

Claire May was beaming. "I love rodeos," she said. "I have been coming to the rodeo nearly every year when the fair is on. Ever since I was a little girl, Will and I would come to the rodeo with Mom and Dad. One year, I even got to ride into the arena holding a flag with the other flag bearers. It was so exciting."

"So, from what you've told me, some of the Summer Prairie cowboys are going to compete," said Nathan.

"It's called a ranch rodeo," said Claire May. "Most of the surrounding ranches send their best cowboys to compete in roping, bull dogging, bronc and bull riding. The winners of the events get points for their events, and the ranch that accumulates the most points wins the overall score, and they get a trophy and a cash prize. Everybody tries so hard that it's lots of fun to watch."

"Has Summer Prairie ever won?" asked Nathan.

"Yes, a couple of times, but not very recently," she said.

They bought paper bags of popcorn from a vendor moving down the rows of bleachers. As they sat munching the salty treat, Nathan glanced over to the side of the bleachers. He watched as a fast-talking man stood in the middle of a group of men who all seemed to be shouting at the same time and were handing money to the odds maker. In exchange for their money, he gave them small slips of paper. It was obvious that money was changing hands and the men were placing bets on the rodeo. Apparently, the practice must be legal, Nathan thought, as the group was not trying to hide their activity.

"I reckon that betting on the rodeo is allowed," said Nathan as he continued watching the men.

"Heavens, I guess so," said Claire May. "I know they do it every year that I've been coming here."

Suddenly, their attention was drawn to the band, which had struck up a stirring march. Gates at one end of the arena opened, and horseback riders carrying flags began loping in a circle around the ring. In a moment, they all stopped and faced the judges' platform. The portly man with the megaphone rose from his chair and asked the audience to join him in a prayer. He led the prayer, asking for the safety of all of the rodeo participants. At the conclusion of the prayer, he motioned to the band that began playing quietly behind him. Then, with the band, the announcer began singing a tune that only a few members of the public had ever before heard. After he and the band concluded the song, he told the crowd that the song was called "Defense of Fort McHenry" and was written by a man called Francis Key. Then the man loudly announced, "Let the rodeo begin."

After making one more lap of the arena, the mounted riders departed, riding out the same gate through which they had entered. Immediately, the first event of the evening's rodeo was announced. Subsequently, Will walked briskly up the bleacher steps and joined Nathan and his sister. "I've been down with our boys. I think they're ready. I believe we stand a good chance this year," he said. On the judges' stand, another man had taken the megaphone and began commenting on the events as they unfolded. Nathan, Will, and Claire May listened and watched intently as each event took place. Nathan couldn't help but notice that at the side of the bleachers, the betting continued non-stop even as the events took place. He found it to be a bit odd.

By their very nature, rodeos are not for the faint of heart and can be very dangerous for the participants. Unfortunately, as can happen in any rodeo, two of the cowboys were injured during their events. One fellow was thrown against a fence surrounding the arena, and another one was stepped on by an ornery steer. "Say, Will," said Nathan. "I understand that the boys competing bring their own horses for the roping and bull dogging events, but where do the rest of the calves and bucking stock come from?" asked Nathan.

"Not sure," answered Will. "I believe they are brought to the rodeo by a contractor that works with the carnival. I've heard the same contractor follows the carnivals from town to town."

The saddle bronc riding event had started and promised to be very competitive. For each ride, the name of the rider and the ranch where they worked was announced. Will and Claire May recognized most of the ranch names and even knew some of the cowboys, but one ranch name that was announced during the events was not familiar to either of them.

"Will, have you ever heard of the 'Bar C' ranch?" asked Claire May.

Will snorted. "Same thought just occurred to me," he said. "Not only have we not heard of them, but they seem to be doing very well in the events. At the rate they are going, they may be hard to beat." Their discussion was interrupted by the announcer.

And now, ladies and gentlemen, in chute number one, we have Tito Ramos, the pride of the Summer Prairie Ranch coming up for his final ride. At the present time, Ramos is leading the field. He's drawn a bronc named 'Busted Buckle,' *a wily old mustang that has never been ridden. Tito's got his work cut out for himself. Looks like he's ready. And the chute is open!*

The rodeo band immediately began playing a quick-time ditty as the wild bronc busted out of the chute with Tito Ramos leaning well back in the saddle, holding the halter rope, and jamming his spurs into the bronc's shoulders. It was plain to see why the horse had never been ridden. He had a strange, head-down twisting buck and would mix it with an occasional front-feet-planted, head-down buck that threatened to throw the cowboy into the air over the horse's head. Clouds of brown dust rose in the air as the wild bronc's hooves crashed to the ground with each attempt to dislodge Ramos. Oddly, as it bucked, the horse was making an eerie screeching sound, as if it was in pain. Will intently watched his ranch hand ride the wild bronc. He thought to himself that he had never heard a horse screech like that as it was being ridden. He wondered if there was something wrong with the bronc. Tito was riding well, but it seemed that the seconds were dragging by. Finally, a large bell on the judges stand was struck, signifying that eight seconds had passed. The rodeo band stopped playing, and an outrider rode to the side of the bucking horse allowing Tito to scramble from the back of the still-bucking bronc to the outrider's horse. Because of the wild spinning action of the bronc, and Tito's spurring ride, Will was sure that Tito's score would be excellent. They would wait for the judges' scores.

The outriders in the arena were still trying to herd *Busted Buckle* out of the arena through an open gate, but the bronc was having none of it. Continuing to make the strange sound, the bronc continued to buck, as if a rider was still on its back. Froth showed around the horse's mouth, and a sheen of sweat glistened on his dark brown coat. The Bronc would not stop bucking and lapped the arena twice. Finally, the bronc jumped up with all four legs off of the ground, but as he did so, he was moving forward. The wild horse crashed into the arena fence rails and fell to the ground. The horse rolled on the ground, breaking the main cinch of the saddle. The horse then stood, blowing the froth from its mouth. With the saddle hanging beneath its belly by the bucking cinch, the horse then hung its head and its legs suddenly collapsed. The bronc fell heavily, rolling onto its side. The crowd was stunned and silent. One of the outriders dismounted and walked to the downed animal. He examined the horse for a moment, then turned his face to the judges stand and shouted. "The horse is dead!" An audible gasp went through the crowd.

Almost immediately, in an effort to calm the spectators, the announcer began speaking to the crowd. He made a few perfunctory remarks about how every precaution is taken for the safety of the riders and the stock animals, remarks to which the crowd paid little attention. But then he said, "And now ladies and gentlemen, the judges are ready with Tito Ramos' score."

The judges were tasked with giving a score to each rider. That score was a composite of scores on the performance of the horse, and the skill of the rider. In this instance, Will was convinced that Tito's ride should score well above any other ride that had taken place that evening. The judges held up cards showing the scores they had given. Instead of Tito's ride being scored fairly, two of the judges had scored Tito's ride well below where it should have been. An audible gasp went through the crowd, followed by shouts and talking from the crowd. Everyone knew that Tito's had been the ride of the day, yet he did not win the event. The announcer spoke again.

Ladies and gentlemen, that concludes the saddle bronc riding event. Our scorekeeper is handing me the results. It appears that our champion saddle bronc rider is cowboy Mike Branson from the Bar C ranch. Congratulations, Mike. And now, ladies and gentlemen, we are going to take a few minutes to get the chutes ready for the bareback event.

Will was on his feet. He was fuming mad as evident by his crimson face. He shouted at the top of his voice, "That saddle bronc event was rigged! It was rigged!"

He was still standing as other people in the stands took to shouting, also expressing their opinion that the event had been rigged. Nathan stood up next to Will. "What makes you think the event was rigged, Will?" he asked.

"Wild broncs don't die from bucking, and they don't just fall over dead after hitting a fence. Hell, we have horses that run into fences all the time and they don't die. And wild broncs don't buck with the crazy stubbornness of that horse Tito was riding. And they don't make a noise like we heard. That was the sound of a horse in pain," said Will.

"So what are you thinking, Will?" asked Nathan.

"Well, I can't prove anything, but I'd be willing to bet that horse was drugged to be wild enough to buck any rider off of it. You saw the crazy way that bronc was bucking," said Will. "And then to keel over dead, that doesn't make sense unless the horse was drugged with something that was poisonous enough to make it wilder and kill it. I think the horse was drugged to keep anyone riding it from qualifying."

Nathan did not reply, but he was listening intently.

"And another thing," said Will. "Our man Tito put in the best ride of the day, and both he and the horse were given low enough scores that another cowboy won the event. Hell, I'm willing to bet that nearly everybody who placed bets on the event, bet on Tito to win. Tito has been a leading contender every year. There was a whole lot of money lost by the bettors on that event. Something just doesn't add up right," said Will.

"I see what you mean," said Nathan.

The attention of the two men was drawn back to the arena, where workers had rigged a set of ropes around the hind quarters of the dead horse. While they finished, a team of two draft horses entered the ring. In moments, the workers connected the ropes to the crossbar of the draft horse hitch, and the dead animal was soon unceremoniously dragged out of the arena. Claire May summed up the scene, saying, "That was a sad way for that horse to die."

Nathan watched as the bareback broncs were being loaded into the chutes. "Will, do have any idea who might be the favorite in the bareback event?"

Will had cooled down a bit and sat down on the bleacher. "I figure that Rich Wells, a fella from Dave Morgan's Circle M should have a real good chance to win it. He's been mighty close for the last two years." Dave Morgan owned the adjoining ranch to the Summer Prairie spread, and Will was engaged to marry Alice Morgan, Dave's daughter.

"I think I'll take a walk," said Nathan. Claire May began to stand up. "Claire May, please stay here with Will. I'll be back in a few minutes."

"Hmmph," muttered Claire May, but she sat back down.

Nathan stepped down from the bleachers and turned toward a knot of men gathered at the side and back of the bleachers. He stood for a moment and watched as money left the hands of the rodeo-goers into the hands of the bookie who handed slips of paper back to the bettors. Nathan watched for a few more seconds, then interrupted the bookie. "Hey, mister, who's the favorite in the bareback event?"

The man answered, "The way the bets are going, it looks like the favorite is Circle M's Rich Wells."

Nathan wasn't through yet and asked the bookie another question. "Who gets the proceeds from your betting operation, mister?"

"I don't believe that's any of your damn business. Now get away from here," the bookie answered.

Nathan was not wearing his badge, but it was in his shirt pocket. He pulled it from the pocket and showed it to the bookie. "Now, let's try this one more time. Who gets the proceeds from the betting?"

The bookie stared at the badge and then shrugged his shoulders. "Don't mean nothin' to me, lawman. Ain't nothing illegal going on here." He turned to face the crowd of men. "Who's my next bettor?"

A hand with a dollar bill in it reached toward the bookie and its owner said, "Put it on Rich Wells." The bookie wrote on a slip of paper and handed it to the bettor. But before he could take the dollar from the bettor, Nathan grabbed the bookie's hand holding a wad of money and snatched the money from the man.

"Hey, gimme that back," said the bookie.

"You'll get it back when you tell me who your boss is," said Nathan.

"Oh, my boss is it? So now you want to hassle my boss. OK, lawman. My boss is Junior Skinner. You can't miss him. He's the big man over by the chutes that will put you in your place. Now gimme my money," said the bookie.

Unseen by the bookie, Nathan gave a slight shudder at the name of the bookie's boss, Skinner. It can't be, thought Nathan. Preoccupied, he handed the wad of bills back to the bookie and did not hear the mumbled curses of the bookie as he walked away.

Nathan did not return to his bleacher seat. Instead, he continued walking to the end of the arena, around the end where the band and judges sat, and as he reached the back side of the chutes, he stood off to the side and watched as the preparations continued for the bareback contest. He saw a knot of cowboys talking and joking with each other, each wearing an assigned number on a placard pinned to their shirts. Some were smoking a quick cigarette. Others spit a dark stream of tobacco juice to the ground. They were young men, having fun yakking with their counterparts from other ranches and bragging about who was going to be the eventual winner. Nathan knew that these were the upcoming contestants. He walked over to the group and asked, "Which one of you is Rich Wells?"

One of the cowboys, who recognized Nathan, answered, "He ain't here yet, Marshal. He walked toward the barn a few minutes ago, but I'm not sure where he is now. But he better be getting ready for his ride." While he was talking, Nathan made a mental note of the colors of their shirts.

"Thanks, fellas," said Nathan. "Good luck to all of you." The cowboys turned back to their conversation as Nathan walked away.

And then he saw him. For a second, his heart thumped as he was aware of the uncanny similarity in appearance between Junior Skinner and Hank Skinner, the man who had shot Nathan many weeks ago near Coffeyville. Nathan could not help but stare for a moment, then he quickly looked away and concentrated on the men working on the chutes. Junior Skinner was just as big as his brother and nearly a dead ringer for him. But his hair was a bit lighter colored, and his eyes did not have the pinched together appearance of Hank. But Nathan now knew that Hank and Junior Skinner must have been brothers, and quite possibly twins. As his attention was on the chute area, he watched as attendants worked above the chutes. The bareback broncs had been moved into their individual chutes and the attendants were there to assist each cowboy onto his bronc and prepare for his ride. But then Nathan's attention was drawn to an attendant who was bent over the bronc in chute number five. Just then the bronc raised its head and Nathan was sure that he saw the attendant shove something into the horse's mouth. Nathan stepped into a shadow and watched the attendant look furtively around to see if anyone had seen his action and then look back down on the bronc.

Nathan turned his head and watched as Skinner moved to the back of the arena toward a row of wagons, many of which were painted in the same color scheme. Nathan followed at a discreet distance. Large printing on the side of the wagons attested that they belonged to a company called "Consolidated Rodeo Stock," and listed its business address as Kansas City, Missouri. He watched as Skinner entered one of the caravan wagons. Then, on a hunch, Nathan continued walking toward the barn. As he walked, he met a cowboy who appeared to be coming from the barn. He was dressed in a black shirt. Nathan paused and asked the man, "Are you Rich Wells?"

The cowboy answered, "Nah, I ain't Wells. I don't know any Rich Wells," and he quickly walked away.

Nathan thought it was a rather odd answer, as most of the competing cowboys knew each other. Nathan continued on and entered the stock barn where the rodeo stock was kept during fair week. Dust hung in the air of the barn and could be seen in light rays that entered the barn door and the cracks in the wall of the barn. A strong odor of hay and manure filled Nathan's nostrils. The dirt aisle where he walked was covered with hay particles and bits of dried manure. It appeared that no one was in the barn, and it was quiet except for the chewing sounds and shuffling movements of the animals. He walked down the aisle between the pens and stopped to look at the massive bulls that would be used later in the bull riding event. He then looked at the adjoining pen of bulls and noticed that the animals were all bunched up on one side of their pen. Nathan thought this was odd, until he noticed a bit of color in the dark corner of the pen. A man in a bright sky-blue shirt lay in the corner, and the man was quietly groaning, as he struggled to get on his hands and knees. Nathan quickly walked to the back corner of the pen and reached through the rails to the man.

"Come out this way," said Nathan, and he helped the man come through the rails of the pen. The cowboy straightened up and hung one arm on the pen railing. His face was covered with cuts and bruises and was ashy pale.

"Are you Rich Wells?" asked Nathan.

The cowboy looked at Nathan and said, "Yeah, I'm Rich. Who are you?"

"I'm Marshal Nathan Wolf. I live at Summer Prairie, next to the Morgans."

Wells shook his head to try to clear the cobwebs. "Oh yeah, I know who you are. Will's brother-in-law."

"Right. Can you tell me what happened to you, Rich?" Nathan asked.

"Not much to tell, I guess. I came down here to the back of the barn to take a leak before my ride. Got done with my business and decided to walk back through the barn." Wells paused to rub his head. "Next thing I knew, I was laying on the ground in the dark and some hombre was beatin' the living hell out of me with a club. I musta' conked out, because the next thing I knew, I was in the bulls' pen, and you were pulling at me through the bars of the pen."

"Did you get a look at this fella that beat on you?" asked Nathan.

"Nope, all I saw was the sleeve of his long-sleeved shirt. It was either dark blue or black, but I never saw his face before I hit the ground," said Wells. He shook his head from side to side again, attempting to clear the cobwebs from his mind. "Hey, wait a minute," he said. "I also remember seeing a ring on the middle finger of his hand, about the second or third time that club came down on me. It was silver, and it had a big turquois rock on it."

Their conversation was interrupted as Wells remembered that the bareback event was going to start. "I've got to go, Marshal. I'm going to ride, in spite of somebody trying to warn me off." Wells took three steps and reached for the pen railing again. He paused for a moment to let a dizzy spell pass and to clear his head. As he did so, he saw the short length of a tree branch laying at his feet. He bent and picked it up, looked at it, and handed it to Nathan.

"That looks a bit familiar, Marshal."

Nathan looked at the short branch, then tossed it aside. Rich Wells began walking again with Nathan at his side. Nathan admired the young cowboy. To take the beating he had and then want to compete in the event took real fortitude. "Here's my handkerchief. Go over and wash your face in that water trough so you don't scare the horses." Both men chuckled, and Wells washed some of the drying blood from his face.

"Much obliged, Marshal. I hope you find the guy that did this. I gotta run," said Wells, attempting to hand the wet handkerchief back to Nathan.

"Keep it, Rich. You be careful now. Somebody means business," said Nathan, and he watched as Wells trotted toward the chutes.

As he followed Wells, Nate saw the cowboy receive a contestant number and pin it to his shirt. He also noticed that Junior Skinner was standing to the side watching Wells. Standing next to Skinner was another cowboy with a number pinned to his black shirt. It was the same cowboy that Nathan had met coming from the stock barn. Then Skinner turned to the black-shirted cowboy next to him and appeared to verbally chastise him. The cowboy heatedly responded. Nathan could not quite make out what they were saying, but he could guess. He was sure that the black-shirted fella was supposed to make sure that Rich Wells did not ride that day. At a distance from the two men, Nathan stopped and studied the cowboy long enough to see that he wore a silver turquoise ring on his right hand. Skinner and the cowboy then saw Nathan watching them, and they turned their attention to the chutes.

Nathan hurried around the arena to take his seat again in the bleachers. But as he rounded the judges stand, he saw that Sheriff Tom Barnes was standing near the judges' platform, idly watching the arena. He walked to the side of Barnes. The two men shook hands. "Tom, do you have any of your deputies with you?" asked Nathan.

"Sure, one of them is standing just over yonder," said Barnes, and pointed his finger toward the bookie's circle.

"Can you get him, and then come up and join us in the bleachers?" Nathan asked.

"Yep, can do. But what's this about?" Tom asked.

"You're going to make an arrest," said Nathan.

Anticipation suddenly showed on Barnes's face. "I am?" said Barnes. He had worked around Nathan long enough to know Nathan was usually right on target, so he did not question him. "Okay, I'll be there in a minute," he said, and walked away to get the deputy.

Nathan took his seat in the stands. "Did you have a nice walk, sweetheart?" asked Claire May. She knew that if Nathan was gone as long as he was, something was stirring.

Nathan looked at her and smiled. "Yep, things might get kinda interesting." Claire May slightly shook her head, then looked back in the direction of the arena. But then she turned back to watch as Tom Barnes and his deputy came into the stands and sat beside Nathan. Will and Claire May looked at each other, raised their eyebrows, and shrugged their shoulders.

The group watched as the first three bareback riders rode. Only one of the riders went the full eight seconds. The fourth rider turned out to be the black-shirted cowboy. The announcer shouted through his megaphone that the cowboy's name was Rowdy Cummins and that he represented the Bar C ranch. His bronc leaped from chute number four and bucked around the arena. It was a good ride, and the cowboy lasted his eight seconds and climbed onto the outrider's horse before dropping down to the arena floor. He raised his hat to acknowledge the applause of the crowd and walked across the arena. Nathan could see the turquoise ring on the cowboy's right hand.

"That's your man, Tom," said Nathan to the sheriff. "He needs to be arrested for assault and battery. He beat up the Circle M's cowboy, Rich Wells. We'll go get him after Wells rides. He's next out of chute five, and he's riding a drugged horse," said Nathan.

"Just how in the hell do you know all this?" asked Tom.

"Observation and patience," said Nathan. "And besides, I've got a witness. Let's wait 'til Rich Wells rides, and then we can go get our man."

Their conversation was interrupted by the announcer. He had just shouted that Rich Wells from the Circle M ranch would be coming out of chute 5. In seconds, the gate opened, and the horse lurched from the chute. The horse's actions were non-stop, with twists, rears, and bucks not seen from any of the other horses. The bucking horse passed in front of the bleachers, its eyes were wild and rolling. White foam flew from the horse's mouth and nose, and it made a strange seemingly pained screeching sound as it passed Nathan and the sheriff. Will had stood and watched the horse and rider pass. He leaned over to Nathan. "That horse looks just like the saddle bronc that I said was drugged," he said.

Eight seconds passed, and the signal bell rang loudly. Rich Wells scrambled from the bucking bronc onto the outrider's horse and then dropped to the arena floor. He acknowledged the cheering crowd by doffing his hat and walked to the side of the arena where he climbed over the fence rails. The crowd was still cheering, and Wells paused on the top rail, waved his hat again, and climbed down the other side. The crowd then became quiet, waiting for the judges' score. It was taking what seemed to be an extraordinarily long time for the score. The holdup seemed to be two of the judges who were animatedly talking to each other.

"What the hell is taking so long?" asked Tom Barnes. "I know one of those fool judges yakking away up there," he said. "He lives here in town. But I don't know the other fella."

Finally, the judges' scores were announced as the judges held up numbers on placards. All of the judges gave Rich Wells a maximum score, except one. He was the judge that Tom Barnes did not know. His score kept Rich Wells' score from maximum, but then the announcer took up his megaphone and announced that Rich Wells had, indeed, won the event, narrowly edging out the black-shirted cowboy. The applause continued, and the crowd cheered for a full thirty seconds.

"Let's go, Tom," said Nathan, and the men left their seats to walk around the arena. As they walked, Nathan asked Tom to approach the judge that he knew after all the events were concluded for the day. "Ask him to come to our office in the morning. Just tell him to drop by for coffee," said Nathan.

"OK," said Tom. "I wouldn't mind talking to him about what he knows about the other judge, and why it took so long to score that last rider."

"I'm pretty certain we'll find out," said Nathan.

They found the black-shirted cowboy leaning against the arena fence. He held a cigarette in his right hand. The cigarette rested next to the finger with the turquoise ring.

Sheriff Tom Barnes walked up to the cowboy and told him to turn around. His deputy stood close by.

"What's this all about, Sheriff?" asked the cowboy.

"You're under arrest for assault and battery," replied Barnes.

"Really, Sheriff? And just who got assaulted," sneered the cowboy.

"Well, we're going to talk all about that in the morning, cowboy. So for now, you're going to have a nice night in my jail," said Barnes.

The cowboy turned and the deputy put handcuffs on him behind his back.

"What the hell is going on here." Junior Skinner was striding purposefully toward Nathan and the sheriff. "You've got no right to take that man away. He ain't done nothin' wrong," said Skinner.

"Just stop where you are, Skinner," said Nathan, and he stepped in front of Skinner. Skinner had a half foot and a burly fifty pounds over Nathan, but Skinner was slightly taken aback. He was confused that Nathan knew his name. But he recovered. "Just who the hell are you?"

"I'm U.S. Marshal Nathan Wolf. Is this man a friend of yours?" asked Nathan.

Nathan was an advocate of asking questions that he was pretty sure he already knew the answer. Earlier he had seen Skinner talking with the cowboy, so he knew they were acquainted, probably involved in something shady.

"I know him. He's one of the Bar C boys, and I know a few of them. So, what's the beef with him?" asked Skinner.

Nathan answered, "Nothing at the moment. We just want to talk with him. And since he is not a friend of yours, I would say that right now, this is none of your business."

The three lawmen began to walk away, but over their shoulder they heard Skinner say, "Keep your mouth shut, Rowdy. Don't say nothin' to them."

Nathan turned around. "Are you his lawyer, Skinner?"

Skinner growled, "I ain't no lawyer."

Nathan responded, "If you aren't his friend, and you aren't his lawyer, then close your yap."

Skinner glared daggers at Nathan but did not respond. Instead, he spat a large glob of brown tobacco juice to the ground in front of him. The lawmen walked away.

"Is your name Rowdy, mister?" asked Tom Barnes, as the men were walking.

"Yeah, so what? I'm Rowdy Cummins, and you have no idea who you're messin' with," said the cowboy.

As the group passed the judges' platform, Tom Barnes called out to the judge with whom he was acquainted. The man leaned down from the back of the stage, talked quietly with the sheriff and nodded. He then returned to his chair on the stage. The two lawmen and Cummins continued around the arena. When they reached the area opposite the bucking chutes, two shots rang out. The crowd all ducked and began looking around. Many in the crowd were shouting and looking in all directions for the shooter. One of the shots had caught Rowdy Cummins in the upper arm. The other shot hit the wooden framework of the judges' platform, narrowly missing the judge who had just finished speaking with Tom Barnes. The lawmen searched the crowd and the opposite side of the arena with their eyes but could see no evident shooter. "Don't bother," said Nathan. "Whoever was shooting is long gone."

Claire May and Will came and met Nathan and the sheriff.

"It always seems to get exciting whenever you're around, Nathan," said Will as he grinned at his brother-in-law.

"We need to take this fella to jail, Claire May. Come and pick me up at the office later, and we'll ride home together," said Nathan.

Sunday Night
Summer Prairie Ranch

It was late in the evening as Nathan and the Summers family ate dinner. Once again, Rosa held the baby at the end of the table while Virginia, Will, Claire May, and Nathan each spooned the last of the peach cobbler from their bowls. The roast beef, mashed potatoes, and fresh boiled squash were long gone from their plates. As Claire May finished eating, Rosa handed Bobby to her and rose to pour coffee for everyone. When they all had their coffee mugs full, they rose from the table and walked out to the front porch where they would sit and sip their coffee.

"So tell me again, Nathan, what in the world was going on at the rodeo?" asked Will. Turning to his mother, he added, "You really missed it, Mom. Lots of excitement this afternoon."

"From what I heard, I think I'm probably glad I wasn't there," said Virginia sipping her coffee.

Nathan began, "It was Will who got the ball rolling. He pointed out that something seemed to be wrong with the rodeo stock. Both the saddle bronc and the bareback events had a horse that appeared absolutely wild."

"Wild? The wild horses were wild?" teased Will. And they all laughed.

"Well, you know what I mean. Guess I should have said wilder than usual," said Nathan. "Anyway, Will said he thought the horses had somehow been drugged. And then when the scoring for the events was announced, it sure looked like the events were rigged with the judges, too. And when I was walking around the arena to the chutes, I'm sure I saw a man put something in the mouth of one of the bucking horses. Finally, when I found Dave Morgan's hired hand, Rich Wells, badly beaten and left for dead, I was sure that somebody wanted him out of the event."

"But why was someone shooting?" asked Claire May.

"I'll get to that. Rich Wells made a partial identification of the man who clubbed him, and we saw him when he competed. We later arrested that hombre for assault. Tom Barnes also asked one of the judges, who we think was in on the fixing of the rodeo riders' scores, to come in and talk with us tomorrow. Not long after that, somebody took pot shots at

Cummins, the outlaw who beat up Rich Wells, and another shot at the judge who is going to meet with us in the morning," said Nathan. "My guess is that somebody doesn't want the two of them talking to us."

"Darn good thing the shooter was a poor shot," said Will.

"So Sheriff Barnes and I are going to have a little session with the cowboy and the rodeo judge tomorrow," said Nathan, as he set his coffee mug down on a side table. "Oh, by the way, Virginia, in all of the years you have lived here, have you ever heard of a ranch called the Bar C?"

Virginia paused only seconds before replying, "No, I never have. I don't believe there is such a place in our territory." She quickly changed the subject, asking, "Nathan, what do you suppose will happen to all the hard-working cowboys that got cheated? The fair board will never be able to score those events properly."

"Yep, you're right. But that's the fair board's problem, thank goodness it isn't mine," he answered. "My guess is that they'll divide the purse up somehow." Nathan slowly rose from the table and stretched. "Now, if you all don't mind, I'm bushed. I'm going to bed, gotta get up early and head for town."

Nathan and Claire May passed back through the kitchen to their room, a room that had been added to the ranch house after they were married, and before the baby was born. The kitchen was cleaned up, and Rosa had already gone to her room. In a moment, Nathan and Claire May stood, their arms around each other's waist, and gazed at little Bobby sleeping peacefully in his crib. "You make mighty cute little cowboys, Mrs. Wolf," said Nathan.

"Couldn't have done it without you, Mr. Wolf," said Claire May just before they hugged each other and went to bed.

Same Day, Late Sunday Night

Under cover of darkness, a freight wagon, owned by the Sterling Traveling Carnival and pulled by a team of horses, rolled from the rear of a large tent. Two men sat on the driver's seat. Both men were armed with pistols and rifles. Behind them, the wagon was nearly full of wooden crates. Even though it was dark, the crates were covered with a canvas tarpaulin to keep prying eyes from seeing the cargo. The men drove the wagon from the Chanute fair grounds and eventually pointed the team and wagon north on the road leaving town. While the wagon driver held the reins, his partner placed his rifle in the wagon's foot well and rolled himself a cigarette. He lit the cigarette and blew a cloud of smoke from his mouth. He picked a bit of tobacco from his tongue and spoke to the driver.

"How many of these trips do you suppose we've made, Fred?" the passenger asked. "I think we could damn near go to sleep and the horses would find their way to the warehouse."

The driver responded. "I don't know how many trips we've made, but I think we've gone to Kansas City from every point of the compass and from all over the country. I don't much care for these night runs, especially those winter trips, but I reckon we're getting paid enough to make up for it."

The men drove on in silence, each left to his own thoughts. The road was by no means smooth, and the wagon lurched over every depression in the roadbed. And there were plenty of holes for the wagon to encounter, bouncing the wagon and the men on the seat. Each time it happened, the wagon protested, making loud creaking and banging noises.

"I hope this wagon stays together 'til Kansas City," said the driver. No sooner were the words out of his mouth than the wagon took a bone jarring lurch as a front wheel fell into a large depression in the road. The wagon made a loud banging noise and repeated it as the rear wheel went through the same hole in the road.

"Ouch," said the driver. "That one hurt my back," he said.

"You and me both," said the passenger as the wagon continued north.

What the men on the wagon did not know was that the last lurching twist of the wagon had flipped one of the wooden crates from the back of the wagon just above the tail gate. The load had shifted slightly, breaking the corner tie-down of the tarp and allowing the wooden crate to fall out of the wagon. With the loud banging of the wagon, the men had not heard the crate hit the roadbed. They continued driving and would not miss the lost crate until they stopped in the daylight to check the load and take a break from riding. By then, it would be too late to retrace their route.

Same Sunday Night, Just Past Midnight
Lone Elm, Kansas

Occasional wispy clouds drifted across its light, but the half-moon partially lit the road and the outskirts of the small farming community of Lone Elm. No lights shown, as the residents were safely in bed, and the town was too small even for kerosene streetlights. The four mounted horsemen kept their animals at a walk to keep sounds to a minimum. The men looked to their right at the darkened makeshift fairgrounds where they had been only two nights ago. It seemed a dark and lonely place without the bright lights that had illuminated it when they were there previously. Ahead, they saw their objective.

One of the men spoke quietly. "It's right there, between those two stores. When we made our deposit for Kansas City, I cased it, and it's a pushover job."

The man was referring to the small-town bank, the keeper of funds and mortgage lender for the owners of many farms and ranches in the surrounding area where two of the men had made a deposit just days prior. The deposit was subsequently wired to a Kansas City bank, but the actual cash remained in the bank vault until it could be shipped to a larger bank. The small-town bank was an unpretentious building with clapboard siding, a front window and door, with a sign that read *Bank of Lone Elm.*

The four men wheeled their horses and moved to the rear of the building. The rear door of the bank opened above a worn path that led to an outhouse that stood well away from the bank building. The men dismounted, and one of the group held the reins of the four horses. Another man withdrew dynamite sticks and lengths of fuse from a saddlebag while the other two men examined the bank's rear door. One of those two men returned to the horses and withdrew a short, steel pry bar from a saddlebag. He returned to the door and skillfully put the end of the bar in the door jamb and twisted it. With a small crunching sound, the jamb and lock were broken. The men entered the bank. Only a small amount of light from the half-moon entered the front window of the bank, but one of the men knew exactly where the upright safe was located. In short order, they spied an oil lantern, lit it, turned down the wick, and set it on the floor so the light could not be seen outside the front window. In the dim light, they strategically placed the dynamite. After lighting the fuse, they retreated to the other side of the room where they crouched and covered their ears. In a moment an explosion that could be heard throughout the village tore the door from the upright safe. The lone outlaw outside at the rear of the bank struggled to calm the four horses. In seconds, the men inside the bank removed all the cash they found in the safe and rushed out the rear door of the bank. They stashed the cash in their saddle bags, mounted their horses, and were only dimly seen galloping into the distance by the first villager on the scene of the robbery. The *Bank of Lone Elm* now held no cash within its four walls. In the subsequent morning light, there seemed to be no clues as to the identity of the bandits.

Chapter Seven: The Fat Lady

Monday Morning 3 a.m.

Chanute Fair Grounds

At three a.m. the next morning, thin and wiry Dennis McCary opened the door of the caravan wagon and entered the dark room where his common-law wife slept soundly, softly snoring in her sleep. McCary was the carnival's senior roustabout. He and a crew of workers erected the tents and stands when the carnival entered each new town, and then disassembled them at the close of the carnival. They then loaded the transport wagons before the carnival traveled to the next location. But McCary was also involved in other enterprises that were overseen by the manager of the carnival. Only a small number of the carnival employees knew about those activities.

McCary stripped down to his under clothes and slipped into bed. His movement roused his wife, Priz Dillman, the carnival's fat lady, whose bulk filled nearly three-fourths of the caravan's small built-in bunk. Priz rolled over to face McCary. She knew where he had been. She knew that his activities for the past two years had involved robbing banks and other misdeeds, and she had remained complicit long enough.

Because of her weight, Priz was confined for the most part to the carnival environ. Going into a town that the carnival visited was out of the question due to her limited mobility. Because of this, she moved slowly about the carnival back lot during the off-hours of the day, spending a considerable amount of time in the dining tent, quietly talking with her fellow workers, and catching up on the gossip and activities of their lives. Over time, those fellow workers had come to like and trust their large friend. Patiently listening to other employees who told her their stories, Priz had learned a great deal about the Sterling Carnival. She knew for fact that the carnival itself was rife with criminal activity including the robbing of banks in the small towns through which they had passed. She knew that the cash taken from those banks was partially paid to the bank robbers with the remaining cash entered into the books of the carnival to appear as gate receipts. She also knew from cautiously implied conversations that there was another enterprise transpiring within the carnival, but she had not identified the nature of that activity. She understood that the mystery activity was run directly by the manager of the carnival, and probably under cover of the manager's tent. What transpired within that tent remained a mystery because carnival employees were not allowed to enter the manager's personal abode. And since that was the only location within the carnival that was off limits to the workers, Priz believed that it could prove very interesting to find out what went on in that tent. Finally, she knew that her husband, Dennis McCary, was a ringleader in the bank robbery scheme, because he had admitted it to her some time ago and had shown her his stash of money, his share from the bank robberies. She was afraid that her husband was also wrapped up in other criminal activities that he had not shared with her.

Sadly, due to her physical appearance, Priz Dillman was a highly insecure woman. Because of her looks, she had been spurned and ignored most of her life, beginning with her own parents. When she had been more or less kidnapped by the carnival and given a role as its fat lady, she finally believed that someone was giving her the attention that she had sorely missed in her life. And when Dennis McCary had shown surprising interest in sharing her bed, her world, albeit a tiny sphere, had become complete. She loved McCary with all her heart, and surprisingly, McCary felt a strong attraction to her, although that attraction was not strong enough and long-lasting enough to be called love. Priz was deathly afraid that Dennis McCary, the love of her life, would be arrested by the law and taken from her to go to prison. She simply could not imagine being without him, and therefore had determined that she would once again confront her husband with an ultimatum.

Priz put her chubby arm across McCary's chest. "I want to talk with you, Dennis," she said.

McCary was dead tired. He knew where this conversation was headed. He had heard Priz's pleas before. He wanted to just roll over and get some sleep, but he knew Priz was not going to let him off that easy.

"Dennis, I'm afraid."

"What are you afraid of Priz?" McCary asked, even though he knew the answer.

"I'm afraid of losing you. I'm afraid that you are going to get caught and sent to prison," said Priz. "I don't want that to happen, and I want you to stop going out and robbing banks."

McCary turned to face his wife. "Now Priz, we've been over this a dozen times. I've told you before, I can't just up and quit. Why, if I tried to quit, the boss would have me killed. He doesn't like loose ends, and since I know too much, he wouldn't give a thought to killing me to keep me quiet, even though I would swear to him that I wouldn't rat him out. You know how he is."

Priz had begun to weep quietly. "Oh yeah, I know how he is. But I love you Dennis, and I couldn't bear to lose you," she said. "What would happen to me if you were gone? If you won't quit this awful business, I don't know what I'll do. But to save your life, I might even have to call the law and plead for your life in exchange for you telling them all about this carnival and its crimes."

"Now Priz. You wouldn't do that," said McCary. "If the boss ever found out about that, why, he'd kill both of us. Even if he didn't, and this carnival closed, we'd both be out of a job." McCary was more alarmed than he let on. His wife had never ever mentioned going to the law, and he could not let that happen.

"I don't care, Dennis. You need to quit that bank gang. I know it will come to a bad end, and I can't live even thinking about that," said Priz. "We have plenty of money saved, and maybe we could both just walk away from the carnival."

In the darkness, McCary was upset. His wife was threatening him with the prospect of going to the law. He could not imagine going to prison for many years if she turned him in. Later today, he would need to consult with the boss on what he should do.

"Go to sleep, Priz. We'll talk more in the morning when I'm not so tired," said McCary. As he was falling asleep, he wondered to himself what the boss would want him to do. Deep inside, he knew what was coming, and he shuddered, but then fell asleep.

Chapter Eight: The Wrens

Monday, Early Morning

On the Road to Chanute

Sam Dixon clucked to his draft mare. His efforts really didn't matter, the old horse pulled the cart at one speed, the speed she wanted to move. The thud of the mare's heavy feet on the packed road remained at the same rhythm, as the buckboard and its passengers rolled toward town, the early morning sunlight dancing off of the leaves of the trees on their left. Even though he knew the answer, Sam asked his wife, Mirriam, "What are you girls going to be up to today?"

Mirriam belonged to a church-related social group of ladies, whose monthly gathering at the church was more a way for the rural ladies to get together and socialize than for any higher purpose. They called themselves "The Wrens." Someone remembered that the name of their group came from one of their husbands saying that the group of small, thin ladies reminded him of friendly wrens that quickly flit here and there in their never-ending search for bugs. At first the ladies disliked their nickname, but later decided to adopt the name for their group, adding the motto "Cheerful, Helpful, and Purposeful for God." They would be meeting at the church in a couple of hours to socialize.

"We're studying Psalms this month, Sam. But we also must decide on a book to review for next month. I do hope they pick *Beside the Bonnie Brier Bush*," said Mirriam. "I like the stories in that book, and I think that '*Boyd's Bible and Miscellaneous Bookstore'* has several copies for the ladies."

"Mmmm, that's nice," mumbled Sam. While seemingly only mildly interested in the inner workings of The Wrens, Sam still enjoyed the company of his wife on these monthly trips into town. He loved his little Wren.

Mirriam continued, "But we are also trying to figure out a way to make a contribution to help the town library fund, so we will talk about that, too," she said. The group of women had been instrumental in contributing funds to enlarge the fledgling city library.

Sam had other things on his mind. Another purpose for going into town was the load of fresh vegetables in the cart that he intended to sell to the general store and in turn, pick up a list of the couple's home supplies for the month. He was hoping that the grocer would be in a better frame of mind than he had been last month, when he did not give what Sam believed to be fair payment for his vegetables. But it was not something that Sam dwelt upon. The couple was at the age when they did not require a great deal for their livelihood.

"Oh, Sam, look," Mirriam suddenly shrieked, startling Sam, who stopped the big mare. Sam had also seen the unusual sight that had Mirriam's attention. A square wooden crate sat squarely in the middle of the road. Sam lowered himself from the cart and examined the wooden box. He turned it over, side to side and end over end. It was nailed shut on all sides. There was no writing or identification anywhere on the box. With effort, he picked it up, noting that it was heavy, and brought it around to the tail gate of the cart.

Impatiently, Mirriam asked, "What is it, Sam?"

"Just give me a minute to find out, Mirriam," said Sam as he reached into the cart's toolbox and retrieved a long broad-head screwdriver. Using the tool, he levered one of the boards up from the crate. Reaching his hand into the box, he lifted up a book from inside the crate and held it up for Mirriam to see. "It appears to be a box full of books, all with the same title. A *Farmer's Almanac*, it says."

"Oh, that's nice," said Mirriam. Sam handed the book to Mirriam and then banged the board back into place on the crate and replaced his tools. He climbed back up onto the seat of the wagon, clucked to the mare, and the couple continued into town.

The Dixons made a stop when they got to town. The couple left their cart in front of the marshal and sheriff's office and walked in the front door, Mirriam carrying the book that Sam had taken from the crate. A man, whom the Dixon's believed to be a shop keeper in town, was sitting in the outer office.

"Have you seen the sheriff?" asked Sam.

The man answered, "I think he's busy in the back office."

Not being shy, Mirriam shouted, "Sheriff, are you here?"

After a moment, Tom Barnes came from the back office, followed by Marshal Nathan Wolf. Deputy U.S. Marshal Bill Ward was at the courthouse filing papers.

Barnes saw the couple and smiled. "Howdy Sam, Mirriam. What can I do for you?"

Sam Dixon looked over at the man who was sitting nearby. "Sheriff, can you come outside and take a look at something?"

"Sure," said Barnes, and he walked out the front door with the farm couple. He looked into the back of their cart. "Mighty fine looking carrots you've got there," he said. Nathan waited in the office and gazed out the window at the discourse between Tom Barnes and the farm couple.

In a few moments, the Dixons had explained their finding the box of books on the road and how the box contained no markings or identification of any sort. Mirriam showed the sheriff the book in her hands. "They're all like this," she said, handing the book to Barnes.

"Frankly, Sam, I don't know what to tell you," said the Sheriff, as he turned the book over in his hands, and then handed the book back to

Mirriam. "But let's do this. Hang onto the box for a week, and if I haven't had anybody ask me about it in that time, I'd say you've got yourself a box of books.

Mirriam squealed. "Oh boy, I know just what to do with those books. We will sell them to raise money for the library," she said.

"Sounds like a good plan, Mirriam, but be sure to give it a week before you do anything with them." Tom Barnes's older sister was also a member of The Wrens and would be at the same meeting with Mirriam. "Say, Mirriam, when you get to the meeting would you please remind my sister that she needs to make a lunch for our prisoner today?"

"I sure will," beamed Mirriam, firmly believing that the box of books would soon belong to the ladies' book club and could be sold to help the library.

"Hope you get a good price for your produce, Sam," said Tom. "I'll be seeing you later," he said and walked back into the office.

When he came back into the office, Nathan asked him, "What was that about?"

"A bit of a strange thing. The Dixon folks found a box of brand-new books on the road and wanted to know what they should do with them," said Barnes. "There's not a bit of identification on the box, so I told them that after a week, if nobody asked about them, they could keep them."

On the street, the Dixons continued on to their church, where The Wrens would soon be meeting. When they arrived at the church, Mirriam said, "Now Sam, don't just sit there. I need you to open that box again and give me eight copies of the almanac. I want to hand them out to the ladies so they can read them and be ready to sell them at our book sale."

"Do you think that's a good idea, Mirriam. The sheriff said to just hang on to the books for a week," said Sam.

"Oh phooey, Sam. It's not like the girls are going to let loose of the books. I just want them to review them so they know how to sell them later," Mirriam answered. "Now hurry up and get me the books, please."

After many years of marriage to Mirriam, Sam knew that compliance was the easiest path to follow when Mirriam got a bug in her bonnet. So he climbed down from the wagon seat, went to the back of the wagon and removed the copies of the almanac. He then gathered up Mirriam's basket of food items for the ladies' lunch, along with the books, and followed his wife into the church basement. He set his load on a kitchen counter and made another trip to bring in the wooden crate that contained the remaining books. He set the crate on the floor in a corner of the kitchen, then told Mirriam when he would return to pick her up and went back outdoors to his wagon. He climbed in the seat, clucked to the horse, and turned back up the street to go to the general store.

At the gathering of The Wrens, the ladies caught up on their visiting and worked through their meeting agenda items. The general, happy consensus was that they could probably charge twenty-five cents at their next book and craft sale for each of the windfall almanacs. Every little bit helped in trying to build a larger library.

Yet one of the women in the group of ladies did not quite fit the mold of the happy Wrens. Sarah Jones had progressed through her life with multiple hardships. She was without true, close friends and had a marriage that bordered on dismal. It was a union based on convenience for her and her husband, a man who moved from job to job and seldom had two nickels to rub together. Sarah lived hand to mouth and found only slight solace in coming to the monthly meeting of The Wrens. She had little to contribute and had joined the group primarily to get out of the house for an hour or two every month. With a little help from her own poor decision-making skills, Sarah Jones would soon be caught up in another of life's complications.

Chapter Nine: A Meeting of Lawmen

Monday Morning 8:30 a.m.
Chanute, Kansas

Tom Barnes turned his attention to his desk where two telegraph office envelopes waited for him. They had been slid under the office door around six a.m. according to the time written on the telegraph envelopes. He tore them open just as Nathan came through the front door.

"Says there has been another bank robbed. This time up by Lone Elm," said Barnes as he laid the telegram aside and opened the other envelope. "This one says we are going to get some visitors today," he said. "Your Director Gilman, some fella from the Pinkertons, and another fella from some kind of secret thing." said Barnes as he scratched his head.

He handed the telegram to Nathan who read it. "That's Secret Service, Tom. I believe they deal with counterfeiting." Nathan put the telegram back on Tom's desk.

Tom had turned his attention to the man waiting in a side chair. "Leroy, let's go get a cup of restaurant coffee." Tom and Nathan wanted to take the rodeo judge out of earshot of Rowdy Cummins, who was locked up in the back.

The two lawmen and the rodeo judge, Leroy Fuller, walked to a table in a back corner of the cafe and ordered coffee. After the waitress left the coffee and walked away, Sheriff Barnes turned to Leroy. "Who told you to jimmy up the rodeo scores?" asked Tom.

Fuller nearly dropped his coffee cup, and it spilled as he set it back on the saucer. His hands trembled. "I don't know what you're talking about, Sheriff," said Fuller.

"Now you see, Leroy," said Tom. "We're out here among the nice people in the restaurant, and I don't want to start a fracas with you that might be embarrassing. We know you're lying, so I suggest you tell us the truth, or we go back to my office with you and throw you in a cell until you decide to tell the truth. Now, what's it going to be?"

Leroy Fuller's lower lip quivered, and he held onto his coffee cup with both hands, as if he expected the cup to jump out of his grip. He said nothing for a moment, continuing to stare downward, setting his cup down on its saucer. Finally, he raised his eyes and looked at Tom Barnes. "I didn't have a choice, Sheriff. They made me do it."

Quietly, Tom Barnes asked, "What do you mean they made you do it? Who made you do it?"

"I can't talk about this," said Fuller. "They'll kill me if I talk to you."

Nathan interjected. "The way I see it, Fuller, unless you talk to us, we can't protect you against whoever made these threats. And secondly, if we just let you go, those same folks are either going to kill you, or make you look just like Rich Wells, that cowboy they beat up. You saw him, didn't you?"

Fuller visibly shuddered. "Yeah, I saw him."

Again, quietly, Tom Barnes said, "Talk to us Leroy."

A tear lapped over Fuller's lower eyelid. He began to talk. "Nobody in town knows this, but I did a stint in Lansing for embezzlement. I did my time and then disappeared. The secret of my past has stayed with me through the years. I finally settled here, got married and have a great family. Even my wife doesn't know about my jail time. My little shop is doing well, and I thought I had finally put the past behind me."

"And then what happened," said Tom Barnes.

"Well, it goes back to Lansing," said Fuller. "There was a fella there that everybody hated. He was a huge man, and everybody knew to stay away from him and not to cross him." Fuller paused, wiped his eyes with a handkerchief, and slowly shook his head. "The word in the pen was that he had killed some people and was also involved with some kind of counterfeiting deal. The word was that he was real good at making metal printing plates." Fuller paused again.

"What else can you tell us about this convict. What's the connection here to your judging a small-town rodeo?" asked Barnes.

"For some odd reason, this convict took a liking to me and never was mean to me or beat on me even though I was a darn sight smaller than he was. He knew I was in for embezzlement, so he kept telling me that he was going to make me his accountant when he got out. He kept going on about a sweet operation that his brother was running around the country, and that he was going to join him."

"Did he say what kind of operation that was?" Barnes asked.

"Not right away," said Fuller. "But he also kept saying he was going to get out of prison soon, and that he had contacted his brother to hire me as one of their accountants when I got out. He made it sound like his brother travelled around a lot."

"So, what did you say to him?" asked Barnes

Fuller blew his nose and cleared his throat before he answered. "Well, I didn't want to make him mad at me. No telling what he would do," said Fuller. "But I had no intention of going back to crime to make a dishonest living. And I sure as hell would never go back to prison for something stupid. I couldn't tell him that, though. So, I simply said we would have to wait and see how things shook out. Later, my time was up, and I got out of Lansing early for good behavior, and I headed south looking for work. I started this little business two years ago, got married, had a sweet baby daughter, and haven't thought about Lansing since."

"What was the name of this convict at Lansing that you're telling us about?" asked Nathan.

"Skinner. Hank Skinner," replied Fuller.

Nathan looked at Barnes, then both lawmen looked back at Fuller.

"Did you know that Skinner broke out of prison?" asked Nathan.

"Yeah, I heard about it, and it scared me to death that he might find me and want me to go to work with him. I was afraid he would upset everything I had done right since I got out of the pen," said Fuller. "Then I heard that he got himself killed and darn near killed you, Marshal."

"Yeah, not a pleasant day in my life," said Nathan. "But I still don't understand your role in the rigging of the rodeo scores."

Leroy Fuller then told the lawmen, "I guess that before he escaped, Hank Skinner somehow got word to his brother that he thought I lived somewhere around here and that the brother should be able to recruit me. So when the rodeo came to town with the carnival, I was working in the shop with my wife, and we had a visitor."

"Let me guess," said Tom Barnes. "Junior Skinner?"

"Yep, Junior Skinner," said Fuller. "When he came in my shop, he started spewing that I needed to join his operation. He didn't tell me what he was doing, but I wanted no part of it."

"So what did you do?" asked Barnes.

"I asked him to go outside with me so we could talk about it so my wife couldn't hear, and we went out on the sidewalk. Well, right away he told me to come to work for him," said Fuller. "He wanted me to be his bookkeeper."

"And what did you say?" asked the sheriff.

"Well, I was curious, so I asked him what he was doing. To my surprise, he told me he was rigging rodeos and taking the betting proceeds. He also told me that nobody could touch him because he was the manager of the rodeo stock company. I think it's called Consolidated. After he got done pressuring me, I told him I wasn't interested, and he just stared at me with a look that made me cringe. He looked like he was going to kill me on the spot." Fuller looked down again and shook his head.

"So, you told him no. So then what happened," asked Barnes.

"Skinner grabbed me by the shoulder and turned me around so we were looking in my shop window. Then he asked me if my wife knew that I was an ex-con. I told him that was none of his business. And then he gripped me up here on the upper shoulder and squeezed it so hard that I thought I would pass out from the pain. He said he was making it his business. Then Skinner pointed to my wife through the window and said that if I didn't go to work for him, that he would tell my wife about my jail time. But he didn't stop there. He then said that it would be a real shame if such a pretty wife was left a widow. And that she might not be quite so pretty when he was done with her. He was scaring me to death. I figured I had no choice, and I asked him what he wanted me to do."

"What did Skinner say," asked Barnes.

"He said I was to go to the fair board and volunteer to be a rodeo judge," said Fuller. "I asked him what would happen if they didn't take me as a judge. Skinner said not to worry about it, they would take me. That made me think that somebody on the fair board had been paid to hire me as a judge. At least that's the way I had it figured," said Fuller.

"Okay, so now you're a rodeo judge, what then?" asked Barnes.

"A day before the rodeo started, Skinner came to see me again. He told me that whatever I did in my scoring, the Bar C cowboys were to win the events. So we were to score other ranch cowboys poorly so that Bar C would win," said Fuller.

Nathan then said, “You said ‘we.’ How many judges had been recruited?”

“I’m pretty sure that there were two of us,” said Fuller. “I didn’t know the man, but there was another judge that seemed to be scoring like I was. And with two of us scoring like that, it made it pretty easy to make sure that Bar C kept winning. I don’t know what happened to that fella after the rodeo.”

“Do you know anything about this Bar C outfit? Where is their ranch located?” asked Nathan.

Fuller replied, “Well, I’m not real sure, but I think it is some kind of a ‘front’ organization. From what I’ve seen, all those Bar C cowboys have caravan trailers to live in. They are parked among the stock trailers owned by Consolidated.”

“So you don’t think there really is a Bar C ranch?” asked Barnes.

“Well, like I said, I don’t know for sure. But since nobody has ever heard of the Bar C in these parts, I think it’s just a sham, and all those Bar C cowboys are employed by Consolidated and travel with the rodeo stock from town to town,” said Fuller. “I’m only guessing, but I’ll bet that the Bar C wins most of the events of the traveling rodeo, and they pocket the prize money and the betting pool. But there’s no telling what else they’re involved in.”

The lawmen looked at each other. “I think I’ve heard enough,” said Barnes. Nathan nodded.

“My advice to you, Leroy, is that you should get out of town for a couple days,” said Barnes. “Do you have a place you can go to stay for a while?”

“Yeah,” said Fuller. “My wife’s sister lives out in the country. We could stay with them.”

“OK. Go back to the shop, close up, get your wife and daughter, and leave town. I’ll get back to you in a couple days,” said Barnes. The men got up from the restaurant table and paid their bill. Fuller left them and walked rapidly to his shop to get his wife. As he walked, he mumbled to himself, wondering how he was going to craft the story he would tell his wife.

Just as Nathan and Tom reached their office, the thundering noise of the approaching daily stagecoach reached their ears, momentarily followed by the sight of the horses and stage rolling into town. The driver held the gathered reins and braked the coach in front of their office, a great cloud of brown dust catching up to the stagecoach. As the dust settled, the driver of the stage leaned down to the side and shouted, "You three gents that were looking for the marshal's office, it's right there, and the marshal and sheriff are standing on the sidewalk."

The stage driver climbed down from his seat, walked to the back of the stagecoach and unbuckled the rear luggage boot. In the meantime, three men climbed out of the coach. Each of them removed his hat and began banging his hat on various parts of his clothing, watching as clouds of dust burst from their clothes and formed around them. Then the three men walked to the rear of the coach and got their bags. Nathan was watching and suddenly grinned and walked toward the three men. Tom Barnes followed.

Nathan reached out and shook the hand of Ralph Gilman, his U.S. Marshal regional boss from Kansas City. "Ralph, mighty good to see you," said Nathan.

"Same here, Nathan," said Gilman, who shook Nathan's hand and then continued beating at the dust in his clothing.

An even bigger grin then crossed Nathan's face as he looked at the other man. "Never thought I would see you around here again, Charlie."

"Marshal, I never thought I would be back here either, but here I am," replied one of the men. It was Charles "Charlie" Rath, a Pinkerton detective, who reached out to grasp Nathan's hand. Rath had come to town over a year ago to help Nathan in the case of a crooked local bank president. The men had mutual respect for each other. Nathan and Tom, however, were confused as they were not certain of the reason for the men's visit to Chanute.

"Nathan, this gentleman here," Gilman pointed to the third man, "is George Conley. He's from the St. Louis office of the Secret Service. When we get to the office, Conley can brief you on why he is here. Should we get out of the street and head to your office?" said Gilman. Just as the men began walking, the stage driver shouted at his team and cracked his whip. Dust again rose from the wheels of the departing stage.

"Why didn't you fellas ride the train to Chanute?" asked Tom Barnes.

Gilman answered, "Rail line is out up north of here, so they shuttled us to the stage service. Between you and me, I don't ever want to ride one of those contraptions again. I think I've swallowed a bucket of dirt. I hope Bill Ward has the coffee pot on to wash this out of my throat."

Bill Ward did, indeed, have a fresh pot of coffee on the stove. They each grabbed a mug and sat down at the outer office table. Tom Barnes made sure to close the adjoining door so that the prisoner could not overhear their conversation. Bill Ward joined the group at the table.

Ralph Gilman was looking at Nathan. "How are you getting along, Nathan? Are you still stove up, or are you pretty much over that?"

"Yeah, I'm doing all right," said Nathan. "Shoulder is still a little stiff, but no more pain, and I can ride a horse with no problems." He flexed his arm and shoulder as if to show Gilman that he had mended.

"I probably shouldn't say this, but I was mighty glad you took care of that Hank Skinner fella. When they heard about it, some of the other marshals would have probably hunted Skinner down and taken the law into their own hands for his shooting you. But you got him even if he almost killed you in the process. Glad that didn't happen to one of my best marshals," said Gilman. He lifted and took a swig of coffee from his mug.

"Appreciate it, Ralph," said Nathan. He continued, "I guess Tom and I are a bit at a loss as to why you fellas have come to visit us."

The trio of visitors looked at each other, and Gilman spoke. "Charlie, why don't you start us off," he said.

Charlie Rath took a sip of his coffee and set the mug back on the table. Referring to Nathan and Tom, he said, "I think Pinkertons sent you a telegram about the bank robbery in Lone Elm."

"Yep," said Tom Barnes. "We just got it this morning."

"Well, I'm here representing a consortium of small bankers in Missouri and Kansas that contacted Pinkerton," said Rath. "Too many of them have been robbed since the start of warm weather. Nobody seems to have seen the robbers because they always hit their target banks in the dead of night. But for some reason, these robberies seem to be following a pattern. The pattern seems to be that recently the robberies are coming down a line headed south from Kansas City. And that line is right in your territory, Nathan. So, I spoke with Ralph and asked him if I could get you to help me find these robbers. He agreed, and that's why I'm here."

"I remember that you two made a good team the last time there was a bank problem in these parts, so I figured we would try it again," said Gilman.

Nathan nodded. "Sounds all right with me," he said.

Gilman turned to George Conley. "Go ahead, George."

Conley scooted his chair closer to the table and rested his arms on the table.

"I think that Ralph sent you fellas a telegram about our rash of counterfeiting," said Conley.

The lawmen nodded their heads.

Conley continued. "As you fellas know, our agency is tasked by the government with finding criminal counterfeiters. It's been that way since the Civil War, when counterfeit money was so prevalent that the country was awash in bogus bills. Well, try as we might, we will probably never be able to stamp out all the counterfeiters, because there are a whole lot of small-time crooks that have a canny ability to make 'funny money.' Even a small-time crook can doctor up a real bill to make it look like it's a higher denomination bill. And there's so many of those small-time crooks that we can never find them all."

"I'm not sure what that has to do with us," said Nathan. "I don't believe we have seen any of those bogus bills around here."

"Well, Marshal, you may be right. We don't know for certain what this has to do with your territory either, but let me show you something," said Conley.

From his papers in front of him on the table, Conley retrieved and unfolded a map that he spread on the table so all could see. "You see Kansas City here in the upper right. And you will notice that I have drawn small circles that seem to radiate from Kansas City. Those circles represent locations in which counterfeit currency was passed to a merchant or bank."

The group intently studied the map.

Conley continued. "You will notice that I have not drawn any dots in Kansas City itself. There are so many instances of counterfeit money in Kansas City that it would take me a week to draw all of them on the map. I'll just say that there is a great deal of bogus currency floating around the city, and it's getting worse all the time."

"Hmm," said Nathan as he studied the map. "I can see a sort of pattern here." He was moving his finger over a line of dots that seemed to meander from Kansas City, through many small towns. "This crooked line seems to be coming into our territory."

"Ah, Marshal. What you are noticing are the instances that are the most recent occurrences," said Conley. "Those circles were drawn only in the past few weeks, and they seem to be marching in a zig zag pattern right here to Chanute. That's why I contacted Ralph Gilman. I figured that I needed more eyes on the picture down your way since we have no Secret Service agent in these parts."

Conley turned to address Charlie Rath. "Charlie, I know you want to comment on this, too."

Rath had a slip of paper in his hand as he leaned over the map. "I want to show you something," he said. "I copied a piece of George's map. And as you can see, I also drew circles on my piece of the map. The circles I drew represent locations where bank robberies have recently occurred. If I lay my piece of the map next to the same area on George's map like this," he said, as he placed the smaller map piece on top of the main map, "what do you see?"

"Well, I'll be," said Bill Ward. "Looks like the lines are sort of running along the same path. What to you suppose would cause that?"

"No doubt about it," said Nathan. "It looks to me like the counterfeit currency and the bank robberies are somehow related. But how?"

Gilman looked at Conley and Rath, then looked at Nathan. "We don't know how they are related, but by God, we're going to find out," he said. "But right now, I'm so hungry from that trip that Bill's hat is starting to look good." The men laughed.

"C'mon, Ralph. Let's go get some dinner," said Rath. "I'm hungry too."

"You men go on ahead," said Nathan. "Tom and I have some business to take care of, and we'll join you in just a bit."

Gilman looked back at Nathan questioningly but said nothing and walked out the door of the office.

Monday, mid-morning
Chanute Fair Grounds

Priz Dillman had finished her breakfast. Earlier, she had gotten out of bed, dressed, and gone to the mess tent, leaving Dennis McCary in bed. She was certain that because of the hour he had returned home this morning, he would sleep at least until noon. After entering the mess tent, she sat at a table occupied by co-worker friends. Out of earshot, at a table in the corner of the mess tent, the carnival boss sat with a few of his usual cronies, some of whom Priz was sure were involved with Dennis McCary in carrying out bank heists.

Priz listened to the conversations around her while sipping coffee, but her thoughts were elsewhere. Her conversation with Dennis in the early morning hours was still fresh in her mind. She was mulling over ideas on how to save her common-law marriage and the life of her husband without both of them being killed. She was well aware of the reputation of the boss of the carnival. He was a man who was seldom seen, seemingly cordial, but everyone knew he had his finger in every aspect of the carnival's operation. But through casual conversations with Dennis, Priz knew that there were other enterprises that the man was involved in, and she intended to see if she could find out more about them. After finishing her coffee, she said goodbye to her co-workers, telling them that she was going back to her wagon, a deliberate lie as she had another plan in mind.

Priz casually, yet purposefully, wandered the midway, which would not open until one p.m. Most of the carnival workers were engrossed in getting their booths restocked and ready for the day's business of catering to the local customers. Since it was Monday, the evening crowd would be smaller as most of the visitors generally attended on the weekend. She spoke to some of her friends as she passed by their booths. Drawing no attention to herself, she then slipped between two of the booths and continued to where many of the carnival's wagons were parked. Her own caravan wagon was down the row a short distance, but she was not going there. Instead, she walked toward a large tent that was nearly twice as tall as a carnival wagon. This tent belonged to the carnival boss and was where he spent most of his time. She knew he was not inside his own tent because she had seen him at his usual table in the mess tent conversing with the small group of employees that hovered around him nearly all the time. She worked her way around the tent until she could see the wooden frame of a stand-alone, wood framed door that led into the tent. The framework was held in place by supporting beams anchored to the ground on the sides of the door. As she got closer, she could see that the door was fastened shut with a closed padlock. She crept closer and was surprised to see that there was a small gap between the edge of the door and the canvas side of the tent. She looked around and could see no one about. She moved closer to the small opening.

Peering in, she could see that the tent was sparsely furnished. The furnishings consisted of two single beds, a small wood table with two chairs, a washstand, and two upholstered chairs. There were also three wooden file cabinets. Various papers lay strewn about on the table, and a stack of paper was on the top of the file cabinets. At the side of the file cabinets was a printing press, used for printing up the fliers that were put up on light poles and the sides of buildings in every town that the carnival visited. She gasped suddenly when a person inside the tent walked across her field of vision. She could see quickly that it was the boss's half-caste manservant. The servant did not see Priz and continued walking until he was standing beside the printing press. He then began arranging the mechanism of the press, presumably to prepare the print bed for a new batch of advertising fliers. Priz straightened up and stood for a few seconds. She had seen nothing that told her what the boss was up to.

Just then, Priz heard hoof beats, jingling harness, and the deeper thumping sounds of an approaching wagon. She moved quickly away from the boss's tent and stood out of sight behind another wagon. She could see two men on the driver's seat of the wagon. She continued watching as the rolling wagon drew up to the door of the boss's tent. The driver of the wagon climbed down and rapped on the tent's wooden door. He got no answer from the manservant who was locked in the tent. She soon heard the servant shouting to the driver, telling him that the boss would be back in a minute. As if on cue, the boss approached his tent, exchanged greetings with the wagon driver, and unlocked the padlocked door. The driver untied a tarp on the wagon, and soon, the boss, the servant, the wagon driver, and the passenger were unloading and carrying wooden boxes into the tent. Priz watched until they finished unloading the wagon, but she learned nothing of what was in the boxes or what the boss was up to. She turned and walked to her own wagon. Dennis was awake and sitting on the wagon steps smoking a cigarette. He looked up at her and asked, "What 'cha up to, Priz?"

"Just out for coffee and a walk, Dennis. Did you sleep good?" Priz asked.

"Yep, feeling OK," said McCary, and he got off the steps to let Priz pass to enter the wagon.

Unbeknownst to Priz Dillman, as the carnival boss had approached his tent, he had seen her peeking into the tent doorway, and subsequently saw her watching the unloading of the crates from the wagon. He intended to talk to McCary about it this afternoon. Something would have to be done.

Marshal and Sheriff's Office

After Gilman, Rath, and Conley left the office, Nathan and Tom walked back to the cell area, opened Rowdy Cummins' cell, pulled him to his feet, and roughly pushed the cowboy into a wooden chair at the table near the cells. Tom Barnes held a shotgun loosely in his hands. Cummins looked at the two lawmen, hate written all over his face.

"What do you two jackasses want?" said Cummins.

Quicker than a flea jump, Nathan's fist slammed into Cummins' right ear, knocking the cowboy to the side and spilling him onto the floor. Tom Barnes righted the chair and stood in back of it. "Sit," said Barnes. Reluctantly, the Bar C cowboy sat in the chair again. "We'll ask the questions here, Cummins, not you," said Barnes.

"You guys think you're pretty tough, don't you," said Cummins. "Let's make this a fair fight and I'll take care of both of you."

Unseen by Cummins, Nathan had retrieved his blackjack from his hip pocket. The blackjack found on its mark Cummins' hand laying flat on the table in front of him. The force of the blow broke two fingers in the cowboy's right hand. He howled in pain and drew his hand to his chest.

Nathan drew close to Cummins pained face and said, "Now, Mr. tough guy. The way this works is, we ask you questions and if we think you're telling the truth, you don't get hurt. But if you lie to us, you won't even be able to lay in that cell without hurting all over. You understand?"

Cummins glared at Nathan and suddenly spit in Nathan's face. Then he smiled. Nathan slowly retrieved a handkerchief from his pocket and wiped his face. He replaced the handkerchief, but as soon as his hand was free, he swung the blackjack, striking Cummins in the face, breaking his nose. Blood began flowing profusely from his broken nose. Again, he howled and cursed the two lawmen.

"OK, Cummins. Just keep on being stupid and you'll just get more busted up. So, I'll start with a real easy question. Tell us who you are working for," said Nathan.

Cummins considered not answering and continued to glare at the lawmen. Blood slowly dripped from one of his nostrils. But then he said, "You already know that Skinner's my boss."

"And what's the name of the company you work for?" asked Nathan.

Again, Cummins hesitated before answering. "You've seen the sign on our trailers, Consolidated Rodeo Stock."

"Does Skinner own that company?" asked Nathan.

Cummins responded. "Hell, I don't know, but I doubt it. Skinner spends money like water. He ain't no businessman. He just ramrods the rodeo stock." Cummins hesitated, but then went on. "But he always seems to have money in his pocket. I don't know where he gets it."

"And the Bar C cowboys," added Nathan. "Does he manage you gents too?"

Cummins did not answer.

"Does Skinner hire you Bar C cowboys?" asked Nathan.

Again, Cummins didn't answer. But Tom Barnes stepped up to the side of Cummins and harshly banged the butt of his shotgun into the wound where Cummins had been shot the day before. And again, Cummins howled. "When I get out of here, I'm gonna get both you bastards."

"Cummins, you might never get out of here if you don't cooperate. As it is, you're going to jail for a good long time," said Tom Barnes.

"Bullshit," said Cummins. "You two tin stars are going to find yourselves full of holes when the Bar C boys come to get me out of this can."

"Big talk, Cummins," said Nathan. "So, let's talk about the Bar C boys as you call them. Skinner hires you cowboys, but there's no such ranch as the Bar C, is there?"

Cummins simply stared at Nathan. His silence was as good as an agreement to Nathan.

"Yeah, I didn't think so," said Nathan. "The Bar C boys are just a bunch of paid cowboys on Consolidated's payroll. And I figure you boys just travel with the stock and fix the judges so that you win most of the prize money wherever you go."

Cummins did not know that the lawmen had already questioned Leroy Fuller, the local rodeo judge who was forced into crookedly judging the rodeo events. "Nice guess, Marshal, but you don't know anything."

It was Nathan's turn to glare at the Bar C cowboy. "I know a lot more than you think, Cummins, but if you're so smart, why don't you tell me where I'm wrong. Let's hear it," said Nathan.

"Go to hell, both of you," replied Cummins, as he tilted back on his chair.

Nathan toyed with the idea of kicking over Cummins' tilted chair, but he checked himself. "If you're not denying what I said, then that means that I'm right," said Nathan.

Cummins simply glared at the marshal. He was also wondering whether he should try to take on both the lawmen and make a break for it. Stupidly, he thought he would give it a try and leaped up from the table, spun around, and caught Tom Barnes with a haymaker right to Tom's jaw, knocking him to the floor. Cummins quickly reached down and grabbed at Barnes' revolver. With the gun in his hand, he was about to spin around when Nathan's blackjack struck Cummins behind his right ear. Cummins crumpled to the floor, temporarily unconscious. Tom Barnes regained his feet and rubbing his jaw, he retrieved his pistol and the shotgun he had dropped and placed the pistol back in its holster. Tom continued rubbing his face and jaw. "Didn't see that coming," said Barnes.

"You'll learn," said Nathan, as he watched Cummins slowly roll over and sit up. Cummins eyes were not yet focused, and he sat blinking and looking around the room.

"Get up and sit in that chair," said Nathan. Slowly, Cummins did as he was told.

"So here's what we know so far," said Nathan. "Junior Skinner is your boss, and he runs the rodeo stock and hires you paid cowboys to follow the rodeo and carnival. Is that right, Cummins?"

Cummins stared at Nathan, but slowly nodded his head and mumbled, "Yeah, that's right. So what. Nothin' illegal about that."

"You're right, Cummins. So far, nothing illegal," said Nathan. "But Skinner didn't stop there. He rigged the rodeos so that the Bar C boys would win and take all the event winnings and the betting pot."

"You're dreaming, Marshal. Just how do you think Skinner would do that?" asked Cummins.

"Cummins, we already know that Skinner fixed the judges so that they would score the Bar C boys higher than the other ranch cowboys," said Tom Barnes.

"You don't know that, you're just guessing," said Cummins.

"You're wrong, Cummins," said Barnes. "We have a statement from one of the judges that Skinner forced him to score the Bar C boys higher than the other ranch cowboys. So that's locked up."

"Yeah, OK, so what if Skinner fixed the judges. I didn't have anything to do with that," said Cummins.

"But you knew he was doing it, didn't you," said Nathan.

"Yeah, but like I said, I didn't have anything to do with it."

"But Skinner didn't stop with rigging the judges, did he," said Nathan.

"I don't know what you're talking about," responded Cummins.

"Well, let me educate you, Cummins." Nathan continued. "Skinner was drugging horses to make them buck extra hard, wasn't he? And maybe you were involved with drugging those horses, too, eh Cummins?"

"Now wait just a damn minute, Marshal. I didn't have anything to do with drugging those horses," said Cummins.

"But you knew about it, didn't you?" asked Nathan.

Cummins did not answer right away. Tom Barns stepped up behind Cummins and squeezed his wounded upper arm.

"Ow," screamed Cummins. "Stop messing with me."

"You knew about the drugging of the horses, didn't you?" Nathan asked again.

Cummins nodded. "Yeah, I knew about it, but I didn't do it. That was all Skinner's doing."

"And now we get to where you come into the picture, Mr. Cummins," said Nathan. "Skinner was determined that you Bar C boys would win at whatever cost. So he drugged the horses that were drawn by the favored cowboy to win an event. But he didn't stop there, either."

Nathan paused, then whacked the table with his blackjack. The ominous bang had Cummins' full attention, while Nathan stared at the cowboy until Cummins looked down. Nathan continued. "Yes, Skinner wanted to win each event. So, in addition to drugging the livestock, he decided to rough up the favored riders a little bit to discourage them from riding in their event. Isn't that right, Cummins?"

Cummins glared at Nathan. "I don't know what you're talking about. You're just making up some story as you go along."

"Yeah, I'm a real storyteller, all right," answered Nathan. The marshal then slowly took a large, bone-handled folding pocketknife from his pocket and carefully cut a sliver of fingernail from his index finger.

"You know, I've carried this knife with me for a long time. A knife will last a lifetime if you take good care of it, keep it oiled and sharpened."

Nathan then drew the knife blade along the edge of the wooden table, cutting off a small sliver that grew in length as the knife advanced.

"See how nice and sharp that blade is?" said Nathan.

Cummins just glared at the marshal, but he was wondering where this little exhibition was heading. He continued watching.

"Cummins, I want you to take that turquoise ring off your finger. I've been admiring it and would like to look at it more closely," said Nathan.

"Like hell I will," answered Cummins.

Expecting that answer, Nathan quickly bent over and stabbed the knife blade into the table, with the knife blade stuck in the table between two of Cummins' fingers. Cummins quickly pulled his hand from the table.

"You're crazy, Marshal. You could have stabbed me," said Cummins.

"Oh, believe me, Cummins. I would have stabbed you if I had wanted to. Now, take the ring off before I cut your finger off to get it," growled Nathan.

Cummins eyes opened slightly wider as he stared into Nathan's unmoving face. He was now of the opinion that this stone-faced lawman really would cut off his finger. He slowly reached over and removed the ring and threw it on the table.

"You better give me my ring back, lawman. That ring cost me plenty, and nobody else has one like it. It was made special for me, and I want it back." said Cummins.

"Well, you might get it back, and maybe you won't," said Nathan. "You see, Cummins, this ring is evidence, so I need to keep it for now."

"Evidence! Evidence!" said Cummins. "That ring ain't evidence. What the hell are you blabbering on about now?"

Nathan paused, closed the blade on the pocketknife, and placed it back in his pocket. "Well, you see, Cummins, this ring is evidence that you beat up Rich Wells, the Circle M cowboy who was competing against you in the bareback riding event." Nathan studied the ring as he turned it over in his hand.

"What?" exclaimed Cummins. You can't get me for that. I wasn't even around when that happened."

"Cummins, that's a damn lie. You were not only in the stock barn when Wells got beat up, but you did the beating," said Nathan. "I saw you walking out of the stock barn just after you beat up Wells."

"You can't pin that on me," said Cummins.

"Unfortunately for you, Cummins, Rich Wells identified you. You beat him up so that he would be discouraged from riding in his event."

"Marshal, that stock barn is dark, with no lights. Wells could not have seen me . . ." Cummins stopped talking, realizing that he was nearly implicating himself.

"It's a bit dim in that barn, all right, Cummins. But this ring of yours stands out like a light, and Rich Wells saw that ring coming down on him several times as he was being beaten," said Nathan. "And you already said that nobody else has such a fancy ring. You beat him up, didn't you, Cummins?"

Cummins took a full minute before he answered. Another drop of blood dripped from his nose. "I might have roughed him up a little, but I was only doing what Skinner told me to do. Hell, Skinner told me to kill Wells, but I ain't no murderer," said Cummins.

"So, Skinner told you to kill Rich Wells?" asked Tom Barnes.

"Yeah, he did. But I figured that Wells was already signed to ride a drugged horse that would buck his ass off so hard that he could get killed anyway, so I didn't need to kill him," said Cummins.

Nathan paused and then turned his attention back to Cummins. "I'm going to ask you one more question," said Nathan. "Who is Junior Skinner's boss?"

"I don't know," answered Cummins.

"One more time," said Nathan. "Who is Skinner's boss?"

"I tell you, I don't know," said Skinner.

The blackjack hit the table with a crash, startling Cummins so that he lurched in his chair.

"Tell me, Cummins, or we make it more difficult," said Nathan, and he struck the table again.

But this time, when Cummins again said he did not know who Skinner reported to, Nathan could see what he had been searching for. Fear had replaced the arrogance in Cummins' eyes. Whether it was fear of being struck again by the lawmen, or fear of telling a piece of information that would get him killed, Nathan could sense that Cummins was telling the truth. In all likelihood, Cummins was a soldier in Skinner's schemes, and to protect the ultimate boss, Cummins was not privy to the information regarding Skinner's boss. For this reason, Nathan was confident that Cummins did not know the answer to his question. There was no point in continuing to question Cummins.

"Cummins, Sheriff Barnes here will be charging you with assault and battery and for being an accomplice in Skinner's extortion racket." Nathan turned to Tom Barnes.

"Put him back in his cell, Tom."

As he entered the cell, Cummins called out. "Hey, I want my ring back."

Nathan answered, "The next time you see this ring, Cummins, it will be at your trial. I told you it was evidence." Tom Barnes locked the cell door, and the two lawmen left the jail area closing the door behind them. As they walked out of the cell area, Nathan quietly advised Tom Barnes to have Cummins sign a paper attesting to owning the turquois ring so that Cummins could not disclaim ownership at a future trial.

Ralph Gilman, Charlie Rath, Bill Ward, and George Conley had returned from noon time dinner, and were sitting in the outer office.

"You fellas have a nice dinner?" asked Nathan.

"Mighty fine," said Gilman. "Is everything OK with you, Nathan?"

"Yep," said Nathan, and he turned to Bill Ward. "Bill, how about going over to see the doctor and bring him over to look at our prisoner. While we were talking to him, he fell over in his chair and busted his nose and a couple fingers. The doc probably needs to look him over."

George Conley looked over at Ralph Gilman, but Gilman's face revealed nothing. They did not see Charlie Rath looking down in his lap smiling nor the smile on Bill Ward's face as he left the office to fetch the doctor.

Marshal and Sheriff's Office
Monday Afternoon

With the lawmen all together again, Nathan spent the next hour briefing Gilman, Rath, and Conley on what had been taking place at the rodeos as they came through the small Kansas towns with the carnival. He told them of the role of Rowdy Cummins, and that Cummins had implicated Junior Skinner, the brother of Hank Skinner, the man who had shot Nathan weeks ago.

"Cummins doesn't know who Skinner's boss is, but Skinner ought to be able to tell us. Cummins is just another soldier in a bigger scheme," said Nathan.

The room became quiet as the men digested what Nathan had told them. But then Gilman spoke up. "I was hoping there might be some connection to our bank robberies and counterfeiting, but these Cummins and Skinner fellas just seem like small time operators to me. Rigging prairie town rodeos seems like to me to be Tom Barnes' responsibility. And since you fellas down here haven't seen any counterfeit money floating around, Conley and I might head back to Kansas City tomorrow. What do you think, George?"

"Guess I have to agree," said Conley. "The trail seems to have temporarily gone cold. I'll give it some thought tonight, but I may catch a train tomorrow too."

Nathan stood up from the table and stretched. "Well," he said, "I've still got a criminal interstate extortion and gambling racket going on out at the fairgrounds, so I figure I'll head out there and bring Skinner in here to spend some time in our luxury jail. Bill and Tom will go with me. Any of you fellas want to go along?" asked Nathan. There was no rodeo that afternoon, but another contest was scheduled for the evening. Nathan wanted to get the arrest completed before the public came to the rodeo arena.

Always ready for excitement, Charlie Rath spoke up. "Yep, I'll go with you Nathan," said the Pinkerton man, and he stood up to join Nathan. They would need to retrieve their horses from the livery stable, as the fairgrounds were on the outskirts of the city. The men began walking toward the stable. Charlie Rath would rent a horse in order to accompany the others.

While the other three men got their horses, Nathan retrieved Wander from the stable's side corral, led him outside the fence, and tied him off while he saddled and bridled the gelding. "Short ride today, fella," he said, and patted the horse on its neck. He waited until the others joined him, and the lawmen then slowly rode from town.

At the fairgrounds, the men approached the rodeo arena and circled it. Various chores were being completed by rodeo staff in preparation for the evening event, but the men saw no sign of Skinner. They saw a man sweeping in the stock barn. They dismounted and tied off their horses and approached the man.

"S'cuze me mister," said Tom Barnes. The man stopped sweeping and looked at Barnes. "Do you know where we might find Junior Skinner?" asked the sheriff.

The man with the broom didn't know whether to answer or not. He wasn't real keen on lawmen, but at that moment he was even less keen on his boss. A half hour ago, Skinner had threatened to fire him if he didn't make more progress with the broom. The man didn't take too kindly with being threatened by Skinner. He decided that he might enjoy seeing his boss get hassled by the lawmen. "Look for the bright blue wagon over on that side of the grounds. You can't miss it. It's sitting right next to the big tent."

Nathan walked outside the barn and looked over at the wagons and spotted the blue one next to the tent. He walked a bit farther where he could see both the blue wagon and the entrance to the tent. He was curious when he noticed that there were several sets of wagon tracks leading to the door of the tent. He walked back into the barn and spoke again to the sweeper. "Mister, what's in that big tent over there next to Skinner's wagon?"

The sweeper looked again at Nathan, then looked at the Marshal's badge. "Marshal, for me to tell you where Skinner is, I could probably get myself killed. If I was to open my yap any more, I wouldn't be here tomorrow. So, if you don't mind, I'll get back to my work." Nathan watched as the man turned, moved away from the group, and went back to pushing the broom.

Nathan and the others posted themselves outside of Skinner's wagon. The wagon sat in a field with tall grass on both sides of the wagon. When they were ready, Nathan knocked on the door of the trailer and shouted, "Skinner, this is U.S. Marshal Nathan Wolf. C'mon out of there. We need to talk."

There was no answer. But Skinner was in the wagon, and he had heard the marshal. He had known that this moment would probably come, especially after Rowdy Cummins had been taken away for questioning, and the Circle M cowboy, Rich Wells, was still able to talk. He also knew that the lawmen did not know that the wagon floor contained a trap door that opened to the ground beneath the wagon. Skinner had constructed this escape door as a precaution years ago. He was determined that the lawman would not take him without a fight. A .44 pistol was tucked into his belt.

Carefully, so as not to make any noise, Skinner tentatively pulled the trap door up and folded it back soundlessly on the wagon floor. He then dropped through the hatch and down to the grass below the wagon. He knew the marshal was at the door, and he saw the legs of one other man to the side of the wagon. Skinner slowly crawled to the opposite side of the wagon and carefully began to stand up. But then he saw a third man standing at the corner of the wagon. In desperation, Skinner quickly stood and fired at the man and watched as the man slumped over dead.

Just as Skinner began to run, two shots rang out. Charlie Rath and Bill Ward fired nearly simultaneously. One bullet found its mark and Skinner sprawled in the grass. Rath quickly overtook the outlaw and wrenched the gun from Skinner's hand. Rath then kneeled in the outlaw's back, pulled Skinner's arms back and watched as Bill Ward put handcuffs on Skinner's wrists. Charlie Rath looked Skinner over and found the bullet entry hole in Skinner's left buttock. "How 'bout that,

Skinner. An ass got shot in the ass. Just about where I was aiming," said Rath.

"Go to hell," said Skinner.

Nathan came around the wagon and joined Charlie and Bill. He walked directly to where Skinner was laying and with great force, kicked the outlaw in the ribs. Skinner cried out in pain.

"Where's Tom?" asked Bill.

"He's dead," replied Nathan. "Skinner's shot caught him in the chest."

"Son of a bitch," said Bill, and he walked to the side of Skinner and kicked him in the other side of the outlaw's rib cage. Skinner screeched again. He now had fractured ribs on both sides of his body. Every breath he took henceforth would pain him greatly until those ribs slowly mended.

Nathan turned to Bill and said, "You boys take Skinner into town. I'm going to carry Tom Barnes over to the barn and see if there is a buckboard I can use to take him to town. Get the doc to come over to the jail to patch up Skinner, and then get a couple of Tom's deputies to come out and guard this trailer around the clock until I can get a warrant to search it. In the meantime, don't let anyone in or out of it until I can get back with a warrant. Nathan turned and walked back to the fallen sheriff. He carefully picked up the inert body of Tom Barnes and began walking toward the barn. Bill and Charlie roughly got Skinner on his feet and also began walking to the barn. Skinner moaned in pain with each step.

Unseen by the lawmen, a set of eyes was watching them through a small opening in the large tent next to Skinner's wagon. The man attached to those eyes knew that he would need to quickly begin planning.

Monday Evening
The Home of Judge Rodney Stephens

He didn't know how the woman always knew he was coming, but before he could rap on the door to Judge Stephens home, the door opened and Millie, the judge's housekeeper stood looking unsmilingly at Nathan. "Good evening, Marshal. 'Fraid you missed supper, but the Judge is in," she said.

"How are you, Millie?" said Nathan. "Guess you saw me coming, huh."

Millie showed only the smallest vestige of a smile at the corners of her mouth. She loved playing this game with the marshal where she would always be one step ahead of him when he came to visit with the judge. "The Judge is in his study," she said. "You want a cup of coffee?"

"Sure, Millie. Thanks," he replied and walked toward the judge's study. As he approached the judge's room, the air became thicker from the pipe smoke. It seemed to Nathan that Rodney Stephens was always puttering with his favorite pipe, either smoking it or scraping and stoking it in preparation to smoking it. To Nathan, the smell was not unpleasant, and was even a bit comforting, knowing that he was going to see his friend of several years.

Judge Stephens had his head down, reading a law book open on his desk, but lifted his head at the sounds of Nathan's boots on the hardwood floors. His steel gray hair was mussed from the judge's hand running through his hair as he studiously read. He stood and extended his hand to his friend. Taking the pipe from his mouth, he said, "Well, well, Nathan. How's the world treating you?"

Nathan replied, "You know me, Rodney. Trouble just seems to follow me around."

Stephens laughed. "I know that. What kind of trouble have you got this time?"

Nathan began telling the judge about the past couple of days including the troubles at the rodeo, the fixing of the rodeo events, the threatening of the judge, the series of bank robberies, and the fact that his boss, a Pinkerton man, and a secret service man were in town. But Nathan had to pause and compose himself before he went on and told his friend about the murder of Sheriff Tom Barnes.

Judge Stephens was shocked. "You mean Tom Barnes was killed?" Nathan simply nodded his head in confirmation.

"My God," said the Judge. "I've known his family for years. Tom was a young man just starting out in life. He was a good man, and I think he was elected on account of everybody knowing his folks, and the people of Chanute wanting a young fella in that job." He paused for a moment. "Do you have any idea who killed him," asked Stephens.

Nathan went on to tell the judge of the events at the fairgrounds, and how Tom Barnes was killed by Junior Skinner during the arrest of Skinner for his participation in the rodeo fixing and extortion scheme. He continued and revealed to Stephens that Skinner was the brother of the man who had shot him weeks ago. Stephens sat silently while Nathan related the events. After Nathan was finished, Stephens sighed audibly and said, "If anybody else had a story like that, I wouldn't believe it. And you have this Skinner character in jail?"

"Yes," Nathan responded. "But Rodney, I think there's more to this Skinner fella than we know right now. And that's why I'm here. I would like a search warrant for Skinner's caravan wagon. I'd like to take a look around and see what I might find there."

The judge responded, "Are you absolutely certain that you will find anything incriminating if you search Skinner's place?"

"No, I'm not," Nathan replied. "But the way I figure it, any man that has an escape hatch in the floor of the place he's living and then shoots a lawman must have something to hide, and I'd like to have a close look at the trailer of Skinner's."

The judge drew on his pipe and blew a cloud of smoke toward the ceiling. He continued to stare at the ceiling for a few seconds longer, and then set his pipe on the desk. He then pushed his law book aside on the desk and reached down to pull out a side drawer. He retrieved a form and began filling in the blanks on the paper. When he was done, he handed the warrant to Nathan. "I hope this helps to make a solid case on your prisoner. I sure feel bad for Tom Barnes' parents. Tom was a good fella who shouldn't have died this way."

"I agree," said Nathan. "It was not a pleasant meeting with Tom's folks this afternoon when I had to break the news of Tom's murder."

Millie brought in a tray with a coffee pot, mugs, and a few fresh made cookies and set it on the side of Stephens' desk. She poured two mugs of coffee, handed them to the two men, and left the room. Nathan and the judge drank their coffee and spoke for a few more minutes before Nathan parted company to return to the office, the search warrant in his hand. As he left the judge's office, he thanked Rodney and continued to the front door.

When he reached the office, he found that Gilman, Rath, and Conley had gone to the hotel for the evening. Bill Ward was cleaning up the office and was nearly ready to head for home.

"Bill, did we get the sheriff's deputies to watch Skinner's wagon?" asked Nathan.

"Yep, they're going to be out there all night standing watch," Bill replied.

"That's good. I want to get an early start in the morning, so I'll stay here tonight," said Nathan. "Can you go to the hotel and tell Gilman and the others that we should meet for breakfast in the morning?"

"Sure," said Bill, and he turned to leave. "See you in the morning," he said.

Nathan locked the door after Bill had gone, and then sat at the telegraph key where he tapped out a message to the Summer Prairie Ranch. Claire May keyed her response. Nathan let her know that he was staying in town, that he loved her, and would see her tomorrow night. She replied, saying she and Bobby loved and missed him, and told him to be careful. When finished, Nathan walked to the back of the office where he could clean up before stretching out on his cot. But as he walked past the jail cells, Junior Skinner shouted at him. "You need to let me out of here, lawman. I've got rights. You can't hold me here without me seeing a lawyer."

Nathan turned toward Skinner. "Don't make me laugh, Skinner. You murdered a county sheriff in addition to your other crimes. You're not going anywhere, and I can make a prediction that you are going to get up close and personal with a rope after your trial. Now shut your face or I'll take away all your rights with a single bullet between your sorry-looking eyes." Nathan blew out the wall lanterns and walked to the back room of the office. He was asleep on his cot within minutes.

Chapter Ten: Search Warrant

Tuesday Morning 7:30 a.m.
Main Street Cafe

The lawmen were in the cafe early enough that they had a back corner table to themselves and away from anyone who might choose to eavesdrop on their conversation. The scrambled eggs, bacon, and toast were gone from their plates, with only a few crumbs to reveal that they had eaten breakfast a few minutes earlier. The waitress was refilling coffee mugs as Nathan pulled the warrant from his pocket.

"I know you fellas mentioned that you might go back to Kansas City today, but I'm going out to search Skinner's wagon this morning and any of you are free to come along, but I don't know that there will be any evidence linking Skinner to the bank jobs or counterfeit money," said Nathan. "Still, we've got him for the murder of Tom Barnes. And I want to talk with him to see if I can find out who his boss is. And something keeps gnawing at me about this carnival rodeo business, but I can't put my finger on it."

It must have been the lack of any new excitement or clues pertaining to their areas of interest, leaving the out-of-town lawmen with time on their hands, because within an hour, all five of the lawmen rode from town on their way to the fair grounds. More importantly, the funeral for Tom Barnes was scheduled for Wednesday, and they wanted to attend, so they had decided to stay in Chanute for a couple more days.

When they reached Skinner's trailer, Nathan thought it was odd that no one seemed to be about. They tied off their horses, and Nathan went to the steps of the trailer and knocked on the door. From within they heard a shout, "Who's there?"

"It's Marshal Wolf," replied Nathan. "Open the door."

In response, the door opened a crack, paused, and then opened wide. A deputy sheriff stared at Nathan, a rifle in his hands. Blood covered his shirt front, and he was ashen faced. "We've had some trouble here, Marshal," he said.

With the door now open, Nathan could see a second deputy lying on the floor of the trailer. He was not moving. It was then that Nathan also noticed a series of bullet holes on the door and end of the trailer.

"What the hell happened?" asked Nathan, as the other lawmen gathered and looked around the Marshal at the blood-stained deputy, and the coagulated blood stain on the trailer floor.

"We were ambushed last night. There were two or three of them that jumped us. Smitty, the other deputy, was sitting on the steps there, when they began shooting," said the deputy. "He hustled to get in here, but they got him before he could get all the way inside. I pulled him in and started shooting back at them. Criminy, they didn't stop shooting for probably fifteen minutes. When they finally quit, I looked at Smitty, but he was already gone."

Bill Ward, seeing the blood-stained shirt on the deputy, asked, "Did they get you too?"

"Naw, don't think so," replied the deputy. "I 'spect that's Smitty's blood on me."

"Dammit," said Nathan. "Two lawmen have died at this pathetic carnival. What the hell is going on?"

The men talked a few more minutes. Bill Ward and Charlie Rath left to get a wagon to take the fallen deputy back to town. The other deputy would ride back to town with them. Nathan, Conley, and Ralph Gilman would begin searching through Skinner's wagon for clues.

It was surprising how many small storage places were built into the living quarters of the caravan wagon. The caravans were built for efficiency and meant to carry all of the essentials of their occupants. In addition to the multitude of storage places, Skinner was a slob, with trash, dirty clothing, and dishes spread willy-nilly within the trailer. But methodically, Nathan, Gilman, and Conley went through every inch of the trailer. They were finding nothing that would implicate Skinner in any other crimes. They were ready to give up. They stood outside of the trailer, and Nathan walked carefully around it. At the front of the wagon, there was a driver's seat for controlling the horse team pulling the wagon. Nathan climbed up to the seat. It was then that he saw the patterned series of holes in the wall of the trailer under the seat. It seemed obvious that the holes were for ventilation. But he then noticed that there were telltale seams in the wood, revealing a compartment underneath the driver's seat. For a moment, he could not figure out if it really was a compartment or just a flaw in the painted wood. But when he pushed on what he felt was probably the door of the compartment, the spring-loaded locking mechanism popped the door outward. Nathan peered into the space. He could not see anything but dirty rags. It seemed odd to him that there would be ventilation holes into a space filled with rags. He began pulling them out until he then saw several tools. A crowbar, an axle nut wrench, and other tools were removed one by one until the compartment was empty. Nathan was still wondering why there were holes in the door to the compartment. He reached to the back of the space and his fingers hit the back of the compartment. But before he drew his hand back out, his fingers touched an empty space at the top of the compartment. His fingers went over the top of the opening, finding that the open space extended downward. Nathan was now convinced that the original use of this opening had been an air vent to allow the inward and outward flow of air into the wagon. Yet, he and the others had not found an opening inside the wagon for the air to escape. He climbed down from the driver's seat. Gilman and Conley joined him as they reentered the wagon.

"I think that there's an air vent that comes into this wagon. The top of the vent is about here." Nathan had his hand up against the wall where the driver's seat would be on the outside of the wagon. The vent probably comes down the wall here, but where is the opening inside the wagon?" The men started searching again. Their search focused on a bed that sat end to end across the front of the wagon.

"This bed might be covering the bottom of the vent," said Gilman.

"We've searched through all of the storage compartments under the bed," said Conley.

Nathan had been studying the sheer bulk of the bed. It was made from heavy walnut, with an intricate carved design in both the headboard and footboard. Under-bed storage drawers spanned from the headboard to the footboard. Compared to the other furnishings in Skinner's caravan, the fancy bed seemed out of place in Skinner's trashy wagon. But then Nathan moved his eyes to the wooden floor next to the legs of the bed. The floor appeared to be scarred, as if something had scraped it. He could think of no other manner in which the floorboards had been scratched except from the weight of the bed. It was obvious that the bed had been moved repeatedly.

"Do you think this bed moves when the wagon is traveling?" asked Nathan. "Is that what would cause these scratches on the floor?" he said as he pointed to the marks on the floor.

The men looked where he was pointing. Then Charlie Rath went to the end of the bed and tried to lift the corner. It was all he could do to lift it. He grunted, "I don't think this bed is moving anywhere. Can't see it moving while the wagon is traveling. But we've all seen the size of Junior Skinner. He could probably lift a corner of this whole wagon."

"I want to find that vent," said Nathan. "Let's pull this bed out so we can see what's behind it."

After a moment of considerable effort, the three men had the bed pulled away from the wall. Sure enough, they could now see an ornate filigreed brass grill. They had found the air vent, designed to take hot air out of the caravan and vent it out a higher location, behind the outside driver's seat. Nathan was looking closely at the grill. He then rose and opened one of the storage drawers and retrieved a wood-handled screwdriver he had seen there. He returned to the grill.

"Look how the screws on the grill are shiny," said Nathan. "Somebody has recently taken them out of this grill." While Gilman and Conley watched, Nathan backed out the screws and removed the grill, placing it on the bed. He bent again to look in the air vent but discovered that the air flow was blocked by a wad of cloth rags. He slowly pulled the rags out of the vent flue as Charlie Rath commented.

"Doesn't make much sense, does it? Stuffing all those rags in there blocks off the ventilation. Why would somebody do that?" asked Rath.

The answer came quickly. After all of the rags had been removed, Nathan's hands found a metal box, which he withdrew from the vent.

"Rags were there just to hide this," said Nathan. "Although nobody could see the vent behind the bed, I guess Skinner wanted to make sure this box couldn't be seen."

He examined it for a few seconds. There was nothing out of the ordinary with the box. It was plainly colored gray metal with a padlock hasp. A small padlock kept the hasp closed. It was the type of box that a merchant would use for cash receipts. While the other men looked at the box, Nathan reached back into the vent. Moving his hand inside the flue, his fingers found another article that he retrieved. It was a rectangular package, about three inches by six inches and two inches in thickness. Newspapers tied with twine secured the package.

"Wonder why someone would want to hide these things in that vent," said Gilman. "Hand me that screwdriver, Nathan. I'm going to see if I can pry this padlock off the box."

It did not take long for the hasp on the box to yield to the prying efforts, and the hasp broke with a loud pop. Gilman opened the metal box and whistled aloud. "Well, would you look at this," he said. "It's full of ten-dollar bills." He lifted a stack of the bills from the box.

George Conley quickly grabbed a few of the bills. After studying them for a moment and holding them up to the light from the window, he laughed, then said, "Gentlemen, I think we may have found a connection between this carnival and our counterfeit money problem." He fanned the stack of bills he held in his hand. "These bills are all counterfeit! Look here at their serial numbers. They're all the same number."

While Conley was speaking, Nathan had drawn his knife from his pocket and used it to cut the twine on the newspaper-wrapped package. He then slowly unwrapped the paper, revealing two, engraved metal plates. Conley looked over at Nathan and again laughed. "What you've got there, Marshal, are the printing plates used to print these bills. Look closely at them and you will see the serial number on the plate matches the number on the bills."

"Looks like we may have found a break in your counterfeiting problem, George," said Gilman.

"Indeed," said Conley. "But you must remember, this is only one set of plates from a small-time carnival. There could be hundreds of these scattered around the country."

"So where do you suppose Skinner's press is?" asked Nathan. "It certainly isn't here in the wagon."

"Ah, and now you see the dilemma," said Conley. "Skinner may have simply jobbed out the printing in small towns that he would go through in exchange for paying unscrupulous printers to keep their mouths shut, or he may have had his own press hidden somewhere." Conley paused. "My point is, it's hard to find a printing press, especially if Skinner used several printing sources."

The men were silent for a moment. Gilman then said, "I think we're done looking here. What do you say we head back to town?" From within the tent next to Skinner's caravan, the lawmen were being watched as they mounted and rode slowly away from the carnival.

Tuesday, Late Morning
The Clyde Jones Home

Sarah Jones was lost in thought. She was reading her copy of the *Farmer's Almanac* given to her by Mirriam Dixon yesterday at the monthly meeting of The Wrens. Even though she was a member of The Wrens reading group, Sarah was not an avid reader. The only books in the house were a copy of the Bible, and a few odds and ends collected through the years. Yet, she found the almanac to be fascinating. It was hard for her to grasp that there were so many facts and figures written in a single book along with predictions for the best time to be setting out tomato plants and other food crops for the best yield. How could anyone know so many wonderful things. She sat in her chair by the light of the window in the small, run-down house in a neighborhood of similar run-down paint-starved houses, the houses of working men and those who only worked occasionally. The Jones house matched those of its neighbors. Sarah's was a life of grit and difficulty. Her unloving husband only worked when he needed drinking money and treated Sarah as an unpaid servant.

She heard him coming in the back door of the house. She waited in trepidation to hear the first signs to indicate whether he was drunk or sober. Even though it was only nearing noon, she knew the local bar had been open since ten a.m., and that Clyde had probably already paid it a visit.

"Sarah, where are you, woman?" she heard. The tone of his voice told her that he had been drinking, but that he was not drunk because he was not bellowing. He came into the small living area and looked at her. She closed the almanac, stood, and put the book in her chair. She would need to go find him something to eat before he got mad. She passed him to go to the kitchen but heard him question her.

"What is that you're reading?" he asked as he went to her chair, picked up the book, and read the title. "*Farmer's Almanac*. What the hell is that? We ain't farmers," said Clyde.

"It's just a book that Mirriam Dixon gave me at our Wren's meeting," Sarah replied.

Clyde, who had quit school after the fourth grade, moved the book in his hands, gave it one more look and then roughly threw the book against the wall. "Reading books is just plain foolishness. It sure as hell ain't going to do us any good. Get my dinner, I'm hungry," he said, and gave Sarah a rough push into the kitchen.

As was his habit, Clyde Jones spread himself out on the soiled, threadbare couch after eating his noon meal, and shortly thereafter began snoring quietly. Sarah had washed the dishes, and then she came into the living area to retrieve her book. She glanced over at her prone husband, then picked up the book. She noticed then that the cover of the book had been damaged by Clyde's throwing it against the wall. She walked back into the kitchen and sat at the table. She could see where a corner of the paper on the cover had lifted from the stiff paste board beneath it. She wondered what it would take to repair the damage, thinking that she might be able to make some flour paste to secure the paper cover. But then she saw it. As she gently and slightly lifted the torn thin cover, she could see the $10 bill between the outer cover paper and the paste board beneath it. Gently, she pulled the corner of the bill. It was not glued into the cover and slid out into her hand. For a full minute, Sarah turned the $10 bill in her hands. She could not remember the last time she had held a ten-dollar bill. She was mesmerized by just the thought of having such a windfall. Suddenly, she heard Clyde stir in the other room. She quickly folded the bill and shoved it to the bottom of her apron pocket. She then rose, returned to the kitchen, and retrieved a small bowl. She spooned a small bit of flour into the bowl, then added some water, and made a paste of the mixture.

"What are you doing now, Sarah?" said Clyde as he got his jacket from the peg by the back door.

"You damaged my book, Clyde, and I'm going to try to paste it back together," she replied.

Clyde just grunted. "I'm going out," he said.

"Do you have work to do." said Sarah.

"It's none of your damn business," he replied. "I'll be home for supper."

To herself, Sarah added, you'll be home drunk, you mean, as Clyde went out the back door.

In a few minutes, Sarah had repaired the paper cover of the almanac. Only careful study of the cover would reveal any previous tear. She knew that Clyde would be gone for several hours. She removed her apron and hung it on its hook by the stove, then walked into the living area and put the book back in her chair. Then she went to the bedroom to comb her hair. Five minutes later, she was walking down the street, headed for the general store. She intended to put the $10 dollars to good use.

A half hour later, Mel Donnelson, the owner of the general store had the items stacked in front of him on the counter of the store. The items included grocery staples, sewing supplies, and ladies' wear. The last item placed on the pile was a pretty, pale green dress, simple yet dressy enough to wear to church or to The Wren's meetings. It had been marked down from its original price in order to get it off of Donnelson's store books. To Sarah, it was an ideal dress for her. She looked at the items resting on the counter and was pleased. She now had a nicer dress to wear, something that Clyde would never seem to have the money to purchase, nor the state of mind to even think of purchasing such a thing for her. Donnelson bundled all the items together and wrapped them in heavy brown paper, which he then tied together with a length of string that he pulled from a dispenser hanging over the counter. Donnelson knew the Joneses and wasn't sure whether Sarah Jones had lost her mind. He knew that she had almost two dollars on the books still owed to him, and she had at least seven dollar's worth of items in the package. He bent over a piece of paper totaling up the final cost.

"Sarah, these items today total nearly seven dollars, and you still owe me a dollar seventy-five. I don't mean to be rude, but do you have the money to pay for this?" said Donnelson.

Sarah quickly took the ten-dollar bill from her purse and handed it to Donnelson.

"My, oh my," said the shop keeper. "Clyde must have come into some good work." He eyed the bill, turning it over in his hands. He then pushed the appropriate keys on his brass, National cash register, and the till drawer opened with a ding from an internal bell. He then withdrew coins from the drawer and handed them to Sarah.

"Much obliged, Sarah. Thank you for paying your bill," said Donnelson. He watched as Sarah put her purse over her wrist and gathered up the package in her arms. She managed a diminutive smile at Donnelson, who held the door open for her as she left. Donnelson continued to watch Sarah as she made her way toward home. He was still astonished that Sarah Jones had made such a substantial purchase, considering that

Clyde Jones hadn't worked a full day for wages for years and spent most of any wages at the local bar close to his home.

Donnelson slowly walked back to his cash register and stood in front of it for a few seconds before he rang up a "no sale" to open the register's drawer. He retrieved the ten-dollar bill and reexamined it. Having been in business for years, Donnelson was no stranger to American currency. Even so, he did not get all that many ten-dollar bills in his trade, and this one looked almost brand new. While he looked at the bill, he discovered that there was a small smudge in the ink on the obverse side of the bill. He thought this was odd, because he had never seen the ink on currency smear, even when it was wet. He was interrupted by other customers coming in the door of the store. He had to make a bank deposit at lunch time, so he decided that he would take the bill with him and show it to the bank manager as an object of interest. He had never seen a bill with smudged ink but had no reason to believe that the bill was anything other than legal tender. He placed it back in the cash drawer and turned to attend to his customers.

Tuesday Noon
Main Street Cafe

At their usual table at the back corner of the cafe, Nathan, Conley, Gilman, Rath, and Bill Ward lingered over their coffee. Remaining pecan pie crust crumbs sprinkled their plates next to the coffee mugs. The men's conversation over lunch had naturally centered on their discovery of the counterfeit bills and printing plates in Skinner's caravan, and what their next steps should be. As they finished their coffee, they were quiet, until Nathan suddenly stood up.

"I'll meet you fellas back at the office," said Nathan, and he went to the cashier, paid his bill and hurried out the door of the cafe.

"Uh, oh," said Bill. "His gears are turning. He's thought of something."

Gilman had to laugh. Other than Bill, he had known how Nathan worked longer than Conley or Rath. "Yep, he's on to something. Just let him have his head and follow along," said Gilman. "Let's go. I'm curious."

When they returned to the office, Nathan was in the front part of the office. The door that led to the cells was closed. He was leaning over the table and had Conley and Rath's maps spread out in front of him. They gathered around him and watched as he suddenly straightened up.

He turned to Gilman and Conley. "Ralph, if you and George can wait here a few minutes, I need to go talk with our prisoner. I need Skinner to put some pieces in this puzzle and tell me if I'm right about a theory I have." Gilman and Conley looked at themselves and shrugged their shoulders.

"Guess we could have stayed at the cafe for another cup of coffee," said Gilman.

"You know, that sounds like a good idea," said Conley and he rose to head out the door. "You coming, Charlie?"

"If you gents don't mind, I'd like to keep Charlie and Bill here to back me up," said Nathan.

Again, Gilman and Conley looked at each other, but then walked out the door to return to the cafe. Nathan locked the front door after they had gone. He opened his desk drawer and withdrew a few of the counterfeit bills and put his pistol in the desk drawer. After patting his back pocket to ensure his blackjack was there, he said, "Get the shotgun, Bill, and you and Charlie come with me."

With a gunshot wound to his buttock, Junior Skinner was laying on his stomach on the cell bunk but rose to a sitting position when Nathan and Charlie unlocked the cell. "Come out here, Skinner. We need to talk," said Nathan as he unlocked the cell door.

Reluctantly, Skinner got up and walked to the table next to the cells. He sat in one of the straight wooden chairs facing the table. "You lawmen get lonely? Need somebody to talk to?" Skinner laughed, then said, "We don't need to talk. I got nothing to say." He folded his arms across his chest and stared at Nathan.

"You see, I think you're wrong Skinner. We can talk about how you have come to stay with us because you're going to be tried for the murder of Sheriff Tom Barnes," said Nathan. "Or we can talk about how you were fixing the rodeos so that your shell ranch would always win the purse from the contest, or we can talk about how you had Circle M's Rich Wells beat up and left for dead. Maybe we should talk about how you threatened Leroy Fuller to fix the rodeo scores, or maybe how you drugged your own rodeo stock."

Nathan paused. Skinner gave no indication of complicity and continued staring at the Marshal.

"So, don't say we don't have anything to talk about, Skinner. But, you know what? I don't want to talk about any of that, because we pretty much have you dead to rights on all of those crimes."

Nathan reached in his back pocket and pulled out the small stack of bogus bills. He then peeled them off one by one and threw them on the table. Skinner watched as they each floated to the table. Skinner knew where they had come from, but he said nothing, until he blurted, "Bein' a lawman must pay better than I thought it did." Then he laughed aloud.

"You're a funny guy, Skinner," said Nathan, and he walked around the table and deftly placed a high kick into Skinner's ribs.

Skinner screamed in pain. "You son of a bitch, Wolf. I'm going to get you for that," said Skinner. Pain was written on his face and he groaned in agony.

"You're getting nobody, Skinner. You're a man just waiting for the rope. So stop trying to be a funny man and answer a few questions for me," said Nathan.

"Go to hell, Wolf," Skinner replied.

"I may just do that, Skinner, but it won't be because of you. So, let's get this started. First of all, as you already know, those beautiful ten-dollar bills are counterfeit. And they came from your caravan, along with a set of printing plates that made these bills," said Nathan.

Skinner knew very well that the bills were his, but he denied it anyway. "Those aren't mine. You would have never found them if I had hidden them. You got these somewhere else and are just trying to pin this on me."

"Well, Skinner. I have to admit that that damn bed of yours was mighty heavy. Seemed to me like a good place to hide something too," said Nathan.

Skinner now looked down instead of glaring at the lawmen.

"So, in addition to all of those charges I mentioned a minute ago, we also have you for possession of counterfeit materials. I figure you printed these bills, but even if you didn't, you're still an accomplice by having the plates. Here's how I figure it, Skinner. You're either going to hang for murder or be in Lansing for the rest of your life. You have nothing to lose. So, I'm going to ask you a couple more questions, and I want straight answers," said Nathan.

"You think I've got nothing to lose, Wolf. I'll tell you nothing. If I start blabbing to you, I know I'll die. But I ain't saying nothin'. That way I might just stay alive," said Skinner, his lower jaw jutted out in defiance.

"Maybe, but nobody cares if you live or die, Skinner." Nathan paused again. "I want to know who you are working for," said Nathan.

Skinner did not reply. Instead, he clenched his jaw and looked past the two lawmen as if he was ignoring them. He was mentally preparing himself for what he knew was forthcoming. Nathan began, physically harassing Skinner, and for ten minutes, Nathan did his best to break Skinner. In the process, Skinner suffered a broken nose, what was sure to become a cauliflower ear, a broken finger, and a re-injury to his broken ribs. But Skinner would not reveal who he was working for. Nathan was at last satisfied that Skinner was not going to give up his boss, and decided to change tactics.

"Skinner, you've been following the carnival for a long time. Am I right?" asked Nathan.

Inwardly, Skinner was suddenly relieved that the Marshal was not asking about his boss. He numbly nodded yes as a drop of blood hung glistening beneath his nose on his upper lip.

"Let's see how good your memory is, Skinner. I'll bet you ten dollars that you can't name the last five towns that the Sterling Carnival and Consolidated Rodeo Stock visited."

At first, Skinner did not look up, but then tilted his head and sneered as he rolled off the names, "Ottowa, Princeton, Garnett, and Lone Elm. Gimme' my ten bucks," he said.

"OK, after you answer one more question. Was the carnival and rodeo scheduled to go to Coffeyville?" asked Nathan.

"Yeah, yeah. So What? Now give me my ten bucks," said Skinner.

"You forgot Chanute, Skinner, but here's your ten dollars," said Nathan as he threw another bogus bill in front of Skinner. Skinner just scowled at Nathan.

"Let's go, Skinner. Back in your luxury suite," said Nathan as he roughly pulled Skinner up by his arm and pushed him into his cell. Nathan then locked the cell and nodded to Bill and Charlie as they went back to the front office and closed the door behind them. Nathan unlocked the front door just as Gilman and Conley were walking up. When they returned to the table, Nathan was already bent over the maps again.

"Take a look at this," said Nathan. "These are Charlie's marks on the map showing the locations of recent bank robberies. Notice that on George Conley's map, it's the same towns where bogus money has shown up."

"So, obviously, there's a link between those crimes," said Conley.

"Right," said Nathan. "And here's the clincher. Ottowa, Princeton, Garnett, and Lone Elm. Those are the towns that the Sterling Carnival most recently visited."

"Well, I'll be," said Gilman. "So the towns that the carnival went to are the same towns where the robberies and counterfeit bills showed up. So the link between the crimes is this damn carnival."

"Well, then I think our bank robbers have to be some of the people who work in that carnival," said Charlie Rath.

"I agree," said Gilman. "But how do we ferret them out?"

Their meeting was interrupted by the office door opening quickly. The lawmen looked up to see Mel Donnelson and one of the local bankers standing in the doorway.

Nathan spoke. "Morning Mel. What brings you here?"

Donnelson was flushed and out of breath as he spoke. Obviously, he had hurried to the marshal's office. He held up his hand and began waving a ten-dollar bill in the air as if he was shooing flies. "Marshal, my banker says this here is a counterfeit ten-dollar bill. One of my customers just handed it to me to pay for a bunch of groceries and a dress. I want her arrested."

"Now hold on, Mel," said Nathan, as George Conley walked over and took the ten-dollar bill from Donnelson's hand. "Nobody is going to get arrested until we hear the whole story."

Conley looked at Nathan. “Phony, all right,” he said.

“All right, Mel. Who gave you the ten dollars?” asked Nathan.

“Sarah Jones,” said Donnelson, and he went on to repeat himself. “I want her arrested. She used this fake money to buy nearly ten dollars’ worth of merchandise, and the banker said the bill is phony. So I’m out ten dollars’ worth of goods.”

Nathan knew Clyde Jones and his wife, Sarah. He also knew that Clyde was a ne’er-do-well. Where he or his wife would have gotten the ten-dollar bill was a mystery.

“All right, Mel. I’ll have a talk with Sarah Jones in the morning. But right now, I just need you and the banker to go back to your work. Keep your mouth shut and don’t tell anybody about this. Keep your eyes open in case any other bills turn up. Will you do that for me?” asked Nathan.

“Sure, we can do that,” said the banker. Mel Donnelson just shrugged his shoulders, seeming to be disappointed that instant action was not to be expected. He nearly blurted out his dissatisfaction of the situation, but then thought better of it and remained silent for a few seconds but could not resist a parting shot. “I still say she should be arrested,” said Donnelson. Then he turned and with the banker, the two men walked out the door and could be seen heading back to their respective places of business.

Nathan was sitting motionless at the table, the maps still in front of him.

“Now what’s on your mind, boss?” asked Bill.

The other lawmen had refilled their coffee mugs and sat down at the table, where their hats were strewn about next to the maps they had been examining. Bill brought a mug and set it down in front of Nathan. “Thanks, Bill,” said Nathan. The Marshal turned the mug absently between his thumb and fingers. Finally, he spoke.

"You fellas were not there when Tom Barnes and I interviewed Leroy Fuller, the shop keeper that Junior Skinner enlisted to carry out the crooked rodeo judging. Something has been nagging at me, and now I remember something that Fuller told us. Fuller was at Lansing the same time as Hank Skinner, and for some reason, Hank Skinner took a liking to Fuller and wanted to enlist him in Junior Skinner's crooked Bar C rodeo scheme. After Fuller's release from prison, Junior Skinner met up with him when the rodeo came to town and threated to harm Fuller's wife if Fuller wouldn't cooperate and become the bookkeeper for Skinner's crooked operation. So Fuller had to cooperate with Skinner. But during the rodeo here, Fuller decided that he was done with crooked rodeo judging and judged one of the events fairly. That resulted in the Bar C cowboy coming in second in the event. Junior Skinner was angry with the double cross, and it was probably him who fired a couple shots at the rodeo. Those shots were meant to hit Bar C cowboy Rowdy Cummins so he wouldn't talk, and Leroy Fuller for double crossing him and to keep Fuller from talking. Since Skinner missed in his attempt to shoot Cummins and Fuller, Fuller is probably still in danger of being killed by Skinner."

"Where is this Fuller fella?" asked Gilman. "We better get him out of the cross hairs of Skinner's friends."

"He's OK, Ralph. We sent him out of town where he would be safe," said Nathan. "But I remembered something else that Fuller told me. He said that at Lansing, Hank Skinner's reputation was common knowledge. Besides being known as a cold-blooded killer, remember it was him who almost put me away, he was also known to be skillful in metal working and was rumored to have made counterfeit printing plates. Fuller also told me that Hank Skinner had said that he was going to get out of the pen and go into his brother's business. And when he escaped from prison, he headed south, the same direction that the carnival was moving."

"Makes sense," said George Conley. "Hank Skinner was going to join his brother in the counterfeiting business. So, he headed south to join the carnival."

"Well, that's my theory," said Nathan. "And Hank Skinner stopped and waited near Coffeyville. Junior Skinner told me that the carnival was scheduled to visit Coffeyville. 'Course Hank Skinner was wounded and couldn't travel very well at that point, but I figure he was just waiting for the carnival to come to Coffeyville so he could join his brother, get nursed back to health, hide out with the carnival, and make a few more of those counterfeit printing plates. Coffeyville was going to be the next stop for the carnival and rodeo after they left here."

"But we still don't know who the head man is in the operation, and we don't know how the printing was getting done," said Gilman.

Nathan drained his coffee mug and stood up and stretched. He slowly folded the maps that were on the table but left them there. "Gentlemen, I was away from home last night, so I am going to head for the ranch. I'll be back in the morning, and we can reconvene, say nine o'clock. Then I'll have a little talk with Sarah Jones. Bill, can you camp out here tonight so nobody tries to grab Skinner? Oh, and can you make sure that Espie gets our prisoner fed?"

"Sure will," said Bill. "I'll go home to have supper with Espie and walk her back here to feed Skinner. Then I'll stay here tonight." Espie Ward was Bill's wife. When the Marshal had a prisoner in jail, she fixed meals for the inmate and was reimbursed by the Marshal Service for her efforts. The same arrangement was made for county prisoners, who were the responsibility of the sheriff's office.

Nathan grabbed his rifle from the gun rack. "I'll see you boys in the morning," he said and walked out the door, turning to head toward the livery stable to get Wander. But before he could get the horse saddled, a tousle-haired delivery boy from the telegraph office came running into the livery barn.

"I saw you walking in here, Marshal," said the boy. "I've got a telegram for Mrs. Summers. Can you give it to her for me? I guess whoever sent this didn't know you have a telegraph out at your ranch, huh?"

"Guess not," said Nathan. He handed the boy a coin and watched as he ran back down the street to the telegraph office. Nathan looked at the official envelope that was sealed, saw that it was indeed addressed to Virginia, folded the envelope, and put it in his shirt pocket. After saddling the horse and heading out of town, Wander automatically fell into the canter, then walk routine to cover the miles to the ranch. Nathan did not need to apply pressure to the reins to control the horse. Wander knew the way home and kept up a steady pace. A little over an hour later, they crested a small rise and could look down at the Summer Prairie ranch house. Wander knew where to go, picked up his pace, and headed directly for the corral next to the barn, where he immediately drank his fill from a water trough. Nathan soon had him unsaddled and brushed down before leading him into a stall for feeding. He put more hay into the feeder and held a shallow pan partly filled with oats for Wander to munch before leaving the barn for the house. As he approached the house, he could see Claire May sitting on the side steps leading into the kitchen. Bobby was on her lap. He was home.

Tuesday Night
Summer Prairie Ranch

Nathan swore that nobody could make fried chicken like Rosa. As the family sat around the supper table, Nathan savored every bite of the moist, buttermilk-battered chicken. As he spread butter on one of Rosa's flaky biscuits, he did his best to recount the events of the past couple of days, telling the story to Claire May, Will, and Virginia. But when he told them of the death of Tom Barnes, it drew an unexpected reaction. Virginia Summers knew Tom's mother and father, and the story of Tom's death prompted tears from her.

"He was such a nice boy," said Virginia. "Perhaps he was just too young and inexperienced to be put in that job."

But then Claire May made a remark that silenced the table. In a barely audible voice, she said, "I don't know what I would do if you were ever taken away from me like that," and she glanced at Nathan. For several seconds, no one made a sound. Finally, the silence was broken by the happy jabbering of Bobby, who was sitting at the end of the table on Rosa's lap grinning at all of them. Two tiny white tooth buds could be seen in both his upper and lower jaw. Claire May held her arms up and Rosa passed the baby to her. In turn, she handed Bobby to Nathan. "He needs his father, you know," said Claire May, as she turned back to her plate. Slowly, she picked up her fork and placed a bite of chicken in her mouth. Her mother and brother followed suit.

Later, as they sat sipping coffee on the front porch, they watched as the sun perched on the line of the horizon before sinking below for the evening. Rays of red, pink, and yellow cloud streaks hung in the western sky, a beautiful sight. The sound of crickets and cicadas slowly grew in volume, and somewhere close by, a lone owl was heard. They said little, taking in the serenity of the pleasant night sounds.

"Oh, I almost forgot, Virginia," said Nathan as he pulled the envelope out of his shirt pocket. "Telegraph office gave me this on my way out of town." He handed the envelope to Virginia. In the dim light of the one oil lantern on the porch, Virginia could not read the telegram so she went in the house. She returned later, sat back in her chair, and picked up her coffee mug.

"Well, aren't you going to tell us what that was about?" asked Claire May.

In a somewhat steely voice, Virginia replied, "Nothing to concern yourself, Claire May. I'll tell you all about it some time when I think the time is right."

Nathan and the two Summers siblings thought that reply was a bit odd, but they knew from Virginia's tone that the matter should probably drop for the time being.

Nathan yawned and stood. "I've got to get washed up and go to bed. Unfortunately, I told Bill and the others that I would be back early in the morning. He picked up his coffee mug and walked back to the kitchen, placing the mug next to the sink.

After he had washed himself at the washstand in their bedroom, Nathan turned to go to bed, but Claire May had beat him into bed. She lay smiling coyly at him as he slipped off his outer clothes. He blew out the lamp and slid between the sheets, happily discovering that Claire May did not have a stitch of clothing on her body. He was quickly in the same condition.

As she stroked his belly, Claire May cooed, "Just how early in the morning were you planning to get up, Marshal?"

Nathan chuckled. "Maybe not as early as I thought," he said and pulled Claire May closer.

Chapter Eleven: The Fat Lady Sings

Midnight, Tuesday Night
On the Midway, Sterling Carnival, Chanute

It was the custom of the carnival employees to celebrate on the last night of their operation in each town before they moved on to the next location. The general public had left the fair grounds at eleven p.m., closing time. The midway once again belonged to the carnival employees. The next morning, they would tear down the rides and concession booths beginning at noon. But tonight, as usual, they would have their own barbecue and beer get-together. In addition, many of the ride operators manned their rides for the first hour of the party so that employees and their children could enjoy the rides. After an hour, the rides would also be shut down so that the operators could join the festivities.

Kegs of beer sat next to tables set with a variety of foods. A portable barbecue pit was wafting smoke skyward as beef, pork, and sausages grilled to perfection. An old wind-up phonograph played scratchy music from years gone by as well as some of the more modern tunes, which prompted some of the adventurous participants to choose dance partners and sway around the trodden dusty ground of the midway. The beer flowed freely resulting in some of the hardier drinkers to imbibe just a bit too much. Hence the noon time tear-down schedule for the following day.

Dennis McCary sat on a wood bench eating a sausage wrapped in bread and drinking a beer. Priz Dillman sat next to him, her hands wrapped adoringly around McCary's upper arm while he ate. When McCary finished the sausage, he tilted the beer cup skyward, draining it before he set it on the bench at his side. "Let's go, Priz," said McCary, slightly slurring the z to the point it sounded like a j. "We're gonna ride the big swing, The Swing of Terror." He stood and pulled Priz's hand and arm. She rose slowly, almost reluctantly, since she had also just eaten. But, she had always liked the big swing, and so, she took McCary's arm as they slowly strolled the midway aisle and made their way to the Swing of Terror. No one was riding that particular ride, probably because there was a sign attached to the turnstile to get into the ride. The sign read, "*Out of Order.*" In truth, the ride was very much operable, and the operator of the ride sat in the nearby shadows out of sight of passersby. He was waiting for only two riders, Dennis McCary and Priz Dillman.

McCary walked to the turnstile of the ride and shouted, "Frankie, me boy, where are ya?" The operator rose from the overturned box he had been sitting on and came forward to man the controls of the ride. McCary met him and the men shook hands. Hidden within that handshake was a small, folded packet of two twenties and a ten-dollar bill. The operator slipped the money into his pocket. McCary took Priz's hand and directed her to a swing and helped her sit on the well-worn wooden seat. McCary directed her to this particular swing, because earlier, by using a pocketknife, the swing had been marked by removing a small wood shaving from the back of the seat so that the fresh woodcut could be seen by McCary. Only the operator and McCary could identify that swing. McCary moved around the pole to the opposite side and took a seat on a swing there. He leaned over and waved around the center pole at Priz, who waved back.

The center pole began to turn very slowly, but with each revolution its speed increased. Before long, the swings extended three feet from the pole, then five feet, then seven feet, and finally to their maximum twelve feet from the pole. The swings had lifted to approximately twenty feet from the ground. With centrifugal force, the swings seemed to fly on their own. Because of the force, the weight pulling on the chains suspending the swings was intensified.

Priz loved the swinging ride. To her, it seemed that her weight was lifted from her, and she was able to soar free just like a bird. She put her arms out straight from her sides as if they were wings, and her billowing dress flew above her knees. Her mind left its earthly cares, and she closed her eyes slightly, imagining herself able to fly. She was truly enjoying the sensation, allowing herself to have a few moments of freedom from care. After a moment, she drew her arms back to rest her hands on the safety bar across the front of the swing. She turned her head to look at Dennis McCary. She noticed that he seemed to be staring at the top of the center pole, or was he? As she continued to look at him, there was a loud bang, much like a gun shot. But there was no gun. In fact, one of the links in the chain that was suspending Priz's swing had broken, and the relief of tension on the lower chain had caused the loud popping sound. Immediately, the swing in which Priz was sitting dropped away on one side, spilling her out of the swing from a height of twenty feet. Terror quickly replaced her euphoria, and she desperately tried to grab the seat of the swing as she slid to the side. It was of no use. She was not adroit enough nor strong enough to grab the remaining suspension chain or the seat of the swing. In seconds, she was airborne and on her way to the ground. She managed only a small scream as the ground rose to meet her. When she hit the ground, there was only a muffled whump sound.

She lay in the dusty dirt beneath the turning swings. The broken chain hung lower than the swings as they turned, and it dragged in the dirt as it circled the center pole. In a short time, the swings slowed and stopped. Dennis McCary exited his swing and rushed to Priz. Priz was not moving, and McCary was sure she was dead.

Priz's fall was no accident. In a course of action worked out a day before, and with the insistence of his boss, McCary and the ride operator had developed a plan to kill Priz Dillman. In accordance with the plan, the ride operator began shouting for help as loud as he could yell. Other employees heard him and made their way to the ride. But before they could get there, McCary, who had a semblance of affection for Priz, whispered to her, "He made me do it Priz. I didn't want to do it, but he made me. He would have killed me if I hadn't done this to you Priz."

McCary believed he was talking to himself, and that his confession was falling on deaf ears. After all, he was certain Priz was dead. He watched as other employees rushed to get a wagon and team. Six stout men lifted the inert body of Priz Dillman into the wagon and placed a folded blanket beneath her head. Quickly, two of the men stepped up into the driver's box and hastily drove the wagon to the doctor's office in town. McCary stood with stooped shoulders, sobbing with tears falling to his cheeks. After receiving comments meant to comfort him from his fellow employees, he wiped the tears from his face and slowly walked until he was out of sight from the other employees. He then quickly walked to the boss's tent, entered, reported the death of Priz Dillman, and drank a congratulatory shot of whiskey with the boss. He would have the whole bed in Priz's caravan to himself that night.

Wednesday 5 a.m.
Summer Prairie Ranch

As it was, it seemed to Nathan that the morning came awfully early. Claire May woke him at five a.m. in the most delightful manner. He reluctantly left her soft, warm embrace, rose, and got out of bed at just past six. He shaved and dressed while Claire May fed Bobby as she sat nude and cross legged on the bed watching him. They could smell coffee and sizzling ham wafting from the kitchen. Claire May eased

Bobby from her breast. "That's all for now, little boy. Go to your daddy while mommy gets dressed." She handed Bobby to Nathan, kissed her husband, and began looking for clothes for the day.

"You and Bobby go to breakfast, and I'll catch up," said Claire May.

He was on his way to the kitchen, but as he passed Virginia's office door, the clickety-clack noise alerted him. The telegraph key was bouncing, making its distinctive sound. He paused, gave a thought to ignoring it, but then translated the clicks in his head. Bill Ward was sending, and the message was, *Bill Ward Sending, Urgent for Marshal Wolf.* Bill repeated his call again and with his free arm, Nathan keyed his answer that he was on the line. With Bobby on one arm, Nathan took a paper and pencil to write down the message with his free hand. Bill began sending the telegraph body:

Accident at Carnival. Fat Lady fell from ride. Lady at Doc Johnsons. Near death. Asking for you to talk with her asap. Carnival due to leave afternoon. Stop.

Nathan read and reread the message. He thought that this was the strangest telegraph message he had ever received. But as he sat at the desk and read the note one more time, he drew the conclusion that everything related to the carnival and the rodeo that followed it had turned out to be not as it seemed, as various and seemingly unrelated crimes had occurred in the atmosphere of those events. He decided that he should consider this message from Bill Ward to be another piece in the puzzle. He would leave immediately for town.

He walked back to the bedroom and found Claire May fully dressed with her hair brushed and pinned up. She looked gorgeous. With his free arm, he grasped his wife and kissed her. "I've got to leave for town," he said. Claire May stuck her lower lip out, playing at pouting. She knew he would not be leaving if he did not think it was important. She teased him, "Are you going to take our son with you?"

Nathan laughed. "Oh, no, I guess not," he said as he handed the baby to Claire May. They kissed each other, and Nathan walked out of the bedroom.

"Well, little man," said Claire May to Bobby. "Just you and me again, eh." She kissed the baby and talked gibberish to him for a bit, then walked to the kitchen. She looked out the kitchen window to watch as Nathan finished saddling Wander. In a few moments, he rode from sight.

Wednesday 8:30 a.m.
Doctor Johnson's Home

Without first knocking, Nathan walked into Doctor Johnson's office door at the side of his home. Doctor Johnson was administering to a young boy with a scraped knee that was oozing a steady splotch of blood. The lad was stoic and seemed transfixed on the blood dripping down the side of his leg while his mother fretted. "He's going to need a stitch or two, Gladys," the doc said, and looked up as Nathan entered.

"Glad you're here, Marshal. She's in the back room and has been asking for you ever since she got here," said the doctor.

"I'm not sure why she is asking for me," said Nathan. "I don't even know the woman."

The doctor stood up. "Gladys, keep this cotton pad on the boy's knee while I talk with the Marshal."

The doctor went down the hallway a short way before he stopped to face Nathan. "Marshal, her name is Priz Dillman. She wouldn't tell me why she wanted to see you so bad, but I gotta' tell you, she seems like a very nice woman, but she is not in very good shape. The fall from that ride jostled up her insides so she is bleeding internally, and I have no way to get that fixed. I don't believe she has much time left. Go on back and introduce yourself."

"You said she fell. What did she fall from?" asked Nathan.

"Those gents that brought her here told me she fell from some kind of carnival ride. They called it the *Swing of Terror*," said the doctor. "They said she probably fell from about twenty feet, which might not kill a person. But when you weigh as much as this woman, that fall is going to do some serious damage internally as well as break several bones. I think the fall may have broken her hip and some ribs as well as dislodging some of her innards. Kind of a sad situation, and I don't figure she will last through the day. That's why I told Bill Ward to contact you right away. She's in the room on the right at the end of the hall."

"Appreciate it, Doc. I'll have a talk with her," said Nathan, and he walked down the hall and entered the room on the right.

Priz Dillman lay on her back in bed. She was in pain even though the doctor had given her enough laudanum of opium to put a pony to sleep. She was intermittently shedding tears between fits of raging madness. If she were able, she had already told herself that she would hunt down Dennis McCary and kill him. McCary's words to her while she lay helpless on the ground beneath the Swing of Terror had psychologically destroyed her, leaving her with no will to live. But first, she was going to see that McCary and his boss were caught in the long tentacles of the law. She knew that she did not have long to live; she did not know why, she just felt it. Maybe it was because McCary's soulless words had taken away her will to live. As a result, she had insisted early this morning that the doctor summon the local marshal. She would have her say.

"Miss Dillman?" asked Nathan.

Priz turned her head and faced Nathan. "Are you the marshal?"

"Yes, ma'am. I understand that you wanted to see me," said Nathan.

"Pull that chair up here, Marshal. I have a story to tell you," she said, as she struggled to breathe. Nathan did as he was asked and pulled a side chair closer to the bed.

The room was quiet except for the labored breathing of the injured woman. Soft murmuring sounds of voices elsewhere in the house could also be heard indistinctly. Morning sun rays edged into the window next to Dillman's bed. She began to speak. "Marshal, I have had a rather unpleasant life," said Priz. She went on.

"I'm lying in this bed waiting for the Lord to take me to a place that will be far better than this life on earth," she said.

Nathan's only comment was, "Yes, ma'am."

"Marshal, there is something really rotten going on in that carnival. And my common law husband, who I truly loved with all my heart, is a part of the wickedness. I'm laying here dying because he tried to kill me," said Priz.

"What makes you think he tried to kill you, Miss Dillman?"

"Marshal, as I lay on the ground after falling off that swing, he told me he did it. I'm sure he thought I was already dead, but he leaned down over me and told me he had to kill me because the boss told him to do it." Tears began to run from her eyes, and she paused in her story, all the while she drew labored breaths.

"He betrayed me, Marshal. I have loved him unconditionally for years, but he didn't really love me. If he loved me, would he have wanted to kill me?" asked Priz.

"What's your husband's name?" asked Nathan.

"McCary. Dennis McCary," she answered as she dabbed at her eyes with a handkerchief.

"But, Miss Dillman, why would your husband want to kill you?" asked Nathan.

"Because I know too much," she said. "And I have been trying to get Dennis to stop robbing banks and God knows what else his boss has him doing. But Dennis wouldn't stop. I think he actually liked being an outlaw and robbing banks." She stopped again to blow her nose and take a few heavy breaths.

"So, your husband, Dennis McCary was robbing banks?" said Nathan.

"Yes, him and a group of men from the carnival go back to the towns that the carnival leaves behind and rob the banks, and then they come back to their jobs in the carnival," said Priz. "That's why they haven't been caught. As Dennis used to say, the trail runs cold when it runs into the carnival." Beads of perspiration showed on Dillman's forehead. Nathan could not help but feel pity for her as she lay dying.

Nathan thought to himself, well, that explains why the recent bank robberies seem to be happening in the same towns that the carnival came through. He thought Charlie Rath would certainly appreciate that bit of information.

"Miss Dillman, how do you suppose your husband was going to kill you when you fell off of a swing at the carnival?" Nathan asked.

"Marshal, I've ridden that swing ride dozens of times. Those chains that hold up the swings are very sturdy. But when we were riding late last night, Dennis kept looking up at the chains above my swing. It was as if he was waiting for something to happen. Well, it did. One of the chains broke and here I am, about to die. Dennis did something to that swing to make it break, I'm just sure of it," she said, trying her best to stifle her sobs as she spoke.

"Miss Dillman, if what you have told me is true, your husband has committed bank robbery and attempted murder. Are you sure you understand what you are doing by saying these things about your husband?" Nathan asked.

Priz rolled her head and stared intently at Nathan and spoke again. "You don't understand, Marshal. Dennis was my rock, he was my world. No other man paid any attention to me, except to laugh about my size. Dennis didn't laugh at me and said that he loved me. I loved him. But I never thought that he would deceive me. Never! But now I know. I know he didn't love me with all his heart. He has betrayed me and wanted me dead. That cannot go unpunished, and I want him to face the law. But, if I don't die from my fall, I feel certain that he will try again to have me killed," said Priz. She paused to catch her breath, then spoke again. "And another thing. Deep inside me, I always had my doubts. I always wondered whether something like this might happen. Because of that, I wrote a letter about the bank robberies, and how Dennis was leading a gang of robbers. I wrote that letter months ago. I don't know why. Maybe it was because of my lifetime insecurities, I don't know. But I just thought I might need it for insurance or something. In that letter, I said everything just like I told you. And I put the letter in a safe place."

Nathan was taken aback and marveled at the foresight of the severely injured woman.

"Where is that letter, Miss Dillman?"

"If you go in my caravan, pull out the drawer that has my underclothes in it. Turn the drawer over, and the letter is glued to the bottom of the drawer," said Priz, and she immediately took several rapid breaths.

"OK, I'll go search for the letter. And I think you may be right that McCary might try again to get rid of you," said Nathan. "I think that I will have someone watch your room tonight to make sure nothing happens to you. In the meantime, I'll have a talk with Mr. McCary and see what I can find out."

Nathan stood to leave but bent down and took Priz's hand. "Thanks for telling me this, Miss Dillman. I'll see about getting to the bottom of it."

But as he turned to go, Priz raised her hand and caught his sleeve. "Wait, Marshal, there's more I want to tell you."

Nathan sat back down on the chair. "Yes, ma'am?"

"Marshal, there's something else going on at that carnival. The boss of the carnival has this big tent that he lives in when we are camped in a new town. No one is allowed in that tent except just a few of his cronies. He lives there with a mulatto man, his servant. The servant is a creamed-coffee colored man with curly hair. But it's plain that the man is half African. Anyway, whenever the boss needs an errand run, he sends the manservant. I tried to look in the tent once, but I couldn't see anything. But you need to look in there, 'cause there's something going on in there that isn't right."

Priz paused to catch her breath. Then she went on. "Why else would a wagon pull up to that tent in every town we're in, and then a couple days later, wagons load up with something out of that tent and drive away again. It happens about once a week when we are camped. I tell you, the boss of the carnival is up to something."

Nathan didn't know what to think, but he remembered that he had seen wagon tracks leading up to the opening in that tent next to Junior Skinner's caravan. "Do you think that the wagons could be carrying supplies for the carnival?" asked Nathan.

"Supply wagons don't generally have two armed men on their wagons, do they?" Priz replied.

"No, I would think not," said Nathan.

Priz was fatigued from talking. "You look into it, Marshal," she said in a labored voice. And then she closed her eyes. The opium was taking effect and causing her return to sleep.

But Nathan was not quite finished. "Miss Dillman. Miss Dillman. I want to ask you one more question."

Priz cracked her eyes open.

"Miss Dillman, what is the name of the boss of the carnival," he asked.

Very weakly, almost in a whisper, Priz Dillman answered. "Zima. His name is Marcus Zima."

Chapter Twelve: Mrs. Jones and The Wrens

10 a.m.

Marshall's Office

Nathan tied Wander to the hitch rail at the side of the office. He would take the horse to the livery later to make sure he got fed and rested. As he began to walk toward the door of the office, a boy on a Whippet bicycle careened around the corner of the building and skidded the back wheel in the dirt. The boy retrieved articles from the basket tied to the handlebars of the bicycle and leaned the machine on a light pole. Nathan watched him as he then began tacking a poster to the wooden pole. Nathan walked over to the boy.

"What do you have there, son?" asked Nathan.

The boy looked up and saw the badge on Nathan's shirt. "Posters, Marshal. I'm putting up these posters," he said.

Nathan read the brightly colored poster. On it was written:

The Sterling Carnival is Coming to Coffeyville.
Tell Your Family, Tell Your Friends.
Join us in Coffeyville, Kansas, July 6-13, 1900.

The poster depicted some of the carnival rides and side show facades as background to the writing. It seemed odd to Nathan that the poster would advertise the Coffeyville carnival days, but then he guessed that the posters were probably put up in surrounding towns where the carnival was to visit. And since farmers and ranchers south of town might participate in the rodeo and crop judging at surrounding fairs, maybe it was a good idea to advertise upcoming fairs in neighboring towns. But a thought suddenly occurred to Nathan. He took one of the posters from the boy's bicycle basket.

"Where did you get these posters, young man?" asked Nathan.

"Oh, it's all legit, Marshal. I get paid a penny for each poster I put up," said the boy.

"Yes, seems like a good way to make a little money. But where did you get the posters?"

"Oh, I got them from a man at the carnival. My two friends and me, we was riding our bikes out at the fair grounds and a man stopped us and asked us if we wanted to make some money. We told him 'sure we did.' Then he gave us these posters, the tacks and a hammer and told us to come back when we were done. And, we get a penny for each one that we put up. Can I go now, Marshal?" asked the boy.

"Just a couple more questions, son. Where was the man who gave you the posters, and did he tell you his name?" asked Nathan.

"He came out of this big tent. He didn't tell us his name, but he looked like a negro, only his skin was lighter colored than most black men," said the boy. "He seemed nice, and I think he'll pay us all right."

Nathan reached in his pocket and handed the boy a penny. "I'm going to keep this poster, son. Is that OK?"

"Sure, Marshal, since you already paid me for it." The boy laughed, climbed on his bicycle, and quickly pedaled to the next lamp post down the street.

Nathan walked through the front door of the office and was not surprised to see Clyde and Sarah Jones sitting in the outer office, each with a tin mug of coffee resting on their respective knees. Bill Ward was sitting near them talking with them, catching up on news items and the weather. One of Tom Barnes's young deputies sat at the table reading a new batch of wanted posters, idly listening to the conversation going on next to him, but paying little attention to Bill and the Joneses. Also seated at the table were Charlie Rath and George Conley.

"Morning, Nathan," said Bill. "I knew you would be coming in, so I asked Clyde and Sarah to come to the office."

"Morning Bill. Morning Clyde, Sarah. Glad you could come talk with us," said Nathan. The deputy gave a nod to Nathan and Nathan returned it.

"Morning, Charlie, George. Where's Ralph?" asked Nathan. Ralph Gilman was not in the office.

"He got called back to Kansas City, Nathan," said Bill. "Left on an early train. Said to tell you he'd be in touch later. Somethin' important up there, I guess."

"Mmm," said Nathan, and he turned to the Joneses. "Clyde and Sarah, you'll need to excuse us, please. I need to talk with these fellas for just a minute," said Nathan. "Bill, George, Charlie, let's step outside for a minute."

While the four lawmen stood on the sidewalk outside the office, Nathan briefed them on what Priz Dillman had told him at the doctor's home and finished up by telling them the name that she had told him.

"Zima, Zima, Zima," said George Conley. "That name is unusual, and for some reason the name rings a bell with me. When I was just a young pup starting out with the service, we were investigating some counterfeiting in the Kansas City area, and that name stuck with me. If you don't mind, I'll send a wire to my office and see if they can help us with any background on this Zima character."

"That might be a great help, George," said Nathan. "Can you give Bill the gist of the message and the address to send the wire, and let him run over to the telegraph office and send the message while you and I talk with the Joneses?"

"Sure," said George. He and Bill conversed for a moment while Nathan and Charlie Rath returned to the office. George Conley soon followed.

Nathan sat back down at the table and turned to the sheriff's deputy, Leonard Holcum, a full-time sheriff's deputy who went by the nickname Len, and who was leafing through a stack of wanted posters. Tom Barnes had had two full time deputies and two part time men. The full-time men were for the day and night shift, and the part timers were used in special cases when more manpower was needed. But one of the part time deputies had been killed at the fairgrounds while guarding Junior Skinner's caravan on Monday night. "Len, I need you to get ahold of the other deputies and tell them to be here at the office in about an hour. They all need to be armed. Can you do that?"

"Sure, Marshal. Can you tell me what's up?" asked Holcum.

"Well, when everybody gets here, I'll brief all of you." The deputy stacked the papers he had been looking at and walked out the office door.

Turning to face the Joneses, Nathan said, "Now, Sarah and Clyde, pull your chairs up to the table here. We want you ask you a couple questions."

After they were seated at the table, Nathan introduced George Conley and Charlie Rath. "Mr. Conley is a member of the U.S. Secret Service, and Mr. Rath is an agent for Pinkertons," said Nathan. "Mr. Conley's job is to track down people who are making counterfeit currency, or fake money."

Clyde and Sarah sat paying attention to every word. "Well, what's that got to do with us, Marshal," asked Clyde.

"Maybe nothing, Clyde, but you see, yesterday, Sarah passed off a counterfeit ten-dollar bill at the general store," said Nathan.

Clyde Jones spilled his coffee on his lap and slowly put the coffee mug on the table. Then he began shouting. "Now you just wait a doggone minute, Marshal. We don't have any money, let alone any fake money. Whatever gave you that idea," he said.

Nathan did not answer right away. He simply turned to Sarah Jones. "Sarah, where did you get that ten-dollar bill you gave Mr. Donnelson?"

She didn't know what to say. On the one hand, she had found the ten dollars 'fair and square' in the almanac she had been reading. That bill had looked like the real thing to her. "That was my ten dollars," she said. "Mel Donnelson had no right to tell you that money was phony. I . . ." and she became quiet.

"Sarah, what have you done?" shouted Clyde. "We don't have any money. Where would you get ten dollars? And why didn't you give it to me?"

Sarah Jones raised her voice. "You're right Clyde. We don't have any money because you drink it all away down at that God-forsaken bar. The ten dollars was mine, mine alone. You've got no say in how I spent it."

Sam grabbed the upper arm of Sarah, tightening his grip. "Now you listen to me, woman. If you're hiding money on me, I want to know about it. You've got no right . . ."

Nathan cut him off. "Knock it off, Clyde. You're hurting Sarah. Now let her go before I put you in a cell in the back room."

Slowly, Clyde Jones let go of his wife. Sarah had begun crying. Tears ran down her cheeks, and she dabbed at them with her handkerchief.

"Are you sure that ten dollars was fake?" asked Sarah

George Conley spoke up. "It was fake, Mrs. Jones. Believe me, I have seen lots of counterfeit money, and that ten-dollar bill was phony. Where did you get it?"

Nathan and George Conley were certain that the Joneses had not made the forgery. Neither Clyde nor Sarah were sophisticated or skillful enough to have been able to print the bill.

Nathan repeated Conley's question, rewording it slightly. "Sarah, we know that you did not make that bill, and I don't think you stole it. But where did you get it?"

Sarah Jones answered. "It was in the book."

"What do you mean it was in the book, Sarah?" asked Conley.

Sarah looked at the government man. "It was in the front cover of a book I got from Mirriam Dixon."

"You got a book from Mirriam Dixon, and it had the ten-dollar bill in it?" asked Nathan.

"Well, it was not in the book," said Sarah. "You see, Clyde tore the cover of the book, and I tried to glue it back together, but then I saw the ten dollars under the front cover of the book. That's where I got it," she said.

"You mean the bill was under the cover of the book?" asked Conley.

"Yeah, it was between the paper cover and the paste board under that," said Sarah.

Nathan was thinking back to a few days ago. He couldn't quite put his finger on it, but then he remembered. "Sarah, you said you got the book from Mirriam Dixon, is that right?"

"Yes, she gave a copy to each of the Wrens to read. It's a *Farmer's Almanac*. We are going to sell lots of copies of the book to raise money for the library," said Sarah.

Conley then asked, "Do you mean that this Mrs. Dixon has more copies of the book."

Sarah Jones had stopped crying. She was now finding these questions fascinating, because she felt certain that she was not being blamed for having made the fake ten-dollar bill. Nothing like this had ever happened to her before. "Yes, Mirriam has a whole box of the books. We're just waiting for the next church bake sale to sell them."

Conley was still trying to piece the details together. "Mrs. Jones, where does Mrs. Dixon have the rest of these books? Are they at her home?"

"Oh, heavens no," said Sarah. "The rest of the books are in their box in the church basement waiting for the church bake sale. But all the Wrens have a copy."

Conley turned to Nathan. "Looks like these Dixon people are the source of the counterfeit money."

"Not so fast, George. I think there's another answer. I seem to recall where the Dixons may have gotten the books."

Nathan turned to Holcum, who had returned to the office. "Len, can you run over to the church and go to the basement and look for that box of books. I think you might be looking for a wooden crate. When you find them, bring them here to the office."

"Sure, Marshal. What church?" asked Holcum.

Clyde Jones spoke up. "Methodist Church."

Deputy Holcum laughed. "Methodist it is." He rose from the table and went out the office door.

Just as the deputy left, Bill Ward returned. "Message sent," he said, and went to get a cup of coffee from the stove. He was stopped by Nathan.

"Bill, I need to send you on another errand."

"OK, boss. What's up?" asked Bill.

"Could you grab Wander? He's tied outside. Ride on out to the Dixon place and have them come into town to talk with us?" asked Nathan. "Right away, please."

Bill hurried out the door, and in a few seconds, he could be seen loping Wander up the street. The Dixon place was only a couple miles, so it would not be long. Nathan looked at the clock that was quietly ticking on the wall. "I think that while Bill is gone, we should take a break for lunch. Sarah and Clyde, I'll buy you a sandwich at the cafe if you want to come along."

Of course, Clyde jumped up from his chair. "Sure, we'll go with you. Maybe get a piece of apple pie, too," he said.

Nathan just smiled. He knew that Clyde Jones wouldn't pass up anything that was free, especially food or drink. The group left the marshal's office and walked to the Main Street Cafe to order noon time dinner. When it came to Clyde ordering, he added a beer to his sandwich along with hash brown potatoes.

Nathan looked up at Clyde and said, "Sorry Clyde, you drink on your own dime. The Marshal Service can't pay for your beer." Clyde looked crestfallen, but then got a look from Sarah that made him pout further. He ate his sandwich and potatoes in silence.

While the group finished their lunch, the telegraph office delivery boy came into the cafe. He stood for a moment and then spotted Nathan and the group at a back table. He quickly made his way to the table. "Marshal, do you know a man named Conley? The telegraph manager said he thought you might know where to find him."

Conley raised his hand. "I'm Conley," he said. The boy handed the telegram to Conley and stood for a few seconds while George opened the envelope and read the message.

The boy then asked, "Any answer, mister?"

"Oh. No answer," said Conley and handed the boy a coin. The boy doffed his cap and hurried out of the cafe.

When the group walked back to the office, the three sheriff's deputies were standing on the wooden sidewalk. They parted to let the group pass. Nathan and Charlie Rath stayed outside to talk with the deputies.

Nathan said, "I know this is going to be a bit strange, but I want you deputies to take your orders from Charlie Rath, here," he said as he pointed to Charlie. "Mr. Rath is a Pinkerton Agent and knows all about the case we are working on. Does anybody have a problem with that?"

None of the deputies raised an objection, so Nathan continued. "I can't tell you any of the details right now because I just don't have time. But I need you men to go out to the carnival at the fairgrounds. As I understand it, they are getting ready to pack up everything out there and head to the next town, Coffeyville. We don't want that to happen. Our investigation of that carnival is not done yet. You men have to keep the carnival from leaving town."

"How do you expect we should do that, Marshal?" asked one of the men.

"Let me put it this way, gents. Anyone from that carnival who won't follow your orders is obstructing an official investigation and can be arrested," said Nathan. "And anyone who decides they want to get physical with you must be stopped, in any way you can. Is that clear enough?"

Charlie Rath and the deputies nodded their understanding.

Nathan added, "Take plenty of pairs of handcuffs and make sure your firearms are ready. I was told that the boss man of the carnival is a fella named Zima. You need to look for him and make sure he stays with the carnival so we can bring him in later. I'm hoping there won't be any trouble, but somebody in that carnival bunch has already killed some folks and tried to kill some others, so be alert out there. I will join you later after I wrap up a couple things here at the office." He paused, then asked, "Everybody ready?" He watched as the men nodded. "All right then, good luck."

Charlie and the deputies left to get their horses. As they walked away, George Conley came back outside to speak with Nathan. "It's what I remembered, Marshal. The answer from my office was that Zima was a part of the Victor Carelli mob of organized crime in St. Louis many years ago. He was believed to be an accountant for Carelli, but for some reason he disappeared roughly twenty years ago. They figure he must have crossed Carelli somehow, and Carelli had him disappear."

"So, twenty years later, he shows up here in Chanute with the carnival?" asked Nathan.

"Well, that's the other part of the message. I mentioned this carnival to the boys back at my office, and they think that Carelli owns some of these traveling shows," said Conley. "So, it appears that there's a link between Zima, Carelli, and the traveling show."

"Wow," said Nathan. "I never would have believed that organized crime would show its ugly face in Kansas, let alone down here in Chanute."

After a bit more conversation, Nathan and Conley went back inside the office. Nathan noticed that the wooden crate of books was now on the table in the outer office and George Conley had picked up two copies of the books from the crate.

Nathan went to the wood stove and poured himself a mug of coffee. "Sarah, would you or Clyde like a coffee?" The Joneses demurred and then declined. At that instant, Nathan looked up to see the Dixon buckboard drive into view. Bill was sitting on the edge of the cargo area while Sam and Mirriam Dixon rode on the driver's seat. Wander was tied to the tailgate of the wagon. Bill and the Dixons got down from the wagon, and Bill led Wander to the side of the building and tied him off. In a few moments they all entered the office.

Mirriam Dixon was surprised to see Sarah Jones and smiled pleasantly and said, "Why hello, Sarah. How've you been?"

Sarah, somewhat caustically answered, "I've been better. But I'm afraid you're going to be in a bit of trouble," her mouth displaying a smug expression.

Mirriam Dixon did not know what to make of such a remark, but rather than reply, decided that she would wait to see what this was all about. But then she noticed the crate of books on the table. "Why, those are our books." She looked up at Nathan and asked, "What are they doing here?"

Nathan looked over at George Conley, who was carefully cutting the front cover paper from one of the almanacs. He soon pulled a ten-dollar bill from the sliced paper. Because he was curious, he turned the book over and did the same cutting on the back cover. Sure enough, he found another ten-dollar bill which he held up to the light from the window. He nodded at Nathan.

"Lord 'amighty would you look at that," said Sam Dixon. He turned to Mirriam. "Did you see that, Mirriam. There's money hidden in them books."

Mirriam replied, "Yes, Sam, I seen it. But it don't make any sense. Why would someone put money in the cover of them books?"

Nathan turned to Sarah and Clyde Jones. "Sarah and Clyde, you folks can go on home. I don't think we will need you anymore."

Clyde Jones immediately stood and walked to the door. "You comin', Sarah?"

Strangely, a smile had returned to Sarah's face. "You go on ahead, Clyde. I'm going to stay here for a few more minutes."

A few more minutes was all it took for Mirriam and Sam Dixon to tell their story of how they had found the crate of books on the north road on their way to town a few days ago. They also mentioned that they had brought the box by the sheriff's office to ask him what to do with the books, and how they had been told that if no one claimed the box, then they could keep it and sell the books for the library fund.

A "hmmph" was heard from Sarah Jones, as if she did not want to believe the Dixons' story.

But she was quickly brought up short when Nathan mentioned that he remembered when they stopped by the office and had Tom Barnes look at the books. He told them that he had been standing at the office window when that took place some days ago.

"Sam and Mirriam, do you have any idea where the box came from?" asked Nathan.

"No, sure don't, Marshal. Like we said, it was laying in the road when we were coming into town. There was another set of tracks from a wagon on the road that morning. The hoof prints showed that it had been going north. Anyhow, I looked at the box, but as you can see, there's no writing on it. So, we have no idea where it came from. But Tom Barnes, rest his soul, told us we could keep it. Are we in some kind of trouble, Marshal?"

"No, you're not in any trouble, Sam," said Nathan.

"Well, what about all that money?" asked Sarah Jones.

Patiently, Nathan answered. "Sarah, I thought you would understand by now. That isn't money. All those bills in the books are fake, they are counterfeit."

"Mmm. Well, what's going to happen to me since I went and spent one of them fake dollar bills. Am I in trouble?" she asked.

"No, Sarah. You aren't in any trouble for trying to spend the ten dollars. You didn't know it was no good. But, I'm afraid you will have to work things out with Mel Donnelson at his store," said Nathan. "You will need to take everything that you bought, back to him, or arrange to pay him back in real money. Will you take care of that?"

Dejectedly, Sarah Jones answered, "I guess I don't have much choice, do I?" She then stood up. It was plain that her spirit was damaged. She was thinking ahead on how in the world she would ever pay Mel Donnelson what she and Clyde owed him. She walked slowly out the office door.

After Sarah had gone, Nathan turned to the Dixons. "Sam, you and Mirriam can go on back home. We won't be needing you anymore," said Nathan. "But thanks for coming in to talk with us."

"Does this mean that we can't sell the books at our church sale?" asked Mirriam.

Nathan and Conley both chuckled. "No, Mirriam. I'm afraid that you won't be able to sell these books. Mr. Conley, here, will probably want to take them with him when he leaves. They will become evidence in a counterfeiting charge if we ever find out who made this phony money."

"Well, darn it!" said Mirriam. Sam Dixon gave a small snort and looked down and smiled. He knew that Mirriam was seldom so expressive.

"One other thing, Mirriam. Can you please be sure to gather up the books from the other Wrens? Just bring them back here to the office when you get a chance."

"OK," said Mirriam. She, too, was disappointed that her plans for raising money for the library had been dashed. She took one more look at the box of books, then took Sam's arm and walked out to climb aboard their buckboard. Sam clucked to the horse and turned the wagon to head north out of town.

11:30 a.m.

Fair Grounds at the Edge of Town

The hair on the back of Charlie Rath's neck tingled. He and the deputies rode slowly but purposefully on to the fair grounds. Dust rose from each horse's hooves as they lifted from the dusty midway. Rath felt that there must have been a hundred sets of eyes on him and the deputies. They dismounted but held their reins. Every deputy had his free hand on the pistol in their respective belt holsters.

Charlie walked up to a knot of men who were dismantling a concession stand. "S'cuze me, gents."

The working men looked at Charlie with hostility. One of the roustabout workers spoke up. "Who are you, and what do you want?"

"I'm looking for the boss of your outfit. I believe the Marshal told me his name is Zima. Can you tell me where I might find him?" Charlie asked.

The man replied, "I don't think he's anywhere around here, mister. So I would advise you to just get on your animal there and head on back out of here."

Charlie replied, "Well, sir, just for your edification, my name is Rath, Charles Rath, and I'm an agent for the Pinkerton Agency. I'm here to investigate the fact that this here carnival is running a criminal operation that robs banks and makes phony money. You wouldn't know anything about that, would you?"

The man spat a glob of tobacco juice in the direction of Rath's boot, narrowly missing it.

"I don't know nothin' about nothin' Mr. Pinkerton. And if I did, I wouldn't think it was any of your business." The roustabout turned and feigned continuing with his work. But Charlie watched as the man slowly picked up a spanner wrench, on the end of which was an ugly hook.

Charlie replied, "Well, sir, since you appear to be the spokesman for this carnival, let me tell you that you need to stop your work. Under the orders of U.S. Marshal Nathan Wolf, this carnival is not going anywhere. You are to remain in Chanute until the marshal tells you that you can leave. Have you got that?"

The roustabout straightened up, the wrench in his hand. "Oh, I got it, Mr. Pinkerton. But that don't mean anything to me. Now I'm going to tell you once more, you need to get on your horse and get the hell out of here while you still can."

Noon
Judge Rodney Stephens' Home

He did not let her see him laugh. He kept his head down while he tied Wander to the hitch rack and walked up the steps onto Judge Stephens' porch. Millie was standing in the doorway with the front door fully open. How the hell does she do that, thought Nathan. Bill Ward and George Conley were with him, and they dismounted and followed Nathan.

"The Judge is about to have lunch. I made enough if you want to join him," said Millie.

With a stoic countenance, Nathan stepped up onto the porch and removed his hat. He noticed the twinkle in her eye and hint of a smile. Millie knew she was jousting with the marshal over the fact that she was always waiting with the door open when he came to the house. "I appreciate the offer, Millie, but I can't stay. I just need to get a warrant and head on out."

"Suit yourself," said Millie. "He's in his study."

For the next thirty minutes, Nathan and George Conley walked the Judge through the last two days and the incriminating statements made by Priz Dillman, the letter she had told him about, and the make up of the bank robbers. Nathan then explained to the judge about the connection between the carnival, the bank robberies, and the counterfeit currency, explaining how they had discovered that the counterfeit bills were being placed in book covers. Conley then told Judge Stephens that they were not sure how the carnival was able to print the currency and then find a way to get rid of the bogus money. He also said that they did not know whether the carnival was placing the money in the books or whether it was done somewhere else. He admitted to the judge that there were still a great many unknowns surrounding the counterfeiting, and that was the reason that they needed the search warrant. Nathan then reminded Stephens that if they wanted to be completely legal, the warrant should cover Priz Dillman's caravan and any other property of the carnival.

"Nathan, that's a pretty broad search warrant," said Stephens. "Are you sure you can't be a bit more specific?"

Conley spoke up. "We probably could, Judge, but the way we found those counterfeit printing plates leads me to believe that our search might lead us to any number of other facilities owned by the carnival. I tend to agree with the Marshal."

Judge Stephens was silent for a few seconds before he reached down and opened one of his desk drawers and drew out a blank warrant. He soon had the blanks filled out on the warrant and signed it. He handed it to Nathan.

Five minutes later, Nathan climbed onto his saddle and with Bill Ward and George Conley at his sides, the three men loped out of town, heading for the fair grounds. In minutes, they arrived at the fairgrounds, just in time to see Charlie Rath and the deputies slowly being surrounded by a group of carnival men, one of whom had a spanner wrench in his hand and was beginning to raise it in the air.

"Bill, put a shotgun blast at the feet of the man with the wrench," said Nathan.

The loud blast and the cloud of dust raised by the pellets hitting the dirt in front of the man with the wrench startled the man and the others in his group, causing them to stop moving forward. Nathan and Bill quickly dismounted. Bill ejected the spent shotgun shell and reloaded. Nathan had drawn his pistol and walked to the side of Charlie Rath.

"Put the wrench down, mister, and walk back from there," said Nathan. "The next shotgun blast will cut you in two."

The man scowled, dropped the wrench, but then shouted over his shoulder as he walked back to join his friends, "We don't need any lousy lawmen here. You need to get on out of here and leave us alone."

Nathan did not answer. He turned to Charlie and asked, "Have you found that Zima character?"

Quietly, Charlie responded, "Naw, and big mouth there says he doesn't know where he is. Claims Zima isn't anywhere around. Good chance he's lyin', of course."

"Cover me close," said Nathan. He holstered his pistol and walked toward the man.

"My name is Wolf," said Nathan. "U.S. Marshal Wolf. What's your name, mister?"

The roughneck simply scowled at Nathan.

"My friend," Nathan said, nodding toward Charlie, "says you seem to be the talker for the carnival at this point. So let's talk."

"Pound sand, lawman," said the roughneck.

"Well, I guess you do know how to talk," said Nathan. "You claim that you don't know where we can find Mr. Zima. Is that right?" The roustabout simply glared and was silent.

"So, let's pretend that you're telling the truth," said Nathan. "If Mr. Zima is gone, who is the next person on the totem pole that we can ask a few questions about your carnival?"

The roustabout said nothing and continued to scowl at Nathan.

"Look, mister. We can do this right here, or I can take you back to town to spend a few nights in our jail. What'll it be?"

The man did not answer.

Nathan's hand came from his back pocket, and the blackjack struck the man on his left temple, knocking the man sideways, but he remained standing.

"Real cute, lawman," said the man. "Why don't you take off that gun belt, and we'll see just how tough you really are."

"Mister, I don't have time to stand here and play patty-cake with you. Tell me who's in charge of this outfit if Zima isn't here. Talk fast, or we take you to town, and I can tell you, you won't like our accommodations."

The roustabout stood glaring for a moment. But then a thought occurred to him. He had been standing near to where Priz Dillman had fallen and was left by her husband to die. The roustabout was one of the men who had helped get Priz into the wagon to get to town for medical help. Priz may not have known it for certain, but she had several earnest friends within the carnival. Those friends respected the trials she had been through and gave her credit for seldom complaining, treating others with respect, and just for being a decent person. The roustabout thought Priz Dillman had received a raw deal at the hands of Dennis McCary. He had noticed that when Priz lay on the ground after her fall, and he and others had lifted her into a wagon to go for help, that McCary had not assisted, but stood and watched as the wagon took her away. As far as the roustabout was concerned, that was no way to treat someone who you claimed you cared about. He also knew that McCary was "on the inside" with Zima and strutted around the carnival like he owned the place. He also had a hunch that McCary was in on some kind of shady dealings. So the roustabout made up his mind.

"Step over here a minute, Marshal," said the roustabout.

Nathan and the man walked to where the other men in his work group could not hear them. "I figure that when Zima is not here, Dennis McCary is the man you need to talk to."

From his conversation with Priz Dillman at the doctor's house, Nathan knew who Dennis McCary was and what he had done, and therefore, he wanted to talk with McCary anyway. "Where do I find this McCary fella?" asked Nathan.

"Look over my shoulder. I'm not going to point to it, but do you see the wagon with the red door?" the man asked.

Nathan looked over the man's shoulder in back of him. "Yeah, I see it," answered Nathan.

"That's Priz's caravan. He's likely to be there. He seems to never want to do any work," said the roustabout.

"OK, I'll check it out," said Nathan. "Did my friend tell you that the carnival is not to leave town?"

"Yeah, he told us. But I don't see why we have to stay here. Marshal, no matter what you think, most of the people in our carnival are just average folks trying to make a living," said the roustabout. "They don't hurt nobody, and they haven't done anything wrong."

"I expect you're right," said Nathan. "And we don't need to make things difficult for you or the other employees who haven't done anything wrong. But, every apple barrel has a couple rotten ones, and we mean to get the rotten folks out of here."

The roustabout shrugged his shoulders and walked back to his friends. Nathan walked over to Bill and Charlie.

"Can you fellas sort of drift along behind me to keep me covered. I don't think we'll have any trouble, but you never know," said Nathan.

Nathan started walking, and the lawmen walked slowly along behind him. But, as he walked, Nathan suddenly saw the tall pole above the midway and made his way toward it. It had not yet been torn down for moving. As Nathan approached, he could see that the swings remained attached to their chains hanging straight down from the top of the pole. But the swing that Priz had fallen from was still hanging from only one chain. The upper portion of the second chain was still attached to the pole. When he reached the center pole of the "Swing of Terror," Nathan began walking slowly in an ever-widening circle around the base of the pole. Periodically he kicked his boot at a clump of dirt but kept walking. Charlie, Bill, and the deputies watched him, but also kept a wary eye on the carnival employees who had followed and were watching the lawmen from a distance. In a moment, Bill came to Nathan's side.

"What are you looking for, boss?"

"I don't know, Bill. But I figure there had to be a reason for that Dillman woman to fall from this . . ." Nathan did not finish what he was saying. He had bent over and was retrieving an article from a clump of grass some distance from the center pole. "What do you make of this, Bill?" he asked as he handed the article to Bill.

"Well, I'll be," said Bill. "This link has been sawed through."

Bill was holding a chain link from the same type of chains that held up the swings on the ride. But the link was stretched open, and the edges of the open link plainly showed that someone had used a hacksaw to saw through the link on its end. The link would have secured the swing for a time until the centrifugal force strain from the turning swings stretched the opening farther, allowing the chain to separate at that point, and spilling the rider from the swing.

"I reckon we know that someone wanted that poor woman to fall, don't we?" said Bill.

"Sure looks that way," Nathan answered. He put the broken chain link in his pocket. As he looked up, he noticed a man wearing a faded denim shirt had separated himself from the crowd that had been following them. The man moved slowly away and disappeared between some of the vendor stalls.

The roustabout who had spoken with Nathan earlier, walked up to the lawmen and spoke to Nathan. "What'd you find over there, Marshal?"

Nathan showed the man the broken chain link and said, "It appears to us that someone sawed through the chain link to cause Miss Dillman to fall."

After studying it, the roustabout gave the split chain link back to Nathan. "McCary may have done this, Marshal. I expect you'll find out for sure. But I'm thinkin' that he had to have help." The man turned and walked back to the group of employees who had gathered nearby.

One p.m.
Priz Dillman's Caravan

With Nathan leading the way, Charlie, Bill, George Conley, and the deputies walked through the knee-high grass to where Priz Dillman's caravan was parked. Several of the carnival employees tagged along and stood watching the lawmen as they worked. Just as the roustabout had predicted, they found Dennis McCary. He was sitting on the steps of the caravan smoking a hand-rolled cigarette. He dropped the cigarette butt in the dirt at the base of the steps and stepped on it with the toe of his shoe.

"Are you Dennis McCary?" asked Nathan.

"Yeah, so what," McCary replied.

"McCary, I'm U.S. Marshal Nathan Wolf. I am arresting you for bank robbery and attempted murder."

McCary laughed. "You ain't arresting me for anything, lawman. I ain't done anything to get arrested."

Nathan tossed a set of handcuffs to Charlie Rath. "Be my guest, Charlie. He's your bank robber. Hook him to that wagon wheel there," said Nathan.

"Now just a damn minute, lawman. You've got nothing on me. I ain't done anything wrong," said McCary.

"Shut up, McCary," said Charlie, who then slapped McCary and pulled him to his feet. He spun McCary around and put a handcuff on one of his wrists. Rath then ratcheted the other cuff onto one of the spokes on the rear wheel of Dillman's caravan. "Sit down, bank robber," said Charlie, and he shoved McCary to the ground.

McCary was mad, glaring at the lawmen.

"C'mon, Bill," said Nathan as he climbed the three steps to the door of the caravan. Bill followed him into the wagon. The caravan looked a bit different from that of Junior Skinner. There were colorful pictures of flowers on the wall and a brightly colored throw rug on the floor. It was apparent that a woman lived here.

The two men began pulling storage drawers open, searching each one, until they found the drawer which contained ladies' undergarments. Dumping the contents of the drawer on the bed, Nathan turned the drawer over. Sure enough, there was an envelope attached to the bottom of the drawer. Nathan removed the letter and opened it. He smiled, and handed the letter to Bill, who read it and then wagged his head from side to side. "Curious that she wrote this," he said. Bill reread the letter Priz Dillman had written:

To whoever finds this:

I have known for quite a while that my common law husband, Dennis McCary, who I dearly love, has been leading a band of men from the Sterling Carnival to rob banks. He has had the blessing of our carnival manager, Marcus Zima, to carry out them robberies. My husband told me that the stolen bank money is divided between the gang members and Zima. I don't know what Dennis has done with his share of the money. I have begged Dennis to stop and he says he will, but he don't. I told him I was going to turn him into the law to save him from hanging. But that didn't stop him none. Deep down I think Dennis might be a good man, but Mr. Zima has done corrupted him. I hope if the law finds this letter that they will go easy on Dennis since he ain't killed anybody, and I still love him. Maybe he could cooperate with the law and not spend any time in prison. I surely hope so.

The letter went on, and in addition to McCary, Priz Dillman named the rest of the members of McCary's bank robbing gang. And since none of the men knew about the letter, they could be easily rounded up later by Nathan and Charlie.

"Sad that the lady still loved McCary, and McCary tried to kill her. Gotta feel sorry for her," said Nathan. "I guess she figured McCary was going to get caught sooner or later, and she wanted the law to go easy on him if she wasn't around to help him."

Bill was scratching his near-week's growth of beard and then said, "So this McCary fella robs banks. Makes me wonder what he did with the money," said Bill.

"These caravans are home to the carnival people," said Nathan. "I figure if he has any money from those bank robberies, its bound to be here somewhere."

Methodically, the two lawmen searched every nook and cranny of the caravan but turned up nothing. The same type of air vent as had been in the Skillman caravan was also searched and revealed nothing. They replaced all of the drawers and their contents.

Nathan and Bill gave up and walked down the steps of the caravan. Nathan walked over to Charlie Rath. He was standing a few feet from McCary, who was sitting on the ground next to the wagon wheel to which his wrist was shackled.

"We didn't find any money in the wagon, Charlie. But I figure it has to be here somewhere. Why don't you have a go at McCary," said Nathan.

Charlie Rath needed no encouragement. He handed his shotgun to Bill and walked over to McCary and kicked the bank robber in the belly. McCary screamed in agony.

"McCary, my name is Rath and I work for Pinkertons. I'm here because you've been robbing banks, and those little banks don't like having their customers' money stolen. So, they asked Pinkertons if we could help find the men who were robbing their banks. And by gum, we found you."

Charlie slowly moved to the side of McCary and kicked him again. McCary screamed in pain. But as he subsided, he raised his head and began yelling.

"Hey Rube! Hey Rube! Hey Rube!" shouted McCary.

None of the lawmen seemed to know why McCary was shouting those words, but as they looked around, they could see more carnival employees running to join the small group that had been watching the lawmen. But then, George Conley spoke up.

"It's some kind of rallying cry," said Conley. "See how the carnival folks came running like they are going to help McCary."

The lawmen now faced the building crowd. There were at least thirty carnival employees now facing the lawmen. Some of the men in the crowd carried clubs. They talked among themselves and appeared to begin walking toward the lawmen."

"If they get within twenty paces of us, start shooting," said Nathan. But then Nathan continued, shouting at the crowd. "You folks need to stop right there," he said. Surprisingly, the crowd paused momentarily. Nathan went on, "This man McCary has been arrested for bank robbery and attempted murder. He tried to kill Priz Dillman. It doesn't concern you. You need to just go on back to your work. We don't intend to harm any of you, but we will shoot to defend ourselves."

A few of the men began shouting insults to the lawmen, tempting the others in the group to move forward.

"Shoot in front of them, Bill," said Nathan, and Bill Ward aimed and fired his shotgun at the ground in front of the crowd. The group stopped again.

"Look around you. You've got a half dozen shotguns aimed at you," said Nathan. "It would be suicide to come any closer. Like I said, we don't mean any harm to you folks. We only want the criminals that are hiding in your outfit. If you will let us do our job, we will leave you so you can get on the road to your next stop."

The lawmen watched as the roustabout who had previously spoken with Nathan came to the front of the crowd. He turned and began talking with the people. Several replied to him and questioned him. The lawmen could not hear all of his words, but they gathered that he was explaining the attempted murder of Priz Dillman. The roustabout turned and walked to Nathan.

“Marshal, they want to see the chain link I told them about. Can I have it to show them?” he asked.

Nathan reached in his pocket, handed the split link to the roustabout, and watched him return to the group of carnival employees. They passed the link among the group and returned it to the roustabout. He turned and walked back to Nathan.

“I don’t think they’ll bother you anymore, Marshal, but a few of them who were friends of Priz will probably hang around and watch you men for a while. A couple of them volunteered to beat the hell out of McCary for you,” he said as he chuckled. He handed the split chain link back to Nathan.

“Thanks, mister,” said Nathan. “We appreciate your help, but I figure that McCary will spend most of the rest of his life in prison. I suppose I ought to go talk to that ride operator, too”

The roustabout slowly nodded his head in agreement and then walked back to the group of carnival employees. Several men in the crowd had already disbanded to return to their work. McCary could not believe what was happening. He watched as several of the men moved away from the crowd. Then he began shouting, “What’s the matter with you people? I’m in trouble here. Come and get me out of this,” he shouted, but the men in the crowd were paying no attention to him.

“You bastards. You lily livered cowards, come and help me here,” shouted McCary. Nobody came to his aid.

“Guess your friends don’t like you very much,” said Bill Ward. “It appears they like Miss Dillman a whole lot better than you, jackass.”

When he knew that the crowd was not coming to help McCary, Nathan moved and stood at the bottom of the doorway to the caravan. He had one boot resting up on the step and he leaned on his upraised knee. Deputy Len Holcum was standing next to him. But then, Holcum began bending at the waist while he looked at the door of the caravan. After he had done it several times, Nathan asked him, "What's got into you, Len? You feeling all right?"

The deputy laughed. "Yep, I feel fine. But look at this, Marshal." He was pointing to the doorway of the caravan. "Look at how the inside floor of the wagon is here," he said as he rested his hand on the floor at the threshold of the door.

"Yeah, OK," said Nathan.

Holcum leaned over at the waist again. "And it you look down here, the floor that you see underneath the wagon is several inches lower than the threshold." He had his second hand resting against the bottom of the wagon.

Nathan leaned over and looked at where the deputy was pointing. "Oh, yeah, it is," he said and smiled. "Gotta be a double floor." But before he finished talking, Holcum had scrambled beneath the caravan and was lying on his back looking at the wagon's lower floor.

In a moment, he shouted, "Here it is Marshal."

Nathan dropped to his hands and knees and slid under the wagon to see what the deputy was pointing at. "Uh, huh," was all he said. He watched as the deputy used his knife blade to loosen four large-headed screws. When they were out, a square panel dropped from the lower floor down onto the belly of the deputy. He set it beside him in the grass. He then reached his hand into the opening and removed several packages wrapped in brown paper. Nathan opened the first one to find a stack of currency. He backed out from beneath the trailer and handed the stack to George Conley. Conley examined several of the bills and said, "These are the real thing, Marshal. I think you found some of the bank money." He handed the first stack to Charlie Rath. When Deputy Holcum had cleaned out the false compartment, the packets were all given to Charlie. He would count all of the bills when they went back to the office and then wire Pinkerton headquarters regarding the finding.

"What now, boss," said Bill.

"Let's leave McCary here for now," said Nathan. "He ain't going anywhere. I want to get over to that big tent to see what we can find."

The lawmen began to move away from the caravan when McCary shouted, "You can't just leave me here. At least take me with you. I'm liable to get myself beat up handcuffed like this."

"Well knucklehead," said Charlie, "they might pound some sense into that space between your ears." The lawmen walked away.

Chapter Thirteen: The Tent

Three p.m.

Back Lot, Carnival Midway

The large tent loomed ahead as the lawmen made their way toward it. When they reached it, they knocked on the wooden entry door. There was no answer. Nathan shouted out.

"Zima, this is U.S. Marshal Nathan Wolf. Open the door. I want to talk with you."

Still, there was no answer. Nathan turned to one of the deputies. "Go get your horse and make sure you have a rope and come on back, pronto."

The deputy took off at a trot and was only a minute before he came riding up on his horse. Nathan asked him, "Tie your rope off on your saddle horn and give me the end."

The men watched as Nathan fed the lariat through the two ropes that supported the wooden door frame and tied the rope back on itself.

"OK, deputy, take a strain on it," said Nathan, and he watched as the rope became taut. "All right, give it a good pull."

The deputy pulled the rope taut again and then spurred his horse. The support ropes creaked against the door frame but did not give. The deputy again spurred the horse and this time yelled at the same instant. With a loud bang, the wooden frame and the attached door came tumbling out of the opening in the tent. The doorway slid a few feet until the deputy calmed his horse.

Almost immediately, a shot was fired from within the tent. It was followed by two more as the lawmen took cover to the sides of the opening. With Charlie Rath on one side of the now-open door and

Nathan on the other, they nodded to each other and rushed into the opening. They saw what first appeared to be a black man standing in the shadows and holding a large revolver in his hand. The lawmen fired nearly simultaneously, and the manservant crumpled to the ground. Nathan and Charlie rushed to the fallen man and retrieved the gun from his hand.

Priz Dillman had told Nathan that Zima had a half-caste servant, so he knew by seeing the man lying in the dirt that he had to be the servant. "Where's your boss?" asked Nathan. "Where's Zima?"

The servant was bleeding, but the extent of his injuries was not serious. Charlie found some clean rags and soon had torn some bandages to stop the bleeding. The rest of the lawmen had spread out and were searching for Zima. After a few minutes, it was evident that he was not in the tent.

Nathan was standing and letting his eyes rove around the tent. Suddenly he shouted to Conley, "Hey George." Conley looked his way.

Nathan pointed to the corner of the tent. "See that tarp over there, George?"

Conley nodded answered affirmatively.

"I'll bet you a stack of bogus money that you will find the printing press you've been looking for under the tarp," said Nathan.

Conley went to the corner of the tent and pulled the tarpaulin from the large object. He immediately gave a whoop. "Wahoo, here's the press. And would you look at this, the plates for ten-dollar bills are still set up to print. How'd you know it would be here?" asked Conley.

"A kid on a bicycle told me," said Nathan and laughed.

Conley looked at him like he was crazy. But then he shouted to the other deputies, "Does anybody see a wooden crate of books?"

"Yes, sir. There's several wooden boxes over here, and they all have books in them," said one of the deputies.

Conley walked to the open boxes and picked up one of the books. He quickly tore the cover off of the book, and sure enough found a bogus ten-dollar bill.

In all of the excitement and noise, the lawmen had not heard the approach of a wagon and team, but they heard someone shouting. “Zima. Hey Zima, are you in there?”

Both Nathan and Charlie drew their pistols and walked toward the door opening. Bill Ward joined them with his shotgun at the ready. They stayed in the shadows until they could clearly see out of the door opening, where they observed two armed men standing in the driver’s foot well of the wagon that they had backed near the door. The wagon contained a shipment of wooden crates, just like the ones in which the lawmen had previously found books.

“You two men drop your weapons and turn around,” shouted Nathan.

“Oh yeah,” said one of the men. “Who the hell do you think you are?”

“I’m U.S. Marshal Nathan Wolf, and I’m also the man that will fill you with lead if you don’t do what I say,” said Nathan. “Now drop those rifles and your gun belts and come over here.”

For a second the two men almost appeared to want to try their hand at facing the lawmen, but then decided that it might be better to stay alive. They put their rifles in the driver’s box and dropped their gun belts to the side of the wagon. They stepped down from the wagon and approached Nathan, Charlie, and Bill. “Keep your hands in the air, you two,” said Nathan.”

“Charlie, check them out.”

Rath frisked the two men and found no other weapons.

“Now, suppose you boys tell us what you are doing here,” said Nathan.

The two men did not seem upset or hostile. It seemed that they were as surprised to see the lawmen as the lawmen were to see them. One of the drivers spoke for them. "We're here to make a delivery and a pick up, that's all. What the hell is this all about?' he asked.

George Conley had joined the lawmen, and he moved close to the wagon. He removed the tarp to find that the wagon was full of wooden crates. He shouted to Nathan, "More wooden crates, Marshal."

"Open one of them, George," said Nathan.

Retrieving a large screwdriver from the tent, George returned and pried two boards from one of the crates. "It's full of books," said Conley. He lifted two of the books from the crate and brought them over to Nathan.

"Look at this," said Conley. "If you open the books, they are the same inside as the other books we've seen. Some kind of *Farmer's Almanac*. But these books don't have covers on them. What's that mean?"

Nathan laughed. "That's what the printing press is for, George. Zima is printing the paper covers and the counterfeit bills right here. Then, when he is finished, my guess is that these drivers load the finished crates on their wagon and take them someplace. Let's ask them."

Conley and Nathan turned to the drivers again. "Were you boys supposed to pick up a shipment here?"

"Sure," said the driver. "We make this run about every two weeks. We bring a load of crates to the carnival and take a load back with us."

"Do you know what is in those crates?" asked Nathan.

"Naw, we don't care what's in them. We're just a couple of teamsters, and we get paid for delivering freight. We don't care what the freight is," said the driver.

"When you pick up your load at the carnival, where do you take it?" asked Conley.

"Same place all the time, Marshal. There's a warehouse in Kansas City that has a fella that contacts us when he wants us to make a run," said the driver. "He tells us that we have to have two armed drivers, and when we bring the load back from the carnival, we get our pay. My friend and me have made this run to the carnival dozens of times. Seems like we just follow the carnival around from place to place."

"And you never knew what you were carrying?" asked Conley.

"Nope," said the driver. "That is until you opened one of those boxes. Who in the world wants books without covers, anyway?"

"Was it always Mr. Zima that you came to see at the carnival?" Conley asked.

"Yep, him and that light-skinned negro fella that works for him. They're the men we delivered to and picked up from. No problem finding him. We always just looked for this here big tent. Say, you sort of messed up that door, didn't you?" said the driver as he looked at the door frame laying on the ground. "Zima probably won't like that very much. Which reminds me, where is Mr. Zima and the other fella?"

Nathan spoke up, "Mr. Zima doesn't seem to be here right now. The servant fellow is in the tent with a couple bullet holes in him. He'll be all right, though. I want you two fellows to stay right where you're at. My deputy will keep an eye on you, so don't make him shoot that shotgun of his. It's too loud and makes a big mess."

The drivers looked at Bill and then at each other. They wouldn't be moving.

"Go ahead and put your hands down and sit right there on the ground, you two," said Bill. He watched as the two teamsters sat down.

Nathan and George Conley walked to the side to converse. "How do you want to handle this, George? I don't think these two drivers know a thing about what is going on. But this counterfeiting problem is your bean pot to stir."

"This is a great opportunity for the Secret Service. I want to hang on to these two drivers," said Conley. "I'll put them up in the hotel for a night or two. That will give me time to get on the telegraph and set up a squad of Secret Service agents to meet this wagon when it goes back to Kansas City. I'll ride along with the drivers to meet the other agents. When the drivers make the delivery, the other agents and I will storm the warehouse where they are delivering the books with the phony money."

"OK, sounds like a good plan to me," said Nathan.

"Oh, Nathan," said Conley. "What did you mean when you said that a boy on a bicycle told you about the printing press?"

Nathan chuckled. "A kid on a bike was putting up handbills advertising the carnival's next stop in Coffeyville, and I asked him where he got the posters. He said he got them from a negro fella in a big tent. So, it stood to reason that the carnival had their own printing press to do up their fliers. The only place big enough to have a press was this tent."

George Conley laughed. "A boy on a bike solves our case. Now I've heard it all," he said, shaking his head.

In less than an hour, the deputies and the wagon drivers had offloaded the crates from the wagon and reloaded it with the crates of books that contained the book covers with the counterfeit bills. The tarp was retied to the wagon, and the drivers were allowed to drive the wagon into town to the livery stable. An armed deputy rode atop the wagon load and George Conley rode alongside the wagon.

Nathan and the rest of the lawmen escorted the half-caste servant and went to get McCary, still cuffed to the Dillman caravan wheel.

"Did you think we forgot about you, McCary?" asked Nathan facetiously.

McCary just glowered at the lawmen.

Nathan unlatched the handcuff that was attached to the wheel, pulled McCary to his feet and cuffed his free wrist.

"Where did Zima go, McCary?" asked Nathan.

McCary did not answer and looked away from the Marshal.

Nathan open handedly slapped McCary on the side of his head. "Apparently you don't hear so good. I asked you where Zima went."

McCary could see now that things were only going to get worse for him. For years, he had worked for Zima and enjoyed the protection of the carnival manager. But with Zima out of the picture, and Priz Dillman likely dead, he had no place to hide. He figured that it was now pointless to try to protect the man that had run out on him. He finally answered Nathan. "I don't know where Zima is."

"All right, you don't know where he is right now. I'll buy that. But you seem to know Zima pretty well. Where do you think he might be headed?" asked Nathan.

"I tell you I don't know. We never talked that much. He once told me, though, that he has no family except his mother. She lives somewhere in St. Louis. That's all I know," said McCary.

"All right, let's go," said Nathan. "I've got a nice cell waiting for you."

The lawmen, with McCary and the manservant in tow, were headed to where they had tied off their horses. But as they walked, they passed by the *Swing of Terror,* and Nathan stopped. He needed to talk with the ride operator. But surprisingly, the tower had been taken down, and the chains and swings detached. The group of lawmen spread out to look for the ride operator and had almost given up their search when one of the deputies shouted out, "Marshal, look there." He was pointing to a man lying nearly out of sight at the base of a clump of nearby bushes. Nathan had also seen the man's body and was walking toward the deputy. He examined the man and confirmed that he was dead. The body was covered with cuts and bruises, but the blow that had probably killed him was the one that broke the man's skull.

Nathan stood and saw a few carnival employees sitting in the shade beneath a cottonwood tree watching him. He walked to them and recognized the roustabout he had spoken with earlier.

"Do any of you know that dead man over there?" asked Nathan.

The roustabout stood and said, "Yeah we know him. He was the operator of that swing ride."

Nathan then asked, "Do any of you know what happened to him?"

"It looks like to us that he had an accident of some sort. My guess is that the center pole of the ride fell on him," said the roustabout.

"Accident, huh," said Nathan. "Looks more like to me that he got hit by several accidents."

Nathan watched the reactions of the group of men. Only a slight smile crossed a couple of their faces. Nathan was quite sure that the death of the man was no accident. Someone, or several men in this group had beat the ride operator to death in retaliation for his complicity in trying to kill Priz Dillman.

Nathan paused and then asked, "How long has he been the operator of that ride?"

"Can't say for sure, Marshal, but it's been a long time," said the man.

"Was he, by chance, operating the ride on the night when Priz Dillman had her fall?" asked Nathan.

"Well, you see, Marshal. Ride operators don't usually let anyone else fool around with their machinery unless the operator has an apprentice," said the roustabout. "And since that dead fella doesn't have an apprentice, then yeah, he was probably operating the ride when she was hurt. In fact, I'm pretty sure he was running the ride."

"Was the ride operator a friend of Dennis McCary?" asked Nathan.

"I think you could say that," said the roustabout. "But then you might also say that they were thick as thieves, if you know what I mean."

"Hmmm. I see," said Nathan. He turned to walk away but paused and turned back to the group of men. "You might want to get that dead fella out of the hot sun. It might not smell so good around here in a little while."

"We'll take care of that little detail," said the roustabout.

"Indeed, I'll bet you will," said Nathan.

The group of men then all seemed to smile. "Yep, we take care of our own, Marshal," said one of the men.

Nathan was now certain that the men had killed the ride operator. But he also knew that they would provide alibis for each other, and no one could ever be convincingly arrested for the murder. He had made up his mind to ignore the crude internal justice system of the traveling carnival, at least in this instance. Nathan thought that Priz Dillman could take satisfaction in knowing that of the two men who had been responsible for her attempted murder, one was dead and the other would stand trial.

"Mister, the carnival is now free to leave town. However, there is a printing press in that big tent," said Nathan. "Leave it behind when you go. The federal man needs it for evidence." Nathan turned to catch up with the other lawmen waiting by their horses. The mulatto man was riding the horse of the deputy who had ridden to town on the wagon. The group soon left the fair grounds and headed to town.

6 p.m.
Marshal's Office

The small three-cell jail was full. Junior Skinner, Dennis McCary, and the manservant would each occupy a cell. But the servant was waiting in the outer office with Bill and Nathan for Doctor Johnson to come and dress the man's wounds. In the meantime, Nathan thanked the sheriff's deputies for their assistance at the fairgrounds. George Conley and Charlie Rath had gone to the Main Street Cafe for supper.

Nathan spoke with the night shift deputy. "I'd like you to head down to the cafe and get something to eat and then go over to Doc Johnson's house to keep an eye on Miss Dillman tonight. I don't know who is out there that might still want to see her dead. When you get over to the Doc's, get a quick nap, but stay alert after dark. I'll be staying here tonight if you need me."

"Will do, Marshal," said the deputy, and he took his shotgun with him as he left the office.

Doctor Johnson had examined the manservant and cleaned and dressed his wounds. "He'll be all right," said the doctor to Nathan. "He's got a couple big holes in him, but I've dressed them, and they will heal just fine. I'll come by tomorrow and check on him again." The doctor repacked his kit and strode to the door. Nathan went with him and when they were just outside the door, Nathan asked about Priz Dillman.

Doctor Johnson replied, "She's mighty weak, Marshal. I ain't real sure she can make it through the night."

"That's too bad, Doc. She seems like a nice person."

The men shook hands, and the doctor turned to leave. "Thanks, Doc," said Nathan as the doctor waved and walked down the wooden sidewalk. Nathan returned to the office, and he and Bill sat down at the table with the manservant.

"What's your name, mister?" asked Nathan.

"Jube. Jube Tedley," said the man.

"Well, Mr. Tedley, you're in a bit of trouble here," said Nathan.

"Yes, sir. I know it," said Tedley.

"All right," said Nathan. "So why don't we start out by you telling me what in the world you were doing in Mr. Zima's tent."

"I work for Mr. Zima," said Tedley. "Been working for him nigh on twenty years, I reckon."

When Tedley spoke, his voice was low, a baritone level, and he spoke ever so slowly through a set of white, perfectly-spaced teeth. Nathan could see that this was going to take time to get the story of this half-caste man.

"Just what is it that you do for Mr. Zima, Tedley?" asked Nathan.

Tedley winced in pain from his gunshot wounds as he shifted position on his chair, his eyebrows knitted in concentration and discomfort. He sighed, settled himself, and then said, "I reckon I do most anything that Mr. Zima needs me for. I keep his place clean, do some repairs and run errands for him, and drive his wagon when the carnival moves. Like I said, I just do whatever Mr. Zima wants me to do."

Charlie Rath and George Conley were back from the cafe and joined Nathan and Bill.

As he resumed questioning Tedley, Nathan watched him carefully. He did not see the usual cockiness of a hardened criminal in the speech and mannerisms of the manservant. Nathan asked, "Tedley, how did you get mixed up with Mr. Zima in the first place?"

Tedley calmly began telling his story. "Mr. Zima and me go back a long ways," he said. "Probably half my lifetime. When I was younger, I was livin' in St. Louis. Livin' on the streets. I didn't have no home. My momma and daddy split up when I was just a kid, and I lived on the street with a bunch of other kids without no homes. We would get on by running errands, cleaning folks' fancy surreys and buggies and such, just to get a bit of money to live on."

Before Nathan could ask him again how he met up with Zima, Tedley continued. "One day, I was down by the taverns in the low district. Me and my friends was sitting on the side of the street, and along comes this beer wagon loaded with barrels of beer." Again, Tedley tried to shift his body to get more comfortable.

"We was watching these two big men loading them barrels onto carts to take into the taverns," said Tedley. "Them were some of the strongest men I ever saw."

Nathan quietly tapped his fingers on the table impatiently and watched Tedley as he resumed his story.

"One of my friends had a couple firecrackers in his pocket, and he decided that it would be funny to see if we could make those beer wagon horses spook and run. So, he lights one of them firecrackers and tosses it in front of the horses. Well, those horses spooked all right. Only when they jumped, they pushed that wagon backwards instead of front ways, and rolled that wagon right over my leg and busted it." Tedley stopped talking.

Impatiently, Nathan asked, "Yes, but what about Zima?"

Tedley went on. "Marshal, you sure are an antsy sort of fella. I'll get to it. Well, when I was laying there screaming my fool head off, those beer men picked me up off the street and carried me into one of the taverns. They took me upstairs and put me in a bed, and a doctor came to look at me. While he was lookin' at me, this beautiful white woman was there with him." Tedley paused again and seemed to be lost in his memories.

"My God, Tedley, what about Zima?" asked Nathan.

"Well," said Tedley. "It turned out that that pretty woman was Mrs. Zima. She worked at that tavern. Well, she let me stay there until my leg healed, and when I could walk again, she took me by the hand and took me to a warehouse close by the tavern. Mr. Zima was her son, and he worked there. Miz Zima, she told him to put me to work. And I've been with Mr. Zima ever since that beer wagon busted my leg."

"Tedley, you know that Mr. Zima is a criminal, don't you," said Nathan.

"Well, I guess I never would call him a criminal," said Tedley. "He's always been fair with me."

"Being fair with you is one thing, Tedley. But you know he was doing things that were against the law, didn't you?"

"I 'spose that some of Mr. Zima's doin's was not according to the law, but seems to me that nobody was getting hurt. Least, I never heard tell of anybody getting hurt," said Tedley. "But then, Mr. Zima never talked to me very much about what he was doing. He just told me what to do."

Nathan was quietly thinking as Tedley told his tale. He thought it was possible that Tedley did not know all of Zima's activities, or he was very naive, or was simply not altogether very smart. Yet, he had lived on the streets when he was younger. He couldn't be that naive, could he? Another possibility was that Tedley was just flat out lying. Nathan decided to take a different approach.

"Tedley, you ran the printing press for Mr. Zima, didn't you?"

"Sure," said Tedley. "I printed up all of the posters for the carnival."

"But that wasn't all that you printed, was it?" asked Nathan.

Tedley hesitated. Up to this point, he had been cooperative with the marshal, but he was having second thoughts. "Marshal, I don't want to get Mr. Zima in any trouble. He's been good to me."

"I understand," said Nathan. "He's been good to you, but you knew that you were printing fake money on that printing press, didn't you?"

"Oh, sure. Mr. Zima had me print that fake money," said Tedley.

"Well, for crying out loud, Tedley. What did you think Mr. Zima was doing with that money?" asked Nathan.

"Mr. Zima had me put the money in the covers of those books," said Tedley.

"He called them *surprise books*, 'cause we sent them to Kansas City to be handed out at as prizes at gambling houses. At least that's what Mr. Zima told me."

Nathan shook his head from side to side, still wondering whether Tedley was so naive that he could not understand the implications of making phony money. "Tedley, do you know what it means when I say that Zima was lying and that he was in the money laundering business?"

Tedley claimed that he truly did not know what money laundering was, but he alleged that he had even more difficulty believing that his boss had lied to him. "Do you mean that Zima was lying about them books?" he asked.

"Exactly," said Nathan. "Oh, the books were surprises, all right, but the fake money was used for criminal purposes."

"Mmm," answered Tedley.

George Conley spoke up. "Tedley, do you understand that making counterfeit money is a crime?"

"Nope. I don't know too much about the law," said Tedley. "Exceptin' what I read in my Bible. Mostly about the ten commandments. Them's God's laws I try to follow."

Nathan decided to ask the manservant one more question. "Tedley, where do you suppose Zima has gone? Where might we find him?"

Tedley didn't answer for a full minute, staring at the table. He was quite sure he knew where Zima had gone, but should he tell these lawmen, he asked himself. Finally, he made up his mind. But he would not be immediately forthcoming. "I'm just not rightly sure I know where he might be," said Tedley, but as he made that statement, one of the man's eyebrows lifted ever so slightly.

Nathan was about to give up after hearing Tedley. But then, he had seen the slight movement of Tedley's eyebrow, and he watched as Tedley's eyes moved reflexively, as if he was searching for a story to tell, or wondering whether the lawmen had believed the story he had just told them. He then looked down at the table again. But those small reflexes by Tedley told their own story. Nathan was sure that Tedley had just lied. Had Tedley made up other lies as he was questioned, Nathan wondered.

Nathan stared at Tedley. In a moment, Tedley looked up at the Marshal, but quickly looked down again.

"Tedley, you just lied to me, didn't you?" asked Nathan.

Tedley looked up at Nathan. "No sir, I ain't lyin'," he said.

Nathan reached across the table and firmly slapped Tedley. "Tedley, I'm going to ask you again. Where did Zima go? And I want a straight answer. If I think you're lying to me, all hell is going to break loose." Nathan could not help but notice the quick anger in Tedley's face after he slapped the man. But just as quickly, a calm demeanor returned to the servant's face.

Tedley had been looking at Nathan. In his gut, he knew that the Marshal was telling him straight up that there would be consequences for lying. It didn't matter to him, he thought, as he had already made up his mind to answer the question, knowing that it would put Zima in the cross hairs of the law and remove himself from the law's interest in him. "Only one place I can think of that Mr. Zima might have high-tailed it to," said Tedley. But he said nothing more.

Thirty seconds went by. "I'm waiting, Tedley," said Nathan.

Tedley twisted in his chair, presumably to find a more comfortable position. Then he answered, "Mr. Zima told me once upon a time that his mother lives in St. Louis. It appears she is the only family he's got," said Tedley. "I reckon he might go to see her."

Nathan was pleased at Tedley's answer. It jibed with McCary's story that Zima may be on his way to St. Louis to see his mother.

"What is Zima's mother's name?" asked Nathan.

“I believe her name is Veronica Zima. Yeah, that’s it,” said Tedley.

Tedley knew that he had ratted out Zima, and he also knew that his life now would need to make some changes, even though by his deceptions, he had thrown the lawmen’s interest away from him for now, and that was exactly his intent.

Nathan was carefully watching Tedley. Tedley returned Nathan’s stare, but this time, his face revealed nothing. Without conflicting evidence, Nathan could see no reason not to believe Tedley. And yet, his gut told him that something was amiss with Tedley, but he could not put a finger on anything specific. He turned to Bill and quietly asked him to put Tedley in the remaining cell, while he, Charlie, and George remained at the table.

When Bill and Tedley had gone to the back room, Nathan spoke to Rath and Conley. “You boys missed some of that conversation, but for now, without any additional information, I’m thinking that Tedley didn’t have much to do with Zima’s operation, other than making the covers for the books and running the press. Zima told him that the books were going to be used as prizes at Kansas City gambling houses. What a bunch of malarkey. Something tells me that Tedley is not as clean as he wants us to believe, but for now, I’ve got nothing more to go on.”

Nathan noticed George Conley, who sat staring at the table and did not comment.

“What’s on your mind, George?” asked Nathan.

“I guess I’m disappointed. We could charge Tedley with being an accessory to counterfeiting, but I don’t think we’ve got any proof to make the charge stick, other than the fact that he admitted to running the press.” Conley continued. “I also don’t think we could get a solid, high-penalty conviction, so I fail to even see the point in charging him. And when word gets around that he might have been mixed up with the fella that shot Tom Barnes, why, that could spark some crazies to try to lynch a half-black man. I feel like we're kinda stuck in the middle. Maybe we just give him a few days in jail for shooting at us."

"I figured you'd say that," said Nathan, "and I agree. But how do you want to proceed with the counterfeiting case?"

"The way I see it," said Conley, "the big fish got away. Zima is long gone by now, but maybe they can catch him in St. Louis."

"Yeah, I was thinking the same thing. I think it's time to send wires to our bosses," said Nathan.

For the next hour, the lawmen drafted telegrams to Ralph Gilman, Nathan's boss, and to Pinkertons and the Secret Service office in St. Louis. They described their activities for the past few days, informed them that Dennis McCary, the leader of the bank robbers had been jailed, and an accessory to the counterfeiting scheme, Jube Tedley, was also incarcerated. In addition, they informed their respective officials that Marcus Zima had fled from the carnival and was thought to be making his way to St. Louis to be sheltered by his mother, Mrs. Veronica Zima. In a short time, they received a reply from their bosses that Zima would soon be the subject of an all-out man hunt in St. Louis.

As the men clustered around the telegraph key, and the last of the wires had been sent, Bill, who had been standing and looking out the front office window turned and said, "Nathan, you've got company coming."

Nathan looked up and said, "Oh no, I've had enough for one day. What is it now?" Bill just laughed, as the office door opened, and Claire May and Will came in. Nathan jumped up from the table and quickly hugged and kissed his wife.

"I sure am glad to see you," Nathan said. The thought had already occurred to him that he might be spending another night alone on the cot in the back room of the jail.

"Will has an errand here in town in the morning, so I came along." She looked at the other men and recognized Charlie Rath. "Hi, Charlie."

"Nice to see you again, Mrs. Wolf," said Rath.

Nathan pointed out George Conley and said, "Claire May, this is George Conley from the Secret Service Agency in St. Louis."

George already had his hand out to shake hands. "Nice to meet you, Mrs. Wolf," he said.

Nathan then turned to Will and introduced him to Conley and Rath, and the men shook hands.

"Have you had supper yet, Nathan?" asked Claire May.

"No, I was waiting for you," said Nathan, and he laughed.

Bill, George, and Charlie watched as Nathan left to go to dinner with Claire May and Will. "Marshal's got himself a real pretty wife," said Conley.

"Yep," said Bill.

8 p.m.
Main Street Cafe

The trio lingered over their coffee. Remnant crumbs of pecan pie were all that remained of dessert. Nathan, Will, and Claire May idly watched the cafe patrons come and go for supper. Nathan was happiest when he was with Claire May, and now that the bank robbery and counterfeiting cases were, for the most part, resolved, he thought that he would be able to spend more evenings at home at Summer Prairie Ranch. His spoon rattled the coffee mug as he stirred the coffee to cool it.

"I've been worried about Mother," said Claire May, breaking into their after-dinner reverie. Will remained silent, but Nathan asked, "What's wrong with Virginia?"

“Well, nothing is wrong with her exactly,” said Claire May. “But she seems to be a little moody and lost in her own thoughts.”

“Is that a bad thing?” asked Nathan.

“I don’t know,” said Claire May. “But she is just not as chipper as usual, and I continually catch her staring at me and Bobby. It’s as if she is afraid of something happening to us. I don’t know what to think. Haven’t you noticed it, Will?”

Will slowly nodded his head. “Yeah, it does seem that she has something on her mind. But I don’t think she’s sick or anything. Maybe it has something to do with Alice and me getting married. Do you suppose she is afraid she is going to be all alone with both of her children married?”

“Maybe,” said Claire May. “But I have another hunch. Do you remember that telegram she got a while back? You remember, the one that she would not share with us.”

“Yeah, I remember,” said Will.

“Well, I think she’s been acting a little funny ever since she got that telegram,” said Claire May.

“Mmm,” said Will. “You could be right. How about you, Nathan. Does Mom seem any different to you?”

“I guess I’m not around her enough to notice any difference. I’m just always amazed at what a nice lady she is and how lucky you two are to have such a great mother.” Claire May understood Nathan’s remark. Nathan had confided to her that his childhood growing up had not always been pleasant, what with having two very demanding individuals as parents.

It’s been a long day,” said Nathan. He yawned as if to put an exclamation point on his remark. “I’ve got to get some sleep. My jailbirds should be all right by themselves tonight and I’ve got a deputy down at the hospital to watch Miss Dillman, so I’m looking forward to a nice soft hotel bed. What say we get out of here." He rose to go pay his supper bill with Claire May and Will following behind.

11 p.m.
At the Hotel

"Good night, sweetheart," said Claire May. She kissed Nathan once more and rolled off of him. Neither she nor he were wearing a stitch of clothing after enjoying a wonderful session of love making. She cuddled up next to Nathan, and they were both asleep in seconds. But there is little rest for a lawman, and shortly after midnight they were awakened abruptly by an insistent knocking on the door to their room. The noise woke Claire May, and she shook Nathan awake.

"Who's there," shouted Nathan.

"It's Deputy Nelson." Nelson was the sheriff's deputy who had been assigned to watch Priz Dillman at Doctor Johnson's home. "We've had some trouble down at Doctor Johnson's place. Can you come down there right away?" he asked.

Nathan was wondering if he would ever again get a good night's sleep, but he knew that such interruptions came with the job. "Yeah, let me get dressed and I'll be right down," he said.

"OK," said the deputy, and the sound of his boots receding down the hall confirmed his departure.

Twenty minutes later, Nathan rapped gently on the front door of Doctor Johnson's house and was admitted by the doctor's wife, who was wearing a light green robe over her night dress. "Evenin'," said Nathan. Mrs. Johnson did not immediately reply, only giving Nathan an icy glare. "They're down the hall," she said. Nathan's boots echoed on the scrubbed wood plank floors as he walked to the room where he knew Priz Dillman had been recuperating. Deputy Nelson was standing in the hall just outside the room, nervously shifting his weight from one leg to the other.

"What's happened?" asked Nathan.

Nelson stammered, but managed to reply, "Well, Marshal, Miss Dillman got shot," he said.

"Well, how in the hell did that happen," asked Nathan. "You were supposed to be guarding her so that she would stay safe." Nathan's face began to color with the anger he felt.

"I was watching her, Marshal. But I must have dozed off for a minute or so. Then I woke up to see that the window had been raised and this hombre was halfway into the room and had a pistol in his hand, and it was aimed at Miss Dillman."

"So, this fella at the window shot Miss Dillman?" asked Nathan.

"I'm afraid so, Marshal. But I shot him too," said Nelson, who was still holding a shotgun. "He's layin' outside the window there," said the deputy, pointing to the open window.

Nathan walked to the window and looked out into the darkness. The oil lamps in the room gave off enough light through the window for Nathan to see the crumpled body of the shooter laying on the ground outside.

Doctor Johnson was leaning over Priz Dillman, but then straightened up to look at Nathan.

"How bad is it, Doc?" asked Nathan.

"Miss Dillman is dead, Marshal," answered the doctor.

Nathan's anger began to surface, and he turned to face Deputy Nelson. "You knucklehead. Your job was to make sure that this would not happen." His face was even more red than previously.

"Now hang on there, Marshal," said Doctor Johnson. "That shooter did not kill Miss Dillman."

"You mean she wasn't shot?" asked Nathan.

"Oh, she was shot all right," said the doctor. "But when she got shot, she was already dead."

"Step over here and put your hand on her face, Marshal," said the doctor.

Nathan did what the doctor asked. He discovered that Priz's face was cold to the touch.

"She has been dead for hours, Marshal," said Johnson. "Apparently, she died some time earlier in the evening from the injuries she received in the fall from that carnival ride. So, the shooter was shooting at a corpse," said the doctor.

More to himself than addressing the others in the room, Nathan said, "I guess that means that McCary, the bank robber I have in jail, is now up for murder instead of attempted murder."

Nathan turned to the doctor, "Doc, hand me that light. I'm going outdoors and look at our shooter," said Nathan.

In a moment, Nathan and deputy Nelson were leaning down to look at the dead man. The shotgun blast from the deputy had resulted in buckshot holes and torn flesh on the face of the shooter, and blood had seeped onto the shirt of the dead man. But Nathan recognized him. "I remember seeing this guy at the carnival. I have a hunch he is one of McCary's henchmen and a fellow bank robber," said Nathan. "Just like McCary, he didn't want Miss Dillman to testify against him for bank robbery. And just like McCary, this fella didn't know that Miss Dillman had already fingered the bank robbers."

"Guess he doesn't have to worry about that anymore, does he," said the deputy.

Nathan scowled at the deputy, but responded, "I guess he doesn't."

When the lawmen went back inside, Nathan said to the doctor, "Doc, I reckon you can release both bodies to the undertaker."

"I'll get hold of him later this morning and let him take them," said the doctor.

"Sorry for all the trouble we've caused," said Nathan.

"Not all your fault, Marshal," said the doctor. "Most of the trouble was caused by that damn carnival." The doctor and his wife went over to examine the broken window while Nathan and the deputy walked from their house.

"Who's going to pay for this window repair, Marshal," asked the doctor's wife as she faced Nathan with a stony scowl on her face and a hand on her hip.

"I don't know for sure, Mrs. Johnson. But I expect that the sheriff's office budget should be able to reimburse you," said Nathan. He turned to the sheriff's deputy.

"Go home and get some sleep, Nelson," said Nathan. "I shouldn't need you the rest of the night."

"OK, Marshal. I'll see you at the office in a few hours," said the deputy, and he walked away.

Back at the hotel, Nathan fell asleep, exhausted, fully clothed, laying on the top of the bed clothes. Claire May reached an arm from beneath the covers and laid it across Nathan's chest as he slept.

Thursday morning, 8:30 a.m.
Main Street Cafe

The sun streaming through the front window of the cafe helped clear the cobwebs from Nathan's head. They also revealed that the cafe window could use a good scrubbing. Nathan's fork followed the path from plate to his mouth, with bite-size loads of pancake and sausage making the trips. "Slow down, sweetheart," said Claire May. "Those pancakes aren't going to run away."

Nathan chuckled. "You're right. I won't let them get away." They both laughed. "Just hungry, I guess."

Will had already finished his breakfast and was coming through the cafe door after completing his business at the general store. He had loaded the buckboard and had come back to pick up Claire May for the return trip to the ranch. He joined them at their table, removed his hat, and ordered one last cup of coffee before they left. Thirty minutes later, Nathan stood on the sidewalk in front of the cafe and waved to Claire May and Will as they left town. He turned as they rode away and saw Bill Ward trotting to him.

"You better come with me," said Bill. "You aren't going to believe this."

The two men strode to the marshal's office. Bill led him back to the cells. They were met with hand clapping and jeers from Junior Skinner and Dennis McCary.

"Ah, the great Marshal Wolf returns," Junior Skinner jeeringly said. "Well, here's a good one on you, Marshal."

At first, Nathan did not know what he was talking about. But then he saw that the cell that had been holding Jube Tedley was empty. He pulled the cell door open and saw the metal lock bolt laying on the floor of the cell. Next to it was a flexible metal chain saw with two small handles on each end of the chain. The saw had been used to cut through the lock bolt.

"Yeah, the great Marshal Wolf didn't even check old Tedley's pant cuffs," said McCary. "He had that saw sewn into the bottom of his pants. Didn't take him long to vamoose, did it, Marshal." Both the prisoners laughed and hooted at Nathan and Bill.

Nathan looked at Bill, a crease of question crossing his face. "Didn't know he was gone until I got here this morning and was going to go out the back door to the privy, and those two yahoos started yappin'," said Bill.

Nathan leaned down and picked up the broken lock and the flexible saw. He and Bill walked back to the front office. "He's probably got an eight-hour head start on us," said Nathan.

The circumstances of the escape nagged at him.

"Why would a manservant be carrying a flexible saw? There was no reason for him to add a charge of escaping jail to his record. He probably would have been acquitted if he had been brought to trial for being an accessory to counterfeiting. It doesn't make sense that he would break out of jail," said Nathan. To himself, he thought that something just didn't add up with Jube Tedley.

Almost as if he was reading Nathan's thoughts, Bill said, "I'm starting to think there might be more to that half-black fella than we thought."

Their musings were broken by the front door opening. They looked up to see Dwight Mullins come in the front door. The men greeted each other and then Dwight said, "It appears that we have a horse thief, Marshal."

Nathan cut him off. "Don't tell me. You're missing a horse," said Nathan.

"Yeah, sure enough. But what made you say that?" asked Dwight.

"'Cause I've got a missing prisoner," said Nathan. "I'd bet a dollar that he took your horse to high tail it away from here."

"Oh, no," said Dwight. "That was one of my best riding horses. Guess I'll never see it again."

"Reckon not," said Bill. "He's long gone."

Nathan and Bill watched as Dwight slowly shook his head and walked back out the door.

"So now Tedley's a horse thief too," said Bill.

"Looks that way," said Nathan. Tedley's theft of the horse was certainly not a surprise, thought Nathan. But he was concerned that there were too many loose ends with the crimes connected to the traveling carnival.

Chapter Fourteen: Zima's Run

Friday, mid-morning

The funeral for Tom Barnes had not been held on Wednesday. To accommodate family wishes to allow time for out-of-town relatives to attend, the funeral was held on a bright, pleasantly-cool Friday morning. The lawmen, Wolf, Ward, Conley, and Rath, stood on one side of the open grave, their hats in their hands, furtively looking across the grave at the parents of Tom Barnes. Mrs. Barnes, dressed in black, held her head down, her shoulders visibly shaking periodically. Her only son, a young man with a bright future, and a man who was well liked by all who knew him, would soon be lowered into the waiting abyss. The strain of losing his son plainly showed on the face of Mr. Barnes. It was unlikely that the Barneses would ever fully get over the death of their son at the hands of an outlaw.

In due time, the pastor finished the graveside service. Attendees slowly began to drift away from the cemetery. Out of respect for Mr. and Mrs. Barnes, the lawmen waited until the oak coffin was lowered into the grave, and the Barneses slowly walked away, their arms entwined, seeming to draw support from each other. Only then, did the lawmen replace their hats and walk back to the office.

On Board the Missouri Pacific Line

Meanwhile, many miles away, the giant 4-6-0 steam engine chuffed loudly as the brakes were applied. The train was slowing as it reached the outlying prairie on its approach into Jefferson City. The change in the rhythmic track noise woke Marcus Zima in his closet-sized compartment on board a passenger car of the Missouri Pacific railroad. He opened his eyes briefly to look out the train car window even though there was nothing to interest him. He had slept for several hours but was still tired. The previous day of hanging onto the saddle horn of the loping horse for hours as he made his way to the rail head at Ottowa had been longer than he had ever ridden a horse. He decided that if it was at all possible, he would never ride another horse. His thigh muscles and groin ached painfully. Then he smiled, remembering how he had duped a farmer waiting at the station into buying his stolen horse for forty-five dollars. He rolled onto his other side and closed his eyes. Maybe I can get a few more hours of sleep, he thought.

As Zima began to doze, his mind drifted back and replayed the past few days, beginning when his world had seemed to be on an even keel. He had been able to run the carnival with little interference, he had well-paying criminal operations at work within the carnival, and he enjoyed the company of fellow ruffians and an acceptable female carnival worker when the urge overcame him. Still, he had never been a happy man. Nearly asleep, his mind went farther back, twenty plus years, when Victor Carelli had spared his life, only to have him shipped off to spend the rest of his life with a seedy carnival that travelled from small non-descript town to another town of the same ilk. He had been humbled into working his way up in the organization, from shoveling up excrement from the carnival animals, to cooking in the mess tent, until finally his skill with numbers put him in the accounting position for the carnival. He had shown Carelli that he had paid for his embezzlement mistake and was actively contributing to the criminal syndicate. Yet, for all of those years of earning his way, he had been forced by threat of death to live with, and listen to the advice of, the overbearing, uncouth mulatto, and put on a front that the half caste was his servant. Being forced to split the proceeds of the bank robberies and counterfeiting operation with that man was also forced upon him. But even with these conditions, Zima thought that at least he was managing to put away a great deal of money from those illicit endeavors.

The bank robberies had been Zima's idea. He had been doing the accounting for the carnival and making the bank deposits and wire transfers to St. Louis after each carnival run. During one bank deposit he had noticed how poorly guarded the small-town banks were, and he decided that he would make an unauthorized withdrawal of the same funds the carnival had deposited the day before. He had recruited Dennis McCary from the band of carnival roustabouts and told him to recruit three more of the men whose skills included those needed to bust into bank vaults. The result was a very lucrative operation. McCary and the rest of the robbers were well paid to keep their mouths shut. But then that damn McCary had told him that Priz Dillman was threatening to go to the law if McCary did not stop robbing banks. With Zima's consent, McCary had taken it upon himself to rid the carnival of the fat woman who threatened their operation. Zima had told McCary that he didn't care how it happened, just get rid of her. After the law had gotten interested in Dillman's fall and the counterfeiting scheme, Zima had come to the conclusion that the snooping lawmen were getting too close for comfort, and he needed to skip out and head for St. Louis before the marshal and his cohorts dragged him to jail. Zima smiled just thinking that the mulatto was left behind to face the law.

Zima was convinced that among other failed criminal acquaintances, Junior Skinner also contributed to his downfall. Zima had hired Skinner to operate the rodeo stock operation. Initially, Skinner had done a satisfactory job with the rodeo venues. The spectator traffic along with the cowboy entry fees at the rodeos had produced a decent profit. But then, Junior Skinner had gotten greedy. He had insisted on rigging the rodeos so that even more money could be pulled from the rodeo operation. Skinner had also insisted that his percentage of the take be increased. To enforce his demand, Skinner had hinted at inflicting physical harm to Zima if his conditions were not met. Zima knew that this was not an empty threat, as Skinner had built up a small cadre of enforcers within the rodeo operation and had forced his way into the counterfeiting operation. Zima blamed Skinner for bringing the law to sniff around the rigged rodeo operation, and the investigation grew from there. He hoped that Skinner would swing from a rope after the law finished with him, right alongside Dennis McCary. And while they were at it, that damn mulatto could make it a dandy trio in a necktie party. God, he hated that man. But there was nothing he could do about Tedley. It seemed that he was well known by St. Louis and was untouchable for some reason. His swirling thoughts got the best of him, disturbing Zima enough that further sleep was out of the question. Resignedly, he rose and pushed the bunk up into the wall so he could sit on the couch. He dressed, put his shoes on, and ambled to the dining car for some breakfast.

Zima was on his way to St. Louis. Throughout his life, especially after his father had died, Zima could always count on his mother for advice, and she would certainly have ideas on how he could hide out until the heat was off. He knew, though, that he could not be seen by Carelli or his network of spies. For abandoning the carnival, Carelli would have him shot on sight. But paying a visit to his mother was not the only reason for returning to St. Louis. There was a blued steel .38 snub nose revolver in his inside vest pocket, and he had a carpet bag with a false bottom full of cash. He now had the resources to take his revenge. He had never forgotten how he was physically beaten and hauled in front of the fat, arrogant gangster, Victor Carelli, and had only been saved from certain death by the pleadings of his mother. The fact that he had stolen money from Carelli was of little significance to Zima. Instead, he dwelled on the fact that he had been demeaned and forced to live with Jube Tedley, whom he despised. The scene of the fat gangster blowing cigar smoke and drinking wine while telling his goons to kill him was burned into his memory. It was that recollection that drove Zima. He now planned to get his revenge by killing Victor Carelli.

In a few hours, he would be in St. Louis. He was hesitant to tell his mother of his intentions. He was sure that she would not agree with his plan and in all likelihood, was still carrying on a relationship with Carelli. But he felt certain that she would not betray him by telling Carelli that he was back in town. Zima smiled as he drank a cup of strong tea in the dining car. Ahh, he thought. He looked forward to exacting sweet revenge.

Summer Prairie Ranch
Two Hours Before Sunset

Nathan, Claire May, Will, and Virginia sat on the front porch of the ranch house. They were watching the quail hen leading her six chicks from the grove of trees. By her actions, the hen was teaching the chicks to feed on grass and weed seeds and an occasional bug she happened upon.

"She better get those chicks back in that grove before she gets spotted by a passing coyote," said Will. As if she knew what Will had said, the hen cocked her head and seemed to measure the day's deepening shadows, then reversed her path, slowly leading her brood back to the safety of the brambles in the grove.

"Oh, Nathan," said Claire May. "I forgot to mention that mother and I went to visit Meezie Jones." Meezie Jones and her grandson, Daniel Chambers lived on an adjoining ranch. Meezie Jones was an elderly black woman, a former slave, and seemed to have the uncanny ability to speak to her daughter, who had been killed many years ago by a rogue Ku Klux Klan group. They had raided the Chambers' small farm and killed Meezie's daughter Dehlia and son-in-law, Jonah Chambers. Daniel and Meezie had survived that raid by hiding from the outlaws during the raid and had been farming their place now for many years.

"How is Meezie?" asked Nathan.

"She's just as spry as ever," said Claire May. "We had quite a talk, and she mentioned several times how kind it was that you had shared the extended acreage and oil rights with them when Crenshaw's gang was broken up."

Two years ago, when outlaw banker Arthur Crenshaw's illegal operations were stopped, the Crenshaw holdings were broken up, and the Summers, the Morgans, and the Chambers families bought and divided the forfeited Crenshaw land and oil rights among them. The combination of greater acreage and a market for their crude oil had greatly increased the profitability of the three ranches and had brought Meezie and Daniel from the brink of eking out an existence, to being much more affluent.

Claire May went on. "Would you believe that Daniel was butchering a hog when we went over there?"

"I didn't know he had any pigs," said Will.

"Oh, he's built a pen for them and has four gilts. He bred the gilts and was butchering the boar. He said that boars are just too hard to handle. He said he would bring us a ham once he had cured it."

"Hogs," said Will. "Nothing stinks worse than those critters. Glad Daniel's place is far enough away that we can't smell them. Gotta say, though, that I sure like bacon and ham," he said and laughed.

"Anyway," continued Claire May, "their little house looks spruced up. It's got a coat of paint on it, and there are some pretty flowers up next to the porch."

"Daniel? Planting flowers?" Nathan and Will said almost simultaneously.

"No, no," said Claire May. "Here's the fun part. While we were there on the porch with Meezie, a pretty dark-skinned girl came out of the house."

"Uh, oh. That's trouble," said Will, and he and Nathan laughed.

"So, Daniel's got himself a girlfriend," said Will.

"No, Mr. smart guy," said Claire May. "He's got himself a wife, and her Name is Gloria. Apparently, Daniel went up to Nicodemus, the black settlement, found himself the right gal, and got married up there. She's real pretty and very nice. We had a long chat with her and Meezie. It was Gloria who planted the flowers."

"I'm glad Daniel found himself a wife," said Nathan. "I like Daniel. He's a good man."

"And that's not all," said Claire May. "Meezie pulled me aside just like she did when I became pregnant with Bobby. She told me that Gloria is going to have a baby, but she and Daniel don't even know it yet."

"Yikes. That old woman is a little scary," said Will. "I'm not sure I want her telling my future."

"Now that would be a scary story," said Nathan. Will gave him a playful poke in the shoulder and they both laughed.

"Well, scoff all you want, you two, but I really admire Meezie," said Claire May. "She's been through a lot in her lifetime, but still has a wonderful disposition. Isn't that right, mother?" she asked.

"In a quiet voice, Virginia answered, "Yes, she surely does."

Changing the subject, Claire May said in a teasing voice, "There's another little story that needs to be told right here on this porch, isn't there, Will?"

"Don't know what you're talking about," said Will.

Claire May laughed, and even Virginia chuckled. "Oh, yes you do. You better tell Nathan, or I will," said Claire May.

"All right, all right. Alice and I have set a date for our wedding," said Will.

Nathan laughed. "That's a good thing. I figure she was fixing to walk out on you if you didn't get around to marrying her pretty soon. When's the big day?"

"Alice says it's going to be September 5. She likes the cooler temperature instead of the hot summer," said Will.

"Well, anyway. Congratulations, it's about time," said Nathan.

In addition to quail watching and yakking, Nathan had also been watching Virginia Summers. Bobby was on her lap, and Nathan's mother-in-law was gently playing with the baby. As usual, Bobby was smiling as Virginia played with his toes and tickled his feet. But as he watched her, Nathan saw a change in Virginia's face. She appeared to have a wistful, faraway look. She raised the baby, kissed Bobby's cheek, and handed the child to Claire May. Virginia rose from her chair and said, "I'm going in to see if Rosa needs any help in the kitchen." She turned and went back into the house. Will and Claire May looked at each other. They said nothing, but they were of one mind, convinced that something was bothering their mother.

"You saw it, didn't you?" asked Claire May of Nathan. "You saw how she changed moods. I saw you watching mother. You saw it."

Nathan was slow to answer. "I saw her change moods, yes. But I still don't know if there is something bothering her." To himself, he thought that it was, indeed, apparent that Virginia had something on her mind that she was not sharing. But he did not feel that he should say that to Claire May and Will as Virginia was not his mother.

"If something is eating at her, I'm sure she will tell us in her own good time," said Nathan.

Will rose from his chair and went into the house. Claire May rose with Bobby. Speaking to Nathan, she said, "I've got to go feed this little guy and get him to bed. I'll come back when I'm through." She reached over and patted Nathan's arm as she left.

Nathan had not told much of the story of the carnival arrests to the family. It was because, in his own thinking, the case was not fully resolved. A thought continued to nag at him. Just like the games of the carnival, wherein patrons were suckered into believing that they could win a prize while not knowing that the games were rigged, Nathan had a disturbing thought that he had somehow been deceived by those running the carnival. But he could not put a finger on the crux of the ruse. However, his underlying thought was still centered on the fact that the half-caste servant had fled from jail and any further inquiry into his background. It did not seem to make sense to Nathan, and the question would not go away. He theorized that the half-caste, Tedley, would have no family nearby, and therefore, would not run far. Nathan was convinced that it was more likely that the carnival was his home and family, and that Tedley might very well flee to rejoin the carnival. Having made up his mind, Nathan went into the office and sat by the telegraph key. He began tapping out his messages. He sent wires to be delivered to Bill Ward's home, the Coffeyville sheriff's office, and to the eastern Oklahoma marshal's office in Tulsa.

Claire May had first looked out on the porch for him, and then joined him in the office. "Why are you sending messages at this hour?" she asked.

"Had to send one to Bill, one to the Coffeyville sheriff, and one to the Tulsa marshall's office," he answered. "I still think there are some loose ends in this carnival mess."

They then talked about the carnival case and several unrelated topics until it was time for bed. As they walked to their bedroom, Nathan said, "If you hear me get up early, don't bother getting up. I'm going to get an early start to catch the train to Coffeyville."

Saturday Afternoon
Coffeyville, Kansas

As the train sat idle at the Coffeyville depot, Nathan, Bill and two sheriff's deputies from Chanute off-loaded their horses from the stock car. Per Nathan's instructions, Bill had enlisted the help of the deputies and made all of the preparations for the trip to Coffeyville. The Coffeyville sheriff, his deputy, and the Tulsa marshal watched from the platform as Nathan's group walked their horses down the stock car ramp. After they had mounted, the seven lawmen rode into town and hitched their horses outside the sheriff's office. The men were soon gathered around a table in the office as Nathan spoke to them.

Nathan briefed them on what had transpired in Chanute over the past few days, telling them of the rigged rodeos and the counterfeiting operation. He wrapped up by sharing his nagging question of why Jube Tedley had fled after escaping from jail in Chanute. He also told them that he was acting on a hunch only, and that there might be nothing to do when they visited the carnival. But he emphasized that he felt he had been fooled by the carnival people, and that he was not taking any chances of getting bushwhacked by the unpredictable carnival hands. He told them that Tedley had appeared docile and claimed that he knew little of the criminal operation, and it was for this reason that he and George Conley had decided not to charge Tedley in the counterfeiting operation. But Tedley's escape had changed his mind.

"I aim to recapture Tedley and wring him out," said Nathan. "There's just something that I'm missing in this carnival mess."

The sheriff spoke up. "Marshal, I don't understand. You say this mulatto fella shot at you and the secret service agent. What was he trying to do?"

"Well, that's a bit of a mystery too," said Nathan. "George Conley and I thought he was trying to protect Marcus Zima, his boss. But now

I'm not so sure. And why in the hell would he want to escape if he suspected that we were not going to press charges against him. It doesn't make sense."

"You expect we'll have any trouble?" asked the Tulsa marshal.

"I don't expect so," said Nathan. "But you never know with those transient carnival folks. That's why I wanted your guns with us."

More questions followed until the men all knew the background and what they might expect to encounter. "All right, we'll meet here in the morning and plan to head out to the fairgrounds right away, hopefully before too many people know what we're up to," said Nathan.

"Sounds good, Marshal. There's a decent hotel just down the block and the livery stable is right across the street," said the sheriff. "Hotel's got a restaurant there, too."

The men filed out to the street. Tired of sitting on the train all afternoon, Nathan and Bill led their horses and walked to the livery stable. After giving instructions to have the horses ready early in the morning, Nathan and Bill walked to the hotel for the night.

Chapter Fifteen: Hot Receptions

Sunday Morning, Fair Grounds
Coffeyville, Kansas

The fairgrounds were quiet in the early morning. Meadowlarks melodiously greeted the group of lawmen as they rode slowly to the midway, where they dismounted and tied off their horses. They passed the open-sided stock barns, a few other sheds, and the usual fairgrounds arena with wood bleachers. Nathan spotted the large tent amidst the rows of caravans. But as the lawmen turned in the direction of the tent, they were met by a group of roustabouts, many with clubs in their hands. But they stopped momentarily, and Nathan could see that one of the men had turned and was speaking to the group. He then left the group and walked toward the lawmen. When he spied Nathan, he walked directly to him. One of his friends accompanied him. The first man to reach Nathan was the same man who had spoken with Nathan when he had visited the carnival in Chanute to investigate the attempted murder of Priz Dillman. Neither of the approaching roustabouts was carrying weapons.

When the roustabout reached Nathan, he said, "Well Marshal, seems like we meet again. What's the problem this time?"

Nathan reached out and shook hands with the man and then his friend. "You've got a fella in your carnival we want to talk with. His name's Jube Tedley."

"The mulatto? What in the world do you want with him?" asked the roustabout.

"We just want to talk with him, that's all," answered Nathan. "Is he over yonder in that tent?"

The roustabout opened his mouth to speak, but as he did so, a gunshot rang out. The man quickly turned his head and ran for cover. His friend stood still for a moment, a look of confusion on his face. His knees then buckled, and he rolled to the ground. Blood began to form a puddle to the side of his body. Nathan leaned down to look at the second man, and as he did so, a second shot rang out. A sheriff's deputy loudly grunted from the impact of the bullet meant for Nathan and clutched his side as blood oozed onto his shirt.

Nathan remained on his knees on the ground and shouted, "Get down." The lawmen scurried for cover while the crowd of carnival employees scattered, running in all directions.

A third shot was fired, this time panging off the wheel rim of a caravan behind which several people were taking cover.

Nathan had run to take cover and found himself next to Bill, crouching by a wagon. "Did you see where those shots were coming from?" asked Nathan.

"More than one place," answered Bill. One may have come from that tent and another one from that clump of bushes," he said as he pointed the barrel of his pistol at some bushes in the distance.

"Bill, make your way around to the other men and tell them to shoot at any location where they think they see a shooter. We want to keep them pinned down. I'm going after the fella in the bushes, so don't let anybody shoot me by mistake," said Nathan. Bill moved off to seek out the other lawmen, while Nathan crouched down and darted between wagons as he made his way toward the clump of bushes.

Nathan ran out of wagons to duck behind. There were now only a few scrub oaks between him and the shooter. Just as he was about to sprint for the trees, another shot rang out, narrowly missing Nathan's head at the corner of the wagon. Knowing that the shooter would need to chamber another round and re-aim, Nathan immediately took off running and flopped down behind the small trees before he could be fired upon again. Behind him, he could hear other shots being fired sporadically. The occasional shots were then replaced by a volley of shots that lasted nearly a full minute. Some of the other lawmen must have found targets, he thought. It then became eerily quiet.

Nathan removed his hat and placed it on the ground. He then rose slightly, and in that second, he could make out the outline of a man crouching in the bushes. Nathan went down on his stomach and inched to the side of the tree. Another shot rang out and peeled bark from the tree next to Nathan. He immediately rose his head slightly, took careful aim, and fired at the man in the bushes. He heard a satisfying yelp from the man. He had been hit.

Not wishing to take a chance of the man still being able to fire his weapon, Nathan remained where he was for a few moments. He then began to slide forward on his belly. He had gotten only a few feet when another shot broke the silence. Nathan felt his foot being twisted. He turned his head and looked at his boot. Where the heel had been higher than his body, the boot had a hole in it. He lay for a moment flexing his foot, moving the boot. He thought it was odd, but he felt no pain. He continued forward, and the man shot again. This time, Nathan immediately stood up and ran, firing his pistol as he ran. Saving his last shot, he crashed into the bushes where he had last seen the shooter. He quickly crouched to fire but held up when he saw the shooter's bleeding body. Blood flowed from two wounds. One of Nathan's shots while he was running must have also hit the shooter. Seeing that there was no longer a threat, Nathan rolled out the cylinder of the pistol, dumped the empty shells, reloaded, and replaced the gun in its holster. He straightened up, walked to the man's body and rolled him face up. He did not recognize him.

"Marshal, Marshal!" From behind the trees where Nathan had been moments before, a man was waving his hands and shouting at Nathan. He crouched again and drew his pistol.

"Who is it?" shouted Nathan.

"It's me," said the man and walked from behind the trees. It was the roustabout that Nathan had spoken to earlier. The man hurriedly walked to Nathan's side.

He looked at the body of the man shot by Nathan. "Yeah, that figures," said the roustabout.

"What figures, Mister?" asked Nathan.

"Do you still have Dennis McCary in your jail, Marshal?" the man asked.

"Yeah, he was there when I left town," said Nathan.

"Well, this fella is one of his henchmen, one of his drinkin' buddies, and a fellow bank robber," said the roustabout.

"How do you know he was a bank robber?" asked Nathan. He did not think that it was common knowledge that McCary and his friends were robbing banks.

"Oh, hell, Marshal, there ain't much that goes on in a carnival that everybody doesn't know. We knew McCary was robbing banks, but none of us wanted to face his gang and Mr. Zima. By the way, did you ever catch Zima?" the man asked.

"Naw," said Nathan. "He was long gone as you know. We think we know where he went, and I figure he is just about at the end of his line."

Just then, Bill Ward joined them. "We've got two more of these hombres over yonder. Somebody went to fetch the undertaker." Occasional shots could still be heard in the vicinity of the big tent.

"What about Tedley?" asked Nathan.

"We ain't seen him," said Bill. "But somebody is still taking pot shots from that tent. I figure Tedley might be in there, but it's so dark on the inside of the tent that we can't see him. He sure as hell can see us though."

Nathan walked back, retrieved his hat, and returned to talk with the roustabout. "Mister, can you make sure that the undertaker gets this fella, too?"

"Sure thing Marshal. You law boys keep this up, and it's gonna be mighty peaceful in this carnival without all these bad boys."

Nathan chuckled. "One more to go, mister. One more to go."

Nathan and Bill began walking quickly to where they could see the Coffeyville sheriff and Tulsa marshal crouched behind a wagon. They were taking occasional shots at the tent and were answered by a shot from within the dark tent.

The Tulsa marshal said, "Nathan, there's no way to get in that tent. He can see us, but we can't see him. Even if we went around back and lifted a tent flap, he'd still see us before we could see him."

Nathan stood looking at the canvas tent. Some of its panels moved gently in the breeze. A brightly colored pennant fluttered at the apex of the center pole. He turned and looked at the other two men and Bill. "As much as I would like to have Tedley alive, he's already done too much damage. Let's burn him out."

Nathan signaled to the roustabout who was watching from a distance. He came running to the lawmen. When he reached the lawmen, Nathan asked him to go find a couple buckets of kerosene. He also advised the man to tell the owners of a couple of the caravans that were close to the tent to move them farther away. The lawmen watched as the roustabout spoke with the other carnival workers. Quickly, a dozen men bent to the task of rolling the two wagons away from the tent. When they were done, they stood watching from a distance.

While the other lawmen covered them, Bill and the Coffeeville sheriff walked around to the sides of the tent. Each carried a pail of kerosene. In moments, they had each saturated a portion of the tent's canvas and quickly lit them on fire. The fire started slowly and seemed to remain at the site where the oil had been put on the canvas. But after a moment, the fire began to build, clawing its way up the dry canvas until three sides of the tent were engulfed in flame. The first of the guyline ropes parted in the flames. It was followed by two others, and the first of the supporting tent poles came crashing down. The other poles would follow shortly. Tedley would either perish in the fire or be forced to come out the main door of the tent. That question was soon answered as a shadowy figure came running through the flaming tent door, indiscriminately firing a rifle he held in his hands. His shots were answered by the lawmen, and in seconds, it was over. The smell of gunpowder mingled with the smell of the burning tent and drifted on the breeze. Nathan walked over to the body sprawled on the ground. Bill joined him. The man's curly black hair and physical features confirmed that their target had, indeed, been Jube Tedley, whose blood now seeped from several bullet wounds and formed a pool beneath the body of the dead man.

"It's Tedley, all right," said Bill.

Nathan stood looking at the body of the dark-skinned man at his feet. "I wanted to find out more from him. Now, I reckon we'll never know what made him escape jail and end up this way. I sure would like to know," said Nathan, as the other lawmen walked up to join him.

"Nathan, the carnival folks say that those other two dead men were part of McCary's bank robbers," said the Tulsa marshal. "Guess that pretty much takes care of that gang."

The men watched as the flames began to grow less intense. From the ground up, the tent was gone, the canvas had all burned away, and the support poles lay askew in the glowing flames and ashes. The fire was now feeding on those articles that had been inside the tent. And even that hungry fire was running out of fuel to feed it.

The roustabout walked to Nathan's side and watched the flames slowly dying. "What do we do now, Marshal?" he asked. His concern was for the livelihood of he and his friends who worked the carnival.

"Well, I surely don't know, mister. Somebody must own this outfit, and they'll likely come and find you. But in the meantime, you might want to choose a couple of your friends and you all take charge of keeping your traveling schedule." Nathan paused and then went on, "When the fire is out, you may want to sift through that tent. Lord knows what you might find. But if you find money, you might want to check with a bank to make sure it's real."

"What if there is some money and it's real. What do we do with it," asked the man.

"I've got a feeling that if there is any money, it was earned by the sweat from all of you and your friends. I'd say you divide it up among yourselves," said Nathan. "Least that's what I would do if I had been working for a bunch of crooks."

"Okay, Marshal. That's what we'll do," said the man, and he hurried away to speak with his friends.

Bill Ward had walked up beside Nathan. The marshal immediately sat down on the ground. "Here, Bill. Help me get that boot off," he said, and held up his leg. Bill straddled Nathan's leg and pulled off the boot. Bill held the boot in the air looking at it.

"Hoowee," said Bill. "I ain't never seen anything like this. Did this happen today?"

Bill handed the boot to Nathan who also examined it. He could see the track of a bullet that had gouged a path through the side of the upper portion of the heel and had continued on to bore a hole that had gone clean through the outer walking part of the heel.

"Another couple inches over and you wouldn't be walking much any more," said Bill.

"Probably better not show this to Claire May," said Nathan, as he pulled the boot back on his foot. Bill looked at Nathan and grinned.

It was late afternoon before the lawmen returned to town. After putting their horses up at the livery, the seven men took a seat in the *Kansoma,* a bar that passed for the nicest watering hole with a restaurant in the town of Coffeyville. A waitress came and took their drink orders. Nathan ordered three fingers of bourbon and watched as the woman made her way around the table. In a few minutes she returned and distributed the glasses.

Before she left the table, the waitress asked, "Sheriff, what was all that shooting we heard this afternoon? Sounded like a war going on out by the fairgrounds," she said.

The sheriff did not think that this was the time and place to tell her that a deputy and a carnival roustabout had been shot. He would tell her the full story later. "Just a little target practice, honey," replied the sheriff. "Just havin' some fun." The waitress smiled at the sheriff. She had known the sheriff for years and knew he wouldn't tell her the real story while the other men were present. So she responded, "That was a whole lot of targets, I guess." She continued to smile as she walked away from the table. The other men watched the sheriff as his eyes followed the waitress back to the bar.

"Friend of yours, Sheriff?" the Tulsa marshal teasingly asked.

The sheriff laughed. "You might say that. Been married to her for ten years."

They all laughed, but other than his deputy, none of them knew whether or not he was telling the truth.

Nathan lifted his glass from the table. "I'd like to thank all of you for helping me out today. I'm mighty glad I had you boys along to put the odds in our favor. This round is on me."

The men drank up and thanked Nathan.

"Don't know what we'll do without you here, Marshal. Things are mighty quiet most of the time. That is, until you come to town," said the sheriff. The men laughed, and the sheriff added, "I've got a deputy in the hospital from a bullet wound, but he'll be just fine. He's got a friendly nurse who's takin' special care of him. Hell, I didn't even know he had a girlfriend." The men laughed.

The sheriff then looked at Nathan and added, "You caused a little excitement in what probably was going to be another boring day."

The men laughed again. The sheriff went on, "Shoot, those Amish folks out at the edge of town still mention you every time they come to town for supplies."

"Say hello to them for me the next time you see them, Sheriff," said Nathan. "They are some mighty fine folks who saved my life. Anyway, thanks again for helping us today. I reckon we'll catch the morning train back to Chanute."

The men ordered another round. When the waitress put the glasses down in front of the men, she came to the sheriff and put his in front of him, and then said, "Last one for you, sheriff." Then she walked away.

"See, I told you I was married to her, now didn't I?" said the sheriff. And the friendly teasing of the sheriff continued.

Chapter Sixteen: Zima and Carelli

The Following Day
Veronica Zima's Apartment
St. Louis, Missouri

An hour before, Veronica Zima had been visited at the bar she managed. Her visitor was her boss and lover, Victor 'Vico' Carelli. He had given her disturbing news regarding her son, Marcus. Carelli explained to her that Marcus had "gummed up the works" at the carnival operation and was on the lam from the law. But most disturbing, Vico told her that over twenty years ago, he had been tolerant and had allowed Marcus to live after she pleaded for his life. Vico told her that this would not happen again, and that if Marcus showed himself in St. Louis, he would be exterminated "like the rat that he is." The last thing that Carelli told her was that he was going to give her a new work assignment. The assignment would be a promotion to her with a substantial increase in pay. Veronica was unsure of the situation, and inwardly she did not want to move to a new assignment where she would likely not see Carelli again. But she had been with Vico for so long that she could read him, and she knew their relationship was changing. The fervent ardor had faded from Carelli's embraces. She reasoned that if Carelli had grown tired of her, and the fact that she knew a great deal about his criminal operations, perhaps it would be best if she were on her own. Out of sight, out of mind, she thought, and maybe by going away she could avoid any more vengeful actions directed toward her by Carelli. Therefore, Veronica had told him that she understood, but inwardly, she was so upset that she had left work and gone home. She sat drinking a strong cup of tea, looking out the window to the street below. The day was overcast with intermittent drizzle that danced on the window as it gathered and ran down the glass.

As she gazed on the street, she watched as a rain-glistening black hansom cab stopped in the street. A man alighted from the carriage, spoke to the driver, and handed him some money, then turned to face her apartment window. From cafe windows facing each other on opposite sides of the same street, the carriage passenger was being observed by two government agents, one of whom hurriedly walked down the street to the public phone in the telegraph office. He gave the telegraph office manager his nickel and placed his call.

Veronica Zima's face blanched, and she nearly spilled her tea on her lap. She jumped up from her chair and rushed to the apartment door, throwing the lock mechanism and dead bolt to ensure they were locked. The man she had seen getting out of the cab had been her son, Marcus.

In a moment, there was a rapping on her apartment door. She knew who it was, and momentarily she did not answer. But after a few seconds, she asked, "Who is it?"

From the other side of the door came the quietly voiced reply. "An old friend. Are you alone?" Zima was taking no chances. If his mother had company, especially if it was Carelli, he would flee to return later.

"Go away, Marcus, before they find you," she said.

It surprised him a bit that his mother knew it was him at the door. "Let me in, mother. I need to talk to you," he replied.

"No Marcus. You're not welcome here," said Veronica. "And if you know what's good for you, you will get out of St. Louis before Carelli's men find you and kill you."

Zima replied, "I'm not going to be killed, mother. Someone else is going to die."

Veronica was confused. What in the world was he talking about, she wondered. And then a faint thought occurred to her. Oh, no, she thought. He can't be that unhinged. She unlocked the door, opened it, and watched her son enter.

"Who is going to die, Marcus?" she asked, already thinking that she knew what he was going to say.

"Carelli, Mother, Carelli's going to die, and I'm going to kill him. And then you and I can leave St. Louis and go somewhere that we can't be found," said Zima, smiling as he spoke.

Veronica looked at her son. Twenty years ago her loyalties were clear cut. Her love for her son at that time had prompted her to plead for his life, and she had been appreciative that her son had been sent to the carnival operation versus being put to death by Carelli. But his appearance here was breaking her heart. She still loved her son, but the man standing before her had changed persona. He no longer exhibited any innocence. His face was hard, his eyes wide open, and the wild look in his eyes told her that he was serious about attempting to reach and kill Victor Carelli. She was certain that he did not have even a remote chance of reaching Carelli, and she owed a great deal to the gangster from their relationship over the years. But she tried one more time to make him understand the situation.

"Marcus, don't be insane," she said. "If Carelli's men find you, they will kill you. If you want to live, you must run. Get away from here. Just coming to visit me puts both our lives in danger. You must go, now!" she said.

Zima laughed. "No, Mother, I'm not going to run. I'm going to take care of business, and then I'll come back for you," he said. He turned and began to walk out the door. "Remember, I'll come back, and we can get out of here," he said as he paused in his walk. "We'll be free of that son of a bitch, Carelli."

Veronica Zima watched as her son walked away. She looked from her window as he boarded the waiting hansom. It drew away from the curb and was soon out of sight. She was now sure that she would never see her son again.

If Veronica Zima had continued to watch from her window, she would have seen two other enclosed cabs pacing briskly down the street. They were following Zima's cab as it made its way through the city. For a time, they followed at a distance, but when Zima's cab finally made a turn into the warehouse district, they knew where he was going. One of the cabs stopped while one of its passengers ran into a sundry store to use a public phone. Completing his call, he ran back outside and reentered the cab. He told the driver to make haste until they could reach the other cab occupied by government agents.

For years, the U.S. Secret Service and the U.S. Marshal Service, as well as local law enforcement entities had monitored the shady business dealings of Victor Carelli. By their careful study, they knew that Veronica Zima was involved with Carelli, both in business and personally, and they knew that many years ago there had been a rift between Mrs. Zima's son and Carelli, and for a considerable time, they had lost contact with Marcus Zima. More recently, however, paid informants had revealed that Carelli had banished Zima to a travelling carnival operation that Carelli owned. When U.S. Marshal Nathan Wolf had wired the Marshal Service after breaking the counterfeiting operation at the carnival in Kansas, he had advised them that Marcus Zima was heading for St. Louis. That information was passed to the Secret Service. Immediately, extensive surveillance was initiated by those agencies to apprehend Zima. In answer to the hasty call made by the agent following Zima's cab, at least a dozen agents had arrived or would soon arrive to surround the warehouse at which Carelli did business. They were there to apprehend Zima, but if Carelli somehow blundered and put himself in a position to be arrested, well, they thought, that would be icing on the cake.

The drizzly mist had stopped. The ground was wet, with puddles standing in the warehouse yard. Large horse-drawn wagons arrived at the warehouse loading docks while other wagons departed. By all appearances, the warehousing business owned by Carelli was thriving. The government agents kept their hansoms and other conveyances parked to the edge of the property, while they discreetly watched the hansom that had brought Zima to the warehouse. As the lead secret service agent on the raid, George Conley sat in one of the carriages. Pulling a side curtain slightly aside, he could see anyone entering or leaving the warehouse. Conley and the other agents were waiting for Zima to step out of the cab, as they intended to rush him as he departed. But minutes went by, and there was still no sign of Zima. Finally, George Conley and three other agents rushed up to the waiting cab in which Zima had been riding, two men on each side. With guns drawn, they quickly opened the doors of the cab, only to find that it was empty.

"Here now, what's this all about?" shouted the cab driver as he tightly held the reins of his fidgeting horse. "Whoa girl, whoa," he shouted to the horse. The animal calmed and turned its head to look at the men standing next to the cab.

"Where's your passenger," cried Conley.

"Well, he's not here," said the driver. "Now what's all the fuss about?"

"Never you mind, mister," said Conley. "Are you waiting for your passenger to return?"

"Yeah, he told me to wait for him," said the driver.

"Well, stay here and keep your mouth shut," said Conley.

Conley and the other agents returned to their carriages to wait for Zima. Conley thought to himself as he sat waiting. He wondered how in the hell Zima left that cab without being seen by us. In addition, he did not know whether Zima was in the warehouse or not. But he figured that since Zima had told the cab to wait, he must be close by.

What the agents had not seen earlier was Zima slowing his cab and leaping out to hide in a stand of bushes near the side of the warehouse after telling the cab driver his intentions and instructing the man to drive up to the warehouse and wait for him. Zima had then waited for the other cabs to pass and then hurriedly walked to the opposite side of the warehouse where he had seen another door. Quietly entering the warehouse, he made his way to the upper floor where he could remain unseen until Carelli came out of his office.

Zima waited behind a building support stanchion in the shadows. Indistinctly, he could hear voices in the offices nearby. He recalled that Carelli had an outer office where his secretary sat and where visitors waited to see the gangster. He wondered where the ever-present bodyguards were posted. He presumed that they would be in Carelli's inner office with him. Zima continued to wait. He tensed and held his breath when he heard a door open. The sound of voices became clearer as the men entered the outer office. Someone was giving instructions to another person. In seconds, Zima watched as the outer office opened and Carelli's secretary rushed out, presumably to carry out the instructions given to him by the other person. Zima then heard the door to Carelli's office close. He knew this was the chance he had been waiting for. Cautiously, he quietly opened the outer office door and crept in. As he suspected, the outer office was now unoccupied. He continued forward and stopped at Carelli's office door. He removed the snub nosed .38 from his pocket and cocked the gun's hammer. He took two deep breaths and turned the doorknob, then hastily pulled the door open.

Carelli was sitting at his desk reading papers that contained handwritten figures. His two bodyguards sat in chairs at each side and behind the desk. A cigar hung from the corner of Carelli's mouth. He looked up when Zima stepped into the office. In that instant, Zima fired the revolver and the bullet struck Carelli in the middle of his chest. The quicker of the two bodyguards jumped from his chair, pulling his own gun as he rose. He fired his gun at Zima, but Zima had already turned to leave. The bullet meant for Zima passed by harmlessly. Zima continued his escape, running down the stairs to the first floor with the bodyguards in hot pursuit.

The government agents waiting outside did not have to wait any longer. They heard two shots, and they poured from the waiting cabs shortly before the side door of the warehouse opened. Marcus Zima ran through the door, closely followed by two other men. One of the men paused and took aim at Zima. He fired and Zima fell to the ground. The Federal agents then opened fire on the two men who were attacking Zima. They fell in a hail of bullets, both mortally wounded. Conley ran to Zima, who while wounded, might live through his ordeal and was looking up at Conley with a dazed look on his face.

"Are you Zima?" asked Conley.

Zima nodded, and Conley reached down and grabbed Zima's gun from his hand. Looking at two of the other agents, he said, "You two get him in a cab and rush him to the hospital. I want him alive, so guard him carefully." The two agents quickly picked up Zima and placed him in a cab. The cab sped away with the horse at a gallop.

Conley and several other agents cautiously entered the warehouse with their guns drawn. Those men who had been working on the ground floor, along with many of the teamsters, stopped working and watched as the agents made their way to the stairs leading to the second floor. In moments, they were in Carelli's office, only to see the corpulent gangster slumped in his chair at his desk. A cigar lay on the desk still smoldering and smoking. Bloody splotches shown on Carelli's vest. Conley walked around Carelli's desk and felt the gangster's neck, checking for a non-existent pulse.

One of the agents slightly lifted Carelli's shoulders. "Looks like he took it right in the pumper," said the agent, who then put Carelli back in the position in which he was found.

"Hmm," mumbled Conley in reply. His interest had shifted from Carelli to the stack of papers laying on the desk, many of which contained coagulating blood droplets. He pulled some of the sheets closer to read them, then quickly began leafing through others. A broad smile crossed Conley's face. "Bingo," he said and began gathering up all of the papers.

Just then there was a disturbance in the outer room, and Carelli's secretary came rushing into the office. He looked at the federal agents, not knowing who they were. But then he saw his boss slumped over in his chair.

"What's going on here?" said the man. "You can't be in here. Where are Mr. Carelli's guards?"

"Who the hell are you, little man?" asked one of the agents.

The secretary puffed up and said, "I am Mr. Carelli's secretary, smart guy. Who are you?" he asked.

The agent pulled his badge from his pocket. "Federal agents, mister, so just calm down and have a seat over there. We'll get to you in a minute."

But the secretary saw George Conley gathering up the papers from Carelli's desk. "Here, you can't do that," he said. "Those are Mr. Carelli's papers. You have no right to take them." The secretary knew exactly what was contained in those papers, as he had written most of them himself. The secretary began to march around the desk and made a grab for the papers from Conley's hands. He was quickly grasped by his collar at the back of his neck by one of the agents. He made a gasping snort of a sound as he was literally lifted off the floor, walked to a side chair, and pushed into the chair.

"I told you to take a seat, Mr. Secretary," said the agent. "Now be a good little boy and stay there so we don't have to be more forceful." The agent walked back to George Conley's side. "What do you have there, boss?" asked the agent.

Conley replied, "What we've got here, my friend, is the ammunition we have been waiting on for years. This data will close down every one of Carelli's crooked operations here in St. Louis and in Kansas City. And our little secretary friend sitting there will be our corroborating witness. That is, if he wants to keep on living without a rope necktie." The deflated secretary looked at Conley and scowled.

Later, as Conley and some of the agents left the warehouse, Conley stepped to the two fallen Carelli bodyguards. Satisfied that they were dead, he continued on with two agents, while the others took Carelli's secretary and returned to their headquarters, where they placed the secretary in a waiting cell. Later, the man sat on the bunk, sullenly staring at the floor. While he knew it probably would not happen, he hoped that some of Mr. Carelli's friends would come and rescue him from this pathetic jail. He could not fathom, after working for arguably the most powerful and ruthless man in St. Louis for many years, that such a powerful organization as the Carelli rackets could be brought to its knees in the blink of an eye. Knowing that Carelli was dead, he pondered his fate. It took only a matter of moments for the quick-thinking accountant/secretary to realize that the Federal agents that had arrested him needed his knowledge and subsequent testimony. He had decided that he would reveal those facts and details, but in exchange, he would insist that he be exonerated and serve no prison time. He looked forward to the negotiations. The secretary smiled inwardly. Years ago, he had witnessed the day that Marcus Zima had been caught stealing from Victor Carelli. After all, it was the secretary that had snitched on Zima. The secretary nearly laughed aloud. Zima was a foolish idiot, he opined to himself. Unbeknownst to Carelli, the secretary had stolen at least ten times the amount of money from the mob boss and Carelli had never suspected him. Yes, he thought, I will leverage the Federal agents for my testimony and then slip away to a foreign land to enjoy my ill-gotten lucre. Then he did laugh out loud.

Three Hours Later
All Saints Hospital, St. Louis

With Carelli dead and his secretary safely ensconced in a holding cell at the Secret Service office, Conley went to the hospital to check on the condition of Marcus Zima. He was greeted by the agents who had taken Zima to the hospital for treatment.

"How is he?" asked Conley.

"The doctor doesn't think he's going to make it," said one of the agents. "They pulled the slug out of him, but they think it caused too much damage. I'll tell you something though. That Zima guy is nuts. In the cab, he kept laughing all the way to the hospital, mumbling something about 'finally getting him.'"

"Can he talk now?" asked Conley.

"I think so, but the doc probably won't like it, you talking to him. He didn't want us hanging around him," said the agent.

"Show me where he is," said Conley. The agents took Conley to a room a short distance down the hall.

"In here, boss," said one of the agents, as he held the door open for his senior agent.

As he stepped into the room, Conley saw a doctor and nurse standing at the sides of Zima's bed. Zima was lying face down on the bed, his head turned to the side. Conley showed the doctor and nurse his badge and introduced himself.

"Can he talk, doctor?" asked Conley.

"Not right now," said the doctor. "He's not completely out of the anesthetic. But he should be coming around in a short while. But I don't know how much you will get out of him. He'll be pretty weak, and it's not likely he's gonna make it."

"I'll wait," said Conley. However, his rumbling stomach was reminding him that he and the other agents had not eaten for several hours. They left Zima's room and found the hospital cafeteria to eat while they waited. After two hours and several mugs of coffee, a nurse came to them to let them know that they could return to Zima's room.

When Conley walked into the hospital room again, he bent down and asked Zima. "Feel like talking?" Zima managed to nod his head, and for nearly an hour, while Zima's strength held out, Conley talked with Victor Carelli's killer. Later, as Conley left Zima's room, he was smiling.

"Everything all right, boss?" asked one of the agents.

"Everything is fine," answered Conley. "Let's plan a meeting for tomorrow morning and I'll brief all the agents. I'll call the Kansas City U.S. Marshal's office and brief Ralph Gilman after our meeting. After all, it was their man in Kansas who started the ball rolling on this whole mess. I met him. He's a good man."

Later that same day, agents who had been watching for Kansas City freight arrivals at the St. Louis railroad depot, intercepted an entire rail car filled with wooden crates addressed to Carelli's warehouse. Those boxes contained stacks of books with a variety of non-descript titles. Every book contained counterfeit bills of various denominations. It was obvious that with the sheer volume of counterfeit money involved, the money was being printed in other locations, as well as at the carnival in

Kansas, and then forwarded to the Kansas City warehouse operation for sorting and forwarding to St. Louis. The Kansas City warehouse would need to be revisited again in an attempt to trace the originating source of each of the phony money shipments prior to closing down that location. George Conley and his secret service agents would be busy for quite some time.

Chapter Seventeen: Phone Call

Sunday Afternoon
Summer Prairie Ranch

Nathan was sure that he had riled every muscle in his body. It was all he could do to continue lifting the sharpshooter shovel and throw it back down into the packed soil. He had lost count of the number of fence post holes he had dug. He paused and looked back down the row of posts already tamped and sitting like brown soldiers at attention. He finished the hole, set down the shovel, and threw a mesquite post into the hole. He walked to where the water jug rested in the prairie grass, picked it up, and took a long swig. He set the jug down and looked up to see Will waving at him several posts back. He knew what he wanted and walked to his brother-in-law. He reached down to the wooden box in the grass, grabbed the hammer and a few staples.

"Ready?" asked Will.

"Pull away," Nathan replied.

Will flexed the wire stretcher and held it tight while Nathan pounded in the staple. They repeated the process for the other four barbed wire strands and moved to the next post, repeating the process until they reached the post that Nathan had just set.

The fencing project had started yesterday at the rail station in town. A shipment of mesquite posts, ordered from Oklahoma, had arrived. Using the wagons from Summer Prairie Ranch and others borrowed from neighbors, every Summer Prairie cowhand had converged on the rail station and physically loaded the wagons from the rail freight car, a process that took nearly the whole day. Back at the ranch, as the neighbors' wagons were unloaded, a ranch hand had driven the wagon and team back to its owner, his own horse tied to the wagon in order to return to Summer Prairie. Today, they were setting posts and stringing wire. Nathan ached everywhere.

"Let's call it a day," said Will. Me and the ranch hands will finish up in the next few days."

They gathered up their tools and put them in one of the wagons. Then they sat in the shade of the wagon to rest and were soon joined by the ranch hands who came and sat in the shade with them. Various patches of wet cloth on the men's shirts attested to their hard physical labor. After resting, they would soon start back to the ranch house.

Will nudged Nathan in the arm. "Sore enough yet," he said.

Nathan looked at him and said, "I think even my eyeballs are sore."

Will laughed and then said, "Hey, hey, watch this." He was pointing to a cluster of four steers. For some reason, they were all facing the same direction.

"There's a pair of coyotes out there in the grass in front of the steers," said Will. "Watch them for a minute."

The cattle stood eyeing the coyotes for another minute. Suddenly the four steers took off running toward the coyotes. Immediately the coyotes began running, yipping as they ran. After a short distance, the four steers stopped running and watched the retreat of the coyotes.

"You can always tell the youngsters," said Will. "I think the young steers do that just to have fun and tease the coyotes. The older cows don't do that. They're more focused on eating. Anyway, it's always fun to watch."

The crack of a rifle shot broke the quiet. One of the hands stood, took careful aim, and fired once more at the retreating coyotes. A high-pitched yelp followed the sound of the shot.

"I don't see the other one, boss," said the cowboy.

Will was still watching where the coyotes had retreated, but he was speaking to Nathan. “A pack of coyotes can single out a straggler newborn calf and chase it until it can’t run any longer. All the momma can do is watch her calf getting eaten by the coyotes. So, we shoot ’em whenever we can,” said Will.

The cow hands mounted up, and Will and Nathan drove the wagon back to the house. After seeing to the horses, Nathan and Will walked to the water pump. They stripped down to their under shorts and pumped the cold water over their heads. Will held the block of soap under the water to wash off the ants that were drawn to the animal fat in the soap. Taking turns, the men washed off, picked up their clothes and went to sit on the front porch to dry in the last rays of the afternoon sun.

The screen door slammed behind them, and they heard, “Now there’s a fine sight to behold. Two cowboys in their drawers,” said Claire May. “I think I should like to hire a photographer.” She laughed, and Nathan and Will could not help but join her.

She held Bobby on her hip with one arm, and she offered her other hand, which was holding two glasses, to Nathan. He took the glasses while Claire May pulled a bottle of bourbon from her apron pocket.

“Now, there’s a girl who knows her men,” said Will, as he poured a stiff shot into his glass.

“Rosa’s got supper cooking and the kitchen smells divine,” said Claire May. “Pork roast and peach pie.”

Claire May was talking to Bobby. “Yes, your daddy looks pretty funny, doesn’t he?” The baby showed his toothy grin. She kissed him and gave him an extra hug.

“You boys might want to get dressed,” said Claire May. “Mother might not appreciate two half-naked cowboys at her dinner table.” She laughed and walked back into the house.

“You got a nice sister,” said Nathan.

"You got a nice wife," Will answered.

They picked up their dusty clothes and went into the house, too tired for further conversation.

After supper, they returned to the porch, a second bourbon in the hands of Nathan, Will, and a short glass of wine in Virginia's.

"I forgot to tell you, Nathan," said Claire May. "While you boys were out playing with fences, you got a telegram from Ralph Gilman."

Nathan looked at Will. Simultaneously, they both spoke, "Playing with fences?" They both laughed.

Claire May grinned. "Anyway," she said, "he wants you to call him in the morning when you get to town."

"Mmm," said Nathan. "Wonder what he wants."

"Maybe he's going to get you a telephone in your office so you don't have to keep going to the judge's house to use his," said Will.

"Yeah, I need to ask him about that," said Nathan. "Millie's starting to get on my nerves." But he smiled as he said it.

Next Morning
On the Road to Chanute

Wander was up to his usual behavior. The horse was watching a rabbit that sat nibbling grass at the edge of the road. Ever so slowly, he was moving toward the rabbit to investigate and was pulled back by Nathan's gentle pull on the rein.

"No dice, bub," said Nathan. Wander reluctantly moved back to the center of the road but eyeballed the rabbit as they passed by. The rabbit did not move, believing that his camouflage and grass cover hid him from the passing rider. After the horse and rider passed, the animal went back to its rapid chewing.

Nathan still ached from the past two days of hard physical work. Plantin' fence is not all that much fun, he thought to himself. But then he remembered what Claire May had done last night to help ease his achy muscles, and he smiled. He said to himself that he could never have found a better wife than his beautiful Claire May, and he loved her dearly.

Later, in town, Nathan tied Wander to the hitch rack at the side of the building, removed his rifle from the scabbard, and walked into the office.

"Mornin' Bill," said Nathan. "Got any coffee?" He knew that Bill always kept the coffee pot full and waiting on the wood stove.

"Mornin' Boss," said Bill. "Got a little sweet cake there too, to go with your coffee. Espie made it last night."

"Mmm, thank Espie for me, please," said Nathan after he had swallowed his first bite. He knew Espie Ward's skill as a fine cook, and the cake reinforced her reputation. He took another bite and sipped a bit of hot coffee into his mouth to mix with the bread. He sat down at the table to enjoy his refreshment.

Bill was standing, gazing out the front window. "Uh, oh," he said. "Looks like trouble."

Nathan swallowed his last bite of the cake and said, "What's up?"

Before Bill could answer, the front door of the office opened and in rushed Millie, Judge Stephens' housekeeper. Nathan smiled. "Well good mornin,' Millie," he said. "What brings you around so early?"

Millie opened her mouth to speak, but before she did, she began to eye the coffee mugs and the sweet cake on the table. Nathan watched her eyes wander to the cake.

"How about a coffee and a piece of sweet bread?" said Nathan.

"Where'd you get that sweet bread?" Millie asked. "Did Espie make that?"

Bill laughed. "Yep, it's Espie's hand all right."

"Well, maybe just a little piece and half a mug of coffee," said Millie.

The men contained their laughter as they watched Millie dive into a piece of cake double the size that they had eaten. A little piece, indeed, thought Nathan.

"I'm going to stay here with Bill and eat my cake," said Millie. "But Marshal, you need to get over to the judge's. He's had two phone calls from your boss in Kansas City this morning. He wants to talk with you real bad. So, you better just go and scoot on over there." She turned her attention back to her cake and coffee.

Nathan couldn't help but laugh at the audacity of Millie giving him orders. "Yes ma'am," he said. "I'll just hop on over there." He took two more swigs of his coffee, drained the mug, then set it on the table.

A few minutes later, he knocked on the front door of Judge Rodney Stephens' home. The judge opened the door. "Mornin' Nathan." He peered over Nathan's shoulder and said, "What happened to Millie. Did she get kidnapped?" He smiled.

"She got captured by a piece of Espie Ward's sweet bread over at my office," Nathan answered.

"Come on in," said the judge. "Your boss has been pestering me this morning. Guess he wants to talk with you real bad."

They walked to the judge's office and library where they took a seat.

"How you been?" asked Stephens.

"I'm so stove up I can barely walk," said Nathan. "I think puttin' up fence is a job for younger fellas." He went on to tell the judge how he and Will had been working to fence a portion of the ranch.

"I would bet it's tough work," said Stephens. "Back a few years, we never worried about fences. Everybody seemed to get along all right without 'em. But I guess too many boundary disputes means that the ranchers have to protect their investment in cattle and grass. Has Will had any problem with his neighbors?"

"No. Summers have real nice neighbors. But like you said, I think everybody is worried about losing cattle," said Nathan.

"Yep, I reckon," said Stephens. "Cattle market's a little low right now, so nobody can afford to lose any cows."

The judge swiveled around in his chair and lifted the telephone earpiece. He paused and said, "Well, let me ring up Ralph Gilman for you, and then I'll leave you to talk with him. I might even go over to your office and get a slice of Espie's sweet bread."

Judge Stephens picked up his telephone earpiece and spoke into the phone, giving instructions to the local switchboard operator. He waited while she placed the call. In a moment, he said, "Hello Ralph. Yes, he's right here with me. I'll give the phone to him." The judge rose from his chair, waited until Nathan came around the desk, and handed the earpiece to him. Nathan took his place at Stephens' desk so that he could speak into the phone. Judge Stephens then walked out of his office, waving as he walked away.

"Hello," said Nathan. "You're at it kind of early, aren't you boss?"

Ralph Gilman chuckled and answered. "Yeah, I guess so. But I've got some news that you really need to hear, and I couldn't wait to tell you."

"Well, fire away," said Nathan.

"In the last couple days, I have gotten two telephone calls. One was from Robert Pinkerton, you know that's the son of Allan Pinkerton, the agency's founder. And I also got a call from George Conley. You know him," said Gilman.

"Are we in some kind of trouble?" asked Nathan.

Gilman laughed. "No, no trouble, in fact, just the opposite."

"Well, that's good to hear," said Nathan.

"So let me start with Pinkerton. I don't know this Robert Pinkerton," said Gilman, "but he surely thinks the world of you."

"Mmm, how so?" asked Nathan.

"Well, it seems that your friend Charlie Rath got promoted to a senior agent, or some such thing, and told Pinkerton that he couldn't have done it without your help. And all of those little banks that the carnival boys robbed have gotten some of their funds back. Well, they all wrote letters to Pinkerton thanking him for his help. But guess what?" said Gilman.

"OK, Ralph. What now?" asked Nathan.

"Well, it seems that there was a standing reward put up by Pinkertons for information leading to the arrest of the bank robbers. So, Pinkerton is sending you a check for five hundred dollars. How's that sound?" asked Gilman.

"That's fine, Ralph," said Nathan. "But, you know, I don't deserve that reward. I had a lot of help from Bill Ward and Charlie Rath. But most of all, I had the help of a very good lady who made her living as the fat lady of that carnival."

"Oh, that's right," said Gilman. "Refresh my memory. What was her name? Was it Dillman? She died, didn't she?"

"Yeah, Priz Dillman was her name. Her killer, Dennis McCary, is waiting in my jail for trial. I know the county undertaker never got paid for her funeral expenses, and I figure I'll square that up with him with part of that reward money."

"Sounds like a good thing to do," said Ralph.

"We also had one of the county sheriff's deputies killed when we conducted a search at that carnival. He's got a wife and a couple of kids that are struggling since he died. I think I can help them out with a bit of this money. I think she'll make good use of it. And I want to give a bit of the money to The Wrens."

"Hmm," said Conley. "All right, I give. What is The Wrens?"

Nathan chuckled. "It's a group of ladies who are raising funds for the library here in Chanute. They'll make good use of the money."

"Okay," said Gilman. "But there is something else that Pinkerton talked with me about."

"Oh, what's that?" asked Nathan.

"Well, he hinted to me that he would like to hire you to work for Pinkertons," said Gilman.

Nathan paused before he responded. Then he said, "That's mighty nice of Pinkerton to consider me. But I don't think their way of doing business is something that interests me."

"Now what do you mean by that, Nathan?" asked Gilman.

"From what I've seen, Pinkerton keeps his boys on a pretty short leash. When we were working together, it seemed like Charlie was sending off a message to his boss every little bit. My job gives me a lot more freedom than that. I don't think that kind of set-up would be right for me," said Nathan.

"Hmm," answered Gilman. "Sometimes I think maybe I let you have a little too much free rein. I worry that you might go and get yourself killed someday."

Nathan chuckled. "Not if I can help it," he replied.

"Anyhow, I told Pinkerton that I would mention it to you," said Gilman. "But I told him that it wasn't very likely that you would say yes. I'll let him know that I talked to you, though."

"Appreciate it, Ralph," said Nathan.

"Okay, so let me tell you about the other call I got," said Gilman. "Remember, it was George Conley that called."

"Uh huh," replied Nathan.

"Well, George wanted me to pass on some information to you. He couldn't get hold of you because you don't have a phone at your office."

"Oh, yeah, I need to talk to you about that," said Nathan.

"No need to talk about it," said Gilman. "I've resisted spending the money for a telephone, but I think Conley embarrassed me into it. I've authorized the funds for a new telephone for your office."

"That's great, Ralph. I think Judge Stephens thinks it's a bit odd that I have to come to his house every time I need to use a telephone," said Nathan.

"All right, now let me get on to why Conley called me," said Gilman. "First of all, he wanted to thank you for your hospitality there in Kansas, but more importantly, he wanted to thank you for getting that case of counterfeiting started down your way."

Gilman paused and then continued. "Conley said he couldn't have solved some of the rest of the counterfeiting crime without your help."

"Well, I appreciate his thoughts," said Nathan.

"I don't think I told you that when Conley followed the carnival's wagon load of counterfeit money to that warehouse in Kansas City, it turned into a mighty big deal."

"Why, what happened?" asked Nathan.

"That warehouse was full of counterfeit money. Most of the money was just like that batch you found in Chanute," said Gilman. "A lot of it was bound into the front covers of all different kinds of books. The rest of it was in stacks, also in unmarked wooden crates. Conley told me that there was probably a million dollars in phony money in that warehouse."

"Ooowee," said Nathan. "What were they going to do with it?"

"Well, it seems that wagon loads of it left that warehouse every day. It was taken to railroad freight cars and loaded onto them. Those rail cars then went to St. Louis and into other warehouses there. Those St. Louis warehouses were owned by one of the city's most notorious gangsters, a fella named Carelli. He took the phony money and laundered it through his illegal operations, and that left a whole lot of merchants and bankers holding the bag for taking in phony money all over the Midwest, from Chicago to Kansas City and on up to Minneapolis and St. Paul."

"That carnival we busted couldn't have been the only place printing all that money," said Nathan.

"Heavens no," said Gilman. "There were small presses all through the Midwest that were sending money to Kansas City for sorting before it went to St. Louis. Conley said that this gangster fella probably figured that if one or two of those small presses got busted by the law, he would still be receiving counterfeit money from the small presses in other locations. Conley figures that the gangsters put the fear of death in those small printer operators so they would keep their mouths shut and couldn't lead the law up the chain to him."

"Guess that's why everybody we talked to was so afraid to spill the beans," said Nathan.

"Probably so," said Gilman. "But Conley also said that if you hadn't gotten to the bottom of the counterfeiting in your location, they might never have discovered the extent of Carelli's counterfeiting operation."

"I had no idea the counterfeiting business was that large," said Nathan.

"It sure is," said Gilman. "Conley says that with your help, they have made a good dent in it, though, at least in the Midwest. And that Carelli fella is out of business."

"Well, that's good," said Nathan. "I expect he'll spend the rest of his life behind bars."

Gilman laughed. "No jail for Carelli," he said. "He's dead."

"That's even better," said Nathan. "Did Conley's boys take care of that?"

"Naw," said Gilman. "And here's where the story gets funny, and why I wanted to talk to you about it. Do you remember the fella that was the ringleader of that carnival operation?"

"Yeah," Nathan answered. "It was a man by the name of Zima."

"And he slipped away from you, didn't he?" asked Gilman.

Nathan did not know whether Gilman was being accusatory or just stating the facts.

"Yeah, when we went to arrest him, he had already left. I feel kinda bad about that."

Gilman laughed. The laugh unsettled Nathan, as he was uncertain why his boss took Zima's escape so lightly. Gilman continued, "Your tip to Conley that Zima might be heading for St. Louis to see his mother turned out to be spot on. He showed up there at his mother's, and Conley's agents stayed on his tail."

"So, did they capture him?" asked Nathan.

"Hang on, my friend, I'll get to that," said Gilman. "Conley and his boys stayed on Zima's tail, and he led them to a warehouse in St. Louis."

"Is that the one that had all the phony money, by chance?" asked Nathan.

"Bingo," said Gilman. "That was this gangster Carelli's headquarters as well as being one of his warehouses holding stolen shipments of goods along with part of the phony money. Conley's boys hit the jackpot."

"So then Conley nabbed Zima at this warehouse?" Nathan asked. He was beginning to wonder what the point of Gilman's story was going to be.

"No, not quite. It seemed that this Zima character had some kind of axe to grind with Carelli. Conley thinks that it may have had something to do with Carelli bouncing him out of town some twenty years ago. Anyway, Zima went into this warehouse, and Conley and his boys waited outside for him to come back out. But after they heard a couple gunshots, Conley decided they had better go into the warehouse. But just as he and his boys were going in, Zima came charging out with a couple of Carelli's heavies chasing and shooting at him."

"Well, who blasts Zima, Carelli's mugs or Conley?" asked Nathan.

"It was Carelli's boys. They shot Zima and then Conley's agents shot the two goons. It must have sounded like the fourth of July at that warehouse," said Gilman.

"So Zima died at the hands of his criminal buddies. Always makes for a happy ending," said Nathan.

Gilman laughed. "Not so fast, my friend," said Gilman. "When Conley and his agents went into the warehouse, they found this Carelli character dead with a bullet in his heart. And guess who did it."

"Okay, I'm betting on Zima," said Nathan.

"You're absolutely right. It was a .38 slug that they dug out of Carelli, and Zima was carrying a .38 special. Carelli's goons had .45's. So Zima took out Carelli," said Gilman. He went on, "Conley said that Carelli's warehouse was full of stolen goods and counterfeit dough. But along with that, Conley said they found a whole bunch of paperwork that implicated Carelli in several other business deals, and Conley's boys and our marshals are closing down all of them even as we speak."

"Wow, you were right. What a bust for Conley and his agents," said Nathan. "Did Zima die in the shootout?"

Gilman laughed again. "Well, you would think he did. He was caught in the crossfire from Carelli's men and Conley's agents. But he didn't. Conley's agents took him to the local hospital, and he lived for a few more hours. And in that time, Conley was able to talk with him. And guess what Zima told him."

"I give Ralph. You've already got me hooked in this yarn," said Nathan. "What did Zima have to say?"

"He implicated Carelli in all of the shenanigans, of course. But you know, we thought Zima was the head of the carnival criminal operations."

"Well, wasn't he?" asked Nathan.

"Nope, he wasn't the leader of that outfit. The carnival ringleader was a fella that Zima said he hated. The man's name was Jube Tonley, or Todley, or something like that," said Gilman.

Nathan groaned. "Tedley. His name was Jube Tedley."

"Yeah, that's it, Tedley. Zima told Conley that this Tedley fella was some kind of half caste, a mulatto, I think he said."

"Yeah, that's right. He was half black and half white," said Nathan. "He also broke out of my jail using a hidden flexible metal saw."

"Okay," said Gilman. "But there's more. According to what Zima told Conley, this Tedley fella was Carelli's bastard son. And because Tedley was Carelli's son, Carelli put Tedley in charge of the carnival many years ago. So it was Tedley who was running the whole criminal operation of that carnival." Gilman paused to catch his breath. There was silence on the other end of the phone.

"Nathan, you still there?" asked Gilman.

"Oh, yeah. I'm still here. Dammit. I knew there was something about that Tedley fella, but I couldn't put my finger on it. I couldn't figure out why he would want to saw his way out of my jail. I guess now I know why. He wasn't about to give up his criminal operation in the carnival, and he knew he had protection from Carelli. I'll tell you what, though, Ralph. You should have seen him when Conley and I interviewed him here. He was cool as a cucumber, playing innocent to everything we asked him. Nathan continued, "George Conley and I both thought the guy was just carrying out Zima's orders, and now it turns out that he was the one giving the orders. He wasn't Zima's manservant.

Zima was working for him." Nathan went on, "Carelli's son. Boy, don't that beat all."

"It sure does. I knew you'd get a bang out of that," said Gilman. "So, it looks like you need to get back on the trail of that carnival and pick up Tedley. George Conley and I want that hombre real bad."

"Well, I'll give you and Conley a present," said Nathan. "I tracked him to the carnival when it was in Coffeyville."

"Tedley?" asked Gilman.

"Yeah, Tedley. He had joined up with the carnival at its next stop. We found him, holed up in a big tent at the carnival. We couldn't get at him in the tent, because we couldn't see him inside that tent, and he had clear shots at us. So, we burned him out. He came out blasting, and we answered. So, you can tell George Conley that Tedley is dead."

"Fitting end," said Gilman. "Saves the taxpayers the cost of a trial. Oh, and one more thing. You got your second job offer during Conley's phone call. He wants you to come work for him and the Secret Service." The phone line was silent for a few seconds.

"Tell George that I appreciate him thinking of me, but my answer to him is the same as my answer to Pinkerton. I kinda like what I'm doing, so figure I'll just stay put," said Nathan.

"Well, I'm glad you said that," said Gilman. "I'd hate to lose you down there."

"Not right away, anyway, Ralph," said Nathan and both men laughed.

"Uh, oh," said Gilman. "Somebody just told me that Washington is calling on one of our other telephones. I better get off the line. Mighty good work you did there, Nathan, and we'll talk again real soon. Gotta go." And with that, the telephone line went dead. Nathan slowly put the earpiece back on the telephone.

Tedley. I sure misread that guy, Nathan thought as he shook his head.

As Nathan left the judge's house, he met the judge and Millie coming in the opposite direction.

"Everything all right?" asked Stephens.

Nathan smiled. "Just fine, Rodney, just fine," he said and kept walking to the office.

When he got to the office, he briefed Bill on Gilman's call. He sat down at his desk and opened the top drawer to retrieve a piece of paper. He was surprised to find in the drawer, a saucer on which sat a piece of Espie's cake.

"Had to hide that from Millie and the Judge," said Bill. "They ate up everything else."

Nathan went to the stove and poured himself a mug of coffee, sat back at his desk, and relished every bite of the cake and washed it down with the warm coffee. "I think I'll take off early today, Bill. Need to spend a little time with Bobby." Nathan finished his coffee, grabbed his rifle, and opened the front door. "I'll see you in the morning, Bill."

"Okay, boss," said Bill. "See you in the morning."

Chapter Eighteen: Virginia's Telegram

Summer Prairie Ranch

"No kiddin'," said Will. "So it wasn't that Zima character who was heading up that carnival?"

"That's right," said Nathan. "As I was thinking about it on the ride home, I guess I wasn't the only one fooled. Everybody we talked to in the carnival thought Zima was the big boss. It turned out that Carelli's son, Tedley, was the big boss and had been running that outfit even before Zima ever got there. Maybe a few of the real old timers in the carnival knew about him, but they had learned a long time ago not to talk about it. Tedley had everyone else fooled into thinking that Zima was their boss."

"Well, I for one, am glad that whole nasty business is over with," said Claire May. "Imagine, you getting shot by the brother of one of the criminals in that carnival. And then, killing that poor Dillman woman. That gives me goosebumps to think about it. Those people were just plain evil."

The family was eating supper in the kitchen. Because he was done eating, Nathan was playing with Bobby on his lap. A small smile, as usual, was on the baby's face. The plates on the table held remnants of rhubarb cobbler, the only remaining evidence of Rosa's supper menu.

"Okay, let me have him, sweetheart," said Claire May. "I need to give him his supper and change his nappy."

Nathan handed the baby to Claire May. His eyes turned to Rosa as she went to the stove to bring over the coffee pot. She refilled the mugs, put the pot back on the stove, and began clearing the dishes from the table. Will, Virginia, and Nathan adjourned to the front porch.

The sun was in its last hour, and the cicadas had already begun their incessant drone, with occasional crickets joining the chorus. As the shadows grew, a lone bat flitted across the yard snatching airborne insects on the fly. He was soon joined by more bats as they began their night-time quest for supper.

Claire May soon joined the others on the porch. Their conversation tended to be the same each night. They discussed the weather, livestock prices, and what their neighbors were up to. It was quiet talk, the kind of talk that lulled Nathan into an appreciation for the steadiness, the normalcy of a family, and the quiet serenity of wide-open spaces. All of these had been lacking in his childhood. His father had been a brash, loud, hard-drinking man who devoted little time to his son, preferring to spend more time in a nearby bar with his like-minded friends. Both of his parents had died shortly after he had become sheriff in Iowa. He missed his mother, who always spoke kindly, but not his father. His family was now Claire May and Bobby, and his extended family included Virginia and Will. He was a contented man.

Virginia left her chair and went indoors. In a moment she returned. A piece of paper was in her hand. "Will, can you light that lantern?" she asked.

Will raised the chimney of the lantern they kept on the porch, struck a match, and lit the wick. He adjusted the flame and set the lantern on the small table by Virginia's chair.

"I've been keeping a secret from all of you," Virginia said. "It has been bothering me for weeks, and I can't keep hiding this from you."

"What are you talking about, mother," asked Will.

"Some time ago I got a telegram."

Claire May looked at Will and said, "Ahh, the telegram," and she smiled as she said it.

"Don't be flippant, Claire May," said Virginia. "I'm trying to be very serious, and, and . . ." Virginia dabbed at her eyes, obviously deeply concerned about something.

"I'm sorry, mother," said Claire May.

"It's all right, dear. I should have told you all about this when I got the telegram," she said, "but I wanted to think about it, and what it might mean to all of us."

For a moment, Virginia said nothing more, looking down at the paper in her hand. Then she said, "Do you two remember anything about your dad's brother, your uncle John?"

Claire May and Will looked at each other. Will was two years older than Claire May. He responded, "Yes, I remember him a bit. He came to the ranch a couple times. I remember him because he took me fishing at our tank when he was here. Seems like he was always laughing, if I recall."

"I remember him, but I was so young I didn't really know him," said Claire May. "Gosh, I haven't heard anything about him in years."

Virginia looked at her children and then spoke. "I haven't heard from him in quite a time also. In the past, we would hear from him once or twice a year, but I think the last time either of us sent a letter to each other was after Robert died. I wrote him and told him about that, but never heard anything back. So, it's been years. I didn't even know if he was still living." Virginia continued. "John was an interesting character, and you're right, Will. He was a happy-go-lucky sort, always ready for a joke and a laugh. He could always make me and Robert laugh at his antics. I remember the year that he was here for Christmas. Robert and I tried to talk him into going to church with us, but he refused. He said he needed to wrap some last-minute gifts. So Robert and I went to church in town without him. When we got back from church, Rosa came out to the barn as we were putting up the horse and buggy. She was all upset."

"Why?" asked Claire May.

"She wouldn't tell us," said Virginia. "She kept saying, 'just wait 'til you get in the house and see what that loco man has done."

"Oh, I remember what he did," said Will. "He . . ." Will couldn't help but laugh. "You finish the story, mother."

"So, your father and I came in the house and put up our coats. Rosa was pointing to the parlor, so we walked in there," said Virginia. "And what did we see? There was Uncle John standing beside the Christmas tree, smiling from ear to ear."

Will laughed again.

"Well, what about it," asked Claire May.

"The tree was upside down," said Virginia. "Uncle John had taken all the decorations off of the tree, hung the tree from the ceiling upside down, and then put the decorations back on to hang down from the tree."

Claire May laughed. "What did you and father do?"

"Robert was so mad, I thought he was going to punch his brother. He was hollering and stamping back and forth, shaking his finger in John's face. Then John said, 'you know, this is the custom in parts of Europe.' Well, that set Robert off again. Robert told him, 'This isn't Europe, you fool.' I didn't know if Robert would ever cool off," said Virginia. "But he did, finally, and even had to laugh at the frivolity of it all."

"Did you leave the tree that way through Christmas?" asked Claire May.

"Yeah, they did," said Will. "I thought it was kind of fun to be the only kid in my brand-new kindergarten class to tell everybody that I had an upside-down Christmas tree. Not sure that Dad appreciated it though."

"Robert got used to it and found the humor in his brother's stunt," said Virginia. "But I can tell you, we never had another upside-down tree in our house. But that's the kind of man that Uncle John was."

"What about the telegram, mother?" asked Will.

Virginia paused again, lost in her thoughts. Then she looked up. "The telegram is from a lawyer in Texas. Uncle John has died, and this lawyer is the executor of John's will. John never married and had no children of his own."

"Why did that lawyer send you the telegram?" asked Claire May.

"Well, as I said, John had no family of his own, but he had some assets in his estate that needed to be passed on to his relatives."

"For crying out loud," said Will. "Are we his only relatives?"

"It looks that way," said Virginia. "And he has left something in his estate to our family. So, when I got the telegram, I waited a day or two and went into town to see our attorney. While I was in his office, he called Uncle John's attorney in Texas to make sure that we knew all the details of John's will."

Even though they were anxious to know the details, neither Claire May nor Will asked the obvious question. Instead, they waited for their mother to fill in the details.

"To be specific, Uncle John had a homestead that he had settled on. He had a section, over six hundred acres that he ranched. Not very large by our standards, but a nice sized property, nevertheless," said Virginia. "He has left that property to you, Claire May."

"What?" said Claire May. She was astounded. "Why would he leave his ranch to me. I didn't even really know him."

"He had no family, Claire May. We were his only relatives, and he remembered you kids fondly," said Virginia. "Why you, Claire May? I don't know. But that was his wish. Maybe he thought that by this time, Will was probably managing our ranch, and he would have been right."

She turned to Will. "He didn't forget you. He left his stock cattle to you for disposition."

"Oh," said Will. Everyone was quiet for a short time. Then Will asked, "All right, mother. So where is Uncle John's property?"

"According to the telegram, it's in Texas," said Virginia. "It's in a county named Wise, and near a place called Decatur. But that's all I know."

Claire May and Will were stunned. Nathan was having a hard time trying to grasp the consequences of his wife's inheritance. Out of the blue, someone had willed Claire May a ranch in Texas. Both Nathan and Claire May had the same thought. What were they supposed to do with it? Their home was here at Summer Prairie Ranch.

Nathan looked more intently at Virginia in the glow of the lantern. His mother-in-law's eyes glistened from tears almost ready to fall. Worry lines crossed her face. He began to understand. Virginia was very concerned that the news in that telegram would fragment her family, perhaps taking her daughter from her, her son-in-law, and her grandchild. That was why she had not shared the telegram with them at the time she received it. He felt helpless to console her. He watched as neither Will nor Claire May said anything. Like their mother, they were also stunned and lost in thought.

Almost in a whisper, Virginia said, "What should we do?"

At first, no one replied. But then, Will responded. "Mother, we don't need to do anything yet. I think that Claire May, Nathan, and I should go into town and call the lawyer that sent that telegram. Maybe we can get some more details and make some decisions. Is that all right with everybody?"

Virginia replied, "Perhaps that's best. I'm sure that Texas attorney will be expecting your call."

Two Days Later
Chanute

"But Nathan, do you know how it works?" asked Claire May. She had pulled up a chair and was sitting beside Nathan at his desk in the marshal's office. Will sat on the other side of Nathan. Just a few days before, a man had come into the office and installed a new telephone. It was a Stromberg Carlson, black candlestick model, and seemed to sit imperiously daring Nathan, Will, and Claire May to avail themselves of its mysterious technology.

"I think so," said Nathan. "I've used Judge Stephens telephone several times. Do you have that telegram?"

Claire May searched in her purse and handed the telegram that had originally been sent to her mother, to Nathan. He studied it for a moment, looking for a telephone number. When he found it, he picked up the earpiece and spoke to the operator. He gave the number to the voice on the other end of the telephone.

"If you will hang up your telephone, sir, I will call you back as soon as I reach the party in Texas. Please stay by your telephone," said the operator.

"Okay," said Nathan, and he hung up the earpiece.

Claire May was looking at him quizzically. "What happened?"

"The operator will call us back when she reaches that Texas lawyer fella," said Nathan.

"Oh," replied Claire May. "It just doesn't seem possible that we can talk to someone hundreds of miles away by talking to that machine thing."

Yesterday, their family attorney in Chanute had placed a call to the attorney in Texas to let him know that Claire May and Will would be calling him today. They waited several minutes before the telephone rang. Nathan picked up the earpiece and answered. After saying a few words, he handed the earpiece to Claire May. "They want to talk to you, Claire May." She took the earpiece and said, "Hello."

A woman spoke from the telephone. "Hello. My name is Esther Burkhart. I am the secretary for Mr. Harold Boone. Am I speaking to Miss Claire May Summers?"

Claire May answered. "Yes, I mean no. I'm Claire May Wolf. My maiden name was Summers, but I'm married now."

"Oh, I see," said Burkhart. "Very well, then. Please stay on the phone for Mr. Boone."

"Yes, ma'am," said Claire May. She turned to Nathan, visibly nervous, and said, "She is getting the attorney."

A deep male voice was then heard on the telephone. "Mrs. Claire May Wolf, then, is it?"

Almost shaking the earpiece because of her nervousness, Claire May answered. "Yes, sir, this is Claire May Wolf."

"What was your father's name, Claire May?" asked Boone.

"Robert, Robert Summers," answered Claire May.

"And what was your uncle's first name?" asked Boone.

"It was Uncle John. He was my father's brother," said Claire May.

Boone chuckled. He could tell from her voice that Claire May was nervous. "Well, then that's fine. All right then, let me tell you the stipulations of your uncle's last will and testament."

Silently, Nathan showed his wife how to hold the earpiece between them, holding it close to their ears so that they could both hear what the attorney had to say. For the next few minutes, he told them about the small Texas ranch, its assets and its detractions. Nathan and Claire May asked many questions, all of which were answered by Attorney Boone.

After the briefing session was concluded with all of their questions answered, Boone made two more comments. "If there are no more questions, I reckon that I need to know whether you want me to try to find a buyer for the property. Shall I do that?"

Nathan was looking at Claire May, and he was shaking his head to signify no.

Claire May answered Boone. "No sir. We don't want to sell it just yet. I think that my husband and I would like to come to Texas and see the property. Would that be all right?"

"Of course. I understand. It's a lovely property, and I was hoping you would say that. It would be a shame to sell the property without you first seeing it. Just send my office a telegram to let me know when you will be arriving," said Boone. "Now, is your brother there with you?"

Claire May handed the earpiece to Will. "He wants to talk to you, Will."

Will spoke into the telephone. "This is Will Summers speaking."

The conversation between Will and the attorney only lasted for a minute or so. Will told Boone that he would not be selling the stock right away and would come to see the ranch and stock with his sister.

Will sat for a few seconds looking at the telephone. "The attorney said goodbye. What do I do?"

"The call is over. Just hang up the earpiece, Will," said Nathan.

Chapter Nineteen: A Decision

August 25
Wise County, Texas

"Look at all the trees, Nathan. Trees and rolling prairie," said Claire May, as she looked out the open window of the train car. "It looks a lot like home, only there are more trees, and they're big." Her cheery disposition had returned after being upset about leaving Bobby at Summer Prairie two days ago. A relative of Rosa's would act as wet nurse for the baby while Claire May was gone, and that had initially worried Claire May a great deal. But Virginia and Rosa had assured her that wet nursing was a common practice, and that Bobby would be just fine while she was gone.

Nathan, Will, and Claire May had spent a tiring two days of monotonous travel by train, rolling through Tulsa yesterday, then Oklahoma City, passing an Indian hunting party's encampment that broke up the scenery, and crossing the Red River early this morning. Late on this second day, they were to reach Decatur, Texas. Will had remarked that the grazing land also looked a lot like Kansas, dotted with many of the same type of mixed breed cattle, many of which had what seemed to be giant horns. With the Texas sun pounding on the roof of the rail car, even with the windows down, the air was stiflingly stale and hot. Black, sooty smoke occasionally wafted into the windows from the laboring train engine. In the course of their journey, they had changed trains several times, moving from one railroad's sectional rails to another as they progressed. They were now riding the Denver and Fort Worth Railroad that would take them into Decatur.

It didn't look like much of a town as they approached. Only a few buildings broke up the prairie, but a larger building and two church spires could be seen rising above the surrounding buildings. A fellow train passenger, in characteristic Texas manner, boasted that he was also going to Decatur and the town had a population of 1,600 people, much smaller than Chanute, that had a population three times that number. Nathan and Claire May kept an open mind. They were there to make decisions, and they would base those decisions on what they observed.

Several minutes later, the engine began chuffing as it applied its brakes, slowing to eventually sit beside the loading platform. A weathered sign hanging on the side of the rough wood depot indicated that they had reached Decatur, Texas, their destination. They stepped down from the rail car onto the platform and looked about. A few folks were meeting up with arriving family and friends and after their greetings they began departing the station. The trio began to wonder if someone would be there to meet them. But, while they waited for the remainder of their luggage, a tall, trim, neatly dressed woman walked briskly toward them. Her black skirt skimmed along just above the ground, and her white, starched blouse was buttoned to her neck. A thin black ribbon encircled the neck of her blouse, and a narrow black belt adorned with silver conches marked the line between her skirt and shirt. Her steel gray hair was neatly coiffed in a braid that was coiled and perched on the back of her head. She reached out her hand to Claire May and firmly shook hands. "Mrs. Wolf?" Claire May nodded. "I'm Esther Burkhart," said the woman. "I'm Mr. Boone's secretary, and I spoke with you on the telephone." She then introduced herself to Will and Nathan, shaking each of their hands. She was a no-nonsense woman, with a firm, dry handshake. Nathan could easily tell that she was a working woman who took her position seriously.

"Mr. Boone is in court this afternoon," said Burkhart. "He sends his apologies, but will meet with you in the morning. In the meantime, I have secured rooms at the Cattlemen's Hotel for you, and I have a surrey waiting to take you over there."

As they rode to the hotel, Esther Burkhart told them that the hotel was not fancy, but it was respectable and clean, with a restaurant on the first floor. "Mr. Boone will meet you at nine o'clock tomorrow morning. There will be three horses tied to that hitch rack in the morning for your use," she said, pointing to the hitch rack at the front of the hotel. "I presume you ride, Mrs. Wolf?" Burkhart asked.

Claire May smiled at Nathan and Will. She was stifling a giggle, but appeared serious when she replied, "Yes, ma'am, I ride." To herself, she said, 'I can outride you any day, lady.'

Burkhart watched as the trio unloaded their luggage from the carriage. "Now remember, nine o'clock tomorrow morning," she said. She then turned to the driver, said a few words, and the carriage moved down the street.

"Now remember, boys, nine o'clock," said Claire May as she looked at Will and Nathan and mimicked the strait-laced secretary. Nathan and Will laughed. They knew Claire May's disdain for pomposity.

Burkhart had been correct. The Cattlemen's Hotel was small, not fancy, but was neat and clean. A savory aroma lingered in the air from the recent dinner service. After checking in at the desk, Claire May said, "Let's take the luggage to the room and go for a walk. I've been cooped up on that train for too long, and I need to stretch my legs."

Later, as they walked around the downtown area, they marveled at the county courthouse, decked out in pink granite. It was this building that they had seen earlier as their train approached town. Stores marched side by side in a square around the large courthouse. There were supply stores for ranchers, mercantile stores, a ladies' shop, lawyers' offices, a newspaper office, a post office, and a barber shop. They all seemed to be thriving, with horse and wagon traffic parked in front of them all. Off of the square, they could see a small building with barred windows, obviously a jail and an office for law enforcement.

"Kind of a nice little town," Will remarked. "Seems to have most everything."

"My goodness that's a big courthouse," said Claire May. She was staring at the tall peak of the building. "Ours doesn't look like that." She dabbed lightly at her face with her handkerchief. The heat was stifling.

They continued around the square until they were in the shade, where they paused for a few minutes, and once again gazed up at the tall courthouse peak. "Mmm, I'm hungry," said Nathan, by then paying less attention to the tall, imposing building.

Claire May and Will continued for another minute to study the courthouse, but turned to see that Nathan was gone. "Where'd he go?" asked Claire May.

Will pointed to Nathan standing in front of the hotel restaurant waving to them to come along. Will laughed. "Well, he said he was hungry. Let's go, I just realized I'm hungry too."

Next Morning

There were only a few customers remaining in the restaurant the following morning when they finished breakfast on the first floor of the Cattlemen's Hotel. The wall clock in the dining room pointed to 8:55 a.m. And it was at that time that a man came to their table. "Are you Claire May Wolf?" he said as he put out his hand.

Claire May shook his hand and acknowledged that she was Mrs. Wolf.

"I'm Harold Boone," said the man, and shook hands with Nathan and Will as they introduced themselves.

Boone was a small, wiry, thin man, half a head shorter than either Nathan or Will. He was dressed in a dark brown suit with a stiff white shirt. He wore a pair of brown boots that displayed a recent shine. At his neck was a bolo tie with black braid and a shiny brown stone at its center that finished off his shirt front. He wore a wire-rimmed set of spectacles and carried a tan, Stetson open road hat that he turned nervously in his hands, as if he was ill at ease. Nathan formed an opinion that maybe this lawyer fella needed the type of no-nonsense secretary that he had, but yet, there was an air of competence to the attorney.

"I assume you met my secretary, Miss Burkhart," said Boone.

"Yes, sir, we did," Nathan replied.

"Esther is my widowed sister," said Boone. "She's my right-hand man, so to speak."

Claire May thought to herself, I guess that explains why Boone had a female secretary.

Boone continued, "I'll wait for you in the lobby, and then we can be on our way."

In a few minutes, they all walked out of the hotel. Sure enough, there were three horses, saddled and waiting at the hitch rack in front of the hotel. Claire May could not help smiling to herself remembering the slightly imperious instructions given to them by Esther Burkhart.

"Those are your horses," said Boone. "I'll take my buggy," he said pointing to a small, black, open-wheeled, one-horse buggy. "If you will just follow me, we'll head on out to John Summers' place." Boone walked quickly and climbed aboard the buggy and waited until the others were mounted. Then he flicked a light whip over the horse and trotted off down the street. When they thought he was out of hearing range, Nathan, Will, and Claire May all seemed to talk at once. The consensus was that Boone was quite the dandy, but also rather independent, as he had made no mention of offering Claire May a ride in his buggy.

"So Nathan, how is it riding a horse that doesn't wander all over the place?" Will asked and laughed. It was a humorous jab at the fact that Nathan's horse, Wander, tended to stray from the path on occasion. Nathan smiled at the humor.

John Summers' place was approximately five miles to the northwest of town. After a time, they left a traveled road and entered a long lane. Branches from live oak and post oak trees hung over the lane. They were met by a large black and white shepherd dog that seemed to bark joyfully at their appearance. The dog trotted to the side of the horses as they moved on, and they soon came to the house in an open area. The small house stood treeless in the front, but had several large oaks to the rear. As they dismounted, Boone remarked, "The dog's name is Sparky. He was John's constant companion."

Turning to the house, Boone said, "As you can see, the house is rather modest. But it has a good well, the fireplace is large, and the cook stove is not very old. I think that Mr. Summers may have used the fireplace to cook before he got the stove. They walked around the house to see a covered porch that extended across the entire back side of the house. The porch looked out on a barn, fenced pasture, and a large, shaded pond to one side. An outhouse stood unobtrusively at one side of the house. As they gazed toward the pond, they saw a doe with a fawn that had lost all but a hint of its spots looking back at them from the trees at the pond's edge.

Opposite the pond at the back side of the house were the barn and a corral. A cattle chute led from the pasture to the corral. Looking out toward the pasture, a variety of hide colors could be seen on the backs of the grazing cattle. Stretching their gaze, they could see the fence line of mesquite posts and barbed wire march over the rise in the pasture and return toward the house from the distant opposite side.

Boone pulled a sheaf of papers from beneath his arm and began to unfold one of the sheets. Holding the paper in front of him, he showed the trio the plat drawing of the property. It revealed that the ranch was nearly six hundred and forty acres, a section roughly one mile square. "As you can see, the property is square shaped. These old homestead claims in the county were laid out in sections, each being six hundred and forty acres. Mr. Summers had one section, and it's a mighty fine property. It is treed in places, which provides plenty of timber for building and makes good shade for the cattle. The whole section is fenced." He was pointing to the plat map. "As you can see, there are two creeks running through the property. One of them feeds that tank over there."

The trio looked at each other. "What's a tank?" asked Will.

"Here in Texas, we call ponds tanks, especially when they were man made," said Boone. "Mr. Summers dammed up the creek to form that tank."

As they looked in the direction of the pond, the doe stepped from the cover of the trees and led her fawn to the tank to drink. When they had their fill, they walked back into the trees and disappeared, their tawny coats blending in with the vegetation. The trio turned their gaze to the barn where they saw a man emerge from the building. He looked at them, then waved and came walking toward them.

"That's Pablo. Pablo Carillo," said Boone. "He's the foreman and caretaker of the place. He stayed on when John Summers died. He's got a room in the barn with a little cook stove where he lives. You'll like him, he's a good man."

Carillo greeted them and introduced himself. He shook hands with all of them. His hands were rough and calloused, his blue denim pants weathered and faded, and he wore a sweat stained slouch hat. His face was nearly the color of coffee, with well-earned weather lines crossing his forehead. In accented English, he answered a few questions posed to him by Claire May, Will, and Nathan. He answered them all, unflinchingly. He's a cow man, Will thought to himself.

When they were through with their questions, Carillo touched the rim of his hat and said, "Nice to meet you all. I've got some harness down in the barn I'm working on, so I better get on." They watched as he turned and walked back to the barn.

"Didn't I tell you," said Boone. "Carillo was John's right hand."

Boone paused, then said, "Let's go up and look in the house."

They followed Boone back to the front of the house where he used a burnished skeleton key to open the front door. The house was small. The entry hall opened into a large center living room and kitchen. Two bedrooms flanked the center rooms. The home had obviously belonged to a bachelor. There was no decoration or color evident in the sparsely furnished home. Two upholstered chairs with a table between them occupied the front room. One of the chairs showed considerable wear. A plain, metal oil lamp and an open book, cover up and laying on its pages, sat on the table between the chairs. A few books lay scattered on the floor near the chairs. In the kitchen there was a small round table and two plain, straight-back wooden chairs near the cook stove. A sink with a pump handle sat between two sets of open shelves that contained cooking pots and pans and a few plates and mugs.

The bedrooms were also sparsely furnished. A bed and washstand were in the bedroom that had been used by John Summers. The other bedroom appeared to have been used for storage and was littered with a variety of supplies. Windows were placed in the walls of each room in the house, giving the house good natural light. All in all, it was a house that was solidly built with hewn oak ridge poles topping off each room.

But the house needed the touches given to homes occupied by families in order to soften its rough masculine look. After a few minutes, Boone led them out the back door where they each took a seat on several handmade wooden chairs on the covered back porch. Sparky the dog laid down next to Claire May's chair. Claire May's hand dropped to the side to scratch behind the dog's ears as she gazed out at the pond and acreage.

"Well, what do you think of the place?" asked Boone.

"It's a beautiful setting," said Claire May.

Nathan and Will expressed no opinions. An observer would speculate that the men were each measuring their own thoughts, deferring to Claire May.

"Mr. Boone, I'd like to ride the perimeter of the property," said Nathan. "Why don't we plan to come back into town and meet you at your office in a couple hours." Will and Claire May agreed with him.

"I think that's a fine idea. I'll leave you all here to explore, and I'll head back to town," said Boone. He gathered up his papers and walked to the front of the house where he climbed back into his surrey. In a moment, he was gone.

"Let's get the horses, but I want to stop at the barn and talk with Pablo Carillo," said Will, and they walked to where the horses were tied, Sparky the dog following at their heels.

Carillo had finished his immediate chore in the barn and came out to meet them as they rode up. The trio dismounted, leaving the horses ground tied to graze on the sparse vegetation while Nathan, Claire May, and Will looked around in the barn. Along with the usual trappings of harnesses, haying equipment, and supplies, three riding horses wandered in from a small corral on the open side of the barn to stand in a half-walled stall area. The horses put their heads over the short wall, curiously looking at the three strangers. In typical fashion, the barn smelled of animals, hay and manure, with dust particles shining in the sun rays that streamed through the doors and windows. But the barn was neat, with equipment and supplies hung from pegs or stacked against the walls. From off the main aisle, a door standing ajar revealed a pallet bed in the small quarters where Carillo lived. Alongside the barn sat a work wagon and buckboard.

As they admired the riding horses, Carillo spoke up. "The red over there, that was Mr. John's horse. The others he kept for visitors."

"Where is your working stock?" asked Will.

"Oh, they're out on pasture. We won't need them until it's time to cut hay," said Carillo.

Claire May seemed anxious as she said, "We're going to ride the perimeter. We'll be back in a bit." She had already moved to her horse and was mounting as she said it.

Will and Nathan walked to their horses. As they walked, Will said quietly to Nathan, "Guess she's in a hurry."

Nathan was curious. He had thought that Claire May would not seem overly interested in the ranch, but he could now see that she was eager to see the rest of the property. They loped the fence line but paused when they came upon the fenced pasture that contained the working stock horses. There were six large draft horses. A smaller, younger horse remained close to one of the horses, obviously a spring foal.

"Must be a stud in with the group," said Will as he studied the group of horses. "Oh, yeah, the big fella over there. He has some of the color markings as the colt. Look at him eyeballing us." Indeed, the stallion held his head erect, ears cocked forward, staring straight at them as if to let them know that this was his territory.

They rode on, keeping with the fence line until they came to a second pasture. They could see that the additional creek made its way along, supplying water to this pasture and continuing on to the horse pasture. But they were surprised to see a dozen head of what appeared to be pure-bred Herefords in this pasture, easily identified by their white and red markings. A larger bull grazed apart from the heifers and the two calves. This small herd was fenced off from the other cattle.

"Those are some mighty fine lookin' animals," said Will. "Wonder what Uncle John was going to do with that little herd."

They rode on, comparing the other cattle on the ranch with the Herefords. "From what I can tell," said Will, "the rest of the ranch cattle are black, white-face cross-breds with a lot of Mexican characteristics, horned, lean, and rangy. I see a few longhorns sprinkled among the herd, too. I'm going to tell Carillo and Boone that they can sell all of them, but keep the Herefords."

They continued on and reached another pasture that contained no animals. "Hay field," said Claire May. The tall green and tan feed grass waved its seed heads gently with each passing breeze.

Their ride finally brought them back to the large tank. Their appearance at the tank spooked another deer that quickly vanished into the woods. Using her handkerchief, Claire May wiped the beads of sweat from her face. "My God, it's hot in Texas," she said. After letting their horses drink, they made their way back to the barn. Carillo was waiting for them in the barn doorway.

Somewhat surprisingly to Nathan and Will, Claire May dismounted and began a rapid-fire questioning of Carillo. She was pleased to discover that Pablo Carillo had been working with Uncle John for over eight years. Carillo explained that he hired casual laborers when it was time to work the cattle, repair fence, and collect the hay. He showed them a hay press near the barn, used to make bales that were stored in the barn loft. The temporary ranch hands loaded hay from the hay field on wagons and brought it to the press where it was baled, tied, and put on a steam driven elevator that carried the bales to the loft. The small, somewhat portable steam engine was moved to drive either the hay press or elevator.

"We don't always need hay," said Carillo. "But sometimes, if there isn't enough dry grass in the pastures in the winter, we have to feed some of the hay. And sometimes we have summers that don't have enough rain, and then we don't have enough good grass. Then we have to use some of the stored hay. It's always better to have some hay stored away, even if we don't have to use it."

Will was still curious about the cattle he had seen. He asked, "Pablo, what was Uncle John going to do with the small group of Herefords?"

Carillo seemed to look off into the distance before looking back at Will and answering. "Them Herefords were Mr. John's pride and joy." Carillo seemed to choke up slightly, but then continued. "You see, Mr. John knew he was going to die. Doctors told him he had something called a tumor that was going to kill him. When he found out, he bought that Hereford bull and a few heifers."

This was all news to Claire May and Will. Their mother had never mentioned that their Uncle John was ill, as his name had never come up in any conversation at home. Perhaps Virginia had not known of his illness either. Claire May asked, "Why in the world did he do that, when he knew he was going to die?"

Carillo gazed past them before he spoke. "Well, you know, he had no family. He was never married. But he remembered his brother Robert's children," said Carillo. "He had made up his mind that when he died, he was going to leave this ranch to you, Mrs. Wolf."

Claire May did not know how to react. The sad story of her uncle moved her deeply.

Carillo saw her reaction and paused. As if fondly remembering his deceased boss, he scuffed his boot on the ground and again looked off into the distance. He then turned to Claire May again. "That little herd of Herefords is his legacy. He wanted them to be the seed of a herd of pure breds for you to inherit. But he ran out of time. He died before he could make the herd larger. He figured that since the herd was so small, it was insignificant. So he told Mr. Boone to just include them with your brother Will's inheritance, not to hold them back."

Claire May's head was bowed as she wiped tears from her cheeks with a handkerchief. She snuffed her nose and wiped it, then raised her head. "Pablo, what are your plans now that Uncle John is no longer here? Will you be staying on at the ranch?" asked Claire May.

"I don't know yet, Mrs. Wolf," Carillo replied. "Mr. Boone told me that it was your ranch now. Are you going to keep it?"

At the question, Claire May was flummoxed. She looked quickly at Nathan and Will. Her face expressed a question. But there was no response from the two of them. This was going to be a decision that required some time to think about.

Claire May turned to look at Carillo. "I don't know yet, Pablo. My family and I will need to discuss our decision," she said. "But, if we decide that we want to live here, I do hope that you will stay on. It seems to me that you have found a permanent home, and you are taking good care of the place."

Pablo did not respond. He looked Claire May in the eyes and slightly nodded his head in agreement. Throughout their conversations, he had quietly studied the woman who now owned the ranch for which he had labored so long. He was of the opinion that Mrs. Wolf could easily run the ranch, and that he would be agreeable to having her as his boss. But for now, he kept his opinion to himself. Sparky sat obediently at Claire May's side, looking up at her with his liquid brown eyes. He had made up his mind too.

Will walked to Carillo and shook his hand. "Pablo, I would like for you to work with Mr. Boone to get the cattle sold."

Carillo held on to Will's hand. "Do you want me to sell all of the cattle, Mr. Summers?"

"No," said Will. "I want you to keep the Herefords. I'll make a decision about them soon."

Later, as they sat in the office of Harold Boone, the attorney asked them virtually the same questions that Pablo had asked. He was told by Claire May and Will that a decision would be made in the near future about the ranch, and that the cattle could be sold, except for the small herd of Herefords. Claire May and Will told him that they would stay in touch with him in the next few weeks, and they bid goodbye to Harold Boone.

As they were leaving Boone's office, they passed Esther Burkhart. She stood and shook their hands. But then, she looked at the small watch that was pinned to the front of her crisp white blouse. "Say," she said, "If you folks don't have to catch a train for home tonight, you might want to go see the horse races this evening."

"Does Decatur have a horse racing track?" asked Nathan.

"Oh, heavens no," said Burkhart. "Decatur is too small to have a real horse racetrack. But we have a course set up in the pasture down at the end of the main street. Once a month, folks bring their own favorite horses to race just for bragging rights. But it's a lot of fun and folks bring food for sale, mostly to help out with charity or civic needs. You are welcome to go and watch."

"We may just do that," said Claire May. "Our train doesn't leave until tomorrow morning."

"Oh," said Burkhart. "I forgot to mention that if you are so inclined, there is generally somebody acting as a promoter and taking bets on the horses. It's not very serious betting since they only allow a one dollar maximum. It's fun just the same, that is if you don't object to horse wagering."

"No objections," said Will. They bid Burkhart goodbye again, and the trio left Boone's office and walked to the hotel.

In the late afternoon, as the sun's intensity lessened slightly and the shadows lengthened, the trio walked to the end of Main Street and joined the crowd of people standing behind a roped off area. Just as Burkhart had mentioned, tables with various foods formed a line well back from the rope, and at the end of the tables a knot of men gathered around a nattily dressed gent who was gathering their money in return for small slips of paper on which he had written their betting preferences. It appeared that those sellers who had set up their tables early had garnered the more favorable locations in the shade of a grove of oak trees. Women, some of whom wore bonnets to shield from the sun, and others who held fringed parasols for the same reason, stood behind the tables on which they displayed their crafts and food items for sale.

A sign on one of the tables caught Nathan's eye. It read, *Old Swayback Church Sale.* Nathan spoke to the woman at the table, while he looked at the tray of frosted cinnamon rolls. His mouth watered a bit. "Excuse me, ma'am. What in the world is the Swayback Church?"

The woman looked at Nathan curiously, sizing him up and down. "You're not from around these parts, are you mister."

Nathan had to laugh. "No, ma'am, I'm not. We're just here for a visit." Claire May had overheard and joined him.

"You see, mister," said the woman. "Everybody from around here knows the Swayback Church, so I knew you were a stranger." Claire May stuck out her hand and introduced herself. The church lady did the same. The two women exchanged pleasantries for a few minutes. Then the woman pointed off across the racecourse. "Look over yonder. Do you see the church steeple?" she asked.

Claire May replied that they saw it.

"Well, look to the back of the steeple and follow the roof line," the woman said.

Nathan and Claire May both spoke at once. "Now we see why you call it the Swayback Church."

The woman told them that when the ridge pole was placed for the roof of the church years ago, it was a stout and straight oak. But over time, with the weight of the roof, the ridge pole bent, taking the roof with it. So, the church now had a "swayback" roof. But since it had stood that way for many years, there seemed to be no danger of the roof collapsing, and the woman told them that a stout upright tree trunk had been placed inside the church to support the ridge pole and prevent any further sag.

"You said it was a Methodist church?" asked Claire May.

"Well, yes," answered the woman. "But other faiths use the building too, and we hold some civic events there too. So, everyone is welcome; you too, when you come to town again. Just like our preacher says, there's no locks on our church's doors."

Nathan and Claire May looked at each other and smiled. Nathan said, "That's a great story about your church. How much for two cinnamon rolls?"

The two women laughed. "He does that a lot," said Claire May, mildly apologizing for Nathan's quick change in subject. After paying the woman for the sweet treats, the couple walked on. It appeared that the horse race was about to begin.

The horses were taking their places, lining up abreast behind a rope being held by a man at each end. A man barked out *One, Two, Three* and at the count of three, the men holding the rope dropped it from their hands. The horses leaped beneath their riders and were soon rounding a turn, racing down a rise until they were out of eyesight. But as the crowd grew quiet, the sound of the thundering hooves could be heard but not seen behind the rise. The sound could be followed by the spectators, and they turned their heads in anticipation. Indeed, the horses soon appeared again as they rounded the long curve that would bring them back to the starting line. In a few seconds, the horses flew past the spectators, one horse clearly in the lead. But a lone horse, less its rider, loped behind the others.

Nathan overheard a man standing nearby remark. "Uh, oh. That's Leroy Madsen's horse. There's gonna be trouble now."

The crowd watched curiously as the winner of the race was announced, a man called Berle Gatton. The bettors once again crowded around the man with whom they had placed their bets. But suddenly, a man could be seen sprinting across the field from the unseen back stretch of the racecourse. In a short time, he reached the circle of horses and riders still at the finish line. He pushed his way through the horses, reached up, and pulled the winning rider from his horse. The other horses and riders quickly drew away from the two men. They knew what was going to happen.

The man who had run across the course was shouting loudly. "Gatton, you son of a bitch. You didn't win this race fairly. You cheated."

The man who had announced the winner asked, "Leroy, what makes you say that?"

"He bumped me off course and then knocked me from my horse," said Madsen.

"I did no such thing," replied Gatton.

The verbal barrage ceased when Madsen wound back and threw a fist at Gatton's jaw. Gatton staggered back but recovered and threw his own punches at his aggressor. The two men stood toe to toe, neither able to land a final knock-down blow. The exchange lasted for several minutes. But apparently to no one's surprise, a tall, burly man walked quickly and purposefully to the dueling racers. He stood a half head taller than either of the two fighting men, and the large tan Stetson on his head added yet a few more inches to his height. He quickly grabbed each man by their shirt collars and held them each at arm's length. What he was saying could not be heard, but his head and mouth movements revealed that the two fighters were receiving a stern dressing down.

The crowd loved the spectacle. They cheered, hooted, and whistled as the man held the two fighters apart.

Nathan turned to a man that was standing near him and asked him, "Who is that fella breaking up the fight out there?"

The man turned to Nathan. "Don't you know him? That's Ben Steele. Texas Ranger Ben Steele."

Nathan had heard of the Texas Rangers, of course. The stories of the Rangers' exploits ranged from mundane to unbelievable. The truth was probably somewhere in between. But Nathan had never worked with a ranger and continued watching as the ranger finally released the two fighters, who, astonishingly, shook hands. As soon as they finished, the peace negotiations were interrupted by the loud clanging of a metal bar striking a metal triangle over and over. The men in the crowd soon began hurriedly walking toward a wagon parked under some trees at the far end of the tables. Two large beer kegs stood on their sides at the tailgate of the wagon. A man with a wooden hammer was pounding a bung valve into the end of one barrel while men lined up to get their mugs, then queued behind the beer barrel, while another man filled their mugs. The two men who had been fighting only moments before could be seen with their arms over the shoulders of each other hoisting their beer mugs. Apparently their on-again off-again friendship was long established and well known by the local townsfolk.

Nathan, Will, and Claire May watched as the beer line slowly got shorter. "These Texans are quick to get mad at each other, but seems like they cool off quick, too," said Nathan.

"Especially if there's a beer keg nearby," Will said as he laughed and turned to walk toward the beer wagon.

As they joined the crowd at the beer wagon, Nathan turned to the stranger he had spoken to earlier. "Does this happen often? I mean, is there a fight during the races on a regular basis?"

The stranger laughed. "Every month, mister. Seems like somebody always takes offense at having their favorite horse shown up by somebody else's horse. But nobody ever gets hurt very bad other than a bloody nose now and again. But then the beer bell gets rung, and the whole thing gets forgotten until next month. It's a pretty harmless way for a bunch of rowdies to blow off steam." The man then quickly walked ahead to take his place in the beer line.

The line moved slowly, and as they stood waiting, Nathan turned to see Ranger Ben Steele overtly watching them. Steele walked over and stuck out his hand to Nathan. His Texas Ranger badge was pinned to his shirt pocket. "You folks aren't from around here, are you."

Nathan's hackles rose a bit. It was the second time he had heard those words. He wondered how in the world Steele would know that they were strangers as they had never had a conversation. Nathan shook the ranger's hand and introduced himself, Claire May, and Will. Nathan acknowledged that they were visiting from Kansas.

"How did you know that we were not from these parts?" asked Nathan.

Steele smiled slightly and replied that he knew most of the faces of the people who lived in the area. He conceded that he did not know all of them by name. But as he explained, he was "good with faces." In the next few moments, during the course of their conversation, Claire May revealed that she was the niece of John Summers, and the new owner of her recently deceased uncle's ranch.

"I knew John," said Steele. "He was a good man. He helped me one time when I had to hunt down a couple renegade Comanches who were causing trouble out west of town and west of his place. Seems the Indians had broken down a section of John's fences to run their horses through his place. They picked up a couple of John's horses while they were at it. John was hoppin' mad, but we never did find those renegades. I always liked him. Shame he had to die so young."

Steele went on in true lawman fashion. He included Will in his gaze as he said, "If you don't mind my asking, what do you fellas do for a living?"

Will explained that he and his family owned a cattle ranch in Kansas, and he had come along with his sister to have a look at John Summers' place. Steele's gaze turned to Nathan. Nathan pulled his badge from his shirt pocket and showed it to Steele. Steele squinted his eyes and then looked up at Nathan, then looked back at the badge.

"U.S. Marshal, huh. In Kansas?" Steele asked.

Nathan nodded. "Chanute," he said.

Steele scratched his mustached face, sizing up Nathan. The two men were of equal height, but Steele was a bit broader through the chest. No sign of excess weight showed on either man. Their pinched front hats were nearly identical, both dark tan. Steele sported a droopy mustache while Nathan was clean shaven. Both of their faces showed miles of saddle time in the sun.

Steele pushed up the front brim of his hat and seemed to look more closely at Nathan. "Say," said Steele. "You wouldn't happen to know the marshal up your way that had something to do with breakin' up a counterfeiting gang, would you?"

Claire May couldn't keep quiet and jumped in the conversation enthusiastically. "I know him," she said smiling and hugging Nathan's arm. "He's my husband."

Steele looked back at Nathan and said, "Well, I'll be damned. Guess you're not like the other marshals we run across. Most of the ones I've met are worthless. We ran off the last one we had in these parts."

Nathan bristled at the remarks but knew better than to try to defend the entire U.S. Marshal Service. "Why was that?" Nathan asked.

"Like I said, worthless," said Steele. "He was friends with the old judge we had here, and neither one of them wanted to go to the effort to clean up the area. Seems they spent most of their time soaking up the liquor at a local bar. We don't have a sheriff. Nobody wants that job, too dangerous, I reckon. So now the marshal is gone, and we booted the judge out at the last election. Wise County is a tad rough around the edges, and we need the help of a good regional marshal to clean it up. Don't suppose you'd have any interest in a transfer to Texas, would you?"

Nathan was slow to answer. "It's not beyond consideration. But I wouldn't make that decision without Claire May and her family's input. We'll give it thought and see what my boss up in Kansas thinks."

"Well, all right. That's all I could hope for right now," said Steele, as he straightened his hat. "It was mighty nice meeting you folks." He touched the rim of his hat again, turned, and walked away.

The Following Morning
Cattlemen's Hotel Restaurant

The Cattlemen's pancakes rivaled Rosa's recipe. They were light and grilled to just the right shade of tan. Generous, thick-sliced bacon formed a circle around the pancakes. Slathered in butter and sweet syrup, the pancakes faded from the plates in front of Nathan, Will, and

Claire May, until the plates were cleared of the hearty fare. The trio sat with their coffee, gazing about the dining room and watching the foot traffic as it passed the front window of the hotel.

Hearing the clomp of boots on the wood floor, they looked to the side of the dining room as Ben Steele strode purposefully into the room, looked about, then smiled slightly and walked to their table. Without asking, he pulled up a fourth chair and caught the attention of a passing waitress. The waitress nodded, obviously familiar with the ranger's tastes. Steele removed his hat and set it in his lap. He then bid good morning to the trio and shook hands around the table. The waitress returned with a mug for Steele, and she refilled the mugs of Nathan, Will, and Claire May.

"I wanted to see you folks before you left town," said Steele. His rough brown hand casually clinked a spoon against the sides of his mug as he stirred his coffee to cool it.

"I'm hoping that I was not too forward toward you folks yesterday," said Steele.

"In what regard, Mr. Steele?" asked Claire May.

Steele continued stirring his coffee, then set the spoon aside and took a somewhat loud slurp of coffee. Small drops of coffee clung to the lower portion of his mustache. He wiped them off with the back of his hand. "If it's all the same to you, Mrs. Wolf, just call me Ben. I figure the less law-abiding types should call me Mr. Steele, but not my friends." He took another swallow of coffee and continued, but he was looking at Nathan.

"I may have been a bit forward when I talked to you about needing the help of a U.S. Marshal in these parts. You folks are here to look at John Summers' place, not to listen to me rattle on about a need for better law enforcement. So I wanted to offer you an apology."

"No apology needed," said Nathan.

"Well, okay then," said Steele. "But I just get so doggone tired of trying to look out for this territory by myself. So, I figure that sometimes it doesn't hurt to ask questions and poke my nose into other folk's business." He paused, but then went on. "You see, people in Texas think that rangers can damn near walk on water. Oh, excuse me, ma'am," Steele said, looking back at Claire May. "But the truth is, rangers are just men with high expectations for law and order." He paused again, then went on.

"Uh, oh, here I go again, rattling on. Anyway, I just wanted it known that the territory could use another good lawman. Think it over, and now, I better get on out of here. You folks have a good trip back to Kansas, and maybe we'll meet again sometime." Steele stood, donned his hat, shook hands around the table, and walked out of the dining room.

"He's quite the character," said Will.

"He seems nice enough," replied Claire May.

Nathan made no response. He was holding his coffee mug in both hands, gazing out the hotel dining room window.

Ten Days Later
Chanute, Kansas
The Courtroom of District Judge Rodney Stephens

In the same court room, four days earlier, the trial of Junior Skinner on the charges of murdering Tom Barnes, extortion, racketeering, and being an accessory to counterfeiting had gone smoothly. Everyone in the court room had known Tom Barnes or his family, and potential jurors were familiar with the rigging of rodeo events. After all, a large number of them had visited the fair and rodeo and had seen the results of Skinner's handiwork in the form of drugged horses in the bareback and saddle bronc events. Nathan had testified to the guilt of Skinner, laying out all the details of the crimes committed by Junior Skinner. The jurors had also heard the key testimony of Leroy Fuller, the merchant who had been forced to participate as a rodeo judge in the rigged grading of the events.

Throughout his trial, Skinner sat with his arms folded across his chest. His attorney could offer very little in his defense. In addition, there were no character witnesses for the defense. Skinner had no real friends to come and offer a favorable character testimony. An odd situation arose when Judge Stephens instructed the jury to leave the court room to deliberate on a verdict. Instead, as the jury left the jury box, their foreman stopped and gathered the jury members around him while still in the court room. After a short, whispered discussion, the jury filed back into the jury box. Their foreman remained standing and announced to Judge Stephens that they had reached a verdict.

Judge Stephens knew that the case against Skinner was airtight, but he was still a bit surprised at the swift action of the jury. "Do I understand correctly that you have already reached a verdict?" asked Stephens. He was answered by the jury foreman, informing the judge that they had.

"Frankly, I am astonished," said Stephens. To confirm the jury's decision, he asked the jurors to raise their hands if they were in agreement with the verdict. Every member of the jury raised his hand, thereby showing that the decision was unanimous. Stephens then asked for their verdict.

"We find Mr. Skinner guilty of all charges," said the foreman. "We reckon that Skinner needs to hang for killing Tom Barnes and all those other things he done."

Judge Stephens was left with no other alternative. Skinner had been found guilty of all counts. The judge sat motionless for half a minute, then turned to address Skinner. "Mr. Skinner, the jury has found you guilty on all counts. Therefore, I am sentencing you to be executed." Several shouts in agreement and a great deal of talking from those in attendance was soon stifled by the rapping of Judge Stephens' gavel.

Turning to the bailiff, Stephens instructed the bailiff and sheriff's deputies to return Skinner to his cell. He was led from the court room in handcuffs and ankle shackles. Skinner's attorney sat motionless and expressionless at the defense table. In a futile last effort for his client, he had pled for a life sentence, even if it meant a lifetime of hard labor for Skinner, but the jury ignored the plea. Skinner would hang.

Ironically, Skinner was transported to Lansing to await his execution. This was done so that Leavenworth County could determine whether it wanted to add another charge for Skinner's assistance in his brother's prison break. After two days, Leavenworth County declined to add the charge, and Skinner was subsequently hanged in the same prison from which his brother had escaped.

Today, in the same court room, the trial for Dennis McCary, charged with the murder of Priz Dillman, and bank robbery, was not going as smoothly. It was speculated that McCary had used some of his hidden robbery funds to buy the services of a skilled defense attorney. The attorney was methodically dragging out the court proceedings by objecting to numerous court actions and belaboring his cross examinations to the point that Judge Stephens was reaching the end of his patience, resulting in the judge admonishing the defense attorney.

"Counsel, the court is tiring of your antics. Your attempts to delay the court are groundless and banal," said Stephens. "Either get on with your defense or rest your case. Do I make myself clear?"

"Yes, your honor," replied the attorney. He knew that his client was clearly guilty, yet he was being paid to clog the wheels of justice. His only defense witness had been one of McCary's bank robbery cronies who had not been caught in the bank robbery charges. The witness had made his appearance, alleging to be an old friend of McCary's who hoped to vouch for the character of the bank robber. He testified as a concerned carnival employee friend of McCary's, swearing that he had known McCary for years, and he attested that a man of McCary's fine and noble character could not possibly have carried out the crimes for which he was charged. The witness's ramblings fell on deaf, more reasonable ears. His testimony did little to lift the shroud of guilt hanging over McCary, and the jury was not impressed. They had already seen Priz Dillman's letter and the story of how the letter had come into the possession of Marshal Wolf.

McCary's attorney decided to employ a different tactic. Knowing full well that he could not personally testify, he seemed to ignore that rule and began to look directly at the jury while attempting to laud the character of his client and proclaim McCary's innocence. "Gentlemen of the jury, I ask for your indulgence and consideration for my client. Mr. McCary knows nothing of the events for which he is accused. Mr. McCary is a man of fine . . ."

McCary's attorney was visibly startled when he was interrupted by the sharp pounding of Judge Stephens' gavel.

"Counselor, if you wish to testify for your client, I suggest you wait until your closing remarks. Otherwise, you may recuse yourself as Mr. McCary's attorney of record, and I'll swear you in as a witness. What are your wishes, Counselor?" asked Stephens.

The visibly chastised attorney for McCary came to the conclusion that he had no more tricks up his sleeve. "Defense rests, your honor."

"I should hope so," Stephens responded.

After a recess for the attorneys to gather their notes together, closing remarks began with the county attorney addressing the jury. He carefully went through the evidence item by item, reminding them of the testimony of the prosecution's witnesses. And once more, in his most somber manner, he read Priz Dillman's letter. Dennis McCary could only squirm uncomfortably in his chair. After his summary, the prosecutor yielded the floor to the defense.

The defense attorney was played out, but decided that he wanted one more chance to sway the jury. "Your honor, if it pleases the court, would you permit my client to retake the stand?"

"Counselor, your client has already had his say in this court. There will be no more testimony from Mr. McCary," said Judge Stephens.

"I understand, your honor," said the attorney. "I just believe that the jury should have an unobstructed look at Mr. McCary while I do my summarization. I am of the opinion that the jury may be able to see for themselves that my client . . ."

The attorney did not finish his statement, as the rapping gavel again punctuated the court room.

Judge Stephens commenced to harangue the attorney, letting him know in no uncertain terms that his grandstanding was not appreciated. While this heated discussion was taking place, all eyes in the court room were focused on the judge and the wayward attorney. That is, almost all eyes. Dennis McCary was paying no attention to the drama taking place on the floor in front of him. Instead, his eyes had searched and found what he was seeking. Three rows behind the attorneys' tables was a man sitting on the right side of the aisle. The man wore a gun and holster on his left hip, the pistol's handle hanging out into the aisle. Before anyone realized what was happening, McCary jumped up from his chair, ran back in the aisle, and reached and drew the pistol from the seated man.

McCary spun around and fired one shot into the ceiling. A few paint chips and dust particles floated down from the bullet hole in the tin ceiling. McCary then turned and pointed the pistol directly at Nathan. "Marshal, don't try anything stupid. Throw your gun out into the aisle.

Everyone else in this courtroom, stay in your seats and don't even think about drawing on me or I'll shoot the marshal."

Just like everyone else in the court room, Nathan had been intently watching the verbal contest between Judge Stephens and McCary's attorney. He cursed to himself for not keeping a better eye on McCary, a known murderer. He was forced to draw his Colt and toss it to the aisle where it made an ominously loud thud as it landed on the floor. McCary bent over and picked up the pistol from the floor, now holding a gun in each hand. McCary then turned and began shouting at the judge.

"Judge, I'm walking out of here, and nobody had better follow me." Then McCary decided that he had not yet said enough and decided to gloatingly pontificate, saying, "Yeah, I killed Priz Dillman, and I may have robbed a bank or two, but I ain't goin' to prison. You'll have to kill me first." Little did he know that his words were prophetic.

While McCary's back was turned as he faced the judge, Nathan's left hand strayed to the hip of the man who was sitting beside him. Nathan's hand found the man's Colt pistol and slid it from its holster, quietly pulling back the hammer. He was hoping that the man had loaded all the cylinders of the gun. Slowly, Nathan rose from his chair while McCary continued his diatribe directed at Judge Stephens.

Aside from McCary's screeching, the room was quiet enough that McCary heard his name being called.

"McCary, turn around," said Nathan.

Alarmed, McCary spun around to find the black hole of a gun muzzle pointing at him. Rather than surrender, McCary quickly raised one of the pistols to firing position. The ear-pounding explosion of Nathan's borrowed pistol reverberated in the court room, followed almost immediately by an equally loud shot from McCary's gun. Nathan's shot found its mark in the center of McCary's chest. McCary's shot went wide and high, hitting nothing but the wall of the court room. Nathan made his way to McCary, who was lying prone and bleeding profusely on the court room floor. Nathan checked McCary, confirming that the outlaw was no longer breathing and nodded to Judge Stephens. He then picked up and re-holstered his Colt. He walked to the aisle and handed the other pistol to its owner, then calmly walked back and took his seat. The murmuring in the court room grew until people were shouting at each other in order to be heard. Men seated all around Nathan reached to shake his hand. Standing at his bench, Rodney Stephens' gavel pounding was having little effect. It was a full ten minutes before quiet was restored to the court room.

With nothing left to be said, Judge Stephens turned to the jury. "Gentlemen of the jury, you are dismissed. This trial is concluded." With those words, Stephens once again rapped his gavel and stood at his bench. Justice had been served for Priz Dillman, and Dennis McCary would never again run afoul of the law.

Judge Rodney Stephens remained standing at his bench in the court room as the spectators made their way to the exit. In a few minutes, only the judge, the bailiff, and Nathan remained behind.

"Well, you've done it again, Marshal," said Stephens, with a stern red-faced demeanor. "Last year, one of your cases resulted in a horse pissing all over the floor and near destroying the place, and now I've got blood staining the floor of this hall of justice. I have half a notion to try all your future cases outdoors." The judge caught himself beginning to smile and then attempted to hide it by lowering his head and appearing to intently look at the papers on his desk. But then, he couldn't contain his mirth and burst out laughing. Nathan joined in.

"Rodney, I'm just going to have to try to arrest a more civil type of criminal in the future," said Nathan, and the men laughed again.

After giving the bailiff instructions on the disposition of the case, the dead man's body, and the cleaning of the court room, Stephens said to

Nathan, "After all that commotion and having that lunatic point a gun at me, I could use a drink. Let's go over to the house." Stephens removed his black robe and hung it on a peg behind the front wall, out of the public view, and the two men walked out of the courthouse.

After a few minutes, Nathan and Rodney Stephens sat on the judge's front porch, each with a glass of amber liquid in their hands. "You know," said Stephens, "I just might be getting too old for this line of work. I've pretty much lost patience in the foibles of men's fallibility. I get angry every time a man like McCary stands before me, and it has damaged my ability to remain impartial. I might just give it all up at the end of this year," he said and then took a sip of his drink.

Nathan had heard this talk from Rodney Stephens a couple times before and knew that his friend would only retire when he was darn good and ready, so he refrained from a response. He and Rodney Stephens had been friends for several years and had respected each other for just as long. Both men held difficult jobs with public responsibilities, and they worked well together. Nathan stood up and set his empty glass on the table between their chairs. "Always a pleasure, Rodney," said Nathan. "I better get back to the office." The men shook hands and Nathan stepped down the first of the two porch steps.

He paused when the judge said, "Remember now. A better class of criminal, if you please." Both men laughed, and Nathan shook his head and put his hat on as he walked down the front path of Stephens' home.

Later, as he sat at his desk in the office, Nathan was finishing a report to be sent to Ralph Gilman in Kansas City. His thoughts were interrupted by Bill Ward, who was looking out the front office window. "Hey boss. Claire May is here," he said, as he watched the buckboard stop in the street. Claire May stepped down from the buckboard and came through the front office door. Nathan was already standing in the entry to greet her, and the couple quickly kissed.

"What brings you to town, sweetheart?" asked Nathan.

"It's a nice day for a ride, and I figured the trial would be over quickly. So I came to town so I could ride back home with you," she answered.

"Well, aren't you the clever one," said Nathan. "I'm ready to go now. That report to Gilman can wait 'til tomorrow."

Outside, Nathan tied off Wander to the back of the buckboard, climbed to the driver's seat next to Claire May, and they rolled out of town. But Nathan knew that Claire May had an ulterior motive. For several days the couple had talked quietly between themselves about what they had seen in Texas. They had tried to be as critical as they could in weighing the decision of whether to stay in Kansas or take the gamble of a new adventure far from the comfort of Summer Prairie Ranch. Nathan had gone so far as calling Ralph Gilman to inquire about transferring to north Texas. Gilman had told Nathan that he would support him in his decision, even if it meant losing his best marshal in Kansas. But Gilman had also told Nathan that getting a marshal to take the job in north Texas, and remain in the job, had been difficult for the Marshal Service because of the larger-than-life presence of the Texas Rangers. Gilman emphasized that gaining the respect of an arm of lone star state law enforcement would be very difficult, a real challenge for any U.S. Marshal. While it sounded discouraging, Nathan was optimistic and felt he could overcome the challenge. He had told Gilman that he would inform him as soon as he made a decision.

But a decision would have to be made, and that was the motive behind Claire May's getting Nathan alone on the ride to Summer Prairie. At home, they had little time and privacy to discuss their decision. They would use a leisurely drive to discuss and finalize their plans.

Some minutes later, the couple had driven the buckboard away from the road and parked in the shade of a cottonwood tree. The sound of blue jays scolding them, and gently flowing water from the creek next to the buckboard formed a background as Claire May spread a blanket on the grass where they sat down, watching the slow flow of the creek water.

"I think I'm talked out, Claire May," said Nathan.

"I know what you mean," she replied. "But, are we in agreement, then?"

"Claire May, I would go with you anywhere you wanted to go. But I don't want it to seem like I am urging you to do anything you don't really want to do," said Nathan. "So, I want you to be very sure that this is what you want to do."

Claire May smiled and responded as she looked into her husband's eyes. "All right then. We're in agreement."

The couple stood and hugged and kissed each other. "I love you sweetheart," said Nathan.

Claire May answered. "I love you, Mr. Wolf," and she giggled while he tickled her ribs. They folded the blanket, climbed back into the buckboard, and resumed their journey home.

At the entrance to their lane from the road, Nathan stopped the buckboard and turned to Claire May. "You know we need to tell them tonight."

"I know," said Claire May. "Just let me find the right moment, and I'll break the news."

They rode on to the ranch house, where Claire May dismounted and Nathan drove the buckboard to the side of the barn where he would tend to the horses before going into the house.

Three Hours Later
Summer Prairie Ranch

The oil lamp sconces on the walls of the kitchen created a soft, nearly-orange light. Rosa had put a clean, yellow tablecloth on the table, heightening the soft colors in the kitchen. Claire May loved the relaxed and comfortable feeling that she got when she sat with her family for meals, but she picked ever so slowly at her venison sausage and late season sweet corn and tomatoes. Bobby had been fed just prior to supper and had fallen asleep on Rosa's lap. His lips puckered involuntarily and moved as if he were nursing while he slept.

Claire May was struggling with the right moment and words that she could say to her mother. She was very worried about how Virginia would take the news of the decision that she and Nathan had made. Her stomach churned, and she continued to pick at her food. She looked over at her mother, who, surprisingly, was staring at her. It was uncanny how it seemed that her mother always knew her thoughts.

"When do you think you'll be leaving?" asked Virginia. Claire May dropped her fork on the plate with a clattering noise. She looked over at Nathan, who had stopped eating and was looking curiously at his mother-in-law.

How does she do that, thought Claire May, as she asked, "How did you know we would be moving to Texas?"

Her mother put down her coffee mug and folded her hands under her chin. "I've known you all your life, Claire May. I think I know how you think. You're a very independent person, and I've known ever since you and Nathan married that someday you would want to establish your own home. And when I received that telegram from Uncle John's attorney, why, I knew that this was probably going to be the situation that would take you away from Summer Prairie. That's why I couldn't bring myself to share it with you at first."

Neither Claire May nor Nathan knew what to say next. But then Claire May said, "I'm sorry I couldn't tell you myself. But Nathan and I just made up our minds this afternoon."

"I knew it, I knew it all along," said Will. He was grinning as he continued, "I saw the way your eyes lit up when you saw the ranch, Claire May, and the way you kept pestering Pablo Carillo when we were down there."

"What is it about me that everybody seems to know what I am thinking, even before I do?" said Claire May. "Mother knew, and now Will says he knew," she said shaking her head.

"Well, I never know what you are thinking," laughed Nathan. The others joined in the laughter, but Virginia's face quickly returned to a more somber mien.

"Anyway," said Will. "That's why I told Harold Boone and Pablo not to sell Uncle John's Herefords. I just knew you would be going back to Texas, and I'm giving you the Herefords to be the start of your own cattle herd."

"Ahh, that's why you didn't sell them," said Claire May. She beamed as she said, "Thank you very much, Will. Now we can grow our own herd. It won't ever be as big as Summer Prairie's, but it will be mine and Nathan's."

Nathan echoed his wife and thanked Will profusely. Then he spoke to Virginia. "To answer your question, Virginia, Ralph Gilman says I can pick my own time to transfer to north Texas. I'm thinkin' we should probably leave in the next few weeks."

"Hmm," said Virginia. "Well, from what you've told me about John's house, one of the first things you should probably think about doing is building another room or two onto that house. I'm going to need a place to sleep when I come down to visit you and the grandbabies."

“Grandbabies?” asked Nathan, and he looked quizzically at Claire May.

In response, she only smiled back at him and said, “You never know, Nathan. You never know.”

About the Author

Counterfeit Rodeos is the third novel in the Nathan Wolf, U.S. Marshal series, preceded by *Trail of the Outlaw* and *Singing Creek,* both of which won silver medals from the Independent Publishers Association. Previous readers of those two books will remember many of the characters from those books that reappear in this novel. Yet, *Counterfeit Rodeos* places Nathan and Claire May in all new and unique situations, especially at the conclusion of the book. I feel confident that you will enjoy reading *Counterfeit Rodeos.*

Thank you to all of my readers, and a special thank you to my wife, Janet, who provides support, guidance, and valuable critique while she edits my work.

www.ingramcontent.com/pod-product-compliance
Lightning Source LLC
Chambersburg PA
CBHW020225260626
47156CB00002B/543

9781645406686